"Hannah Gregory is my kind of gal: smart, feisty, loyal, and resilient. *When Love Calls* is a delightful story filled with entertaining, endearing characters. Lorna Seilstad's trademark is to embroider her novels with historical detail while providing a wonderfully satisfying read."

—**Suzanne Woods Fisher**, bestselling author of the Stoney Ridge Seasons series and host of a weekly radio show on the Amish

"Lorna Seilstad has a way of dropping her characters into interesting times, and she's done it again in *When Love Calls*. Readers will like getting to know Hannah, the oldest Gregory sister, as she finds out that giving up one dream doesn't mean doors won't open up to new opportunities—and, even better, the chance to answer when love calls. With engaging characters and neat history, this new series about the Gregory sisters promises much reading entertainment."

—**Ann H. Gabhart**, author of *Angel Sister*, *Words Spoken True*, and *The Gifted*

"Seilstad delivers a heartwarming story of a delightful heroine who enjoys taking the lead on everything, including solving a mystery—until love comes calling and she's compelled to answer. Filled with witty prose and engaging characters, *When Love Calls* is a thoroughly charming love story."

—**Maggie Brendan**, author of the Heart of the West series and the Blue Willow Brides series

Praise for Lorna Seilstad

"Her quick wit and captivating characters are mixed into a little-known slice of history that will keep you turning the pages and wishing for more when the story ends."

—**Judith Miller**, author of *Somewhere to Belong*

"In a story as refreshing and invigorating as lemonade, Seilstad raises deep questions about a woman's relationship with God, her dreams, and the people in her life—while making me laugh so loudly my kids came running to get in on the joke."

—**Sarah Sundin**, author of the Wings of Glory series

"With a sparkle of humor, heart-pumping romance, and a writing style that is fresh, fun, and addictive, Lorna Seilstad takes you on *The Ride of Her Life*—and yours—along the fun-filled shores of 1906 Lake Manawa."

—**Julie Lessman**, award-winning author of the Daughters of Boston and the Winds of Change series

WHEN
LOVE CALLS

Books by Lorna Seilstad

WHEN LOVE CALLS

A NOVEL

LORNA SEILSTAD

Revell

a division of Baker Publishing Group
Grand Rapids, Michigan

© 2013 by Lorna Seilstad

Published by Revell
a division of Baker Publishing Group
P.O. Box 6287, Grand Rapids, MI 49516-6287
www.revellbooks.com

Printed in the United States of America

Library of Congress Cataloging-in-Publication Data
Seilstad, Lorna.
    When love calls : a novel / Lorna Seilstad.
        pages cm. — (The Gregory Sisters ; Book 1)
    ISBN 978-0-8007-2181-7 (pbk.)
    1. Sisters—Fiction. 2. Christian fiction. 3. Love stories. I. Title.
PS3619.E425W48 2013
813'.6—dc23   2012046735

Unless otherwise indicated, Scripture quotations are from the King James Version of the Bible.

Scripture quotations labeled NIV are from the Holy Bible, New International Version®. NIV®. Copyright © 1973, 1978, 1984, 2011 by Biblica, Inc.™ Used by permission of Zondervan. All rights reserved worldwide. www.zondervan.com

The internet addresses, email addresses, and phone numbers in this book are accurate at the time of publication. They are provided as a resource. Baker Publishing Group does not endorse them or vouch for their content or permanence.

Published in association with Wendy Lawton of Books & Such Literary Agency.

13 14 15 16 17 18 19   7 6 5 4 3 2 1

To Vivian,
my mother-in-love

When love called,
you stuck a Popsicle in your back pocket
and answered.

Thank you for loving us,
encouraging us,
and praying for us every day.

May the LORD repay you for what you have done. May you be richly rewarded by the LORD, the God of Israel, under whose wings you have come to take refuge.

Ruth 2:12 NIV

1

Did she dare?

Hannah eyed the wheeled grocery store ladder resting against the shelves. If she went up that ladder again this week, she might give poor Mr. Reilly heart failure.

Despite the risk of Mr. Reilly's demise, Hannah wrapped her hand around the ladder's rung. If the little man had a conniption, that was his fault. He should have kept his shelves better stocked or at least offered to help her. After all, she'd been waiting for nearly five minutes, and her sisters were home waiting for dinner.

One can of stewed tomatoes, and her meager grocery shopping list would be complete. From its position on the upper shelf beyond her reach, the can taunted her with its flashy red label and bright green letters. It practically goaded her to come and get it.

Her gaze darted to the plaque hung from a nail on the center shelf: "Please Let Us Assist You." She'd be happy to if Mr. Reilly noticed anyone in the store besides the customers with money. As it was, she had no choice but to take matters into her own hands.

Hannah glanced from the sign to the stout, long-nosed grocer. Behind the counter, he continued his chatty dialogue with the banker's wife, turning a blind eye as her five-year-old son skipped around the mercantile like a child at the fair.

Easing the wheeled ladder back and forth a few inches on its rail, Hannah watched to see if Mr. Reilly noticed. When he didn't turn her direction, she hiked up her skirt. With one foot firmly planted on the ladder's first step, Hannah rolled the ladder a yard to the right. After stopping beneath the elusive tomatoes, she scurried up the three flat rungs and clasped the can in her hand before hoisting it aloft like a trophy.

Don't show off. She tucked the can against her side. *Just hurry up and get back down.*

"Giddyap!"

Hannah caught a glimpse of the naughty little boy riding a broom straight toward the ladder. Her breath caught.

"Whoa!" The boy smacked the ladder with the broom handle.

Like a ball on a billiards table, the ladder flew down the row of shelves. With the tomato can in one hand, Hannah clung to the rungs with her other. The ladder jolted to a stop at the end of the shelves. To keep from falling, she dropped the can and gripped the rungs with both hands. The can thunked into Mr. Reilly's potato bin and sent the piled spuds cascading to the floor.

Hannah scrambled off the ladder and began gathering the fallen victims of the tomato can fiasco. She headed for one of the spuds in the middle of the aisle, but the boy reached it first and gave it a hard kick. The potato thumped across the floor and rolled under the yard goods table.

Mr. Reilly's shadow loomed over her. "You? Again?"

Dropping an armload of potatoes into the bin, Hannah brushed the dirt from the front of her skirt. "I apologize, Mr. Reilly. You seemed otherwise occupied with Mrs. Young, and the boy—"

"The boy is lucky you didn't kill him." Mr. Reilly scowled and looked inside Hannah's basket, where the tomato can now lay nestled next to a small sack of flour and a few potatoes. "Is that all you're getting?"

"Actually, I have a bit more shopping to do." Hannah squared her shoulders. He didn't need to know she only planned on purchasing those three items. The funds they had left needed to stretch for quite a while. "And in the future, may I recommend you don't let small children run amok in your store."

"Humph!" The banker's wife gathered her son to her side.

"Now, if you'll excuse me, I have some items left to get." Hannah lifted her chin.

Her heart pounded against her rib cage. That had been close. If Mr. Reilly refused to sell groceries to her, she'd have to take a streetcar halfway across town to buy groceries. Three months ago, when her father had been alive, Mr. Reilly would never have treated one of the Gregory girls like that. He'd be jumping to fill her orders like he was for the banker's wife.

Three months ago, she wouldn't have been in Mr. Reilly's store. She'd have been in a law lecture at Drake University, and she would have been writing theme papers, not grocery lists.

Tears pricked Hannah's eyes. She blinked and forced the tears away. That time in her life was over now. Her parents were gone, and she had new responsibilities—two sisters to raise and care for. *Too bad my law classes didn't make me a stenographer. All the good jobs for women require shorthand, not Latin.*

She and her sisters had survived on what her father had left since her parents' death, but the money wouldn't last much longer. If she didn't find work soon, she, Charlotte, and Tessa would starve.

Hannah set a green-labeled can of Heinz oven-baked pork and beans into her basket. *Or we'll die of a bean overdose.*

She traced each of the thick letters on a coffee can's label. She and her sisters had been out of her favorite brew for three weeks, two days, and six hours. Not that she'd been counting. If they did without the flour, she could have her coffee, but that wasn't fair. Her sisters could live without coffee a lot easier than bread, even if she was finding it very hard to do so.

After paying a still grumpy Mr. Reilly for the groceries, she hurried toward the door. Hannah spotted an advertisement tacked on the grocer's corkboard and came to an abrupt halt.

11

SWITCHBOARD OPERATORS wanted.

The switchboard operator has a mission in life—to serve the public.

A switchboard operator? Hope bubbled in her chest. She could do that. The advertisement said that the selected candidates would even be paid while attending operators' school. Perhaps this advertisement was the answer to her prayers.

She continued to read the post.

Quickness, intelligence, accuracy, and courtesy are essential qualifications, as are courage to handle emergencies and the ability to keep one's presence of mind.

Hannah smiled. It was a perfect fit. She was certainly intelligent, and when Charlotte cut her finger last week, she'd kept a cool head and hadn't fainted at the sight of the blood.

Candidates between sixteen and twenty-five years of age must possess excellent eyesight and hearing.

She mentally checked off each part as she whispered the words aloud.

Patience, a good disposition, excellent character, and a quiet and obedient nature are a must.

She coughed. Obedient nature? So much for that perfect fit.

Sighing, she began to walk away and then stopped. So what if obedience had never been her strong suit? She could do anything she put her mind to. She always had and she always would.

She read the last line, emphasizing the words.

Only candidates who meet these stringent guidelines need apply.

She tugged the advertisement from the tack, folded it, and slipped it into her pocket. She had the qualifications. She was intelligent and articulate, and she could be quiet and obedient if she had to be. In this case, she did, if they were going to survive.

12

Doubt tugged at the corners of her mind. Could she really follow a litany of rules—even for her sisters?

⁂

"This doesn't look like what I purchased." Hannah eyed the fare as Charlotte set a steaming platter of fish and a heaping bowl of mashed potatoes on the table.

After sliding into place at the round oak table, Charlotte spread her napkin in her lap. "Tessa caught a fish after school, and I fried it up. I made mashed potatoes to go along with a jar of Momma's peaches." She smiled at Tessa. "A right proper meal."

At the mention of their mother, Hannah's chest throbbed. Three months had not lessened the pain of losing her parents. She swallowed the ache and surveyed her youngest sister. At the tender age of fourteen, Tessa was still more tomboy than she was young lady. What was she going to do with her?

"The fish looks delicious, Tessa, but you should have asked before you went fishing." She poured water into her glass. "Didn't I tell you to practice your piano after school?"

Anger flared in Tessa's eyes. "No matter how hard you try to sound like her, you're not Momma."

"Tessa Gregory, you should be ashamed of yourself." Charlotte glanced between the two sisters. "Hannah didn't ask to be responsible for us, but she is now."

Hannah uttered a silent prayer for wisdom and laid her hand on Charlotte's arm. "It's all right. This is hard on all of us. Tess, I know I'm not Momma, but I am your guardian now."

The girl yanked her napkin from the table so hard her silverware clanged against her chipped china plate. "The only reason you want me to play the piano is so I'll be more eligible for marriage and you can be rid of me all the sooner."

"What are you talking about?" Hannah said with more patience than she felt. Had she given her parents this much grief? "I want you to practice because every young woman should have a rudimentary understanding of music in order to appreciate it better."

She held out her hands, signaling the others to join her in prayer. "Now, why don't you say grace?"

Charlotte dipped her head and whispered, "And you'd better ask God for some forgiveness for your brash tongue."

Tessa stuck her tongue out at her sister as she lowered her own head. "Dear God, thank you for this fish and the potatoes. I've eaten so many beans I think I could sprout. Lord, will you tell Momma and Daddy hello from us? Tell them we love them and miss them. Tell Momma I've been getting the soil ready to plant the early seeds, and tell Daddy I wish I could go fishing with him. It's not the same when you have to go alone. And Lord, please make my sisters sweeter, and while you're at it, you can spoon a little sugar on Mrs. Wilson too. In Jesus's name we pray. Amen."

Hannah gave her youngest sister a reassuring smile, but the prayer betrayed the turmoil in her sister's heart. No wonder Tessa had snapped at her. It seemed the three of them took turns having difficult days, and today appeared to be one of Tessa's.

After flaking off a piece of fish, Hannah slipped the bite between her lips and savored the taste. "Mmm. Cooked to perfection, Charlotte, and Tessa, it is a nice change. Thank you for catching it."

"You're welcome." Tessa slurped a slice of peach from her spoon.

Despite the breach of etiquette, Hannah didn't correct her. "So, Tess, how was school today?"

"I got my essay back. You remember the one about the plans for my future?" Tessa added a sliver of butter to her mashed potatoes. "Mrs. Wilson wasn't impressed. She kept me after class to tell me I needed to be more practical. According to her, young ladies shouldn't aspire to work in a man's world."

"Poppycock." Hannah pressed her backbone against the hard chair. Through the kitchen doorway, she could see the large photograph of her parents hanging on the wall in the parlor. Like so many things that had gone undone lately, the oval frame needed dusting, but her parents' warm expressions still shone through. What would her father have said about Mrs. Wilson's remark? Would he go and speak to the offensive teacher, or would he tell Tessa to ignore her?

Hannah relaxed and grinned as a thought came to her. "Women are making all kinds of contributions to the world. Remember what Daddy always said: 'If Annie Edson Taylor could go over Niagara Falls in a barrel, then you can do anything you set your mind to.'"

Tessa dabbed her lips with her napkin. "I put that in my paper, but Mrs. Wilson said, 'Miss Taylor's foolhardy choice doesn't make her a worthy candidate for your admiration. You, young lady, should set your mind to making yourself into a marriageable young woman—especially now.'"

Hannah clenched her hand around her water glass. So that's what had prompted Tessa's earlier remark about marriage. Hannah cleared her throat. "I've been thinking."

Charlotte's eyes widened. "About marriage? To whom?"

"No, not about marriage. I've been thinking about our futures." Hannah eyed Charlotte, then Tessa. "I don't think any of us should feel we have to marry in order to survive. We have each other and the dreams God gave us."

"Like becoming a switchboard operator?" Charlotte giggled. "I still can't believe you think you can do that. They'll see right through you and realize you can't follow rules for ten minutes, let alone nine hours a day."

"Like Daddy said, if I have to, I can do anything." Hannah sighed. "Besides, that's a temporary solution to our situation. I'm talking about our long-term goals. Charlotte, I know you want to go to some special cooking school. Tessa, you have a whole world of possibilities, and I eventually would like to return to law school and maybe even learn to fly an airplane. We don't know what the future holds, but we can face it together and support one another. I think we should make a promise that we'll do whatever it takes to help each other achieve those dreams. I think that's what Daddy and Momma would have wanted."

"Yes, Momma said we should stick together." Charlotte held up her right hand. "I pledge to help you both however I can, and not to make Tessa marry some old rich guy at the age of fifteen so we don't have to eat beans every night."

Tessa swatted her arm. "For that, I should promise to support Hannah's dreams and not yours."

Charlotte waved her finger in the air. "Uh-uh-uh. We're sisters. We're in this together."

Setting her napkin aside, Tessa stood. She covered her heart with her hand. "I promise to help you two make your dreams come true, even if I have to push your wheelchairs around when you're old and gray to do it."

Hannah wadded her napkin in a ball and tossed it at her youngest sister. Charlotte followed with her own balled serviette. Tessa caught the second napkin and hurled it back. Soon a volley of white left all three sisters in giggles.

A knock on the door startled them. Hannah stood and dropped the napkins she'd collected in her chair. "You two stay here and eat. I'll get it."

She pushed aside the drapes in the parlor to catch a glimpse of the visitor. She didn't recognize the handsome man, whom she guessed to be in his late twenties. Dressed in a gray tweed suit, the man appeared out of place on the porch of their country home. He knocked again and removed his bowler hat, revealing wavy Coca-Cola-colored hair combed straight back.

After smoothing the sides of her loose bun, she opened the door and spoke through the screen door. "Hello."

"Miss, I'm Lincoln Cole. I'm an attorney representing Iowa Bank and Trust. This concerns your father's estate."

His somber voice chilled her. "My father's estate?"

"Yes. May I speak to your mother?"

"My mother passed as well. I'm the oldest heir."

He withdrew a paper from inside his suit coat and perused the contents. "You're Hannah Gregory?"

"Yes, that's me."

He glanced over her shoulder. "Miss, would you care to step out here on the porch to discuss some matters with me?"

Following his line of sight, she spotted her sisters standing in the parlor's doorway. "Perhaps that would be wise."

He pulled the screen door open for her and motioned to the two rockers separated by a small table on the porch. "Please have a seat, Miss Gregory."

Hannah settled in the chair and clasped her hands in her lap. Her stomach churned with ominous dread. Why was the bank contacting her? When she'd received their letters, she'd sent them back a letter explaining her family's circumstances. Since she hadn't heard from them again, she assumed they'd accepted her terms. But had they?

Mr. Cole turned the chair a bit in her direction before he sat down. He cleared his throat once, twice, three times, before speaking. "Miss Gregory, are you aware your father took out a second mortgage on the farm?"

"A second mortgage?" Her heart plummeted. *No! Please, God, don't let this be happening.*

"Last year, your father lost money in the financial panic and again when his crops failed."

"But I've written the bank and asked for their understanding."

Mr. Cole looked down at his hands. "Miss Gregory, banks cannot extend you credit simply because you ask for it politely. I realize you may not understand matters of business—"

"Go on with what you've come to tell me."

Anger began to burn from deep within. Did this man believe she was going to let him take their home?

"Miss Gregory, your father was indebted to the bank for a considerable sum."

"How much?"

"Unless you have other means of which we are unaware, I think—"

"I said, how much?"

He removed a paper from his pocket and passed it to her.

The numbers blurred into a mixture of blue and black ink beneath her watery gaze. "We don't have that kind of money. We barely have enough to feed ourselves."

He glanced around the farm, and Hannah saw his gaze flit from the broken gate near the barn to the chipped paint on the porch railing. "I can see that."

"But I have someone who will sharecrop the farm this year. Like I told the bank, they will have to be patient until fall."

With a sigh, he folded the paper. "You haven't made any payments since your father's death. Do you honestly believe they are going to let you live here without paying a cent toward this rather large mortgage? The bank's patience has run out, and they are foreclosing on the property. Do you know what that means?"

"Of course I know what it means." She snapped her sentence like a cowpoke's brandishing whip. "But you can't just take our home away."

"It isn't my choice, Miss Gregory." He stood and replaced his hat. "You have one week to make other living arrangements. Do you have relatives?"

"No. No one. Both of my parents were only children." She wrapped her arms around her midsection. Her thoughts spun. How could this man stand there and strip away the last hold she had on her parents?

Mr. Cole's lips clamped in a thin, silent line.

"You have no problem helping the bank take away the only place my sisters and I have ever lived?" The words seethed from her lips. "This is all so easy for you. You probably do it every day. Can you even fathom what this is like? We've already lost our parents and now you're stealing our farm? My sisters don't deserve to lose everything they love."

His Adam's apple bobbed, and he stuffed his hands in his pockets. "Take the basics of what you need from the house to set up your new place—dishes, beds, your personal belongings. Anything you don't take will be auctioned off."

She pressed her hand to her quivering, nauseous stomach. Her head felt like a hot air balloon ready to burst. Moving? Finding a new home? Starting over?

How could she possibly do it all on her own?

2

Marching through the law office, Lincoln shoved open the door in his path, banging it against the wall. Picture frames rattled and heads turned, a sure signal he'd gained the attention of everyone at the prestigious Williams and Harlington Law Firm. But he didn't care. He'd been thinking about this moment all night long.

He halted in front of Cedric Knox's desk and flung an envelope onto the surface.

Cedric looked up. "What's this?"

"It's a hundred and fifty dollars. Cash."

"Why, you shouldn't have. It's not even my birthday." Cedric smirked, his thin, dark brows rising as if he'd said the funniest thing in the world.

Lincoln clenched his fists at his sides. Why did everything about this man, from his weaselly eyes to his prematurely balding head, irritate him so? "It's the money for the Gregory girls' household belongings."

Cedric opened his top drawer and deposited the envelope inside. "If they have that kind of cash, it goes into paying off their father's debt, not to buying back their beds and lamps."

Lincoln felt the eyes of onlookers on his back. How many of them had gathered at the door? "The money's mine. I'm buying their things."

A slow smile spread across Cedric's face. "Well, well, you're

finally learning to take advantage of some of the benefits we attorneys enjoy." He chuckled. "Too bad. I can't let you pay for
their things."

Slamming his hand onto the desk blotter, Lincoln leaned over
him.

"Lincoln!"

He recognized the heavy bass bark of the man behind him as
sure as if it were his own father's voice. After giving Cedric a final
glare, Lincoln turned. Pete Williams, his mentor, his friend, and
the senior partner, scowled at him but said nothing.

"They were orphans, Pete! He sent *me* to foreclose on three
helpless girls. The eldest daughter honestly thought she could get
the bank to extend their loan by writing them a letter."

Pete drew in a long breath, extending his thick waist until the
buttons of his double-breasted suit appeared ready to burst. He
turned to Cedric and raised his eyebrows. "Really, Cedric? You
sent Lincoln?"

The bald man shrugged. "According to Mr. Harlington, I can
assign the bank's foreclosures to whomever I want, which means
I can choose Lincoln whether he's your pet or not."

Lincoln took a step forward, but Pete held out a restraining arm.
"There's no room in this firm for petty jealousies. In the future,
Mr. Knox, I expect you to use better judgment if you hope to make
full partner."

"Then maybe you can explain to Mr. Perfect why he has to wait
until the auction to buy their household items."

Lincoln released an exasperated breath. "Can't we at least spare
those girls the indignity of having their things put on the auction
block? I gave him a hundred and fifty dollars, Pete. We all know
that's more than double what they'd get for the things inside the
house."

"Normally, yes, the items would need to be auctioned." The
corners of Pete's mouth curled beneath a cloud of white mustache.
"But I think the bank will have no problem with that sum for the
purchase of the household goods, and if I remember correctly,

Cedric, you made a similar purchase when you discovered a rather attractive Widow Glidden a few years ago. Lincoln's reasons are a bit more altruistic, don't you agree?"

With a flick of his wrist, he motioned to the hovering clerks, who quickly dispersed, then glanced from Lincoln to Cedric. "Now, I expect the two of you to play nice from now on. I meant what I said about petty jealousies. If they continue, someone won't be remaining in my employ."

<hr>

Despite the cool April morning, the small room at the Iowa Telephone Company felt stuffy. Hannah ran a finger beneath the collar of her white shirtwaist and looked around at the number of girls who'd come to apply for a position as a switchboard operator. *There must be at least two dozen girls present.* Did they need the job as much as she?

Hannah fingered the reference letters in her hand. Perhaps securing one from Dean Ackenridge from Drake College would have been helpful. But taking time to do so would have made her miss today's interviews.

A middle-aged woman with a long, angular face stepped to the front of the room. "Girls, please take your seats."

Hannah sat down in the third row of wooden folding chairs beside a young woman with a mass of strawberry curls. The young woman seemed intent on examining the seam of her skirt.

When she glanced up, Hannah smiled and whispered, "Hi, I'm Hannah."

"Rosie."

The woman at the front held up her hand, and the room grew silent. "My name is Mrs. Reuff, and I'm the chief instructor at the operators' school." Her smooth voice contrasted sharply with her severe looks. "I want to welcome all of you and give you some information about this position and the selection process for all of our Hello Girls."

Mrs. Reuff swept the room with a critical gaze. "Over half of you will not make it through the selection process. Of the half admitted to the school, only a fourth will finish and advance to positions as Iowa Telephone operators."

Muffled voices in the room mirrored the surprise Hannah felt. Only a fourth of them would be hired?

"Our selection process is unparalleled. Naturally, we choose only girls with good health, good hearing, and good eyesight. However, we are also looking for young women who possess natural intelligence and outstanding moral character. Our operators must follow stringent guidelines, and we want only those young ladies who will comply with the rules under all circumstances."

Hannah swallowed hard and rubbed her damp hands on her striped skirt. Rosie shifted beside her.

Another woman handed Mrs. Reuff a piece of paper. "Our vice president is ready to begin. Please wait here until your name is called."

"I don't think I can do this," Rosie breathed. "But I so want to become an operator."

"Of course you can. Simply go in there and be yourself."

"Is that what you're going to do?"

Hannah smiled. "More or less."

"Rosie Murphy?" a woman called from the front. "Hannah Gregory?"

Hannah squeezed Rosie's hand. "I'll be praying for you."

"I'll be praying for you too."

Once she reached the front, Hannah was directed to a room down the hall. Hannah stepped onto a scale and waited while a plump woman who introduced herself as Mrs. Nesbit shifted the weights on the scale. She then directed Hannah to stand against the wall. Mrs. Nesbit placed a ruler on top of Hannah's head and eyed the marks on the wall indicating Hannah's height.

"You'll do," Mrs. Nesbit said, marking Hannah's measurements on a tablet. "Next."

She looked up at Rosie and frowned. "Miss, I can tell by looking at you that you're not tall enough."

"What does that have to do with being an operator?" The words were out of Hannah's mouth before she could stop herself.

The plump lady scowled. "Operators must be able to reach the top of the board, and Miss Gregory, you'd do well to keep your questions under your hat."

Tears filled Rosie's eyes, and Hannah's heart squeezed for the girl. "Can you please measure her anyway?"

Mrs. Nesbit reluctantly indicated for Rosie to step on the scale. Once finished, Rosie moved to the wall and stood beneath the heavy markings.

Hannah shoved a stack of papers from Mrs. Nesbit's desk. "Oh no! Look what I've done."

As she expected, the plump woman bent to retrieve the papers with an aggravated huff. Hannah knelt beside her but motioned with her hand for Rosie to stand on tiptoe.

Once the papers were back in hand, Mrs. Nesbit returned to measure Rosie. Leaning over her round belly, she eyed the mark on the wall. "Well, I'll be. You made it. Barely, but you did." Her eyes narrowed. "You're not on your tiptoes, are you?"

As she pulled back Rosie's skirt to check, Hannah began to fiddle with the model telephones on the desk. "Is this one of the practice telephones?"

Mrs. Nesbit grabbed it out of her hand. "You are not here to play around, Miss Gregory."

"No, ma'am."

Mrs. Nesbit turned to list Rosie's height on her card, and Hannah grinned.

This was going to be easier than she thought.

After Hannah had her hearing and eyesight tested, Mrs. Reuff returned and made Hannah read a selection from *First Lessons in Telephone Operating*. Then, without giving Hannah so much as a smile, Mrs. Reuff led her to an office. Gold letters adorned the door of Vice President Victor Bradford.

Mrs. Reuff knocked softly, then opened the door and laid Hannah's paperwork on Mr. Bradford's desk. "Miss Hannah Gregory, sir."

Hannah took a deep breath and waited for the door to click shut behind her, signaling Mrs. Reuff's departure.

An impeccably tailored Mr. Bradford stood and nodded to a chair across the desk from him. "Miss Gregory, please have a seat." When she'd complied, he picked up her paperwork and a pen. "I'll need the name of your druggist, your physician, and your grocer."

Hannah gulped. "My grocer, sir?" So much for things going well.

"Yes, yes. For references."

"Will you speak to each of these people?"

"Generally that's what one does with references." Impatience tinged his voice. He looked at her over the rim of his glasses. "Do you have a reason for not wanting us to speak to your grocer? Outstanding debt, maybe?"

"No, sir." She rattled off the names and watched Mr. Bradford record them in a heavy script on her application, then he gave the document careful perusal. "Everything seems to be in order. I see you have attended college, and your marks were excellent. What were you studying?"

"Law, sir."

"Unusual course of study for a woman." He quirked an eyebrow and made a note on the paper. "Tell me about your family."

"There are only my sisters and myself, sir. My parents died earlier this year."

"Good, good." He noted it on the form.

"I beg your pardon?"

He looked up. "I'm sorry. What I meant was we've learned that young ladies who need employment are more conscientious workers." He cleared his throat. "Have you letters of reference?"

She passed the letters to him and waited while he perused them. "Your preacher speaks highly of you, as does your former teacher. They mention your intelligence and your excellent character, but I also notice they both mention you are quite affable."

"Is friendliness not an asset as an operator?"

"Of course it is, but talkativeness is not."

"I can be verbose, but I also know the value of silence." She clasped her hands in her lap. "Sir, I need this position. I learn quickly, and I assure you I can do this."

He seemed to study her for a moment. "Miss Gregory, I believe we'll give you a try. School begins next Monday."

3

Hugging herself, Hannah leaned against the wall at the top of the telephone company stairs and waited for Rosie to leave the building. Not only had she been chosen, but she'd learned she'd make five dollars a week while in the operators' school and eight when she became a full-fledged operator. *I know I don't deserve it, but thank you, Lord, for your provision.*

The steady clack of hooves on the paved brick street drew her attention. A delivery wagon lumbered along. Soon a couple of carriages passed in the opposite direction. If it were later in the day, the city street would be bustling.

"Rosie!" she called as her new friend stepped through the doors.

Rosie spun and pressed a hand to her chest. "You startled me. Were you waiting for me?"

"I was. I couldn't leave until I knew how you did."

Rosie blushed, apparently not used to that kind of attention.

"Tell me. How did you do?"

A smile curled the corners of Rosie's lips. "I was selected. You?"

"I guess we're both on our way to becoming Iowa Telephone's newest Hello Girls."

Rosie clapped. "I'm so glad. It will be much easier coming to school on Monday knowing someone—not that we really know each other, but I hope we will, and that we can become friends."

Hannah covered Rosie's clasped hands. "We are friends, and I hope we'll become fast friends." She started down the steps, and Rosie fell in beside her.

When they reached the sidewalk, Rosie turned to her. "I don't live far from here. Perhaps you can join me for some refreshments. My mother will be happy to know another student operator."

Rosie looked so hopeful, Hannah didn't have the heart to disappoint her. "Maybe I could for a little while, but then I need to begin looking for a room to rent."

"You need a place to stay?"

"My sisters and I do. Our parents passed this winter, and now we need to move off our family farm." She swallowed against the wave of compounded loss. "The bank owns it now."

"That has to be awful for all three of you." Rosie patted her arm. "But let me talk to my mother. We might be able to help."

"What do you mean?"

"You'll see."

～⁓◦⟡◦⁓～

Hannah sat down on the couch and surveyed the parlor of the Murphy home. White curlicues embellished the cornflower-blue wallpaper, reminding her of a cherished dresser scarf her grandmother had once embroidered. The scarf still adorned the highboy in her parents' bedroom.

Her parents' bedroom. What would they do with the beautiful bedroom furniture now? It would never fit in a rented room.

The scent of gingerbread reached her nose, and her stomach growled. She pressed her hand to her midsection. Maybe she should have eaten more than a biscuit for breakfast.

Rosie entered with a plate of sandwiches cut in neat quarters and set it on the table. She sat across from Hannah and dropped her gaze to the plate. "Egg salad. I hope you like it."

"I do." Hannah unfolded one of the napkins on her pinstriped skirt. "And to be honest, I'm starving."

Rosie's mother waddled into the room with a mismatched china tea service on a silver tray and set it beside the sandwiches. "Oh,

I like a lass who's not afraid to admit she's hungry." She removed a plate of gingersnaps from the tray before pouring a cup of tea and passing it to Hannah. "Eat up."

"Thank you, Mrs. Murphy."

"It's you I should thank, dearie. My Rosie told me how you helped her today. All she's talked about for a year is how much she wants to be a Hello Girl."

Hannah selected a sandwich from the plate. "I didn't do anything. Having to be a certain height to answer the telephone seems like a silly rule to me."

Rosie added sugar to her cup and stirred it. The spoon tinkled against the porcelain. "I'm sure they have their reasons for everything they do, Hannah."

"Then why do you think they hired only the prettiest girls?"

From her neck to her forehead, Rosie's face blossomed pink. "I . . . uh . . ."

"I'll tell you why." Hannah lowered her sandwich. "Those men think if they hire only the prettiest young ladies, it'll make their company look good."

Rosie gasped, but her mother chuckled. "You certainly speak your mind, Hannah Gregory. I bet you're a surprise a minute." She held out the plate of cookies. "Now, I have a surprise for you. Rosie said you're needin' a place to rent, aye?"

"Yes, ma'am. My sisters and I need a room with a stove."

Mrs. Murphy crossed her thick arms over her rounded midsection. "Well, lass, I believe I may be able to help. I have a small cottage, and the renters up and left only last week."

"But I don't have—"

Holding up her hand to silence Hannah's protests, the woman continued. "And I won't accept a cent until you're a bona fide operator."

"I don't know what to say."

"Say yes." Rosie captured her hand. "It will be such fun to be neighbors."

"Are you sure?"

"Yes, lassie," Mrs. Murphy said. "God placed you in our path for a reason, and he's smilin' on you."

Hannah smiled. "Then who am I to argue with God?"

～～⌘～～

With April rain clouds threatening an afternoon shower, Hannah stepped off the streetcar at its northernmost stop and hurried down the street toward their farm. In a half mile, the street gave way to the familiar dirt-packed road. She sent up a prayer asking God to hold off the rain until she'd made the two-mile walk home. Still, even if she were soaked in a downpour, nothing could dampen her spirits today. Not only had she secured a position with the phone company, she'd also found a small house to rent.

Only one concern still prodded her. On Saturday, they'd need to move out. And while she and her sisters could handle most of the things in the house, a few larger pieces might require a man's muscle. Worst of all, she'd need a wagon to transport their belongings. Surely they could use her father's. Even if it now belonged to the bank, borrowing it for one day wouldn't be the same as stealing it, would it? But if uppity Mr. Cole didn't agree, there'd be an argument for sure.

Lord, help me work this all out. My sisters need me.

Her rapid pace ate up the road, but not quickly enough. Raindrops began to sprinkle her face.

"Hannah!" Mrs. Calloway spotted her walking and called from her porch. "Come on in here and get out of the rain before you catch your death."

Hannah hurried up the brick path to the Calloways' farmhouse and onto the porch. "Thank you for the shelter. I don't mind getting a little wet, but I would rather not get soaked."

"No, I wouldn't think so. Why don't you come in and dry off?"

"If you don't mind, I think I'll stay out here and watch the rain. I'm sure this spring shower will be over in no time."

Mrs. Calloway eyed her for a minute. "You like the rain?"

"Yes, ma'am." Hannah drew in a deep breath. "Especially in spring. I love the fresh smell."

"Humph. All I smell is the hog lot." Mrs. Calloway chuckled. "But you go right ahead and sniff all you want." She wiped her hands on her apron. "I've been meaning to ask you, how are you girls doing?"

"We're fine."

"Then the rumors aren't true?" She glanced across the yard to the road, refusing to meet Hannah's gaze. "I heard you may be losing the farm, and Mr. Calloway and I feel badly about not being able to help you girls more."

Hannah swallowed hard but forced an indifferent shrug. "We've had a lot of neighbors and church friends offer to help, but the farm is still too much for three girls to tend. I found us a place in town, and I'm starting operators' school on Monday."

"That's wonderful, dear!" She draped her arm around Hannah's shoulders and squeezed. "Congratulations. I heard they only hire the loveliest and the brightest young women to be operators." She pulled a dishcloth from her pocket and knocked down a cobweb in the corner of the porch. "And with your silky voice, I'm sure they snatched you up."

Her heart grabbed. That same silky voice, her father had said, would help win cases in front of a jury. Would he be disappointed to know she'd quit college?

Holding her hand out over the porch railing, Hannah noted only a few raindrops dampened her palm. "I think it's beginning to clear."

Mrs. Calloway laid her hand on Hannah's arm. "If you girls need anything . . ."

Hannah's first impulse was to turn down the offer, but something stopped her, and warmth spread over her chest. Had God answered her prayer so quickly? She and the Calloways' son, Walt, had been friends for years.

She turned to Mrs. Calloway. "We could use help moving on Saturday."

The middle-aged woman withdrew her hand. "You're moving so soon? This Saturday? I sure wish I could promise Ethan and Walt's help, but with spring plowing, I don't dare, Hannah. You understand."

She forced a smile. "Of course, Mrs. Calloway. Thanks all the same."

Stepping off the porch, she made a mental list of others who had wagons. All of them would be plowing. She sighed. Oh well, she and her sisters would move themselves, heavy pieces and all, using her father's wagon and his matched pair of plow horses. The only one she could count on was herself, and she might as well get used to it.

Mr. Cole would simply have to understand if they borrowed the wagon. If he didn't, he'd soon learn she could argue as well as any uptown lawyer.

4

Hannah leaned against the door frame of the parlor and waited for her bickering sisters to notice her. Spending every evening packing up their possessions—and their memories—had taken its toll on all of them, and now it was moving day. They'd be moving across town, and everything would change—their schools, their friends, and their whole way of life.

"We can't take it all, Tessa." Charlotte wrapped a footed cake plate in a dish towel and set it in the wooden crate.

"But we can't leave the rosebushes."

"Where will we plant them? At the rental house?" Charlotte shot a stern look at Tessa. "Don't be ridiculous. Roses aren't a necessity."

Tessa swept her arm over the boxes. "And all these pots and pans are? How many could you possibly cook with at the same time?" She jammed her fists on her hips. "And besides, the roses were Momma's favorite."

Hannah stepped into the room. "They certainly were, Tessa. Yellow tea roses."

"We can take them, can't we?"

Flowers meant as much to Tessa as they had to their mother. Both of them loved tending the garden and watching things spring to life. The roses were as important to Tessa, she supposed, as the pots and pans and rolling pin were to Charlotte, who had so lovingly packed them to take along. Charlotte and her mother had shared a love of cooking and baking. Hannah sighed. She and her mother had shared a love of knowledge, and that was more difficult to pack up in a box and take with them.

"How long have you been standing there?" Charlotte secured another dish in the box.

Hannah grinned. "I came in somewhere between roses and ridiculous."

"So we can take Momma's roses?"

Hannah drew in a long breath. The roses probably wouldn't survive, and digging them up would take time they needed to finish packing, but surely they could squeeze in a few bushes.

"Dig up three of them. No more. That way we can each have a bush in our own homes someday."

"Got it!" Beaming, Tessa headed for the door.

The screen door banged shut, and Charlotte frowned. "You know we don't need those flowers."

"*We* don't, but Tessa does."

Charlotte pushed the filled crate of dishes to the center of the table. "Maybe you're right. This is hard on her."

"It's hard on all of us."

Hannah laid her hand on a stack of books. She and her mother had read and discussed nearly every one, and each represented a treasured moment in time. But they couldn't take all the tomes. Pots and pans they would need, and rosebushes they could squeeze in, but cases of books? Where would they possibly go in the little house?

She picked up a volume of Henry Wadsworth Longfellow's *The Song of Hiawatha* and traced the gold swirls on the moss-green hardbound cover. It transported her to the day her parents had given her the book—her sixteenth birthday. She opened the front page and found her mother's familiar script.

You're a young woman now, and I pray daily that God is preparing a man for you like he prepared your father for me. Remember, nobility knows no race or station. Always judge a man by his heart and actions.

She closed the book and slipped it beside the cake plate in Charlotte's box. This little book she'd take.

Charlotte picked up a different volume. "Aren't you taking them all?"

"No, we won't have room."

"I'm sorry, Hannah. I know how much they mean to you."

Hannah caressed the pebbled surface of one of the larger tomes, then pulled her hand away. "I'm going to go hook up the wagon." She lifted her cape from a peg by the back door. "Let's be ready to load in an hour."

Outside, the April dawn had given way to morning. Her gaze swept the farm. Today she'd be saying goodbye to all of it. If only she could keep the image of the barn door, hanging cockeyed on its broken hinge, etched in her memory forever. And what about the spreading oak tree where Tessa had once broken her arm, or the cluster of daffodils sitting at the base of the windmill that made the perfect bouquet on their Easter table? How would she remember them?

She swiped the chilled tears from her cheek with the back of her hand before tugging open the barn door. This was no time for nostalgia. She needed to focus on what needed to be done. Her sisters were counting on her.

After she hitched the wagon to the sweet-tempered plow horses, she led them to the front of the house. Her sisters came outside to join her, and she explained they needed to put the largest items in first. "Let's start with the chiffonier in your bedroom, Charlotte. If we take out the five drawers, it should be lighter to move."

"It's still not going to be easy to get it down the stairs." Tessa held the door for her sisters to enter.

Hannah climbed the staircase. "Since when did difficulty stop any of us?"

⁓⦿⁓

"Easy, now. One more step." Hannah and her sisters lowered the dresser onto the floor at the bottom of the staircase. Pressing her hands to the small of her back, she sighed. At their current rate, they might be packed by Christmas. She glanced at the chiffonier. There had to be an easier way.

"I've got an idea." Hannah tapped her finger against her lips, then hiked up her skirt and climbed into the hollowed-out dresser. Once inside, she stood and lifted the dresser as if she were carrying a large box.

"You look like you're a turtle." Charlotte hurried to open the door as Hannah waddled toward it beneath her shell.

With the wagon backed up to the porch, all she had to do was walk directly into the bed of the wagon. "Tess, go hold the horses. I don't want them moving while I'm getting in."

As soon as Tessa shouted that she had the horses in hand, Hannah moved the dresser from the porch to the back of the wagon. The wagon shifted beneath her feet a bit, but she steadied herself and managed to move the awkward piece to the front of the wagon.

Applause sounded from the ground near the porch, and she looked up. Who was this man? Her cheeks flushed ember hot, and she collected her skirts in her fist and climbed back through one of the wide drawer openings. Quickly she shook out her skirt and adjusted the folds. "How may I help you?"

"You can kindly get out of the bank's wagon." A slow smirk formed on the man's face, and his eyes seemed to say he enjoyed the one-sided game he was playing.

"Excuse me, but who are you?"

He removed his hat, revealing a balding head. "I'm Cedric Knox, attorney from the law firm of Williams and Harlington. We represent the bank to which that wagon now belongs."

Hannah marched out of the wagon and onto the porch. "Hasn't your law firm done enough damage? We're moving like you asked. How are we supposed to get our things to the new house?"

Mr. Knox set his hat back on his head and hooked his thumbs in the pockets of his vest. "I don't really care how you do it, as long as it doesn't involve stealing the bank's property."

"Stealing!" Charlotte nearly dropped the crate in her arms. "It was our father's wagon."

The sound of a second wagon approaching drew their attention. The driver pulled his wagon in front of Hannah's, and her eyes widened in recognition—Mr. Cole. What was he doing here?

She sucked in her breath and squared her shoulders. If he thought he could team up with this Cedric Knox fellow, then she'd set them both straight.

Mr. Cole climbed out of the wagon and joined Charlotte on the porch. He eyed Mr. Knox. "Why are you here?"

Mr. Knox frowned. "I could ask you the same."

Hannah held up her hand. "Gentleman, my sisters and I don't have all day. Let me explain to both of you that we were simply planning to borrow the wagon to transport our things to our new home in town. Then we were going to return the wagon and horses to the barn before the auction this afternoon."

Mr. Knox chuckled. "I'm well aware of what you're *planning* to do, Miss Gregory, but as I said before, you won't be using this wagon. It belongs to the bank now."

"What is the harm in us using it?" Charlotte looked from Mr. Knox to Mr. Cole. "The auction isn't until four this afternoon."

"And what if you break an axle or a wheel? Have you the money to pay for the repairs?" Mr. Knox rocked on the heels of his well-polished black boots. "I know from your state of affairs you do not. Therefore, this wagon isn't going anywhere."

"But nothing is going to happen," Hannah said. "What are we supposed to do with our things?"

Mr. Knox shrugged. "Leave them. They'll be auctioned off with the rest of the farm goods."

"Cedric." Mr. Cole crossed his arms over his chest. "You and I both know there's no harm in letting them use that wagon."

"The law's on my side, Lincoln, and you know it. Do I need to get the sheriff?" He raised his thick eyebrows.

"Leave the sheriff out of this," Mr. Cole growled.

Hannah glared at the newcomer. "What kind of game is this?

Last week you took our farm, and today you act like you're on our side?"

"I'm not on anyone's side. The bank took your home. Not me. Today I came to help you move. I thought maybe you could use a second wagon, but it looks like it may be the only one at your disposal—thanks to him."

He came to help them move? Hannah took in Mr. Cole's dungarees, chambray work shirt, and leather-gloved hands. If she hadn't seen him dressed in a fine suit earlier in the week, she'd never have guessed he was a lawyer. But why would he come to help them? What was in this for him?

"Mr. Cole, you're the last person on earth I'd ask for help." She glanced at the mealy Mr. Knox and scowled. "Next to him."

Mr. Cole pushed past her and climbed into the back of her wagon. "In that case, it's a good thing I'm offering, so you don't have to ask." He lifted the shell of the chiffonier and carried it off the wagon and back onto the porch.

"And where do you think you're taking that?" Her voice rose with each word.

"To my wagon. Or, rather, the wagon I rented." He tipped the chiffonier backward, and Tessa grabbed the bottom.

Hannah gasped. "Tessa, put that down!"

Her youngest sister heaved her end of the dresser into the air, the braid down her back swinging like a pendulum. "We need his help, and we need his wagon. You might be too stubborn to admit it, but I'm not."

Her middle sister, too, began carting her crate to the second wagon, and Hannah shot her a glare. "Look at him, Charlotte. Don't you realize who he is?"

Charlotte tipped her head to the side. "What else are we going to do? Leave all our things here?"

The traitors! What were they thinking? He was the reason they were moving!

She glanced at Mr. Knox, who looked rather pleased with himself and showed no sign of relenting.

Fine. They'd take Mr. Cole's help today—only because they had no alternative—but she'd find a way to pay back every cent of the wagon rental.

Mr. Cole climbed in the back of his wagon, and he and Tessa hoisted the dresser onto the wagon bed. "Cedric, since you're determined to be a fool about this, take that rig to the barn and unhitch it. Then get back here to help me load their things."

"Me?" Mr. Knox coughed.

"Well, I don't see any other men around. You can't let these three beautiful ladies do all this heavy lifting by themselves. What would Pete think about that?"

"I didn't come here to work." He took hold of the horses' bridle.

"No, you came here to do as much damage as you could. So either get busy or get out of here. We've got work to do."

5

Cedric didn't return to the house, and Lincoln wasn't surprised. The man hadn't done an extra stitch of work in the two years he'd known him unless it was to his advantage.

It had taken nearly an hour to load the wagon and another hour to deliver the items to town. Thankfully, the landlady, Mrs. Murphy, had a few neighbors ready to help unload the belongings. As soon as they'd deposited the items in the parlor, Lincoln returned to the wagon and headed back to the farm, praying Cedric wasn't giving the girls any more grief.

Girls. He could hardly call Miss Hannah Gregory a girl. She was probably about twenty, which was five years younger than he. If she'd only smile once in a while, she'd be one of the prettiest young ladies he'd met in a long time.

All three of the Gregory sisters had hair the color of autumn leaves. Hannah's, he guessed, was like apple cider, Charlotte's was a richer amber, and Tessa's, the color of brandy. But all three sisters shared the same hazel eyes.

If he'd had brothers or sisters, would they resemble one another?

He pulled up in front of the house and set the brake. It had been a while since he'd driven a wagon, but he'd not forgotten how to do the job. Taking two steps at a time, he climbed onto the porch and found the front door propped open.

Inside, he heard the girls gabbing upstairs and hurried up to see if they'd finished their packing.

"I may break a few rules, but I've never done anything dangerous."

Recognizing Miss Gregory's—Hannah's—voice, Lincoln paused before opening the door to the bedroom. Through the crack in the door, he could pick out the three sisters gathered in the room, boxing up the remnants of their belongings.

"Have you forgotten the ice incident, sister?" Charlotte laid a decoupaged glove box in a valise.

"Ice incident? Have I heard about this?" Tessa plopped on the bed, and the springs of the brass bed creaked.

"No, and for good reason," Hannah said.

He shouldn't be spying like a gossip-loving old lady, but he couldn't tear himself away. Was this how siblings spoke to one another?

He should leave them to finish packing. They obviously weren't ready for him to take the furniture from this room yet. He began to back away, and a board groaned beneath his boot.

The girls stopped and turned his direction, but he ducked away. On second thought, maybe listening to a little more of the story would be fine. He peered back through the crack and smiled as Charlotte continued the tale.

"It was one of the first snows of the winter, and Daddy was taking Hannah and me to go sledding. Of course, Hannah didn't wait for him. She ran ahead."

So, Miss Gregory was a little impulsive. Why didn't that surprise him?

"And naturally, Lottie, you followed." Tessa giggled.

"I didn't want to miss anything." Charlotte accepted a silver brush and mirror from Hannah and added them to her bag. "Anyway, when Hannah reached the pond, she saw a fawn on the new ice, struggling to walk."

"His little legs were going every which way." Hannah demonstrated the movement with her hands. "He was slipping and sliding, and he couldn't get off. It broke my heart."

Charlotte snapped the valise shut. "So Hannah went out on the ice, even though Daddy strictly told us to stay away from the pond because he didn't know if it was safe yet."

Tessa let out a mocking gasp.

"Like you wouldn't do the same thing, missy." Hannah flicked her sister's blue hair ribbon.

"So you rescued the fawn?"

Charlotte giggled. "No, it rescued itself and ran off—about the same time Daddy came over the hill and spotted Hannah in the middle of the pond. I don't think I ever saw him that mad again."

"I was only trying to help." Hannah moved toward the door. "I don't think a child should get punished for that."

"He punished you because you risked your life. If I remember right, he made it quite clear you should have asked for help and not tried to do it all yourself."

Tessa shook her head. "She hasn't changed a bit."

"What?" Hannah held up her hands. "I'm telling you, we should send Mr. Cole away. We could figure out another way."

Lincoln sighed. Even after all the work he'd done this morning, she still wanted to be rid of him. Didn't this stubborn woman have a lick of sense? How was he going to convince her of the truth? The only reason he'd come to deliver that awful news the first time was because it was his job. But he was here today because he wanted to be.

"It doesn't make a difference." Tessa hopped off the bed. "Hannah, you've been outvoted. We like Mr. Cole, and we're smart enough to see he's an answer to our prayers."

He wished he were the answer to the Gregory sisters' prayers, but he doubted Hannah would accept any additional help from him after today. Even though he barely knew her, he recognized a stubborn streak mirroring his own. After today, he'd never see her or her sisters again.

Strange. That thought shouldn't bother him. But it did.

⚬◦≈◦⚬○⚬◦≈◦⚬

"Your friend Mr. Knox sure rushed out of here." Hannah passed a wrench to Mr. Cole after he lay down on the floor to unscrew sections of the brass bed in her bedroom. Her mother would have been appalled that she'd let a man into her private quarters, but there was little she could do about it now. They needed to take the beds apart, and Mr. Cole had offered. She wanted to refuse his assistance, but since Charlotte and Tessa had both welcomed him in like a long-lost brother, how could she refuse?

"First of all, Cedric Knox is not my friend." He shoved the wrench hard to the left, then twisted the loosened nut off the screw. "He's a colleague who works in the same law office, and that is where all similarities end." He handed Hannah the screw. "Second, he's a first-class troublemaker—especially if I'm involved."

"And why is that?"

Mr. Cole shrugged. "He sees me as a threat, I guess."

"But what does that have to do with my sisters or myself?"

He moved to the other end of the rail. "Nothing. Like I said, he's a troublemaker. If I hadn't showed up, he might have . . ."

"He might have what?"

He undid the next screw, lowered the rail to the floor, and hopped to his feet. "He might have made good on his threat or made an offer to look the other way in exchange for certain favors."

"Favors?" Her cheeks burned hot.

"Nothing like that, Miss Gregory. The cad might have strongly suggested you agree to an outing with him to take in a show or go out for dinner." He moved to the other side of the bed to finish his task.

"Do your law partners know he does this? It's terribly unethical. Why is it tolerated?"

"Whoa. It's not. But he knows it would be his word against yours. He takes advantage of any opportunity he can." He pointed to the rail. "Better grab that before I undo this screw. Hold on tight and watch your toes."

"But why the interest in us?"

"Not all three of you, Miss Gregory." He looked up from his position on the floor and met her gaze. "I'm guessing as soon as he arrived, he would have directed his interest solely upon you."

Hannah dropped the rail. It landed on her toe and she yelped.

"You okay?" Mr. Cole was on his feet in seconds, ready to help her to a chair.

She limped there on her own. "I'm fine."

Apparently, she was fine thanks to his appearance today, but she had no intention of telling him so. Would Mr. Knox really have suggested the favor of her company in exchange for the use of the wagon? Somehow the thought made her feel tawdry.

"Why don't you rest a minute while I take down the bed rails? Then I'll be up for the headboard." He scooped up the long bed rails, his muscles cording beneath his rolled-up shirtsleeves. "I shouldn't have maligned Cedric. I apologize. It's not a very good Christian witness." He swallowed hard. "And I'm sorry about your home too. If there was another way . . ."

He didn't finish the thought and let the words fall away as he walked from the room.

Was he genuinely sorry? She simply refused to believe that. Christian witness? No good Christian man went around putting orphans out of their homes. Why hadn't he offered his help that day? A good attorney should have been able to see a way to let them keep the farm.

Still, he had gone out of his way today. Was she being too hard on him?

She shook her head. No matter how kind Mr. Cole was today, she needed to remember it was his fault they were in this predicament in the first place, and she didn't plan to forget that anytime soon.

❦

"Hannah, I'll get that!" Lincoln hurried to the landing at the top of the stairs and lifted the brass bed's headboard from her shoulder.

"I have it, Mr. Cole." She yanked the bed back, saying his name as if it were as distasteful on her tongue as a swig of castor oil.

"I see." He let go of the bed and watched her shoulders sag beneath its weight.

"And I do not remember offering permission for you to use my Christian name."

He stepped back, his jaw set firm. "I apologize, and since you have this headboard well in hand, I'll leave you to it."

He stood at the top of the stairs and watched her heave the monstrous piece down the stairs. The back end clunked on each of the wooden stairs, possibly denting them, but he didn't intervene. With her chin set and determination showing in her hazel eyes, she managed to get the headboard to the front door and onto the porch without a single glance back at him.

Lincoln shook his head. Hannah Gregory was one stubborn woman. He headed to the bedroom they'd been emptying and relieved Charlotte of the footboard.

"Thank you, Mr. Cole." She picked up a pile of quilts. "But I thought you were helping Hannah."

"She said she didn't need my help."

"And you believed her?"

He chuckled, remembering her slight limp. "No, but she sure tried to look convincing."

"That's her problem. She'll help anyone, but she never wants anyone to help her. I guess it's part of being the oldest." She glanced around the room. "Looks like we're finished up here now. How much room is left in the wagon?"

"It's getting tight, but we should be fine. Why?" He followed Charlotte from the room and down the stairs.

"There are two crates in the parlor that Hannah said we had to leave until last. They belong to her."

"And you think she should have them?" He smiled. In the hours he'd spent with the three sisters, he'd noticed two things. One, stubbornness must be a Gregory family trait, and two, the girls were fiercely loyal to one another. "Don't worry, Charlotte. We'll make room."

They met Hannah and Tessa at the wagon. Somehow, the oldest sister had managed to get the headboard into the wagon without his help. Impressive.

She tucked quilts around the headboards and footboards in the back of the wagon and then wiped her hands on her apron. "That should be it, right?"

"Except for your crates in the parlor." Tessa peeked over the top. "But I'm afraid it looks pretty full already."

Lincoln shifted a set of chairs to the right. "See? There's still a little room left." He turned to Tessa. "Why don't you show me where those crates are?"

"Mr. Cole, those crates aren't necessary. We can leave—"

Ignoring Hannah's protests, he followed Tessa inside. Behind him, he heard the click of Charlotte's and Hannah's shoes as they crossed the porch, hurrying to join them inside.

Tessa pointed to a corner of the living room. "The crates are really heavy. They're filled with Hannah's books."

"What kind of books?" He picked up two volumes from the top of the pile and read the titles. Tipping his head to the side, he glanced at Hannah as she entered the room. "This is a law book, and this one is on ballooning."

Hannah's eyebrows rose. "Yes, they are. You read quite well."

"Why do you have a law book?"

"She has a lot of them." Tessa pointed to a second crate. "They're her schoolbooks—from college."

He spotted a Drake College pendant sticking out of the side of one of the crates. "You're a law student?"

"Don't look so surprised. Weren't there any women in your law class?"

"A couple, but you have to admit it's a rare course of study for a lady. I believe there are less than a thousand women practicing law today."

"Well, you needn't worry about me adding to their ranks." Hannah plucked them from his hands. "I'm going to be a switchboard operator now."

"You aren't going back to college?"

She glared at him.

He bristled. If looks could kill, he'd be a buried out back in a matter of minutes.

"Actually," she said, "you and the bank have helped me make that decision, and I find I prefer ensuring my sisters have food on the table to obtaining my law degree. So, as I said, I really don't need these books any longer."

"And the book on ballooning?"

She set the books back in the crate. "That's none of your business."

Tessa flapped her arms. "Hannah is fascinated by anything that flies—birds, balloons, kites, and especially that new flying machine those brothers made."

"Mr. Cole isn't interested in my hobbies, Tessa."

"Quite the contrary." He lifted the crate into his arms. "And all of these books are going in the wagon. Who knows what the Lord has planned?"

≈≈≈◦◯◦≈≈≈

With Tessa already wedged in the bed of the wagon and Charlotte passing out sandwiches to everyone, Hannah slipped back inside the house to say goodbye. All twenty years of her life had been spent in these walls.

She took a deep breath and wished she could carry the memory with her always. How would she recall the outdoorsy scent of her father after he'd put up hay all afternoon? Or the smell of her mother's wonderful molasses rolls fresh from the oven?

Running her hand along the fireplace mantel, she recalled their Christmas stockings hung near the fire and how they'd rushed downstairs to discover what they were filled with. Somehow her parents had always managed to get them candy in addition to an apple or an orange. Under the tree, there'd always been a gift— sometimes store-bought, sometimes homemade.

She wandered upstairs to Tessa's room and then to the room she shared with Charlotte. The view from her window overlooked the fields where she'd so often watched her father plow or harvest the corn crop. Tears burned behind her eyes. Within a few weeks, someone new would be planting rows of corn on his land.

She entered her parents' room. She and her sisters had taken little from it—a special box filled with Momma's locket, cameo, and earrings, Papa's watch, Momma's silver dresser set, and Papa's shaving mug, razor, and pocketknife. The fancy oak bedroom set would never fit in the rented house, and they had no need of her father's clothes. Their mother's, they'd packed. Some of the dresses could be remade.

Dropping to the bed, she buried her face in the feather tick. The tears she'd been keeping at bay released in a torrent.

Lord, why does this have to be so hard? This isn't fair. If only I'd have come home when Momma first got sick, maybe—

Mr. Cole cleared his throat.

She rolled over and looked at him, but his back was to her.

"Miss Gregory, are you ready to go? Folks are starting to arrive for the auction, and I don't think you'll want to see them."

She patted her face dry. "Thank you. I'll be out in a minute."

What was she doing thanking him? This whole thing had started with him representing the bank. The only reason he'd come today was to ease his conscience. Of that she was certain.

He pulled a white handkerchief from his pocket and waved it in the air like a surrender flag. "If you need this, I'm putting it on the banister at the top of the stairs."

He had been kind.

Too bad it was a lie.

Standing, she smoothed the sides of her hair and checked her appearance in the mirror. Before slipping out of the room, she kissed her fingertips and pressed them to the dressing table. She found Mr. Cole's monogrammed handkerchief and traced the embroidered C. She dabbed her eyes with the fine linen cloth and stuffed it in the pocket of her apron.

After glancing around the house one last time, she stepped out on the porch. With her heart as heavy as the crate of law books, she closed the door to the Gregory home behind her.

No, it wasn't fair, but it was happening all the same.

6

"Who are you?" The man in front of Lincoln stood with his arms crossed and his brows furrowed.

Lincoln came to a halt, set down the last crate of books in the wagon bed, and extended his hand. "Lincoln Cole. I'm helping the Gregory girls move into the city. And you are . . . ?"

"Walt Calloway."

Hannah slipped out the front door. When she spotted Walt, her eyes lit up. "Walt!" She hiked up her skirt and hurried down the porch steps. To Lincoln's surprise, reserved Hannah hugged the lanky young man. She turned to Lincoln. "This is Walt Calloway. He's been a dear friend since we shared a reader in second grade."

"My mother said you were moving today. There was a problem with one of the telegraph lines, so I had to make the repairs before I could come out and help, or I'd have been here earlier." Walt kept one hand on Hannah's back as he met Lincoln's eyes. "But it looks like you have everything well in hand."

"Walt works for the Western Union as a lineman." Hannah moved to pat the back of the wagon. "Mr. Cole's already taken one load into town, and we're about to take the other. Can you come and help us unload?"

"I suppose."

"Perfect." She glanced at his wagon and smiled. "I can ride with you, and that way Charlotte can ride up front in Mr. Cole's wagon."

An unfamiliar knot twisted in his gut. Who was this Walt, and why did his appearance make Lincoln feel so uneasy? He'd been looking forward to the drive into town, but he certainly didn't have any designs on Hannah Gregory. She might seem like a breath of fresh air to him, but he was barn-lot stench to her.

He hated that she had such a low opinion of him. Couldn't she see he was not the kind of man she'd originally pictured?

All his work today seemed to do little to change her mind.

Well, that wouldn't stop him from doing what was right. For whatever reason, God had put this family in his path, and he'd make sure the Gregory sisters were taken care of—even if Hannah killed him in the process.

⌁⌁⌁

Every muscle hurt from the move, but Hannah ignored the pain. Excitement and nerves tangled inside her like the telephone wires crisscrossing the street over her head. Rosie walked beside her. In a few minutes, they would cross the threshold of the operators' school, and her new career would begin.

Please, Lord, help me keep my mouth closed.

"I don't know about you, but I'm as nervous as a turkey before Thanksgiving." Rosie pressed her hand to her stomach. "What if I can't remember everything they teach us? What if I can't remember my own name?"

"You're going to do fine." Hannah hoped she sounded convincing. "And they won't let us become real operators until they think we're ready."

"I wonder what the inside of the telephone building looks like." Rosie stopped in front of the Iowa Telephone Company and looked up. The operators' school was housed next door.

Hannah compared the two buildings. The school lacked the fancy cornice work and big windows of the telephone building. She, too, wondered what the Iowa Telephone Company held. Perhaps they'd get a tour of the actual switchboard area today.

Spring scented the air. She drew in a deep breath and smiled at Rosie. "Ready?"

Rosie smoothed her black skirt and adjusted the collar on her white shirtwaist. "Do I look all right?"

After eyeing her own matching outfit—the uniform of all the Hello Girls—Hannah nodded. "Remember to breathe."

At the front door, they were directed by the plump Mrs. Nesbit, the woman who'd weighed and measured them, to join the others. Hannah took a seat and glanced around the classroom. If this wasn't the operators' school, she would have almost been able to convince herself she was back in college. Neat rows of desks filled the room, and a blackboard proclaimed "Welcome" in an elegant script. Charts and maps of the city lined the walls. But where was the switchboard? How could they learn to be operators without that essential piece of equipment?

All around her, young women chattered until Mrs. Reuff, the woman who'd said she was the school's supervisor on the day they'd applied, glided to the front of the room.

"Good morning, ladies." While her voice was warm and smooth, her crooked nose and long, thin face made her expression sharp. "Today you begin your operator training. In your classes, we will teach you to speak in a low, melodious tone. We will teach you about the mechanics of telephony, and we'll explain traffic curves by volume of calls."

Hannah stifled a smile. Was *telephony* a real word?

Mrs. Reuff seemed to pin her with her dark eyes. "Most importantly, you will be trained daily in the proper phraseology to be used with subscribers, and you'll be allowed to use no others."

A young woman in the second row raised her hand. "What if the subscriber says something rude?"

"You will learn how to be courteous to all callers, no matter how difficult they may be." Mrs. Reuff dipped her chin, ending the discussion. "And most of all, you will be trained in a separate, miniature operating room on the switchboard apparatus until you meet our proficiency standards." She swept the room with her gaze. "Then, and only then, will you advance to work as an actual operator."

Rosie opened her notepad and began to jot down everything Mrs. Reuff said. The supervisor smiled in her direction, clearly pleased. "As you know, you were selected because you are intelligent, healthy, painstaking, and agreeable young ladies. Only half of the young ladies who applied reached this point. However, if at any point during your month of training we find you do not meet those qualifications, we will not hesitate to dismiss you."

Hannah felt as if someone had pulled her corset strings taut. Agreeable? For a whole month?

"If any of you show an aptitude for operator's work"—Mrs. Reuff frowned in Hannah's direction—"which at this point remains doubtful, you may advance prior to the end of the four weeks."

Hannah drew in a long breath as the instructor again explained the pay scale. But Mrs. Reuff was quick to emphasize that half of them would prove to be unfit during the training period and would be dropped.

Quick mental calculations told Hannah she'd make thirty-two dollars a month as an operator but only about twenty during her month as a student. If she could move on more quickly, she'd make more money, and she and her sisters needed those extra funds. She'd do whatever it took to fly through the course work and be one of the first promoted to the actual switchboard.

Mrs. Reuff walked over to a cream-colored poster hanging on the wall and picked up a long, pointed stick. "A high-class service in an operating room is the fruit of good discipline, so let's begin with the rules."

Hannah bristled. Why did they have to call them *rules*? Couldn't they refer to them as *guidelines*, or better yet, *suggestions for conduct*?

She bit back a smile, recalling her mother once teasing her about law being a strange profession for someone with such a dislike for rules. She'd explained to her mother that she liked the order of the law—how black-and-white things were and how the law applied to everyone regardless of station or gender. What she didn't like about rules was the indiscriminate way they were handled, where women were restricted and men were allowed to do as they pleased. She hated being confined.

The instructor droned on for nearly half an hour, emphasizing the importance of punctual attendance, mental alertness, and courteous responses to all of the instructor's directives.

All of them? Hannah's tongue was already sore from biting it. She would need to pray extra hard tonight.

Mrs. Reuff went on to explain that the students would be taking several exams and would need to be diligent in their studies. "You must learn to do all things after a certain set form," she said, "using the habitual actions we teach you, and making no mistakes in the process."

Hannah raised her hand. "But I thought—"

"Your first mistake, Miss Gregory." Mrs. Reuff's brow pinched. "Everything you do will be completed by rote. There will be no thinking done here."

She tapped the long pointer against the final rule on the poster. "Because you each now represent Iowa Telephone, Mr. Bradford and I will be checking on your moral character." Mrs. Reuff tapped rule five. "Church attendance is mandatory, and none of you are to receive male callers during the month-long training period. Ladies, do I make myself clear?"

A few girls in the room gasped, but Hannah smiled.

Finally, a rule that would be easy for her to follow.

7

Smoke hung in the air.

Lincoln stepped off the streetcar on Grand Avenue and scanned the sky. Thick, gray billows formed in the air two blocks down, not far from Pete Williams's home. His chest tightened. Pete had gone home from the law office early. What if this was his house?

Jogging down the sidewalk, he zigzagged around the people crowding the sidewalk, all of them trying to determine the fire's location. He nearly tripped over a little girl who stepped into his path, but caught himself and raced on. A bell clanged to his right. He halted. A hook and ladder cart, pulled by three massive-necked, dapple-gray horses, whipped around the corner.

Lincoln passed the first three houses on the blocks, ticking off the names of their owners in his mind—the Kauffmans, the Walkers, the Mennigs. Smoke belched from behind Pete's house.

He finally drew near enough to see the flames. The crowd of gawkers grew so thick he had to slow.

"I heard the whole thing." An elderly woman pointed with her cane toward the smoke. "There was a boom, and then all that smoke filled the air."

Lincoln skirted around her. A gas explosion, maybe? If so, no one was safe around here.

He came to a stop in front of Pete's palatial mansion and breathed a sigh of relief. Whatever was on fire was behind Pete's house, perhaps even in the neighbor's house or yard. He pushed his way through until he was in front of the crowd and then scanned Pete's yard for any sign of his friend. Pete and his grown son, Albert, stood beneath the side portico watching the action behind their house.

"Pete!" Lincoln jogged up the steps of the portico, and Pete and Albert turned. "What's going on? Are you all okay?"

"We're fine. The windows sure shook, but nothing broke." He pointed to the roaring blaze in the back of the house behind him. "Elias Ferguson's carriage house is going up like a piece of kindling."

Lincoln stared at the flames licking the trees around the carriage house, trying to recall the name Elias Ferguson. "The division manager of the Western Union?"

"Yes, that's him."

"How do you think it started?"

Pete looked first at Lincoln and then at his son. "There was an explosion of some sort. I'm sure of that."

Albert didn't take his gaze from the blaze. "With all the talk about striking again, there's sure to be an investigation of this."

"You think it was deliberately set?" Lincoln asked.

Albert, the studious type, shrugged. He seldom spoke more than a few words to Lincoln. For some reason, the young man had a chip on his shoulder when it came to Lincoln.

Pete laid a hand on his son's shoulder. "Unfortunately, Albert's probably right. With all the union problems, this doesn't look good."

Lincoln heard the snap of a beam from inside the burning structure. If the union wanted things to change, setting a fire at the home of the manager hardly seemed the best way to gain the man's cooperation. Then again, frustrated men didn't always think straight.

⁂

What was Walt doing on the front porch of her new home?

After a quick glance about her to see if anyone from the school was around, Hannah quickened her pace. Thankfully, Rosie had made a stop at the drugstore on their way home.

Her heart thudded against her rib cage. What if anyone saw him there, especially with the new rules by which she had to abide?

Walt was bent over with his hands on his knees, his chest rapidly rising and falling. Clearly, he'd run to get there.

Please, Lord, don't let there be any more trouble.

She climbed the steps, and he straightened, pulling the hat from his head. A smile lit his familiar face. "I'm glad you're home. I—"

She held up her hand to cut him off. "We can't talk here. What if someone sees?"

"Sees what?" He held his palms faceup in a perplexed gesture.

"You've got to go." Pressing both hands against his back, she started to push him toward the steps.

"Stop shoving me. I just got here." He turned and frowned. "Why are you acting so crazy? Did you put your finger in one of those switchboard holes?"

She fired an exasperated glare at him. "I can't have gentleman callers while I'm in school, so you have to leave."

"Not until I say my piece. You've known me my whole life, so I don't need to tell you I didn't run all the way here for the exercise."

Hannah bit her lip. If her oldest friend needed to talk to her, why should she let rules stand in her way? A few months ago, that would never have happened.

She started to unlock the door. "Let's go inside."

"Inside? We can't do that. Your sisters aren't home yet. I know because I've been knocking for at least a minute."

"Move it. Now." She grabbed his arm and pulled him through the door.

"Did anyone ever tell you that you're a bossy lady?"

"Yes. Frequently." She stopped inside the front parlor, closed the door behind them, and spun toward him. "So, what's so important you'd risk my job?"

"That job is exactly why I'm here." Without being asked to do so, he crossed the room in three long strides and sat down on the tapestry-covered sofa.

"Why don't you make yourself comfortable?" Sarcasm dripped from her voice.

"Thank you. I don't mind if I do."

"You are as annoying as a brother." Hannah went to the window and closed the inch-long gap in the lace curtains as if doing so would keep out any prying eyes. "Get on with it. Why are you here?"

"I'm worried about you."

"Me? Why?" She sat down on one of the matching parlor chairs, folded her hands in her lap, and studied Walt. The way he casually crossed his ankle over his knee didn't fool her. His green eyes, always so easy to read, said he'd come because of genuine concern.

He placed his hand on his knee. "You know, when you become a full-fledged operator, you'll have a choice of whether to join the union or not."

"I hadn't thought about that, but I suppose you're right. Why is that a problem? I know how active you are in the telegraphers' union. Last year's strike lasted for weeks."

He ran his hand over his chin. "There may be another strike. That's why I'm here."

"What does that have to do with me? I'm sorry, Walt, but I am not following you."

"After last year's strike, six telegraphers—four men and two women—were fired and blacklisted by Western Union management because of their union involvement."

Hannah pressed her back against the chair. Since second grade, she'd been beside him, and she'd never heard him speak with as much venom as when he spoke about the management. The sound unnerved her, but she remained silent to let him finish.

"Those six telegraphers deserve their jobs back, and we're willing to strike to get that done. That is, if our other plans fail." He paced the small room. "Hannah, if we strike, the telephone operators might have to join us. They'd have to honor our strike. Union power lies in stopping the work, or in this case, all communication."

"Then I won't join. I need this job to support my sisters."

"I know, but haven't you heard of some of the things that can happen to folks who break union lines? For your own safety, you have to join or at least honor any strike lines." He stopped and pulled her to her feet. "Please."

"I'll do the best I can."

"I know you will. There's one more thing." Walt removed his hat and raked his hand through his sandy hair. "There may be some trouble. Stay clear of Mulberry Street."

Her stomach cinched tight. She laid her hand on his arm. "Please, don't do anything you might get in trouble for, or anything dangerous."

"Me?" He gave her an impish grin. "You should know better than anyone I'm good at not getting caught." He tapped her nose. "Should I sneak out the back door now?"

She giggled. "How about I dress you up like Charlotte and you can come and go as you please?"

"Don't tempt me, Hannah. We're not in grade school anymore."

"What do you mean by that?"

He didn't answer, but the look he gave her was far from brotherly.

8

What had Walt truly meant by his last few comments?

Hannah set a crate they'd yet to unpack on the kitchen table, her thoughts spinning from Walt's words. Was he implying he wanted to court her? No, she had to be reading too much into his words. They were friends. More like brother and sister. Not once had she looked at Walt that way. Well, maybe once or twice, but she'd still been wearing braids then.

She pulled a cake pan from the crate. Walt loved cake. All kinds, but plain white cake was his favorite. She'd made him one for his birthday last year, and he'd grinned for half the day.

Tessa bounced in, plopped into one of the straight-backed dining chairs, tossed a tablet on the table, and snapped open a newspaper. "'City may be cut off from the rest of the world.'"

"What are you talking about?" Hannah shook the thoughts of Walt from her mind.

"It's the headline in today's paper. I've decided to become a journalist, so I'm keeping track of the best headlines. This story is about the Chicago telegraph union considering another strike, which would cut off Chicago from receiving any communication." Tessa set down the paper.

So this strike talk went beyond Des Moines.

"But I could do a better job writing the story. This is boring."

Hannah smiled at her sister. Lately Tessa wanted to do something different nearly every day. "What would you put in it?"

"Blood. Turmoil. Rioting. People are fascinated by that stuff." Tessa pointed to another headline. "This one is good. 'Victims roasted alive in train wreck.'"

"Tess, that's horrible!"

"But it gets your attention, doesn't it?" Tessa tapped her pencil against the tablet. "So, now I'm going to interview you. Ready?"

With an eye roll, Hannah removed a plate from its wrappings. "Sure."

"Was spending a whole day in classes at operators' school as boring as it sounds?"

After wiping the plate with a towel, Hannah set it in the cupboard, looked at Tessa, and chuckled. Naturally, her younger sister would think spending a full day in classes would be less than exciting.

"It was actually quite fascinating, Tess." Hannah freed another plate from its wrappings. "Professor Phillip E. Tubman came in to teach us about how the telephone works. Did you know a telephone has 201 parts?"

"Do I need to know that?" Tessa jotted the information down. "Did this professor talk all day?"

"No, his class lasted for an hour. Besides the introduction this morning, we had his class on the mechanics of telephony, and Mrs. Nesbit gave us our first voice lesson."

"Why do you have voice lessons? You aren't learning to sing."

"We are learning how to breathe."

Tessa cocked an eyebrow. "You seem to be doing that just fine."

Hannah straightened and pressed a hand to her stomach. She took a deep breath and felt her stomach expand beneath her palm. "See? There's a way to breathe that allows you to project your voice more effectively. You must expand your diaphragm."

"If you say so."

Charlotte strolled into the room. "If you say what?"

Hannah lifted the next crate onto the table and passed Charlotte the heavy cast-iron skillet from within. "I was telling Tessa about what I learned today."

"She learned to breathe." Tessa grinned. "And she says it was fascinating. Makes you want to run out and apply to join her, doesn't it?"

"Tess." Hannah frowned.

"What? That's what you said." She held up her tablet. "See? It's right here. I quoted you."

Charlotte giggled and set the skillet on top of the stove. "I'm afraid it doesn't appear you impressed our little sister."

"But Lottie, you could impress me." Tessa opened the door to the icebox, and cool air whooshed into the room. "By making a delicious supper. I'm starving."

"It's hard to make something delicious when our cupboards are bare." Nudging her younger sister aside, Charlotte opened a cupboard door and held up a can of beans. "Anyone interested in beans du jour?"

"Beans again?" Tessa moaned.

"Sorry. It's all there is."

Guilt tugged on Hannah, and she sank onto a chair at the table. "I know it's hard, but we've used up everything Mother had canned except for a half dozen jars of jelly. And if you recall, we haven't had beans every day. We had fish last week, remember? And Mrs. Murphy brought a housewarming supper over when we moved in. I'll get paid at the end of the week, and we can get some groceries then."

Tessa folded her hands. "Lord, please send us something other than beans to eat. Please, please, please."

A knock on the door interrupted her dramatic prayer and made all three of them turn. Hannah pushed up from the table. "I'll get it."

The oak door groaned as she opened it. Before her, a freckle-faced boy stood, his checked cap askew atop his chestnut hair. In his arms he held a crate with "Zenith Oats: Iowa's Choicest White Oats" displayed across the front.

Hannah smiled at the boy. "Hello, may I help you?"

"This is your delivery from Maxwell Grocery."

"There must be some kind of mistake. I didn't place an order."

He shifted the crate under one arm and pulled out a sheet of paper from the top. "Are you Miss Hannah Gregory?"

"Yes."

"Then it's for you. My paper says it's a housewarming gift for you and your sisters from a Mr. Lincoln Cole."

Him again. Her blood boiled. How dare he try to appease his guilt by sending them food? Did he think they wanted his charity? She ought to march down there right now and give him a piece of her mind.

The boy shifted the crate. "So, where do you want it? The kitchen?"

"We can't accept the order." She took a step back, ready to shut the door.

"Lady, wait! What am I supposed to do with all this?"

"Take it back to the mercantile, please, and explain to Mr. Becker I refused it."

The boy shifted the box again. "But it's my last delivery, and then I can go home."

Hannah took a deep breath. Perhaps she should return it herself. After all, it wasn't fair to make this boy go out of his way because Lincoln Cole thought he could buy his penance.

Tessa stepped between her and the door and slipped outside. "I'll take the box."

"Tessa Gregory, you will not!"

"Hey, I prayed and the Lord answered. Are you gonna argue with God?"

The boy passed the groceries to Tessa's waiting arms in the blink of an eye and was gone down the steps before Hannah could say another word. She glared at her sister. "Now what are we going to do with it?"

"I have one suggestion." Tessa balanced the crate on her right arm, reached inside, and pulled out an apple. She bit into it with a loud crunch. With her mouth still full, she mumbled, "Let's eat."

Hannah tried to remove the crate from her sister's arms, but the girl was too fast. Tessa hurried inside and deposited the groceries on the kitchen table.

Charlotte's eyes widened. "Where did all this come from?"

"Mr. Cole." Tessa took another bite from her apple and swiped the juices from her chin.

"And before you start making menus, we can't keep it." Hannah laid her hand on the box's rough wood slats.

"Why not?" Tessa asked. "I heard the boy say it was a house-warming gift."

"Because it's not right." Hannah sighed. "Mr. Cole shouldn't be sending us gifts."

"But Daddy always said you never know how the Lord is going to provide when you pray." Tessa raised a can of Folgers coffee beans in the air and shook it with fire-and-brimstone furor. Beans rattled inside. "Well, I prayed and the Lord provided." She shook the tin again. "How long has it been since you had any coffee? We all know how much you love it."

Hannah's mouth watered at the thought of sipping a cup of the dark brew enhanced with sugar and cream, but they couldn't keep this gift. It simply wasn't right.

Charlotte moved some items around in the box. "There's a quart of milk and a couple packages from the butcher in here too. We should probably get those in the icebox."

"You think we should keep this too?" She glared at them. Had they all gone mad? "Need I remind you it was Mr. Cole who made us lose our home? He's an egotistical, arrogant, know-it-all man who feels guilty about putting out three orphans."

"Mr. Cole's been nothing but kind, Hannah. I don't think it's fair to read other things into his thoughtful gesture." Charlotte picked up the quart of milk and set it in the icebox. "Besides, he didn't take the house. The bank did. He was simply the messenger, and it isn't fair to shoot the messenger."

"I'd like to shoot this one with Daddy's shotgun," Hannah mumbled.

Charlotte shook the butcher's package in her direction. "I'm surprised at you. Besides, it is a gift, and Momma wouldn't want us to be rude and turn it away."

"Fine." Hannah crossed her arms over her chest. "It might take a while, but I'll pay him back for every crumb."

Charlotte took the Folgers tin from Tessa and pried open the lid. She waved the tin beneath Hannah's nose. "In the meantime, what do you say to a cup of coffee provided by the egotistical, arrogant, know-it-all man who was thoughtful enough to include coffee?"

The scent filled Hannah's nostrils, and she licked her lips.

One cup couldn't hurt.

He owed her for everything he'd put her through.

<hr />

One more set of contracts to process, and Lincoln could call it a day. It had been a long week, and he couldn't wait to spend some time on the golf course. Holding the stack in his hands, he tapped the edges against the surface of his desk to line up the papers, then began reading the first page. By page two, the words blurred beneath his gaze.

He leaned back in his chair and propped his feet on the edge of his desk. Lulled by the rat-a-tat of the stenographer's typewriter, the low, steady hum of conversation, and the crinkling of paper, he closed his eyes. He gave in to the urge for a quick nap. A few minutes of sleep couldn't hurt.

A blow to his feet startled him, and he jerked upright, nearly toppling from the chair.

"Here!"

He grabbed the desk to regain his balance and looked up to see Hannah Gregory thrusting her palm toward him with two shiny quarters in the center.

"Take it." She pushed her upturned hand forward. "I know it doesn't cover the groceries, but it's a start."

He shook his head, feeling more muddled than awake. How long had he been dozing? He heard snickering and glanced around the office. Cedric. He imagined the weasel was enjoying this scene far too much.

Lincoln lowered his voice. "Hannah, what are you talking about?"

"It's Miss Gregory to you." She jammed her fists onto her hips. "And I'm referring to the gift you had delivered to my sisters and me after we moved in."

"The food?"

"Yes." She extended the coins toward him again. "I intend to pay you back."

He scowled and pushed her hand away. "Sit down."

She didn't budge.

"Please, have a seat, Miss Gregory." He sighed. "I'd prefer to talk to you face-to-face rather than have you hover over me like my overbearing grade-school teacher. A woman, as a matter of fact, I didn't much care for."

"The best I can promise is not to rap your knuckles with a ruler." She squared her shoulders. "Besides, I prefer to do this standing."

"Do what?"

Slowly she raised her hand over his desk blotter. First one coin and then the other fell with a ping, rolled in a circle, and came to a rest.

Lightning fast, he snatched up the coins and rounded his desk. "I am not accepting these." He grabbed her wrist and shoved the coins back in her hand.

"Yes you are!"

Laughter from his officemate tickled his ears, and his face heated. The pulse in his jaw thrummed. He leaned closer to her and forced the words to come out calm. "Let's talk about this in private."

"I'm not going anywhere."

"Well, I am. You can stand here all day if you want." With that, he headed out of the office and toward the elevator, praying she'd follow. What if she stayed in the office and made a scene?

After reaching the elevator, he punched the button and forced himself not to turn around to see if Hannah was behind him. His patience was rewarded when he heard the telltale click of her pounding heels on the hardwood floor, and from the speed of the clicks, he guessed her anger still ran red-hot.

The elevator rumbled to a stop, and Mr. Welch, the white-haired elevator operator, pulled open the wire-cage door. Lincoln motioned toward the entrance, and Hannah marched inside. He followed.

"Where can I take you, Mr. Cole?" Mr. Welch asked.

"First floor, please. We're going for a walk."

Hannah shot him a fiery glare.

Mr. Welch chuckled and shoved the brass lever to the side. "Pardon my saying, but the lady doesn't look like she cares for your idea."

Hannah crossed her arms over her chest as if to punctuate her agreement with Mr. Welch's observation. Lincoln grinned and counted the floors of the office building as they descended.

Nine, eight, seven. Ramrod straight, Hannah pressed her back against the wall. What was she thinking? As an attorney, he'd been trained to anticipate the enemy's next move, but she wasn't an easy woman to read.

Five, four. He chuckled. Even as clearly irate as she was, he found it hard to think of her as the enemy. Still, he was willing to bet a week's worth of paperwork that she was preparing to deliver an earful of ugliness at her earliest convenience. Well, if she wanted a fight . . .

Three, two. The elevator jolted and came to a halt. Caught off balance, Hannah stumbled into him. Lincoln caught her, and her cheeks filled with color.

"Hmm." Mr. Welch rubbed his beard. "Looks like she's warming up to you already, Mr. Cole."

9

Despite Hannah's best efforts to break free without causing a scene, Lincoln Cole kept hold of her elbow and directed her out of the building. He didn't slow at the sidewalk but led her across the paved brick street to the green space of Court House Square.

"Unhand me."

He yanked his hand away as if he didn't realize he'd still been holding on to her. "I apologize."

"Now, if you'll kindly take this"—she held out the money again—"I can be on my way."

He crossed his arms over his chest. "I told you I'm not accepting that. Those groceries were a gift."

"It's not appropriate for me to accept a gift from you." Even though she'd planned this moment for days, it was not going the way she wanted.

He hiked a shoulder. "Well, they weren't for you. They were for Tessa. Is it wrong to give a gift to a starving orphan?"

"I would never let my sister starve!"

"That's not how she makes it sound." He straightened his tie.

Had Tessa truly told him that? She was going to give her sister a thorough tongue-lashing for her tall tales as soon as she got this infuriating man to accept her payment. "Tessa is melodramatic. She makes everything sound like it's the end of the world."

"That may be, but I was doing my Christian duty. The Scriptures say taking care of widows and orphans is pure and undefiled religion. So if you have a problem with it, you'll have to take it up with God."

Oh, he knew he had her, and it irked her to the very soles of her feet. Why couldn't he understand she didn't want anyone's help, but especially his?

She took a deep, cleansing breath and glanced around the open area. Some businesses closed early on Fridays, so the streets already bustled with activity.

The streetcar jingled its bell as it approached. It stopped at the corner, and the passengers hurried off. Mrs. Reuff, the supervisor of the operators' school, stepped from the streetcar bearing a package. Hannah's breath caught. What was the instructor doing here? Apparently, mailing a package, as the post office was in the Federal Building. But what if she spotted Hannah?

"Hannah, is something wrong?"

She turned away from the streetcar. "I can't be seen with you."

"Why not?"

"See that woman over there in the big peach hat? It's Mrs. Reuff, one of the instructors at my operators' school." Hannah glanced back at Mrs. Reuff.

"And?"

"The operators' school has rules about gentleman acquaintances." She held out her hand. "Please, take this so I can go home. I can't afford to jeopardize my position."

"Mrs. Reuff can't say anything if you're consulting your attorney."

"But you're not my—"

He inclined his head toward the approaching instructor. "Come on. Let's get out of here."

A few minutes later, Mr. Cole had secured a table near the window at one of the small restaurants on Mulberry Street. He signaled the waitress and ordered them each a cup of coffee.

"I shouldn't be here, Mr. Cole." She sipped from her porcelain cup. The scent of cinnamon wafted through the air, and she wondered if a pie had recently come out of the oven. Her mouth watered at the thought.

Two businessmen at the window table behind them must have had the same idea and called the waitress over to add to their order. Mr. Cole did likewise.

"I don't need any pie, Mr. Cole."

"Please call me Lincoln." He peeked over his own cup. "Remember, that's my name."

"If Mrs. Reuff sees us—"

He set the cup down. "Then you'll explain we were dealing with matters of your parents' estate."

"But we aren't."

"Did your parents have any life insurance?"

"You know they didn't." She pressed her cold hands to the sides of the warm cup.

"See? We've already addressed one facet of the estate." His blue-gray eyes flickered as though he were pleased with his own subterfuge.

"Does lying always come so easily to you?"

His scowl made her regret the sharpness in her words. "No. In fact, honesty is a trait I greatly admire. And as long as we're on the subject, why don't we start with you telling me the truth about why you came to see me today?"

"I came to pay you back for the groceries."

"But that's not why *you* personally came when you could have easily mailed me the money and saved yourself the trip."

"But . . . I . . . It didn't seem proper to mail it."

His brows peaked. "You know what I think? I think you wanted to see me again."

"That's ridiculous." Her face and neck grew warm, and she gathered her handbag and stood. "This is strictly business, Mr. Cole. I apologize for entering your office in such a—"

"A huff?"

"No, I was going to say for entering your office in such a way that I drew attention to your nap." She slapped her napkin beside her plate. "Next week, I can assure you I'll mail the money."

～◦◟◯◞◦～

Lincoln heard glass shatter behind him, and Hannah screamed. He grabbed her waist, pulled her to the floor, and covered her body with his own. A second window splintered, and shards rained around them.

"Hannah?" He rolled off her and reached for her arm. "Are you hurt anywhere?"

She sat up and brushed herself off. "No. I'm fine. What about the others?"

He looked around. The two businessmen were being aided by the waitress but seemed mostly unharmed. He carefully drew Hannah to her feet and studied her.

"Lincoln, you're bleeding."

"So are you." A long, thin scratch marred her pale cheek. He pulled out his handkerchief and dabbed at the blood. He'd deal with his own wound later.

"What happened?" Hannah looked around the scene.

Lincoln pointed to two bricks lying on the floor with notes tied to them. "I think someone threw those and broke the windows, and apparently, they were sending a message."

"To whom?"

He picked up one of the bricks and removed the note. He turned to the other restaurant patrons. "Are any of you with the telegraph company?"

The two men who'd been at the other window nodded.

"Then this special delivery is for you." He offered them the notes.

"Lincoln, what are you talking about?"

He led her toward the door, glass crunching under their feet. "Apparently, this whole mess is due to a union problem."

"Someone from the telegraph company smashed the windows?"

"According to that note, yes."

All color seemed to wash from her face, and she swayed.

69

He steadied her. "Are you all right?"

"I need to get home."

"As soon as we speak to the police, I'll get a hansom cab and take you home." They stepped outside onto the sidewalk, and he watched her scan the crowd.

Who was she looking for? Her instructor? A prickly feeling inched up his spine. Or was it someone else?

⊱⋅ ⊰

Hannah's sisters would be worried sick by now. She sat in a hansom cab beside Lincoln with the sunlight rapidly fading. She should've been home over two hours ago, but by the time they'd bandaged Lincoln's arm and spoken to the police, her hopes of getting home early had shattered like the restaurant's windows.

"You sure you're not hurt? I tackled you pretty hard." Lincoln touched her arm.

"I'm fine." But she'd be sore tomorrow. "I suppose I owe you a debt of gratitude."

"You make it sound so painful." His blue eyes teased her.

"Every time I'm sure I want nothing to do with you, you do something nice and almost convince me otherwise."

"Almost?"

She didn't answer. Kindness oozed from Lincoln, but he had taken their farm. Did he expect her to forget that? "Can you ask the cab to stop here?"

"But we're nearly three blocks away."

"Getting out now is for the best. I can't risk being seen with you escorting me home."

He informed the driver, and she adjusted her hat. "Any more glass shards?"

Gripping her chin between his thumb and forefinger, he tilted her head to one side and then the other. "You look perfect." He brushed over the scratch with the pad of his thumb. "Except for this."

The cab stopped, and Lincoln helped her out. "I'd feel better walking you all the way home."

She held up her hand. "Thank you for the offer, but you can't." She dipped her head in a brief nod and began to walk away.

"Hannah," Lincoln called, "if you need anything, anything at all—"

"Thanks, but I won't." She flipped up her hand without turning around. "Don't worry about me. I'll be fine."

10

What if he wanted to worry about her?

Lincoln climbed back in the hansom cab and told the driver to follow Hannah at a distance until she got home. She never turned to see if he was still there, but that didn't surprise him. When she finally reached the front porch of the tiny rented home, the driver snapped the reins, and Lincoln felt an odd tug at leaving her. Why did he feel so responsible for Hannah Gregory when she seemed so determined to have nothing to do with him?

He leaned his head back against the cushioned leather seat and closed his eyes. His stomach rumbled, reminding him it was well past dinnertime. He should have insisted on taking Hannah some place nice after the ordeal she'd gone through, but she probably would have declined. He laughed wryly. Probably? No, she certainly would have declined. If he was a smart man, and he was, he'd put Hannah Gregory out of his thoughts.

Unfortunately, his thoughts didn't seem to care a whit about his intelligence.

Charlotte removed another sliver of glass from Hannah's hair. Even after thirty minutes of picking through her older sister's tresses, she'd yet to learn anything from Hannah, other than her sister had been at a restaurant where someone had thrown a brick through the front window.

Rattled—that was the word Charlotte would have to use to describe Hannah, but that seemed strange. Hannah always took chances. A little danger didn't usually bother her.

"So you heard the glass break, and then what did you do?" Tessa flopped across Hannah's bed with a tablet in hand.

"I screamed. It surprised me, but I don't want to talk about it anymore."

"Aw, come on. This is my first real story."

"And you aren't writing this one either," she snapped.

A close call didn't usually make Hannah sharp-tongued.

"What did Mr. Cole do after you screamed?"

Charlotte watched Hannah's cheeks grow rosy in the mirror's reflection. Using tweezers, she removed another chunk of glass from Hannah's hair and dropped it into the china saucer on the dressing table. Oh! The truth dawned on Charlotte, and her cheeks spread wide in a grin. It wasn't the window breaking agitating Hannah. It was Lincoln's reaction to it—or perhaps it was Hannah's reaction to Lincoln.

Tessa sat up on the edge of the bed. "Did he dive under the table like a coward?"

"No!"

Hmm. She'd certainly come to his defense.

"Well?" Tessa motioned with her hand for Hannah to continue.

"He pulled me to the floor."

"And?" Charlotte couldn't resist a little prodding of her own. There were things a sister deserved to know.

"And he shielded my body with his own."

"How romantic!" Tessa feigned a swoon and fell back on the coverlet.

Hannah looked up at Charlotte's reflection in the mirror. "Why are you smiling? It was an instinctive act."

She forced her lips into a straight line. "Whatever you say, Hannah."

Tessa bolted upright. "Did Mr. Cole get hurt? Was his handsome face disfigured in any way?"

"Lincoln got a cut on his arm, but his face is fine."

Charlotte picked up the brush and began to draw it through Hannah's long tresses. "Lincoln, huh?"

Hannah didn't respond. Rather, she lifted her hand to touch the scratch on her cheek. From the dreamy look in her sister's eyes, Charlotte guessed Lincoln Cole was beginning to build an irrefutable case for himself.

⌘

Hannah took a deep whiff. The familiar mixture of old ladies' perfumes and freshly oiled pews mingled in the air. Home. Well, almost home. Their church home. Their actual home had been auctioned off, and another family was now filling its rooms. Glad her sisters had agreed to take the streetcar to the edge of town and walk to the church where they'd regularly attended, Hannah shook off her melancholy and began to greet their friends.

Sally Gerard smiled when she entered. The girl was a few years younger than Charlotte and had her hair done in a grown-up style for the first time. After telling her how pretty she looked, Hannah caught sight of little Tommy Vincent. She hoped the Vincents would end up sitting in front of her. Their freckle-faced boy's church antics always proved to be great fun. She could still remember the summer when he'd taken a snake out of his pocket right when the preacher brought up Satan's appearance in the Garden of Eden. Another time, he'd emptied a jar of frogs during an especially long sermon, bringing it to a rapid conclusion.

The boy certainly had good timing.

Walt's angular face lit up when he spotted her. He sidestepped plump Mrs. Witherspoon and made a beeline for her. "What happened to your face?"

Tessa's eyes lit up. "She was at a restaurant when a brick was thrown through the window."

"You were *there*?"

Hannah looked at her sisters, dismissing them with a tilt of her head. Charlotte caught the hint and dragged Tessa away.

Walt pressed closer. "Why didn't you listen to me? I told you to avoid that street."

"I'm fine. Thank you for your concern."

"I'm sorry. That came out wrong, but if I knew you were there, I . . ."

"Walt, please tell me you didn't have anything to do with what happened."

Before Walt could answer, Mrs. Reuff entered the foyer, and Hannah jumped. What was she doing here? Of course, she'd warned the girls she would personally check up on each of them and their moral turpitude, but Hannah didn't know Mrs. Reuff went as far as to visit their churches.

She glanced Hannah's way, seemed to take in Hannah's proximity to Walt, and raised her thick eyebrows. She then glided past Hannah, offering a casual "good morning" on her way.

Walt leaned toward Hannah's ear. "Who is that?"

"Don't do that!" She pressed her hand against Walt's chest. "She's my instructor at operators' school. She must be here to check up on me. You have to get out of here."

"Out of church?"

"Yes—no—I mean at least away from me."

"Hannah, I'm beginning to think you have a few wires switched of your own." A frown suddenly pulled the corners of Walt's lips downward. "Why's he here?"

She turned. Dressed in a sporty Sack Suit jacket, lemon-yellow shirt, and stiff collars and cuffs, Lincoln Cole breezed through the church doors. He sauntered toward her.

"What are you doing here?" she hissed.

He straightened his tie. "Attending church services. I go every Sunday."

"But you don't go *here*."

He faced Walt and tugged on the lapel of his suit jacket. "I may now."

Good grief. She didn't need this. She glanced in the sanctuary and caught Mrs. Reuff watching her. "I'm leaving you both this instant. Don't either of you dare sit by me."

Lincoln held up his hands in mock surrender. "I wouldn't dream of it."

She faced her oldest friend. "Walt?"

"But we sit together every Sunday."

"Walt." Her voice was firm. "Do you want me to lose my position?"

"No." He gave Lincoln a cold look. "But I don't want to lose mine either."

She rolled her eyes and walked away. Men. She'd never understand them. But thanks to Mrs. Reuff and the operators' school, she didn't need to—at least for the next few weeks.

Walt and Lincoln followed her into the sanctuary a few minutes later. They took a seat on either end of her pew, like enormous male bookends. What were these two doing?

When the service concluded, she brushed past Walt and hurried to greet Mrs. Reuff. She had to wait a few seconds as her instructor had snagged the preacher, and they seemed deep in conversation.

Little Billy Carstens, who'd only started walking a few months ago, toddled up to Hannah and extended his chubby arms. "Momma! Momma!"

Hannah lifted the little cherub into her arms, and he hugged her neck. She pressed a kiss to the top of his blond head, surprised by how much she'd missed this little fellow.

Billy deposited a slobbery kiss on her cheek. "Momma."

Mrs. Reuff turned toward her, her eyebrows raised high.

"I'm not his—he's not my—"

"Momma!" He lunged for Mrs. Reuff, but Hannah pulled him back. "Say hi to Mrs. Reuff."

"There you are, Billy." Claire Carstens, clearly in the family way, waddled over. "Thank you for grabbing him, Hannah. He gets away from me so easily these days."

He reached for his real mother. She took him and balanced him on her hip. "I'm Claire Carstens, this ornery little fellow's momma."

"I'm Abigail Reuff, one of Miss Gregory's instructors at the operators' school."

"Operators' school?" Claire frowned. "What happened to law school?"

"It's not in my future anymore."

"Oh." Claire forced a weak smile, then turned to Mrs. Reuff. "It's nice of you to join us today, ma'am."

After Claire had slipped away, Mrs. Reuff adjusted her cape. "As you know, we make every effort to check out the recommendations each of the young women provided. Brother Molden spoke highly of your moral character in his letter." She eyed Walt and then Lincoln. "It surprised me, as you seem to be a popular young lady."

"Those two? Walt is a childhood friend, and Mr. Cole is an attorney."

"Oh yes. I'm sure you are still settling your parents' affairs." She touched the brooch at the nape of her neck. "You have a bright future with the telephone company. I'd hate to see you let any-thing—or anyone—damage that. Do I make myself clear?"

"As clear as the connection on an Iowa Telephone line."

◦∾◦⟨⊙⟩◦∾◦

Why had Lincoln shown up in her little country congregation yesterday?

Hannah jotted the question on her tablet as Mrs. Reuff droned on and on and on. Was he possibly interested in her? No, they were from two different worlds. She simply wasn't in his social class.

"Miss Gregory?"

She jerked her head up, her chest coiled tight. "Could you repeat the question, ma'am?"

Mrs. Reuff's lips formed a perfect upside-down *U*. "If I must. How many seconds should each call be limited to?"

Hannah let out the breath she'd been holding. She knew this. "Six seconds from answer to connection."

"And what is the biggest obstacle in reaching that goal?"

"Inattentiveness on the part of the operator."

Mrs. Reuff tapped Hannah's tablet. "You might do well to remember that."

"Yes, ma'am."

"Now, ladies, I have your scores from the exam Professor Tubman gave on Friday over the science of telephony. I'll pass the exams out now, but please keep your score to yourself. If your score is below 70 percent, there is no need for you to return tomorrow."

Although before the exam they'd been told half of the students would probably not make it beyond this point, Hannah heard a few gasps. The shifting of chairs and the mounting tension in the air told her she wasn't the only one who was worried. That test, which included the mechanics of the switchboard, had been as hard as any of her college Latin exams, but she was certain she'd passed it. She glanced at Rosie, her complexion pale, her hands clasped in front of her as if she were praying. They'd studied together, and the information hadn't come easy to her friend. If the test was hard for Hannah, she knew it had been doubly so for Rosie.

Mrs. Reuff riffled through her stack of papers as she walked down the row, passing a graded exam to each young woman. Rosie accepted hers, and a slight smile appeared on her face. She cocked the paper so Hannah could see her score of seventy-one. But when Mrs. Reuff reached Hannah, she didn't hand her a copy of the test. Instead, she skipped her and moved on to the next student.

Hannah's stomach twisted like the wires in the back of the switchboard. Had she really failed the exam? Was Mrs. Reuff going to give her the bad news privately? Or had her problems earlier put her in danger of losing her position in the training school?

With only one paper still in hand, Mrs. Reuff again addressed the class. "Tomorrow we will begin drills on the practice switchboards, so please review the procedure manual. It will be a trying day, so be sure to get your rest. But before you all go, I'd like to announce who received the highest score on Professor Tubman's exam." She looked at Hannah. "Congratulations, Miss Gregory. You scored a ninety-six."

"A ninety-six? She cheated," a voice whispered behind Hannah. One stern look from Mrs. Reuff silenced the rude speaker.

Hannah whirled in her seat to see who had uttered the lie and discovered snooty Ginger Smith. Martha Cavanaugh pinned Hannah with a livid glare.

So much for making friends.

After the class was dismissed, a few girls congratulated Hannah, but she could tell being publicly recognized had not done her any service. When she spotted tears coursing down one of the girl's cheeks, guilt jabbed her. Some of these young women would not be returning. She swallowed her joy and put on a somber face.

Rosie squeezed her arm. "I'm so proud of you!"

"Thank you." Hannah picked up her books and nestled them against her hip. "I'm glad we both made it. That wasn't an easy test."

"I really didn't think I'd pass." Rosie skirted the desks and walked down the hallway beside Hannah.

"Take comfort in knowing they said that was the hardest one. The rest should be easy."

"Easy for you." Rosie laughed. "But at least we're in this together."

Hannah tried to hide her joy, but it came out in the bounce of her steps as they left the building. She could never tell her sisters this, but she missed her college studies terribly. Nothing felt better than to know she'd done well on an exam.

"Hannah." Martha Cavanaugh stepped in front of her, no warmth coming from her voice. "Don't make the rest of us look bad again. Some of us need this job."

"Yes, and I'm one of them." Hannah offered a sweet smile. "If you need any help with your studies, Martha, let me know. You can always study with Rosie and me." She nudged Rosie, and they left a gaping Martha in their wake.

"Why'd you offer to do that?" Rosie asked.

"My mother always said to render a blessing rather than a curse."

"Well, I can almost guarantee you someone is still doing some cursing."

"Rosie! I'm shocked."

"What? I've known her all my life. Martha learned how to rule the sandbox by the end of first grade."

Hannah shrugged. "I don't think she'll give me any trouble."

"You may have been as sweet as pie back there, but mark my words, Martha Cavanaugh has your name at the top of her 'least favorites' list."

"Maybe she'll forget about it."

Rosie shook her head. "She never forgets."

Great. And with my luck, she'll remember at the most inopportune moment.

11

Charlotte couldn't believe her ears. Dreamy-eyed George Donnelly had actually asked if he could walk her, the new girl, home from school.

After forcing her smile not to betray her fluttering heart, Charlotte nodded. "I guess that would be all right."

He took her books and stacked them on his own. "You live on Chestnut Street, right?"

She nodded. *Oh my stars, he knows where I live.* "I . . . I have to wait for my little sister."

"Really? Are you sure?" He frowned. "I need to get to baseball practice, but I guess we can wait if we have to."

George didn't seem at all pleased to wait, despite what he said. What if he decided to go on without her? An invitation from someone like George didn't come every day. Besides, she wasn't Tessa's nursemaid. Her sister was old enough to take care of herself.

She tilted her head to the side. "I guess Tessa will be fine. She can find her own way home."

A broad smile creased his face. "Good. Let's go then."

The six-block walk might as well have been on air, and it was over much too soon. She'd learned George was an only child and had no idea what he wanted to do with his life. He laughed with ease and had no trouble expressing his opinions. And his grass-green eyes? They were as lethal as any weapons, and he knew how to use them.

When she reached the top of the porch steps, she turned to

George and held out her hands for her books. "Thank you for walking me home. I enjoyed it."

George held the books tight against his hip. "Why don't you come watch my practice?"

"Now? I can't. I need to make dinner."

"You should make one of your sisters do it."

She laughed. "Tessa isn't much of a cook yet, and I can't make Hannah do anything. She'd tell me I should do what I'm asked."

"She's not your mother."

"No." Charlotte let out a long breath. "But she feels responsible for us, and she's working hard to give us a home. I want to do what I can to help."

He shrugged and passed the stack of books her way. "The way I see it, she expects you to take your mother's place in the kitchen— like hired help. I guess I was hoping for more. I'll see you around."

"At school tomorrow?"

"Sure."

"Bye." She waved her fingers at him as he turned. With his shoulders slumped, he looked so dejected her heart squeezed. Maybe he was right. Her sister expected too much from her. Hannah hadn't thought twice about leaving them the other day to go see Lincoln Cole. Why should things be different for Charlotte? Shouldn't she have the opportunity to spend time with a boy?

"George, wait. Let me put these inside, and I'll go with you after all."

❧❧❧

Smoke billowed from the kitchen. Hannah threw down her books and raced into the room to find Tessa removing a charred pan from the oven. Tessa dropped the pan in the sink and shoved the oven door shut with the toe of her shoe. She pumped water onto the charred contents, and smoke rose with a hiss.

"What happened? Where's Charlotte?"

Tessa wiped her hands on a flour-dusted apron. "Heaven knows. She left me a note that said to make supper."

"You?"

Tessa jutted out her chin. "I can cook."

The remains of the biscuits slid out of the pan in a congealed black blob, but Hannah chose not to point out the serious doubts she had about her youngest sister's cooking abilities at the moment. "I mean, why isn't Charlotte cooking dinner? Is she ill?"

"I don't know. I haven't seen her."

"Didn't you see Charlotte after school?"

"No, she didn't wait for me. Here's the note she left." Tessa snagged a piece of paper off the table and thrust it at Hannah. "Now, if you'll excuse me, I have some stew to stir before it goes the unfortunate way of the biscuits."

Hannah read the missive. It was so unlike Charlotte not to fulfill her obligations. Where Hannah struggled with rules, Charlotte was a rule keeper. She wouldn't take off without a good reason. Something had to be wrong.

"Tess, listen. I'm going to go look for Charlotte. If she comes back—" The front door banged open, and Hannah's heart skipped. *Thank you, Lord, for bringing her home.* "Charlotte?"

Her middle sister breezed into the house with a wide smile on her face. She walked straight to the kitchen and poured herself a glass of milk.

Hannah frowned. Charlotte hadn't even commented on the acrid smoke still lingering in the air. "Where have you been, and why did you have Tessa make supper?"

"I went somewhere with a friend." Charlotte plucked a cookie from the jar on the counter. "Besides, it shouldn't be my job to cook every day. It's only fair we share the responsibility for meals."

"That may be so, but you don't go changing the plans willy-nilly, and you can't leave Tessa making meals unsupervised. She's not ready for that."

"And where were you after school?" Tessa pointed at her sister with a stew-dripping spoon.

"Tessa! Watch what you're doing." Charlotte pointed to the spot on the floor.

Hannah wiped the spot with a cloth. "You had me worried. I was about to go looking for you."

"Oh, good grief, Hannah. I went out with a friend for one afternoon. It isn't like I burned the house down." She sniffed the air. "But it smells like Tessa sure tried."

"Charlotte, what's gotten into you? Who is this friend?"

Another smile blossomed on Charlotte's face, and her cheeks pinked. "Only the most handsome boy in my class. His name is George Donnelly. He asked me to go watch his baseball practice. I'm sorry, Hannah. I know I should have told him no, but he made so much sense at the time, and he looked so sad when I said I couldn't join him."

"So you left the note and went anyway—even though you knew we'd be upset with you?"

Charlotte gave a weak smile. "If you saw his dreamy eyes, you'd understand."

Hannah crossed her arms over her chest. "Don't do this again, Charlotte. It's not fair to make us worry. Now help Tessa finish supper. I have a test to study for."

Charlotte lifted her apron from a hook on the back of the door and draped it over her shirtwaist. "Your work is always the most important, isn't it?"

"Did George say that too?" Hannah shook her head in disbelief. This wasn't the Charlotte who'd left this morning. Hannah was beginning to think she didn't like this George boy one bit. "Yes, my work is important. If I don't pass, we don't eat, and we're all in this together, remember?"

Hannah received no immediate response, but she heard her sister mumble as she left the room. What would her mother and father have done about this George? While her mother probably would have given Charlotte time to discern this young man's character for herself, her father most likely would have run him off with a shotgun. Hannah chuckled. For the first time in her life, she was beginning to like the way her father thought.

12

"Num-bah, puh-leez." Hannah stood in front of the mirror watching her lips as she formed the words so often repeated when working as an operator.

"I don't know what you're worried about." Rosie laid her hands on the open volume in front of her. "You seem like you've been connecting calls all your life."

Hannah smiled. Their first week at the practice switchboard had been fun. Some of the girls had become quite frazzled at trying to remember all the details, but Hannah found it much easier to pick up than she'd expected. Still, Saturday offered her the perfect opportunity to practice.

"Mrs. Reuff said I needed to work on my enunciation." She faced the mirror again. "What do you think? Are the vowels open enough when I say *puh-leez*?"

Tessa turned from her seat on the sofa. "Would you two *puh-leez* be quiet? I'm working."

"Collecting more headlines?" Hannah joined her on the sofa.

"Tessa, I'd like to hear them—puh-leez." Rosie giggled.

Hannah moaned. "Don't encourage her."

"I thought you Gregory girls were all about encouraging each other's dreams." Rosie closed her book. "Read me one, Tessa."

"Your mother gave me some older newspapers. This article is

from a paper that came out the day we moved here. 'Groom waits while bride suicides.'"

"Tess, that's horrible!"

Hannah's youngest sister bit her lip but didn't look remotely contrite. "But I bet everyone who saw that headline read the article. Wouldn't you?"

Rosie raised her brows, laughter dancing in her eyes.

"That's not the point." Hannah removed her hat pin and hat and set them on the table. "Was there any news we *needed* to know in that paper?"

"There was another fire."

"Really? Where?"

"Hmm." Tessa paused to read the article. "It was at one of the Western Union supply buildings. They think it was arson. Some kind of explosion. It says they have several suspects."

Fear spiraled up Hannah's spine. Another fire linked to Western Union. She prayed Walt had not been involved.

~~~✸~~~

Lincoln stepped up to the fairway and turned to his caddie. The young man handed Lincoln a wood from the canvas and leather golf bag. Lincoln thanked him and stepped around Pete Williams to tee off. After positioning himself on the side of the golf ball, he drew in a deep breath of spring air and said a prayer of thanks. Only the second day of May, and he was already enjoying the golf course at the country club.

Muscles tense, Lincoln twisted his body and swung the club. The ball sailed into the air until it became a white dot against the pale blue sky. It came down just short of the putting green.

"Not bad, Linc. Good loft." Pete clapped him on the shoulder and chuckled. "Now, let me show you how it's really done."

Lincoln laughed and stepped aside. Pete bent over the ball, his rounded belly hanging low. He swung the golf club, and the shot went wide.

"So that's how it's done? Funny, I thought the goal was to get the ball in the hole."

"Yeah, yeah. Always a smart guy." Pete fell in step beside Lincoln as they walked down the fairway. Their caddies fell in behind. "I heard the Gregory girl came in the office the other day and put you in your place."

"Who said that?"

"Cedric. Who else?" Pete walked to his ball and lined up the shot. He chipped it onto the putting green.

Lincoln removed an iron from his golf bag and approached his ball. "Cedric should have been a fiction writer. He always has his own version of things." He drew the club back and watched the ball bounce onto the green, then roll closer to the hole.

"So what's your version? Did she put you in your place, or vice versa?"

"I plead the fifth." With a grin, Lincoln turned to the caddie and exchanged his iron for a putter.

"Well, well, well. I guess you don't need to say anything. That smile on your face is as self-incriminating as it can get. Do we need to have you and Miss Gregory over for dinner one evening?"

"No." Lincoln shook his head and practiced a couple of putting shots. "Hannah Gregory might be a fascinating young woman, but she isn't interested in the man who took her home." He tapped the ball. It rolled two yards and circled the hole without going in. Emitting a groan, he tapped it. The ball dropped with a ping into the cup.

"It's not like you to let one by." Pete easily sank his putt, then shot Lincoln a challenging grin.

Lincoln handed his caddie the club. "Are you talking about my putt or Miss Gregory?"

"Both." He wrapped his arm around Lincoln's shoulder. "Now, let's go get something to eat, and thanks to my last stellar putt, I believe you're buying. But we need to hurry. Ever since that fire, Elise has been on edge."

They started back to the clubhouse, and Lincoln considered

how to ask about Elise's mental health. She'd always been prone to periods of melancholy. "Is everything okay with Elise?"

Pete nodded. "She's a little rattled, is all. She's better since they made an arrest."

"An arrest?"

"A disgruntled telegraph employee." Pete tugged on the points of his vest. "And since Albert came home, I must say Elise's spirits are better. One thing I know is that I'll never send him away again. It's too hard on her. She's too fragile."

Rounding a bend in the path, Lincoln picked up the pace. He grieved for Pete as he struggled to find answers to his wife's and his son's disturbances and melancholy.

"And how is Albert doing?" Like Pete, he'd hoped Albert's stay at the special home in Germany would help him overcome any of the tendencies he'd inherited from his mother.

"The doctors there declared him cured." Pete huffed and puffed up the last incline. "A complete success, they say." They reached the clubhouse, and Pete paused at the door. "He seems like his old self. He's talking of returning to college next year."

"I hope he does. He's a brilliant young man."

Pete's eyes lit up at the compliment. "And he needs to do something with his life so he can take care of me when I'm old."

"*When* you're old?" Lincoln clapped him on the shoulder. "You'll always have me, old man."

"That's what I'm afraid of."

"Hey!" Lincoln opened the door to the clubhouse. "For that, you're buying your own steak."

"I'll buy if you promise to join Elise and me for Sunday dinner. You can see Albert for yourself and get reacquainted."

"I'm not his favorite person, Pete. You know that."

"I'm telling you, he's changed. Come see for yourself."

Lincoln smiled and agreed. He'd do anything Pete asked, including sitting through an uncomfortable dinner. He owed too much to the man, who'd been like a father to him, to ever say no to anything he asked.

The last notes from the closing hymn lingered in the air. Trying to remain inconspicuous, Hannah turned around and scanned the back of the church where the latecomers usually sat. No Lincoln. Disappointment rippled through her. But that was ridiculous. Why would she care if Lincoln Cole visited her congregation again?

Charlotte touched Hannah's arm. "Where's your friend Walt?"

"Isn't he here?" Hannah's gaze swept the room, and guilt nudged her. She'd noticed Lincoln was absent but not Walt, her oldest friend?

Walt's mother and father, clearly upset, huddled in the corner, speaking to the preacher. How odd. Was Walt ill?

"Can we go? I'm hungry." Tessa's stomach growled as if on cue.

Hannah waved her aside. "Not yet. I want to check on Walt."

She smoothed the bodice of her yellow calico dress and made her way through the congregants. She waited at the side for Mr. and Mrs. Calloway to finish their conversation. But when Mrs. Calloway saw her, she motioned her over.

Feeling like an intruder, Hannah reluctantly joined them.

Mrs. Calloway latched on to her arm as soon as she was within reach. "Oh, Hannah, Walt desperately needs your help."

"Why? What's wrong?"

Mrs. Calloway leaned close and whispered, "He's been arrested."

Hannah gasped. "What happened?"

A deep frown dug crevices in Mr. Calloway's face. "He got himself into this, Grace. He can get himself out. All this union nonsense. He should have joined me on the farm like we always wanted."

"It wasn't his way, Ethan." Tears welled in Mrs. Calloway's eyes. "And you know he needs a lawyer."

Mr. Calloway pulled his wife close. "I'm sorry, Grace, but we can't afford a fancy lawyer, even if we wanted to. We're not set to do that, and we've got the other children to tend to."

"I know. That's why we need Hannah. She's been to law school. Who would fight for him more than Hannah?"

Hannah pressed her hand against her throat. "You want me to represent him?"

"Please, Hannah."

"But I'm not a lawyer. I didn't even finish law school." Hannah's chest constricted when a tear slipped from Mrs. Calloway's eyes. "What's he been charged with?"

"Arson." The woman paused to wipe away her tear. "They think he might have something to do with a supply shed fire, but they arrested him for burning down a carriage house over all this union nonsense."

A glimmer of hope flickered inside Hannah. Walt couldn't have been involved in either fire. He'd been helping her and her sisters move when the first fire occurred, and he'd been with her the afternoon of the second. When she'd arrived home from operators' school, he'd been waiting on her porch. All she'd have to do is explain that to the authorities.

Oh no.

As if someone had blown out her candle, the flame of hope extinguished and a crater formed in her stomach. If she told anyone Walt had been with her, she'd lose her position with the telephone company. She and her sisters would be penniless.

"You'll help us, won't you?" Mrs. Calloway squeezed her arm.

She glanced toward her sisters, and Tessa gave her an impatient glare. She was all her sisters had. But how could she let Walt suffer in jail when she knew he was innocent? *Please, Lord, help me think of a way out of this for both Walt and me.*

No answer came, but she didn't truly expect one. She turned to the one thing she could always count on—her own ability to think things through. Could Walt have had time to start the second fire and then come see her? It was doubtful, but she'd seen his passion about those men being blacklisted by Western Union. But sweet Walt starting a fire? Did the police have evidence to convict him? Or were they counting on the court's often poor attitude toward unions?

She needed more time, she needed more information, and most

of all, she needed to consider the ramifications of her silence. Surely she could find a way to help him without disclosing where he'd been.

Taking a deep breath, she offered Mrs. Calloway a weak smile. "I can't make any promises, but I'll do what I can."

⌇⌇⌇

Hannah couldn't sleep. She rolled onto her stomach, and the bed creaked. She bunched the feather pillow beneath her head. If only she could have spoken to Walt, maybe they could have come up with something, but the jailer on duty had refused her request to see him. She wasn't family, she wasn't Walt's fiancée, and she certainly wasn't his lawyer.

Poor Walt. He had to be scared to death in that jail. How could she even consider not telling the police about his alibi?

The iron bed squeaked again when she rolled on her side.

Charlotte groaned. "Hannah, you're worse than Tessa."

A soft snore came from the bed on the other side of Charlotte. At least Tessa could sleep through almost anything. Poor Charlotte could not.

Sharing this one room wasn't easy, but at least they had a place to live. If she did tell the truth, where would they end up?

After tossing back the covers, Hannah climbed out of bed, grabbed her robe, and padded from the bedroom. She made her way to the kitchen and soon had milk warming on the stove. Warm milk flavored with vanilla, a bit of sugar, and a sprinkle of nutmeg had been her mother's solution to bouts of insomnia. She'd always tell Hannah the best way to fight the monsters of the night was with warm milk and prayer.

As she waited for bubbles to form around the edges of the milk, she decided to apply the second half of her mother's monster-fighting advice and again ask God for a solution to this dilemma, because this giant of a problem threatened to consume her.

She absently stirred the white liquid, her mind wandering in the middle of her prayer. What she needed was someone who knew how to fight this giant. She needed her own personal David—someone who could find the right five stones and use only one to take the giant down.

Hannah opened the Hoosier cabinet door to locate the vanilla extract, and her eyes lit on a can of Hershey's cocoa. She bit her lip. That would most certainly be a treat, but where had the cocoa powder come from? They hadn't been able to afford those kinds of extras for months.

She lifted the nearly full can from the shelf, and the answer came to her. Lincoln. He'd sent it with the groceries.

Her stomach knotted. Was God pointing her to her giant fighter? No, it couldn't be. Not him. She'd sworn to herself to never ask Lincoln for help. She'd flatly refused every offer he'd made. Could she now swallow her pride and ask the man who'd taken their home to save her friend?

She stirred cocoa powder into the milk and ladled the hot liquid into a china cup. One sip told her she'd forgotten the sugar.

Frowning, she spooned in two teaspoons of sugar. Sugar made the bitter cocoa easier to swallow, but what could possibly make swallowing the bitter pill of pride easier?

⚜

"Miss Gregory?" Lincoln stuffed a folder into his desk drawer and shoved the drawer closed before standing. "To what do I owe the pleasure?"

She didn't answer but stood before him dressed in a pretty, dark rust-colored dress with her lips pressed together. Her soft amber hair was swept upward. Her wide-brimmed hat, beribboned in plum, sported satin roses.

"I—" She started to speak and stopped, clutching her purse to her waist.

"You aren't here to make another payment, are you? Because I thought we had that settled."

"No. No, I'm not."

Her honey-coated voice washed over him. If ever God had called someone to be a Hello Girl, it was Hannah Gregory. But if she wasn't here to blister him for sending the groceries, why was she here, and why was she acting so hesitant to speak? Was she in some kind of trouble?

He motioned to the chair in front of his desk. "Why don't you please have a seat?"

She shook her head and kept her voice low. "Is there anywhere else we could speak—in private?"

His heart began to beat faster, but he kept his voice calm. "Certainly." He pressed his hand to the small of her back and directed her toward one of their meeting rooms. A walnut conference table stood sentry in the center of the room, surrounded by leather-covered chairs. After making certain he'd left the door ajar to protect her honor, he stepped to the table and pulled out a chair for her. With the grace of a Boston debutante, she lowered herself into place and laid her hands in her lap. Still, her calm demeanor didn't match the worry in her eyes.

"Hannah, what's going on? Are you in some kind of trouble?"

"No."

He released the breath he'd been holding. Whatever it was, if she was all right, it wasn't as serious as she was making it out to be. She was probably overreacting to some imaginary offense again. He racked his brain for any possibilities. He'd sent no more gifts and made no surprise visits. And after seeing Walt's interest in her, he'd even attended his own regular church services and avoided hers.

He leaned against the doorjamb and crossed his arms over his chest. "So, what is it? Why did you need to see me in private? What have I done now to step on your pretty little toes?"

13

Hannah fisted the chain of her handbag to keep from hurling it at Lincoln Cole. In a matter of seconds, his apparent concern had transformed into a look of smug satisfaction.

"Hannah?" He impatiently tapped his finger against his forearm. "I don't have all day."

Jutting her chin, she met his gaze. "Do you remember meeting my friend Walt Calloway?"

He nodded, and a frown marred the rapscallion's face. Great. He didn't like Walt. This was not going well at all.

"Mr. Calloway's been arrested." Hannah released her tight hold on the purse and wrapped the dainty chain over her wrist, thankful the news was out at last.

Lincoln stood up straighter. "What's the charge?"

"Arson."

"The Western Union fires?" He pulled out a chair and arranged it so he could sit facing her. "I've heard about those. But why are you here? If he needs representation, he or his family should be the ones seeking counsel."

"They don't have the financial means to do so." Hannah kept her tone businesslike. "Because I had some law schooling, they asked for my help, and now I'm . . ."

"You're what?" The corner of his lips lifted in an irksome manner. Was he enjoying making this difficult?

"I think you already know."

He leaned back in his chair and folded his hands across his stomach. "I have a pretty good guess, but I want to hear it from you. I seem to remember you didn't need my help."

She squared her shoulders. Her discomfort seemed to amuse him. The insufferable man! He was not going to unnerve her. Walt needed her help, and that was that.

"Well, I don't, but he does."

"Say it."

"Mr. Cole—" The words stuck in her throat like one of Charlotte's cooking experiments gone horribly wrong.

He leaned forward, grinning. "Say it."

Lincoln Cole wouldn't get the best of her—not when Walt's future hung in the balance. She swallowed hard and clutched her hands together. "Mr. Cole, my friend needs your help, and as I said, his parents don't have the money for a lawyer." She exhaled. Surely that would be the end of this.

"I see." Lincoln pressed harder as if he were driving the point home in a court of law. "I've heard the police have a good case against your friend."

"But he didn't do it. The first fire was set on the day my sisters and I moved in. Remember, he was with us, so he couldn't have set that one. And I can promise you he didn't set the second one either." Her traitorous voice had an edge of desperation.

His brow furled. "And you know that because . . . ?"

Hannah pressed her sweaty palms against her dark wool skirt and swallowed again. "He stopped by my house that afternoon, but you and I both know that if it gets out he was there, I'll lose my position at the operators' school. Mrs. Reuff wouldn't believe I didn't know he was coming."

Lincoln stood up and walked the floor between her and the door as if he had a jury in the room. "So let me see if I have this correct. As far as I can tell, you need my help as much as he does. If you provide his alibi for the second fire, you lose your job. If you don't, you have to live with knowing you sent your *friend* to prison for

95

something he didn't do." He turned and met her gaze, a smirk on his face. "I'd say you're in a pickle, Hannah."

She shot to her feet and marched to the door. She did not have to take this kind of humiliation. There had to be another way.

Lincoln barred the door with his arm. "Ask me."

"Ask you what?" She took a step back. "Do you want me to get on my knees to ask the great young lawyer to represent my poor, unfortunate friend?"

"Not exactly." He quirked an eyebrow. "If I remember right, you said you wouldn't ask me for help if I was the last man on earth."

"So?"

His eyes lit with mischief. "I want to hear you say, 'Lincoln, will you help me, *please*?'"

"Mr. Cole." Even she could hear the anger seething through her words. She refused to say his Christian name. This was a business deal. Nothing more. Everything in her wanted to announce she'd take care of Walt's defense on her own, but she didn't know enough to gamble with Walt's future. Lincoln Cole was Walt's best chance. And her own.

She strangled the chain of her chatelaine purse and ground out the words. "Will you help me, please?"

A slow grin spread across his face. "I'd be happy to." He motioned her toward the door. So, let's get started."

She blinked. "Us?"

"Yes, Hannah, you and I are going to team up. We're going to work on his defense together."

A thrill shot through her. She was going to work on an actual case.

Her mind spun. A minute ago she wanted to throttle the man, and now she wanted to hug him. What was Lincoln Cole doing to her?

⊰∾⊱⊰∾⊱⊰∾⊱

Defending Walt Calloway was not going to be an easy task.

Lincoln walked beside Hannah toward the jail, mulling over what he'd heard about the charges against Walt. He hated that

Hannah had gotten wrapped up in this, and he vowed to himself to ensure she wouldn't have to come forward.

An ice delivery wagon rolled by, the horse's hooves clopping on the paved brick. A couple of police officers approached them and tipped their hats to Hannah.

Lincoln glanced at her. Still ramrod stiff, she marched beside him like a soldier. He'd probably toyed with her emotions too much today, but oh, it was fun. He found Hannah's fierce independent streak fascinating, but it was time for her to realize one thing.

He was on her side.

Walt Calloway's life was no game. If she cared for the man—and Lincoln thought she probably did since she'd come for his help—he owed it to her to do his best to clear Calloway's name. He may not like Calloway, but if this made Hannah happy, it was all that mattered. She'd been through enough in the last few months.

Known for his work with the telegraph union, Walt had publicly voiced his opinion of the Western Union managers who'd blacklisted some employees after last year's strike. Lincoln had no doubt the employees had been wronged, but how far would the disgruntled man go to make his point? Would Hannah's friend set fire to any number of structures?

They climbed the steps to the jail, and he held open the door for her. She paused and looked at him. "They won't let me see him. I tried the other day, and they refused because I wasn't family or his fiancée."

She'd come to the jail alone? Unescorted? Was there no end to her gumption?

He motioned her inside. "They'll let you see him today. I promise."

It took some convincing, but soon the jailer on duty escorted them to a cell in the back of the jail. Lincoln slipped his hand around Hannah's elbow and felt her shiver. He watched her hazel eyes open wide, taking in the stark surroundings—the rows and rows of bars, the dampness of the brick walls, the iron cots, and the stench of too many unwashed bodies. He remembered his first visit inside a jail. All the law books in the world couldn't have prepared him for the moment when the laws became about people—some innocent, some guilty, all waiting inside cold jail cells for their day in court.

A barred door clanged to the left, and she jolted. A prisoner whistled as they passed his cell, and Lincoln shot him a silencing glare.

"If you want to go back, I'll take you." He'd had more than one client's wife become hysterical in the jail. Even though Hannah didn't seem the type, he didn't want her to feel like she was trapped there.

"No." She smiled at him for the first time since he'd pressured her in his office. "I want to see Walt."

The jailer stopped and pointed. "Last one on the right."

"Can you open it, please?" Lincoln stepped forward. "It's customary for an attorney to speak face-to-face with his client."

The jailer grumbled, walked past the other cells, and pushed his key into the lock. "I'm telling you, you're wasting your time with this one. You can see he's guilty. Look at his eyes." He swung the door wide.

Hannah rushed inside, and Walt embraced her. Something unwelcome pricked Lincoln. Jealousy? He shoved the thought aside.

"Step away from the prisoner, ma'am."

Hannah jumped away from Walt.

The jailer pulled the cell door shut. "Sorry, ma'am. I have to lock the door while you folks are in the cell."

Hannah scowled. "I don't think Mr. Calloway is at risk of escaping."

The jailer clicked the lock and withdrew his key. "Rules is rules. I'll be back in twenty minutes."

Lincoln watched Hannah gather her courage and put on a pleasant expression before turning back to Walt. "Are they treating you well? Do you need anything?"

"To get out of this place." He sank onto the iron cot and punched the pillow. He stopped and glanced up. For the first time, he seemed to notice Lincoln. "Why are you here?"

Lincoln stepped beside Hannah, wishing he'd have brought a chair in for her. With no place to sit except on the cot beside Walt, she'd be forced to stand while they interviewed her friend. He hoped his nearness eased her discomfort at being locked in the cell with the two men. Then again, he hadn't exactly made life easier for her in the last hour or so.

"Mr. Calloway, Hannah asked me to represent you. If you agree, we can begin working on your defense."

Walt raked his fingers through his greasy hair. "Listen, Mr. Cole, I'm sure you're good, but I don't have the money to pay fancy attorney fees."

"I'm doing this pro bono—for free—because Hannah asked."

"Hannah asked you for help?" Relief washed over the man's face, and he locked his gaze on Hannah. "Thank you."

She offered him a weak smile. "I did it for both of us. Please let Lincoln help."

Walt shifted his gaze to Lincoln and nodded.

Lincoln pulled out a small notebook and pencil. "First of all, I need to know if you did it."

"Of course not." Walt stood and began pacing the tiny cell like a caged lion. Another prisoner two cells over called out to Hannah, asking her to come to his cell and cure what ailed him.

"Shut up, you fool!" Walt called back. He stopped in front of Hannah. "You shouldn't be here. This is no place for a lady."

"I'm fine." She touched his arm. "Now, when you came to my house that afternoon, you warned me about some impending trouble. So, if you had no part in this, do you know who did?"

Walt looked from her to Lincoln. Apparently, she'd said more than Walt thought she would. "No, I don't know who started the fires."

Lincoln rubbed his chin. "No, as in 'absolutely not,' or no, as in 'I have a good guess, but I'm not certain'?"

Walt whirled toward Lincoln. "I won't turn on my union brothers." His gaze darted to the side. "They don't deserve that."

"Walt, please." Hannah gripped his arm. "We can't help you unless we know the truth."

Frustration began to grow inside Lincoln. This wasn't going well. The way Walt met his eye then looked away told Lincoln the man was guilty of something, but what? And as much as he didn't want it to be so, he had a niggling feeling Walt had a possible role in all of this. Maybe he didn't strike the match, but he could easily be covering for the man who did.

Lincoln tapped his notebook with the tip of his pencil. "Why do you think the police believe you started the fires?"

"Good grief, I don't know!" Walt leaned against the barred door. "I'm an easy scapegoat. I've made my feelings known about those crooked managers, but I'm telling you, I didn't start any fires."

Lincoln stepped closer. "But you've done other things."

Walt's gaze jumped to the faint scratch still evident on Hannah's cheek, and she turned away.

Anger surged through Lincoln. He yanked the man's arm, forcing him to turn in his direction. "You threw the bricks through those windows? Hannah was in that restaurant!"

Walt's fists clenched at his sides, the veins in his neck bulging. "I told her to stay off that street. Besides, you took her to that restaurant, not me."

"Enough!" Hannah stepped between the two of them. "I'm mad as a cat dunked in water right now, Walt Calloway, so if you know what's good for you, you'll back off and sit down." She whirled toward Lincoln and jabbed her finger at his chest. "And you're here to help. Remember?"

"Hannah, he could have killed you!"

Her chest heaved beneath the frills of her shirtwaist. She glared at Walt. "It really was you? You threw the bricks?"

Walt's gaze dropped to the floor. "I didn't know you were there."

"But you still could have murdered someone." Tears glistened in her eyes. "Up till this moment, I never thought you'd be capable of hurting anyone."

"I wouldn't, Hannah." He stood and tried to take her in his arms. She jerked away.

"You have to believe me. I got carried away—wrapped up in wanting to get those men their jobs back. Please tell me you believe me."

Lincoln waited several seconds before speaking. "Hannah, I don't blame you for being mad at him. Personally, I'd still like to deck him, but we don't have much time left before the jailer returns."

"I know." She blinked and took a deep breath. "I've known you nearly all my life, Walt. I'm furious with you, but I do believe you."

"You're a lucky man, Calloway." Lincoln forced his own anger to subside. If Hannah could forgive Walt, surely he could try, but the image of blood on a beautiful face was hard to forget. He turned the page of his notebook. "Tell us everything you did on the days of both fires."

Walt sank to the cot, his shoulders slumped. "During the first fire, I was helping Hannah move, and during the second, I came to see her." He rubbed his hand over his mouth. "Hannah, if you let the police know you were with me—"

"She can't do that." Lincoln rubbed the nape of his neck with his palm.

"And why not?"

The jailer approached and unlocked the door.

Lincoln snapped his notebook shut. "Because you're lying."

14

"Lincoln, what were you talking about?" As soon as they were outside the jailhouse, Hannah launched into a barrage of questions. "He's not lying. Why did you accuse him of that? Is it some kind of tactic to get him to tell us what he really knows?"

"Let's take a walk around Court House Square, and we'll talk."

Glancing at the clock tower atop the Federal Building, she noted the late hour. Worry grew inside her like a bad itch. She should be home with her sisters. What if Charlotte hadn't come home like she was supposed to?

"I should get home and check on my sisters." She bit her lip.

"Then I guess your answers will have to wait until tomorrow." His mouth curved upward, the outer corners of his eyes crinkling.

"You do realize you're incorrigible."

"Me?" He placed his hand over his chest. "I'm hurt. But surely after you've been in jail, a few minutes of fresh air will do you good. I'm only thinking about your health."

She lowered her lashes and sighed. What difference would a few minutes make at this point?

They walked down the sidewalk until they reached the green space of the square. Lilac bushes greeted them, and Hannah itched to pluck a fragrant blossom and carry it home. "I love lilacs." She paused and pressed her nose to the bush. "My mother loved them. Roses were her favorite, but lilacs were a close second. What about your mother?"

Lincoln shoved his hands into his pockets. "I don't know what her favorite flowers were."

It figured. A man like Lincoln was certainly more in tune with his own wishes and needs than he was with anyone else's.

"How could you not know her favorites?" How insensitive could he be? Suddenly she snapped her mouth shut and turned to him. "You said 'were,' didn't you?"

He nodded.

"How long has your mother been gone?"

"Twenty-five years." He glanced off into the distance. "She died giving birth to me. I never knew her."

"Lincoln, I'm so sorry. And your father? Did he remarry?"

He touched her elbow. "Let's keep walking."

They followed the paved brick path toward the fountain. Even the lilacs couldn't hide the fishy stench of the river to the east, but with the two lofty courthouses on one end and the grass now awakened from winter, the square had beauty all its own.

In front of them, a mother pushed a baby carriage, and a toddler wobbled beside her. Up ahead, a squirrel darted onto the path, grabbed something from the sidewalk, and scurried away. Still, Lincoln remained silent. Why wasn't he speaking? Perhaps the subject of his family was too personal. Maybe she should change the topic. Just as she was about to go back to Walt's innocence, Lincoln pointed to a park bench, and they both sat down.

"My father didn't remarry."

"Where is he now?"

Lincoln gave a deep sigh. "Beside my mother."

Hannah's hand shot to her mouth to keep any wrong words from bursting forth. Lincoln's voice, normally so strong, now held a powerful undercurrent of sadness. "How old were you when he passed?"

"Fourteen."

The same age as Tessa. So young.

"I know what it's like to be alone, that's why I'm sorry I had any part in the bank taking your farm from you. I didn't know you'd just lost your parents. If I had . . ."

"You didn't know?" The words came out weak. Had she misjudged him all along?

Lincoln paused when a train at the nearby Union Depot sent up a shrill whistle. "My dad was a good man. He, too, was a lawyer, and he was a senator right here in Des Moines, but he managed to juggle it all. He did his best to be both mom and dad. Everything I do is to be worthy to carry his name."

"What happened to you after you were orphaned?"

He stood up and offered her his hand. "I have an aunt in Saint Paul. She took me in, and I lived there until I moved here to study law. She sent me to the best schools, and when she found out I wanted to become a lawyer, she sent me to Drake. Studying at Drake was only part of her plan. Working for her old friend Pete Williams was the other. He and my uncle went way back." The wind sent a tendril of her hair dancing, and he tucked it behind her ear. "Now, what's this long face? I don't need your pity. Haven't I turned out to be a fine figure of a fellow?"

His touch sent a current through her, but she dared not let it show. She smacked his arm playfully. "Don't we need to talk about Walt?"

With a frown, he dropped his hand. She followed him to the fountain. Water cascaded over the ironwork swans and splashed into the large stone basin beneath them. Lincoln pulled two pennies from his pocket. He bounced one in his hand before tossing it into the fountain. "Walt's never far from your mind, is he?"

"Jail is an awful place to be." The rank odors seemed to cling to her clothes, and she couldn't get Walt's dejected face from her thoughts. She took the second penny Lincoln offered and tossed it into the fountain. When it landed beside Lincoln's, she smiled. Maybe they made a good pair—at least when it came to helping Walt. "Why do you say Walt is lying?"

"It's something I've learned during my practice. It's not a science, but I think there are two kinds of talking. You can communicate with your words, but you can also communicate with your body, your hands, or your eyes." His gaze locked on hers and lingered there.

What his eyes were saying scared Hannah witless. She gulped. "Please continue."

He nudged her back toward the sidewalk. "Has your sister Tessa ever told you something but you knew she was lying?"

"Yes, Tessa never looks you in the eye when she's telling a falsehood."

"Exactly."

"But Walt didn't do that."

"No, he didn't, but he did something I've seen people do over and over when they lie. He touched his face when he told us about those fires. He practically covered his mouth when he spoke. It was like his hand was trying to keep the truth in."

"But he . . ." Hannah stopped on the path and faced Lincoln. Gone was the teasing arrogance from his eyes. Compassion now flickered on his face. She closed her eyes and tried to picture Walt in the jail. The scene replayed in her mind.

She gasped. Lincoln was right. Walt had done that. Tears pricked the back of her eyes. "But that doesn't mean it was a lie."

"It's not a science. It's only my experience." He pulled her to the side to let a bicyclist pass. "Hannah, on the day he came to help you move, that fire could have already been set by the time he arrived."

"I thought about that too."

"When he came to see you that afternoon at your new home, what time was it? How did he seem to you?"

What was Lincoln getting at? She looked down at the brick pavers, and with each step, fear dug at her heart.

"Hannah, was he nervous or anxious?"

Everything in her wanted to hike up her skirts and run. Would Lincoln refuse to help Walt if he knew how strangely he'd acted that night?

"He was fine." She moved to the side of the walk and crushed a lilac bloom to her nose. "What do we need to do to get him out?"

Lincoln snapped a small branch off and passed her the blossom. "You know another way to tell if someone is lying?"

She shook her head, staring down at the grouping of tiny purple flowers.

"They change the subject." He tipped her chin up with his knuckle, his lips flattening. "Hannah Gregory, I can't help your beau if you won't tell me the truth."

She sputtered, "My—my—my what?"

❦

What was Charlotte supposed to do? She'd completed all her assigned tasks. She'd come home right after school and made dinner. She'd made sure Tessa did her homework. She'd even gathered the sheets off the line. But now George was on her porch and wanted to sit and talk.

"Aw, Charlotte. I did like you asked," he said through the screen door. "I waited until after supper to come see you. I'm sure your sister won't mind if we sit out here for a while."

Charlotte bit her lip. Hannah would most likely disapprove, but it wasn't like she wasn't chaperoned. Tessa was home. The porch was in public view, and Hannah wouldn't think twice about it if a fellow as handsome as George Donnelly was sparking with her. Besides, she'd been the one to tell Charlotte to take more chances.

Drawing a hand down the length of her braid, she pushed the door open. "Thank you for being patient, George."

He tugged on her braid. "I thought you were going to make me sit out here all night. I don't much like waiting, Charlotte."

"Then I'll try not to make you wait again." She motioned to the swing. "Want to sit down?"

He slid in beside her. "Where's that bossy sister of yours off to now?"

She frowned at his reference to Hannah but chose not to address his comment. "I'm not sure where Hannah is. She hasn't come home yet."

"How'd we get so lucky?" His eyes lit up, and his hand inched across his thigh and captured her hand in a tight hold.

The screen door banged open, and Tessa traipsed out the door. With a flourish, she turned a wicker porch chair to face the swing and plopped down in it.

"Tessa Gregory, what are you doing out here?" Charlotte snapped.

Propping her hand beneath her chin, she stared at George. "Chaperoning."

Charlotte jumped to her feet, rattling the chains of the swing. She grabbed her sister's hand and yanked her out of the chair. "You get back inside this instant. We want some privacy."

"So you can . . ." Tessa puckered her lips and gave an exaggerated smack in George's direction.

With a firm grasp around Tessa's arm, Charlotte opened the screen door, shoved her sister inside, and slammed the door shut.

Instead of disappearing, Tessa stood at the screen, adding a few more loud smacking noises.

"Children." Charlotte sidled back beside George and tried to sound older. "Please ignore her."

"Aw, I don't know. I kind of like her suggestion." His eyes dropped to Charlotte's lips.

Heat rushed from the top of Charlotte's head to the tips of her toes. As much as the thought of kissing George thrilled her, something about the way his voice sounded made her stomach churn. Not wanting to hurt his feelings, she laid her hand on his. "You're such a tease. Now, tell me about practice today. Did you hit any of those homey things?"

"It's a home run, Charlotte. I told you that the other day."

She giggled. "Oh yes. I forgot."

He drew her hand up to his lips. "As long as you don't forget to ask about the box social on Friday. I'd hate to have to buy someone else's box."

"I'm sure Hannah will agree."

A voice cleared from the sidewalk. Charlotte looked up to find Hannah standing with her hands planted on her hips. "And to what am I sure to agree?"

Lincoln opened the front door to his home and sighed. He wanted nothing more than to eat a good meal and finish the last chapters of Jack London's *White Fang*. Compared to many of the houses on Grand, his Victorian was rather small, but it was home, and it was certainly larger than he needed. He hoped his father would have been proud of his purchase.

When he'd bought the house, he'd hoped to find someone to share it with. Even though he'd met many young ladies, he didn't want to pursue any of them. At least he hadn't until Miss Gregory entered his life. Everything about her bespoke of passion. She was passionate about her sisters, passionate about her friends, and passionate about God. Did he dare hope she might someday direct her passion in his direction?

Still thinking about the look on her face when he'd brought up her relationship to Walt, he took off his hat and hung it on the hook. My, she was cute when she was flustered. He wanted to believe her protests about Walt simply being a friend, but the way Walt had looked at her said anything but that. Technically, Walt had first rights to her since they'd been friends forever. Maybe Lincoln should step aside.

Then again, he'd never been good at stepping aside from anything, and besides, Walt was guilty of something.

His housekeeper met him in the hallway.

"Good afternoon, Mrs. Reynolds."

"Humph." She reached for his coat. "I doubt you'll still be thinking it's so good when you're eating your dry pot roast."

"You say that every time I'm late, but dinner is always delicious." He flashed the older woman a grin. Somewhere along the line, she'd become more like a second mother than an employee, and he thought she secretly delighted in his praise. "Why are you still here? I told you that you didn't have to stay until I get home. Mr. Reynolds will be worried about you."

She draped his coat over her arm. "Don't you worry about my

mister. He came by earlier and had his dinner with me in the kitchen. He's happy as a lark as long as his belly is full. Now give me a minute to hang up your coat, and I'll set out your dinner."

In a playful lunge, he snagged the coat. "I'll see to my own jacket and dinner."

She propped her thick hands on her ample hips. "But that's my job, Mr. Cole. Your aunt would be quite displeased if she learned otherwise. She hired me to make sure you were well cared for."

"And you do a wonderful job of that." He winked. "If it makes you feel better, I won't wash the dishes when I'm done."

Two red splotches formed on her wrinkled face. "What a pert young man," she muttered as she departed for the kitchen. He heard the banging of what he guessed was the oven door. Poor woman. She simply couldn't let him do it for himself. Hannah would like her.

Lincoln scooped up the mail from the entry table and carried it with him into the dining room. The aroma of hot beef hit him hard, and his stomach growled. Before he even reached the table, he heard the back door slam shut. At least Mrs. Reynolds didn't stay to do the dishes. He grinned. Good. He'd surprise her and wash them. No woman should have to start off the day facing dirty dishes.

A knock on the front door surprised him. Perhaps Mrs. Reynolds had forgotten something, but it was hard to believe she'd consider using the front door. It wouldn't bother him if she did, but it would certainly unnerve his housekeeper.

After setting the letters beside his plate, he strode to the door and swung it open to find his law firm colleague on his doorstep. "Cedric?"

"We need to talk." The man stepped inside without an invitation. He passed Lincoln his hat and cane. "Let me get to the point. You need to give up the Calloway case."

15

Lincoln regarded his associate with a critical eye. Cedric had pushed his way inside and ignored the fact that an untouched dinner, visible through the arched doorway, waited on the dining room table. Did the man honestly believe Lincoln would relinquish his case because Cedric hoped to entice a potential client?

"So you agree?" Cedric sat in a leather chair in Lincoln's parlor.

"I didn't say that."

Cedric withdrew a cigar from his coat pocket and bit off the end. "With your political aspirations, aligning yourself with a union man could be career suicide."

"Maybe it could be." Or maybe it would help. Lincoln had already considered both possibilities. With the growth of unions in the state, representing Walt might actually win him the votes he would most need for a seat in the house. However, it could kill his chances with the men with the deepest pockets.

"I can't imagine you'll drum up much support if you go forward with this." Cedric lit the cigar and puffed smoke in the air.

The room filled with the sweet, heavy scent of tobacco, and Lincoln frowned. The cigar smoke annoyed him, but not nearly as much as the smoker. Even if it killed his political career, he needed to do what was right. Walt Calloway may have been involved or at least know the identity of the firebug, but he didn't deserve to go to jail for something he didn't do.

"Cedric, I'm keeping the Calloway case. I understand securing the Farmers Insurance Company as a client would be a nice feather in your cap, but they are not yet our clients, and therefore, I see no conflict of interest that would make me give up representing Walt."

"Why do you care? He's an arsonist." Cedric pounced on the last word.

"He's accused of arson. Counselor, you should know better." Lincoln moved to the fireplace and set another log on the grate. It popped and snapped, sending sparks into the air.

"You realize you're about to lose the firm a great deal of money because that pretty Gregory girl batted her eyes in your direction."

"Leave Miss Gregory out of this." He turned to Cedric. "Walt Calloway is in need of representation, and I agreed to do it. Unlike some people, I keep my word." He paused to let the words deliver their intended sting. "Now, if that's all, I'd like to eat my dinner."

"We're not finished until you agree to let the case go." Cedric tossed his cigar butt into the fireplace. "I'll take this to Charles if I need to."

Lincoln stiffened at the mention of Charles Harlington, the other senior partner in the Williams and Harlington Law Firm. While Pete had mentored Lincoln, Cedric had been brought to the firm by Charles, and the senior partner had come to Cedric's aid on more than one occasion.

Lincoln met Cedric's stare and held it until the man looked away. Good. He'd won that battle. Cedric couldn't know that the threat concerned him. He had an uncanny ability to grab on to a man's weakness. Like a snake whose fangs sank into fresh prey, he'd hold on to the weakness until the victim succumbed. Besides, would Charles intervene in something like this? And if he did, would Pete stand up for Lincoln's decision? What would Hannah say if he were forced to abandon Walt's case?

Lincoln followed his colleague to the door. "I'd say we should do this again, but you and I both know the truth. We're like oil and water, but we should try to work together for the good of the firm."

"Now you care about the good of the firm?" Cedric snorted. "If you really feel that way, then you'll turn the Calloway case over to someone else. We can all make a lot of money from a client like Farmers Insurance."

"Some things are more important than money."

Cedric opened the front door. "Not many—and certainly not a woman like Miss Gregory. She has no connections and no money. I find it hard to fathom why you're even considering fighting me over this insignificant case."

"I said to leave her out of this." Red-hot anger flared in Lincoln's chest, and he had to clench his fists at his side. "I'm representing Walt. End of discussion."

He slammed the door behind the conniving, unprincipled man. It had been a long time since anyone had made him that angry, but his front door didn't deserve his wrath. At least it was better than slamming his fist into Cedric's ugly face.

-ᴈ⌇ⵀⵊⵀⵋⵀⵋ⌇ᴃ-

Hannah sipped the heavenly brew from her favorite china cup and let it awaken her from the inside out. Only one week and four days left of operators' school, and it couldn't come soon enough. She'd followed all of the rules, but having to spend time with Lincoln while working on Walt's defense worried her a great deal. Along with that, irritation at two of her classmates' petty jealousy was taking the joy out of her days.

She yawned. All the other things going on were robbing her of sleep as well. Last night, her concerns about Charlotte and George, Walt and his lies, and her future as an operator rattled around in her mind. And to make matters worse, Lincoln's face kept appearing.

She'd not made a fuss about Charlotte and the young man keeping company on the porch. After all, she was the one who'd been late getting home, and Tessa had been there. Even though something about George bothered Hannah, she'd agreed to Charlotte attending the box social with him. Hannah couldn't pin down her concern any more than she could grab the steam coming from her coffee cup, but it was there all the same.

Another sip sent a fresh wave of pleasure through her. Coffee had to be one of God's greatest gifts to humankind. She'd heard both coffee and tea were offered free of charge to the operators at the Iowa Telephone Company, along with rolls. Butter, of course, was extra. What a treat that would be when she became a full-fledged operator!

"Hannah, Rosie's here!" Tessa bellowed from the parlor.

After washing down her last two bites of toast with the rest of the coffee in her cup, Hannah hurried to meet her friend at the door. Charlotte and Tessa were there too, slipping into their wraps.

"Girls," Hannah said, "I may be late again. I need to go back into the city to see Mr. Cole."

"Can't you call him on the telephone?" Tessa huffed as she picked up her books from a table by the door. "You do know how to work one."

Hannah scowled at her. "We need to work on Walt's defense."

"And Mr. Cole needs *your* help to do that? What kind of lawyer is he?"

"Tessa, we'd better get out of here before Hannah gives you a week's worth of extra chores." Charlotte pushed her little sister out the door.

Hannah could still hear Tessa on the porch. "I know what kind of lawyer he is," Tessa said. "He's a very handsome one. Handsomer than your George, that's for sure."

Rosie laughed. "There's never a dull moment here, is there? I wish I had two sisters."

"Well." Hannah linked her arm with Rosie's when they stepped onto the porch. She raised her voice. "I may have a deal for you. Two sisters for sale. Very cheap."

"I heard that!" Tessa called back.

By the time they neared the operators' school, Hannah had filled Rosie in on Walt's situation. Rosie seemed especially interested in the part about Lincoln believing she and Walt were a couple.

"You set him straight, right?" Rosie held open the door to the school.

"Yes, but I'm not sure he was convinced. I'm not sure why he cared anyway."

Rosie's eyebrows rose, and her eyes twinkled. "Do you want me to believe you honestly have no idea?"

Warmth pooled in Hannah's stomach, and she smiled. She couldn't deny she felt something—a tiny spark, maybe—when she was with Lincoln, but he was an up-and-coming attorney. He'd never pick a poor Hello Girl when he could have any of the eligible young woman society had to offer.

Bossy Martha Cavanaugh and her snooty cohort Ginger Smith approached as soon as Hannah and Rosie entered the room. Hannah bristled. Until recently, the class's two troublemakers had avoided her. But lately they seemed determined to make her look bad—unplugging her wires, mixing up her circuits, and starting gossip about her whenever they got the chance—all because she'd been a quick study at the practice switchboard.

"Good morning, Hannah." Martha tilted her body in Hannah's direction, deliberately snubbing Rosie.

"Hello, Martha. Ginger." She motioned toward her friend. "Rosie and I were about to take our seats."

"Rosie, you go on ahead." Martha waved her hand in the air as if she were shooing a fly. "You too, Ginger. I'd like to speak with Hannah. Alone."

Ginger's lower lip jutted out in a pout at being dismissed. Rosie glanced at Hannah, waiting for a sign that it was okay to leave her alone with Martha.

Hannah nodded. No need for Rosie to suffer through Martha's ugliness so early in the morning. It was liable to make Rosie's breakfast not sit well.

After the two women departed, Martha leaned against the wall. "Did you know my sister is in the same class as your youngest sister?"

"No, I didn't. Then again, there are a lot of students at East High."

"Your sister is quite a storyteller."

"Tessa does have a vivid imagination." Where was Martha going with this?

"Well, according to my sister, Tessa said you have a friend—a dear *male* friend—who has been arrested." Martha's lips curled in a smug smile.

Hannah's mouth went dry, and her pulse quickened. Why did Martha, of all people, have to find out about Walt?

"Cat got your tongue, Miss Know-It-All?" Martha's voice was low and menacing. "And don't worry about telling Mrs. Reuff. I knew it would be much too difficult for you to confess this unsavory friendship to her, so I took care of relaying the information on your behalf." She gave a smug chuckle. "I told you not to make us look bad again, but you had to keep showing off."

Mrs. Reuff strode to the front of the room, and Hannah walked to her seat, her legs weak. The instructor offered the class a prim greeting. "Today one of you will be leaving us."

A stone dropped in Hannah's stomach. Just like that, she'd be dismissed? Without so much as a chance to refute the accusations?

"As I've told you all before, the telephone company is a place of systems and rules. These systems and rules are in place to ensure the customers receive the highest level of service from the most reputable employees."

Her gaze swept the room and seemed to rest on Hannah.

Tears pricked Hannah's eyes. She'd worked so hard, and she needed this job so badly. How would she take care of her sisters now?

"Miss Gregory, please come up here."

The blood whooshed from Hannah's face, and her heart beat like a telegraph machine. Rosie gasped beside her. Hannah wiped her damp palms on her skirt. Not only was she to be dismissed, but she was to be made a public spectacle as well. Could this get any worse?

She slowly stood and walked to the front of the classroom.

Mrs. Reuff turned to her. "Miss Gregory, while these systems and rules often help us discover young women unsuitable for the profession of operator, they also help us reward those who seem to have a knack for the job."

Hannah blinked. This didn't sound like a dismissal.

Mrs. Reuff handed her a sheet of rolled-up paper and smiled. "Congratulations. You are the first student in your class to graduate and be promoted to the work of a full-fledged switchboard operator. Tomorrow they are expecting you at the Iowa Telephone Company. Report to the third floor. Please, make me proud. And do try to follow the rules."

⤜⟋⟍⊙⟋⟍⤛

After snagging a straight-back wooden chair from the hallway, Lincoln waited for the jailer on duty to open Walt's cell door. Once inside, he set the chair down and straddled it. Across from him his client sat on the iron cot. Walt cocked his head to one side and then the other, stretching his neck. He avoided Lincoln's probing gaze and began cracking his knuckles. If Walt had any idea how hard Lincoln had had to fight to convince Pete and Charles to let him keep this case, he might be more cooperative.

Cedric had gotten to Charles first thing in the morning and built quite a case as to why Lincoln should forego representing Walt to smooth the way for better relations with their potential paying clients. The whole idea made Lincoln's blood run hot.

Pete intervened, explaining how important it was to follow through since the firm's name had already appeared in the newspapers in relation to the case. Then privately, he'd quizzed Lincoln on why he was so determined to hold on to this case.

Like Cedric, Pete pointed out that representing a disgruntled union employee could have dire consequences for Lincoln's future political career. He added that the men who had the most influence in the city often saw unions as their enemy, and if Lincoln wanted to get a representative's position next term, he, too, should start thinking of Walt as just that.

Was he representing his enemy? *Enemy* was a strange word.

Lincoln's competitive instinct embraced the word, but his heart told him it was wrong to do so.

He studied Hannah's friend sitting across from him. A shave would do the man wonders. Dark circles rimmed his eyes, and he seemed paler than he had only weeks ago at the Gregory farm.

Lincoln let the silence lengthen between them, a technique he'd learned from his aunt when she was probing for the truth.

Walt rubbed his hand over his whiskered chin. "So?"

"So, are you ready to tell me the truth?"

Walt met his eye. "I told you the truth. I didn't start any fires."

Impressive. Straightforward. Not overly defensive. Yes, the man was telling the truth.

"But you know who set the fires."

Walt looked to the corner of the cell and finally sighed. "There are a couple of fellows who might do something like that. They're real hotheads, but I don't know anything for certain."

"I'll need their names."

"I can't tell you." He lifted his eyes and met Lincoln's gaze. "I won't tell you."

"You're willing to go to prison for these men?"

"I don't think it will go that far. I'm innocent." Walt drew his hand through his oily hair. "If Hannah will just—"

Lincoln stood up. "No. I won't let her do that."

"I doubt you can stop her, and I think I know her a little better than you."

"You've known her longer, but that doesn't guarantee you know her better."

Anger flickered in Walt's eyes. "When this is over . . ."

Lincoln glared at the man. *Friends, my eye!* Friends didn't react so possessively. Did Hannah really have no idea how Walt felt? Despite her claims to the contrary, did she harbor feelings for Walt as well? She'd certainly gone to great lengths to get her "friend" legal assistance. Maybe she simply hadn't come to realize her own feelings ran so deep for Walt.

The thought felt like a burr under his skin. He didn't trust Walt, but if he were truthful, it was more than that. He had feelings for Hannah.

Lincoln shook his head. Right now, he needed to focus on Walt as his client, not as his competition for Hannah's affection.

"Listen, we both want what's best for her," Lincoln said. Walt needed to understand they were on the same side if he was going to get him off this charge. "If word gets out she's your alibi, she'll lose her job, and we both know she needs that job too much to do that unless it's absolutely necessary."

Walt took a deep breath and nodded. "You're right. Sorry."

"I need one name, Walt. One person I can do a little research on. If this goes to trial, which I'm hoping it won't, all we have to do is create reasonable doubt. We won't be trying him."

"But you'll be pointing the police in his direction." Walt stood and walked to the cell door. He wrapped his hands around the bars. "No thanks."

Lincoln clenched his fists. Why was Walt fighting him? Didn't the man see that Lincoln was his only hope? He forced his voice to show a calm he didn't feel. "All right, why do you think they arrested you?"

Walt turned and shrugged. "How would I know?"

"What kind of questions did they ask you?"

"They asked me a lot about what I do for Western Union."

Lincoln held out his hand, palm up. "And you said . . . ?"

"I told them I mainly repair the wires."

"What else?"

For the next half hour, Lincoln began to get an inkling of the case the prosecution was most likely building. Walt, a disgruntled employee, had ample motive and opportunity. He'd been identified as one of the men who threw the bricks through the restaurant window, and he'd been quite vocal about his blacklisted friends. As for means, Lincoln imagined the detective suspected that with Walt's lineman abilities, he could design and install any number of incendiary devices.

Lincoln stood up. "That about covers it."

"So what happens next?"

"There's a hearing to be held next Monday to see if there's enough evidence to hand you over for trial." Lincoln stood and called to the jailer. "I won't lie to you, Walt. Without another possible suspect, I think we have our work cut out for us. Hannah and I will speak with the city fire marshal and see what we can learn about the fires."

"Hannah?"

"She's helping me with your defense."

"*She's* helping you?" Walt's eyes widened, his jaw tensed.

The jailer unlocked the door, and Lincoln picked up the chair he'd brought in. "Actually, she's helping me help you."

"Just don't put her in any danger."

Lincoln snorted. "No, you've done enough of that already."

16

Seven church spires rose on Piety Hill, strong and constant against the mellowing sky. Hannah's cheeks burned from smiling too much as the streetcar lumbered down Mulberry Street. She'd stopped by home to share the news of her graduation with her sisters, and they'd both been thrilled for her.

Taking the streetcar was a luxury she didn't usually allow herself, and from now on, she would walk the few blocks from the Iowa Telephone Company to Lincoln's office.

What was she saying? That was only *if* she met Lincoln again after work. If they were soon able to secure Walt's freedom like she hoped, she'd have no reason to frequent Lincoln's workplace.

An odd melancholy washed over her, but it was followed by a faint whisper of hope deep in her heart. Did Lincoln feel this strange pull too? No. She mustn't think that way. She and Lincoln were volatile together. Even if there was a remote interest on his part, she was not a good fit for a man with political aspirations. She couldn't follow the rules of society any better than she could those of the telephone company—she was worried enough about that.

The streetcar stopped at the grand Polk County Courthouse to let the patrons get off. On the sidewalk, she shook out the folds of her walking-length spring cloak. The brown-checked mohair had been her mother's selection, not her own, but she was grateful she had the longer cloak on these nippy spring days, even if it lacked the flair of the latest fashions.

A man bumped into her from behind, and she nearly lost her balance. He apologized and moved on. After adjusting her wide-brimmed, ostrich-plumed hat, she headed toward the building that housed Lincoln's law office.

"Hannah?"

She turned to see Eleanor Goodenow, her former Drake classmate, approaching. Eleanor sported a lovely walking suit in lavender, which made her moon-sized brown eyes stand out even more.

"Eleanor!"

The two women embraced, and Eleanor kept hold of Hannah's arms as she stepped back. "We've missed you so much. How are you doing? I was so sorry to hear about your parents. Will you be returning to classes in the fall?"

"I'm afraid not." Hannah forced a smile. "I'm working as a switchboard operator now, and my sisters and I have moved into the city."

"Can you sneak away for lunch so we can catch up?"

"I'm afraid she already has plans."

She jolted and whirled toward the male voice behind her. "Lincoln! You startled me."

"Sorry about that." His dove-blue eyes held a half-excited, half-mischievous glint in them that said he was anything but apologetic.

"Miss Eleanor Goodenow, may I introduce Mr. Lincoln Cole." She squeezed Eleanor's hand. "Eleanor and I were coeds at Drake."

"A pleasure to meet you, Miss Goodenow." He tipped his hat in her direction. "And Hannah, if you'd rather spend some time with your friend, I can speak with the fire marshal alone."

"The fire marshal? No, I need to be there."

Eleanor smiled. "Well, my friend, I can see you are in good hands. Ring my parents' house sometime so we can get together."

"I'll do that. It was so nice to see you." Hannah hugged Eleanor again and watched her walk away before turning back to Lincoln.

Her gaze dropped to his attire. Why was he wearing a full-length driving coat?

"I wanted to save you the trip of walking to our building. I made us an appointment to speak with the fire marshal at his home. I telephoned him and he's expecting us." He swept his arm toward the street, where a shiny, rooster-red automobile was parked. The sun glinted off the brass trim, and the two gas lamps on each side of the automobile seemed to wink at her.

She gasped. "Is it yours?"

"It is. A birthday gift from my aunt. I picked it up from the automobile dealer this afternoon." His grin widened even more. "She told me she ordered it months ago, but it arrived today. I wanted you to be the first to ride in it." His brow suddenly furled. "Wait a minute. Will this get you in trouble with the operators' school? To be seen with me?"

She dropped her gaze to the sidewalk. "Not anymore."

His excitement crumbled. "No, it can't be. Hannah, what happened?"

She tried to maintain her somber expression, but a smile exploded on her face. "I graduated today. The first one in my class to be promoted to the real switchboard."

Lincoln grabbed her waist and hoisted her in the air. She squealed, and he lowered her back to the ground. One woman glared her disapproval, but an older couple approaching them chuckled. Hannah's cheeks flamed, both from the public spectacle and from the electricity that surged through her at Lincoln's touch. He, however, didn't seem to notice her reaction or that of any onlookers.

"We need to celebrate!" He slipped his fingers under her elbow and led her toward the car. "After we see the fire marshal, we're going for ice cream, and I won't take no for an answer this time."

Another lightning strike passed through her. If she did agree to a social outing like this, was she starting down a road that would only bring her grief? She'd had enough of that in the last few months. But when she was with Lincoln, she forgot about the loss of her parents. She might be wanting to kill him, but at least she didn't think about what she no longer had.

Hannah glanced at the automobile. Lincoln, obviously thrilled with his new toy, nearly bounced with excitement. Her fingers tingled at the thought of touching the red automobile. Since she'd first laid eyes on one of the contraptions, she'd wanted to ride in it.

"Lincoln, what about my sisters?"

"We'll telephone them." He flashed her a grin that said he'd won this battle. "You're a graduate now. You officially know how to use one of those."

She swatted his arm. "You're as bad as Tessa."

"No, I'm good for you." He helped her step into the automobile.

"Is that a fact, counselor?"

"Yes, miss, I believe it is." Seriousness flitted across his face, and then the grin bounced back. "But you'll have to give me the chance to prove it."

She swallowed. *Oh my.* What was she doing? She was with a man who, a few weeks ago, helped the bank take her family's farm. Now he was about to take her out in an automobile, of all things, to who knows where. She'd always prided herself on her ability to take risks, but perhaps this was going too far.

Lincoln went to the back of the automobile and opened the trunk. He donned a leather cap, pulled on a pair of long, leather driving gloves, and reached inside the vehicle to flip a switch. Then he moved to the side of the automobile and, bending low, heaved a crank. The engine rumbled to life. As if he'd done it a hundred times, he climbed in behind the wheel. With a flourish, he pulled a wide silk scarf from his coat pocket. "The dealer recommended I purchase this too, so the lady in my life could secure her hat."

The lady in his life? *Calm down. It's just a phrase. He meant nothing by the statement.* Still, her stomach rippled like a buggy on a rough road. Another gift? She couldn't accept this one or any other. Didn't he remember her feelings about the groceries he'd provided?

The automobile vibrated, itching to take off. Unless she wanted her hat to fly down Court Street like tumbleweed in the desert, she needed to use the scarf he offered. Besides, he bubbled so with excitement, she didn't want to do anything to squash it.

She accepted the ivory scarf from his gloved hand and ran her hand along the scarf's soft length. It was truly a fine piece of fabric. Maybe if she borrowed it just for the afternoon, it would be all right.

He adjusted his driving goggles. "As soon as you put it on, we can go."

With a deft swoop, she draped the scarf over her hat and tied it beneath her chin. "Please tell me you know how to drive this?"

He chuckled. "I guess you're about to find out."

With a jolt, the automobile lurched forward, but soon they were puttering along, navigating around carriages, streetcars, delivery wagons, and pedestrians. She relaxed into the cushion of the black leather seats.

"What kind of automobile is this?" Hannah asked as the automobile slowed.

"It's a Reo Gentleman's Roadster." He adjusted something on the steering column. "It has a two-cylinder engine and can reach up to forty-five miles per hour."

"Forty-five miles in one hour? Can a person even breathe going that fast?"

He laughed. "Mr. Vanderbilt himself broke the record a few years ago by driving ninety-two miles an hour at the Daytona Beach Road Course in a Mercedes. What do you think of that?"

"I think I'm glad you have a Reo and not a Mercedes."

Conversation came easily to the two of them as he parked the Reo, and Hannah discovered Lincoln's favorite foods were sugar cookies, mashed potatoes, and beef steaks—in that order. He forced her to admit her affection for coffee, and she happened to mention being partial to chocolate as well.

Since the distance to the fire marshal's home wasn't far from the street, she didn't have time to ask the questions burning inside her about Lincoln's aunt. And how did one ask how wealthy his aunt was without sounding rude? A person could probably buy twenty fine carriages for what this Reo cost.

Jealousy pinched her. Life didn't seem fair. She and her sisters had to scrounge for every cent, and Lincoln was being given extravagant gifts.

Lord, forgive me. What an ugly thought. You and you alone choose who to bless and how to bless them, and I thank you for all of the provisions you've made for me and my sisters.

By the time they reached the fire marshal's home, all jealousy had dissipated like a puff of smoke. Instead, Hannah's heart was filled with thankfulness for this opportunity and this man who was going out of his way to help her friend.

The fire marshal introduced himself as Samuel Stock and led them to his parlor. His wife slipped in with a pot of tea and deposited it on the table before leaving. Hannah's gaze fell on the plate of cookies the woman had left as well. Sugar cookies. Glancing at Lincoln beside her on the couch, she shared a smile and watched him lick his lips.

Hannah surveyed the modest home. The parlor furniture and carpet were worn, but the tidiness of every dust-free corner told her the Stocks were quite proud of their home.

Mr. Stock snagged a cookie, then leaned back in his tapestry-covered chair. "What can I tell you, counselor, that I haven't already told the police?"

Lincoln leaned forward and clasped his hands in front of him. "Sir, I read your excellent report, but would you mind walking us through your findings?"

"In front of the lady?" The fire marshal's voice was gravelly.

"I find the study of fire investigation quite fascinating." Hannah poured the tea and passed the fire marshal a cup.

"In that case, let me get a piece of paper, and maybe I can sketch it out for you." He looked at Hannah. "It's easier for you ladyfolk to understand with pictures."

When the fire marshal went to his rolltop desk to retrieve paper, Lincoln snickered. "Apparently, he doesn't realize how intelligent you are."

"It's so frustrating! He assumes I'm not able to understand because I'm a woman." She scowled at the man, whose back was still to them. "And by the way, how do you know if I'm intelligent? You barely know me."

"I knew the first day we met. You challenge everything." He broke off a piece of sugar cookie. "For the record, I'm not stupid either."

Mr. Stock returned with a pad of paper and set it on the table in front of him. "A fire will talk to you if you let it."

"Excuse me?" Hannah set down her cup.

He repeated the statement more slowly, as if that would help her "inferior" womanly mind grasp what he was saying. She wanted to throw her tea right in the lap of the condescending man, fire marshal or not.

Lincoln laid a hand on her arm as if reading her mind. "You mean the remains of the fire will tell you how it was started?"

Mr. Stock beamed at him. "Yes, my boy, you got it. First thing I do is dig through the ashes when I get to a scene. I'm looking for various signs and patterns formed by the fire." He drew a box on the paper. "Let's say this is a wall and the fire started on the floor in front of it."

Hannah watched him draw a crude fire at the base of the wall. "So you determine the point of origin by the heaviest char, correct?"

Mr. Stock jerked his head up. "Well, as a matter of fact, I do, young lady—among other things. I look for the place where the most damage was done. Was your father a fireman?"

"No, sir. It seemed like a logical thing to look for. But how can you tell if a fire has been deliberately set?"

"Hold your horses." The fire marshal marked a V on the paper wall. "Fire normally follows a V pattern on the wall unless some kind of flammable liquid was used. If there was, you might find other patterns depending on what was used to start the fire."

"Can you give us an example of what you would be looking for?" Lincoln asked.

"Seeing patterns on wood floors or linoleum, finding rags, or smelling kerosene are all clues to arson." He drew three different boxes on a second sheet of paper and a bottle on its side in one box. "About a month and a half ago, before these two recent fires, there was a fire set in a Western Union repair cart. We'll probably never find who did that one, but we think it was set with a bottle of whiskey with a rag stuffed in it, because we found glass shards." He looked at Hannah. "He would have had to light the rag on fire, you understand?"

She clenched her teacup. "Yes, I do."

"Why haven't we heard about that one?" Lincoln asked.

"A supply cart isn't as newsworthy as a building." Mr. Stock scratched his temple with the end of the pencil. "It could have been the first fire this arsonist started, or it could have been someone else altogether—even some kids pulling a prank. Like I said, we'll probably never know."

"How were the two recent fires started?"

Mr. Stock drew a stick of dynamite in the middle box. "The April 18 fire, the one at the Western Union supply shed, was caused by an explosion. Most likely dynamite."

Hannah gasped. "Are you certain? Perhaps it was a natural gas explosion."

He shook his head. "It's easy to tell the difference between a regular fire and when something explodes, because the burn damage is deep and jagged. Things are broken and burned to different degrees. It wasn't gas because of the location of the crater." He tapped the box. "We found evidence that shows whoever did this one understood how wires and switches work."

Which must have led to Walt becoming a suspect. Hannah glanced at Lincoln and shivered. This didn't bode well for her friend.

"In the April 20 fire, the one at the Western Union manager's carriage house, the arsonist used a strange tactic." Mr. Stock drew a thick line across the third box, with several balloon-shaped objects hanging from it. "He used several rubber hot water bottles filled with oil and tacked them to the rafters. When the bladders heated, each one exploded, spurring the fire on."

Lincoln's brow scrunched. "If they all exploded, then how do you know this is what happened?"

Mr. Stock looked at him as if Hannah's stupidity was catching. "Because we found them still hanging. We were able to put the fire out before they all caught fire."

Lincoln straightened his shoulders. "Sir, have you discovered many arsonists who have set more than one fire?"

"A few."

"Do they usually change the way they start the fires?" He pointed to the three boxes. "From a bottle of whiskey to dynamite to oil-filled water bottles—it seems like a stretch to think it's the same person."

The fire marshal scowled. "I gave the detective my findings. They're all connected to the Western Union, so it seems fitting whoever set the fires has a beef with them." He stood up. "I'm sure the Western Union people are resting easier, now that we've got the right man in jail."

"Why do you say that?" Lincoln helped Hannah to her feet.

"Stands to reason. There hasn't been another fire since he's been there."

Hannah sucked in a breath. She hadn't thought about that, but it was true. An arrow of fear shot through her. If Walt wasn't the arsonist, then whoever did it was still out there. What if his next fire wasn't a shed or an empty building?

17

Controlling the power of the engine gave Lincoln a heady feeling. No wonder Mr. Vanderbilt enjoyed racing automobiles. Racing these beauties would be an easy thing to love.

He glanced at Hannah. She'd complained about the pins coming out of her hair and flying to who knows where. Secretly, Lincoln was glad the pins were gone. Her hair had blown loose despite the hat and scarf. He liked seeing her silky hair down—very much.

He gripped the steering wheel to keep from reaching out and touching her tresses. "Hannah, you're awfully quiet. What's wrong?"

"I was thinking."

"About?"

"We know Walt didn't do this, but who did? There's a fire starter out there. What if someone is hurt or killed in another fire because they've stopped looking for the real arsonist?"

Lincoln pushed up the throttle on the steering column, and the Reo responded with more speed. His gut clenched at Hannah's words. He'd been thinking the same things and pondering the fire marshal's comment about there not being any fires set since Walt's arrest. That would not bode well for them in next Monday's hearing. He didn't want to upset Hannah, but the way things looked, he feared Walt would be bound over for trial.

"Let's put the case out of our minds for now." Lincoln turned onto Locust Street. "I believe you and I have a graduation to celebrate, and I know just where to take you."

"Remember, you said ice cream. I'm not dressed for anything else."

He glanced at her. She looked beautiful in her sailor-collared white shirtwaist and black walking skirt. He had no trouble imagining taking her anywhere. Still, he understood her concern. "What you're wearing will be fine where we're going. I promise."

Even at driving less than the Reo's full speed, they neared their destination on Walnut Street in half the time it would take in a carriage. Lincoln pulled the automobile to the side of the street in front of Rogg's Drug. After tugging off his goggles and hat, he smoothed his hair with his hand and turned to Hannah. "This okay?"

"Absolutely, but for the record, I generally don't indulge before dinner."

He chuckled. "Hannah, I'm surprised at you. You seem like a girl who'd be happy to eat dessert first."

"W-well, I am." Her cheeks took on a rosy glow. "You simply caught me off guard. That's all."

"Don't worry. They have food too, and I plan on us having both." He exited the Reo and came around to assist her. "Haven't you been here before?"

She shook her head and scanned the front of the drugstore. "If we were lucky enough to get ice cream treats, it was at a little drugstore nearer our home. But I'd heard some of my Drake classmates talk about Rogg's."

A bell jangled on the drugstore's door as they entered. Hannah stepped inside the doorway and gasped. He didn't blame her. Lights illuminated the long marble-topped fountain and flickered off the polished nickel spigots. Soda glasses and leaded shades sparkled in the mirror behind the elaborate fountain.

Slipping his hand beneath Hannah's elbow, Lincoln led her toward the display. "May I introduce you to the longest soda counter in the world."

"Is it really?"

"According to the owner, Mr. Namur, it is, but I doubt if he's taken a yardstick around the world to check." Since Rogg's offered no other type of seating, he located two empty wood-seated metal stools at the crowded counter and pulled one out for her. He sat down beside her and pointed to a blackboard with the menu choices for the day on it. "Looks like it's a choice between potato soup or a sausage on a bun. Do either of those sound good to you? You can have both if you'd like."

"And ice cream?" She giggled. "I don't think even your new car would be able to carry me home if I ate all that." She tapped her finger against her chin. "I think I'd like the soup."

When the young man approached to take their order, Lincoln told him they would each start with a bowl of soup. The fountain clerk returned a few minutes later and set their orders in front of them, declaring he'd be back to take the rest of their order when they were finished.

Lincoln licked his lips. Cubes of ham dotted the thick white surface, and the fresh rolls on the plates begged to be eaten. Steam rose off the bowls. He leaned over her bowl and drew in a long breath. "If it tastes half as good as it smells, we're in luck."

He glanced at Hannah, who'd not yet taken up her spoon. Would she be comfortable if he offered to say grace in a crowded place like this?

As if she'd read his mind, she turned to him.

It was the only signal he needed. Not only did he want to thank God for the food, but he wanted to put in a word of appreciation for finally having a moment alone to enjoy the company of Miss Hannah Gregory.

❧❧❧❧❧

Hannah scooped creamy vanilla ice cream from her tall glass and slipped it between her lips. How long had it been since she'd had an ice cream treat?

Lincoln took a spoonful of his root beer float. "I never would have guessed you to be a black cow girl."

"I've never had one, but I wanted to try something new, and it's absolutely delicious." She tapped the side of her glass with her spoon. "See the chocolate syrup here? It goes perfectly with the root beer and ice cream. Do you want a bite?"

"No thank you. I prefer my root beer float unadulterated, even by chocolate syrup." He held up his glass. "To Hannah, switchboard operator graduate and first in her class."

"And to your new automobile." She clinked her glass with his and sealed the toast with a sip of spicy root beer.

"So, are you excited about tomorrow?"

"Yes, and nervous too." She took a deep breath. "There's a lot to remember, and I want to do a good job. Mrs. Reuff says central exchange operators have even more rules than the student operators, and rule keeping isn't my forte."

Mirth crinkled his eyes and curled his mouth. "You'll do fine. And when your day is done tomorrow, I'll be able to tell you if I discovered anything new on Walt's case."

The idea of talking to Lincoln after her first day tomorrow warmed her. "Can I ask you a question?"

"Anything."

She stirred her black cow, considering if she really wanted to know Lincoln's answer to the question plaguing her. But she needed to know what he thought. How else would she prepare herself?

"Lincoln, is Walt going to go to trial?"

He didn't answer right away. Instead, he seemed to study her for a moment. "If we don't find out something new, I'm afraid so."

Tears pricked her eyes, and she blinked them away. He'd confirmed something she had already guessed, but the news still made her heart ache.

"Thank you for being honest with me."

"I'll always be honest with you." Lincoln scooped a bite of ice cream into his mouth. "My turn. I get to ask you something."

She tilted her head to the side. My, but his pirate grin was infectious. "All right, I guess."

"Remember, you have to be as honest with me as I was with you, understand?" She nodded, and he continued. "Do you still want to become an attorney?"

She sucked in a quick breath. Did she? She hadn't allowed herself to think about it much lately. Well, that wasn't exactly true. Whenever the desire awakened in her, she quickly put it back to bed.

Lifting her glass to her lips, she downed what was left of her soda. "I can't pursue that dream right now."

He laid his hand on her arm. "That isn't what I asked."

She gave him a wry laugh. "If God had put me in charge of the world, things would be different, but he didn't. My parents would be alive, my sisters would still be living on the farm, I'd be in college, and I never would have met you. But in God's great wisdom, he decided against letting me call all of the shots. Imagine, he thought that he could do a better job running things than I."

"Yes, imagine that." Lincoln's eyes sparkled. "And for the record, I'm sorry about the loss of your parents and your home, but I'm glad I was given the opportunity to meet you." He slurped the last of his root beer from his glass.

Hannah smiled.

After placing some coins on the counter to cover their dinner and ice cream, Lincoln held the door for Hannah to exit.

"There's no reason you can't go back someday," he said.

"Here? To Rogg's?"

"No, to college, to finish law school."

She fired him a glare, and he held up his hands in mock surrender. "Okay. I get it. The subject is off-limits. I only wanted you to know I think you have what it takes to be an excellent attorney."

A slight smile softened her features. "It's getting late."

Before taking Hannah home, Lincoln drove them to a lesser-traveled road outside the city. What a marvel the Reo's gas lanterns were as they lit the road ahead of them.

Lincoln adjusted his goggles. "Are you ready to go fast?"

"Now?" Hannah peered into the dusky shadows in front of them. "Wouldn't it be safer in daylight?"

"And here I had you pegged for a risk taker," he teased.

"I am." She tipped her chin upward, her voice almost sounding courageous. She couldn't let him think she was afraid. "All right. Let's see how fast this automobile can go."

Lincoln pressed his foot to a pedal on the floor and placed his hand on the steering column lever. "This is the throttle, and it controls the speed." He pushed the throttle upward, and the Reo responded. Soon the wind whipped Hannah's hair in all directions, and exhilaration surged through her.

Pressing her hand to her hat, Hannah laughed aloud as her stomach flip-flopped when they sailed over a rise in the road.

Lincoln whooped and glanced at her.

"Look out!" Hannah spotted a cow in the road up ahead.

Lincoln cut the throttle and swerved. The Reo reached for the ditch. Lincoln fought against the loose dirt to keep the automobile on the road—and won.

He reached his gloved hand across the seat and touched her arm. "Are you okay?"

"Absolutely." Her heart hammered, but she felt more alive than she had in a long time. "Can we do that again?"

She could hear a smile in his voice. "Maybe not tonight."

❧

Once they arrived back in the city, Hannah discovered it was much easier to see as they drove. Round-globed electric lights sparkled against the darkened sky and illuminated the streets. The automobile rumbled over the Locust Street Bridge. When he didn't turn toward her home, she sat up straighter. "Lincoln, do you remember my address?"

"Yes, ma'am."

"Then why are we going this way?" She turned to her side to see the street name as they passed a sign.

He pulled up in front of a lovely "painted lady"—a Victorian home with gingerbread trim and what she guessed was a beautiful stained-glass window. Too bad she couldn't have seen it in the daylight. "Does Mr. Williams live here?"

"No." He chuckled. "Pete's house is three times this size. This little thing is all mine."

"Little?" With fresh eyes, she looked at the house again. Two stories, possibly three if you counted the attic. Her present home would fit in half of this. How did a single man care for such a monstrosity? Furthermore, how did he possibly have the funds with which to purchase it?

"Was this another birthday present, or did Saint Nicolas put this under your Christmas tree?"

He puffed out his chest. "This one I bought all by myself. Earned every penny." He glanced at her and smiled. "I think my dad would have wanted it that way, and I wanted to show it to you."

Hannah regretted her sarcastic words. Naturally, he was proud of his home. "It's beautiful, and your dad would be proud of you. Now tell me about your aunt."

For the rest of the ride, Lincoln shared about both his aunt and his uncle. He explained that his uncle had made a fortune in railroading, and the couple had never had any children of their own. Even though his uncle had passed away a few years ago, his aunt seemed to grow younger with each passing year.

"My aunt is quite a character. She says every person has two ages—the one they really are and the one they feel like they are." He laughed as they hit a dip in the road. "According to Aunt Sam, she's sixty going on sixteen."

"Did you ever want for anything?"

He turned onto Hannah's street. "If you're asking if I ever wanted for anything tangible, I'd say no. But I longed for other things. I wanted to be at home with my family when I was sent to boarding school. I wanted to study medicine to help people, but my uncle declared I should study law."

"You help people there too."

"I realize that now. Another thing I really wanted was brothers and sisters." He chuckled. "Money can't buy those."

"I don't know. I have two sisters I'd be happy to sell sometimes." She relaxed into the seat. "If you wanted to study medicine, why didn't you?"

"My uncle was right. He said my mouth was more gifted than my hands. Eventually, after a lot of prayer, his dream became my own."

Could her dream change? If she prayed hard enough, would she be content as a switchboard operator instead of becoming an attorney?

The wind blew against her face despite the Roadster's glass pane. She tightened the silk scarf beneath her chin.

He pulled the Reo to the curb outside her rented home, shut off the engine, and came around to assist her in stepping down. When she reached the front porch, she spotted Tessa's face pressed against the parlor's windowpane, eyes wide at the sight of the automobile. Hannah glared at her and then saw Charlotte yank Tessa away.

"Tess will be out here hounding you for a ride if I don't get inside soon."

Lincoln laughed, a full, warm sound that made her smile and her insides flutter. "Tell her I'll give her a ride tomorrow when I bring you home."

Just like that, he'd anchored himself to her life as if she didn't have a say in the matter. Even though she'd been excited to see him after work and talk about the case, assuming he'd take her home was another thing entirely.

She stiffened at the idea. She didn't want anyone telling her how things were going to be, no matter how striking his dove-blue eyes were. The whole evening had had an almost magical effect on her, and she must not have been thinking straight. She must have been wooed by a black cow and a beautiful automobile.

Neighbors began to come out on their porches to catch a glimpse of the Reo Roadster on the street, even though it was difficult to see in the dark. They gawked at it and then at her.

Hannah's cheeks heated. She glanced at the automobile. When

the Reo sat in front of Lincoln's fine home, it seemed to fit, but here it looked out of place in front of the little houses. It simply didn't belong.

Any more than she belonged in his world.

She undid the silk scarf from around her head and held it out to him.

"That's yours, remember?" He pushed it back toward her.

She couldn't meet his gaze. "No, Lincoln, the man said this was for your lady, and I'm afraid that can't be me."

18

The elevator clanked and shook as it rose, and Hannah reminded herself to breathe. It wouldn't do to faint on the way up to the third floor's central exchange on her first day as an official switchboard operator. Making a good first impression was imperative.

She stepped off the elevator and scanned the hallway. It wasn't Drake College, but the building was bright and clean. A few young women stood talking in groups, probably awaiting the beginning of their shift. She glanced at the large wall clock and took a deep breath. Half an hour early. Good. Being late would not accomplish her goal. Mrs. Reuff had told her to report to Mr. Cayhill, the chief operator, well before her scheduled eight o'clock shift.

Hannah slipped down the hallway until it opened into the immense exchange room. She sucked in her breath as she scanned the area. On two sides of the room, switchboards rose to within four feet of the high ceiling. At least fifty operators worked, nimble hands flying, as they connected the calls. Above the boards, sunlight streamed in through the cross-paned windows.

Operators sat crowded elbow to elbow, perched in straight-back chairs, before each switchboard. Crowning the blonde, brown, black, or red hair of each operator was a metal band. Hannah recognized the band that held the receiver in place over the operator's ear and wondered when and where she'd get her own set.

To her surprise, the only noise in the room, save the rustle of women's skirts and the footsteps of supervisors, was the low, buzzing murmur of operators saying, "Number, please" and "Thank you." The lights on the switchboards twinkled like the stars in the sky as customers placed their first calls of the day.

Overwhelmed by the large room and the number of people, she felt dizzy for a moment. She pressed her hand to her churning stomach. Was she ready for this?

She searched the room for the chief operator and found him busy at the switchboards on the third wall. The sign above these boards indicated they were the long-distance switchboards. On the final, short wall, Hannah noted the three small information operators' desks bearing books and newspapers as well as a switch box.

A few desks sat in the center of the room on raised platforms. These, Hannah had been warned more than once, belonged to the monitors, operators assigned to listen in on calls and watch the other operators for rule violations. Mrs. Reuff had explained the monitors kept a deportment card on each operator, and these cards were reviewed by the supervisors and the chief operator on a regular basis.

Hannah took a step forward and stopped. How odd it was that none of the operators turned their heads from their boards to see the stranger in the room.

Mr. Cayhill, the only man present, walked from station to station. When he spotted her, he approached and smiled. "Miss Gregory, nice to see you."

She smiled and dipped her head. "And you as well, sir."

"I'm glad you arrived early." He glanced at the wall clock. "As you've undoubtedly been told, this isn't our busiest time, but we're gearing up for the day. We won't put you to work quite yet. I want you to meet Miss Frogge. She'll be your supervisor and in charge of acclimating you to our operating room."

She followed Mr. Cayhill down the row of switchboards. He stopped in front of a tall woman with spectacles and bulging eyes. Hannah stifled a grin. If this was Miss Frogge, she couldn't have been more aptly named.

After introductions had been made, Mr. Cayhill excused himself, and Miss Frogge gave Hannah a critical once-over. "I'm too busy to work with you right now, so go sit down at station thirteen, and don't touch anything, you understand?"

Hannah blinked. "Yes, ma'am."

Sliding into the chair at station thirteen, Hannah glanced around for other empty stations. Seeing no others, she guessed this one would become hers. While she wasn't superstitious, being assigned to thirteen was slightly unnerving. She needed all the luck she could get.

No, Hannah. Not luck. God's blessings. She sent up another prayer asking him to bless her with a meek and gentle spirit—two qualities God had not given her in abundance.

She turned to the operators on either side of the station. Neither looked in her direction or offered any welcoming words. Their hands continued to jam the white-corded jacks into the plugs at an amazing rate. Hannah's stomach flip-flopped. How would she ever keep up?

At five until eight, the door to the exchange opened and a line of operators filed in. Each young woman stood behind a currently seated operator. When the bell rang, the two women switched places with clocklike precision. All seated operators moved to their left to exit, and all the fresh operators sat down in the chair from the other side. Hannah doubted a single call was missed during the flawless exchange.

She spent the next half hour watching the workings of the exchange. Finally, Miss Frogge motioned for Hannah to follow her. In the hallway, the supervisor peered over her spectacles. "First in your class?"

"Yes, ma'am."

"Just so you know, that doesn't mean a thing here. You'll have to prove yourself all over again, and you'll get no special treatment from me."

Hannah nodded. "I understand. I'll work hard."

"Of course you will." Miss Frogge turned and marched down the hallway, her shoes clacking on the tiled floor.

Hannah fell in behind her.

The supervisor stopped in front of a large coat closet with a plethora of hangers and hooks. "You may put your wrap here, but leave nothing of value in your pockets. Despite our unparalleled screening process, occasionally we have a young woman with sticky fingers."

Miss Frogge continued the tour, showing Hannah where to pick up her operator's headset, where the infirmary was, and where to speak to the clerk to obtain her schedule. She pointed to an oak door with a window in the top half. "This is the operators' parlor, Miss Gregory."

She indicated for Hannah to enter. The room held a piano, comfortable seating, and even sewing supplies.

"It's lovely."

"The telephone company understands the stress their operators are under and the fragile constitution of most young women." Miss Frogge ran her finger along a shelf and puffed away the dust she'd collected on her fingertip. "They want you to have the opportunity to relax during lunch and on your breaks." She swept her hand toward a table bearing scissors, bright paper, and ribbons. "Right now a scrapbook competition is being held for the operators. Many of the girls are quite witty with their prose. The telephone company is providing the prize for the best scrapbook—a new hat from Younkers."

The thought that the company cared warmed Hannah, but she had a hard time imagining that writing witty prose would fill her free time. She spotted a smaller room off the main parlor, filled with shelves and books. "What is that room for?"

"That's the reading room. It's well stocked, and there's a literary club that meets on Thursdays at five. The telephone company has provided a place for a container garden on the roof as well, if you enjoy that sort of thing." She started for the door. "Please feel free to use any of these amenities as long as you are not on the clock."

A library? Hannah fought the urge to race into the room and examine the volumes. Would they have any of the newest books she'd heard so much about, like Edith Wharton's *Madame de Treymes*? Perhaps they'd even have a new bird-watching manual. That would be a treat.

"Miss Gregory, are you coming?" Impatience tinged Miss Frogge's voice, and Hannah hurried to follow the woman.

The supervisor led her to another room, passed through a set of wide double doors, and spread her arms wide. "This is the cafeteria. Coffee, tea, and bread are provided free of charge. Everything else on the menu is less than five cents, so please do not skip meals. The telephone company says healthy operators are important and less apt to be absent from their posts."

"I suppose that would be true." Hannah smiled, hoping to win a bit of favor with her new supervisor.

"Of course it is. If Iowa Telephone says it is so, then it is." With the brisk pace of someone much younger, Miss Frogge marched from the cafeteria and headed back toward the central exchange.

Hannah hurried to walk beside her. "When do I begin working, Miss Frogge?"

"Our busiest time is between ten and noon. We will need you at your board, but there's no need to fret, as I will be nearby to instruct you." She stopped outside the door to the exchange and pointed to a poster on the wall bearing the rules for operators. "You will be given a paper copy of these rules as well, but there are a few I'd like to point out to you right now."

Hannah glanced at the long list of over a hundred rules and swallowed. Mrs. Reuff had said there were many rules, but she hadn't done the list justice.

"Do not cross your legs or ankles. Both feet should remain on the floor at all times." Miss Frogge held up her hand and checked off the rule by touching a long, tapered finger. "There is to be no gum chewing, no tardiness, and no asking to leave early."

"Yes, ma'am."

"Don't interrupt me." Miss Frogge glared at her. "There will be no conversing with callers. You are to use only the approved phrases, and local calls should take less than six seconds to complete."

Hannah only nodded this time, her chest tightening with each new restriction.

"Eyes should be kept forward at all times. There's no need to glance in the direction of any of the other operators. Your work is in front of you."

So that explained why no one looked around. At the school, they'd had a similar rule, but she had no idea it would be so strictly adhered to.

Having now used up her first hand, Miss Frogge held up the other to continue. "If you must blow your nose or wipe your brow, raise your hand for permission before you do so."

Swallowing, Hannah fought the urge to roll her eyes. That was ridiculous. Did they think all of these intelligent young women were children?

"There is to be no union talk. The telephone company treats you well. You have no need of that. And most of all"—Miss Frogge pinned Hannah with her gaze—"there will be no conversing with the other operators while in the exchange. This includes exchanging notes or pictures. I will not tolerate those who do not follow these rules. Do I make myself clear, Miss Gregory?"

A suffocating cloud descended over Hannah. What had she gotten herself into? Maybe her sister was right. Perhaps it was impossible for Hannah to follow these restrictions. Unlike sweet Rosie, it wasn't in Hannah's nature to be so compliant. She wanted to argue about the absurdity of it all. Raising your hand to blow your nose or wipe your brow? What were these people thinking?

It wasn't natural not to look at the person sitting next to you. She wanted to tell Miss Frogge that there were more important things going on in the world than whether a call took longer than the prescribed six seconds.

She should turn around right now and leave. March out that door and back to college where she belonged.

But she couldn't.

Her sisters needed her.

Like she'd told Lincoln, that time in her life was over, and it was up to her and her alone to see they were taken care of.

She drew in a long breath and dipped her head in a brief nod. "Yes, ma'am. You've made yourself quite clear."

⁓⁓⟨◦⟩⁓⁓

Lincoln had moved too fast and pushed her. His office chair squeaked when he shifted. He pinched the bridge of his nose and tried to focus on writing Roderick McGowan's last will and testament, but Hannah's words from the previous night kept resurfacing in his mind. *No, Lincoln, the man said this was for your lady, and I'm afraid that can't be me.*

What was going on in her beautiful mind? Surely ice cream didn't amount to asking her to be his lady. He'd said nothing about officially courting. Then again, it wasn't like the idea hadn't crossed his mind, and Hannah was too smart not to notice his interest. But everything had been going so well. When had the evening taken a hairpin turn?

"So, did you hear? A celebration is in order." Pete Williams stood before Lincoln's desk, his thumbs hooked in his suspenders. "It's not every day I beat Samuel Appleton in court, so I'm going to let you buy me lunch."

Lincoln chuckled. "I feel so honored."

Pete leaned closer and tried to read the document on the desk. "What are you working on?"

"The McGowan will." Lincoln set his fountain pen back in its stand and sighed. "But it's taking much too long."

"Really? Writing a will doesn't usually give you any difficulty."

"I'm afraid my mind wasn't on the will. It was on something else."

Pete lifted his bushy gray eyebrows. "Or maybe *someone* else?"

"Maybe."

"Miss Gregory, I presume." Pete patted his rounded belly. "Come on. Let's get some food. I'm wasting away even as we speak."

Bright sunlight greeted them outside the building as they headed toward their favorite downtown café and took their seats. After ordering meatloaf and mashed potatoes, Pete spread his napkin in his lap. "How are things going with the arson case? Are you and the lovely Miss Gregory getting together later to work on her friend's defense?"

"I doubt it. It's her first day as a Hello Girl." Lincoln withdrew his pocket watch and calculated the time. She'd been there for about five hours. The eight-and-a-half-hour shift would leave her exhausted, and then she'd need to see to her sisters. Who was he kidding? She'd made her feelings clear about him.

He tucked the watch back in his pocket. "Besides, I'm not sure she wants to see me."

"Did you two have a row?"

"No. She's . . . reticent."

"Do you blame her?" Pete lifted his coffee cup to his lips. "She's fighting to feed her family, and you come rolling up in a brand-new automobile."

"I suppose it was callous of me."

"No, it wasn't, but from what you've said, she's a smart young woman. It probably underscored that she's not in your social class."

The words struck him. "Social class doesn't mean a thing to me."

"If you want a political career, it probably should."

Lincoln scowled, and Pete held up his hand. "Don't get your feathers ruffled. I only want you to think about what you really want."

"What would you do? Would you put love, or even potential love, above your law practice?"

"Son, you know I would. I've been married for over twenty years. I know the value of both coming home to the woman I love and having the career I wanted. But I can tell you this. I'd throw my law practice away in a heartbeat for my Elise. Even on her dark days, she makes me happy, and I would do anything for her. Anything in the world."

"Be careful, or Samuel Appleton might get wind of what a softy you are." Lincoln paused when the waitress brought their meatloaf-laden plates. "I don't know why I'm worried about it. Hannah won't even agree to see me."

"You're approaching it all wrong." Pete scooped up his mashed potatoes. "Love is war, Lincoln."

"I didn't say I was in love."

Waving off his comment with his fork, Pete went on. "You simply need to fill your arsenal with better weapons, develop a battle plan, make allies."

Lincoln hit the table with his fist. "Pete Williams, you're a genius!"

19

It didn't take a genius to know Miss Frogge wasn't planning to leave Hannah's side all day. The supervisor hovered above Hannah. With her operator's set plugged into the special jack at the top of the switchboard, Miss Frogge could listen in on every one of Hannah's calls.

"Hello, Main." Hannah tried to put a smile into her voice. "Number, please."

The man on the other end of the line mumbled, and his words blurred together.

"Three-three-five. Thank you." Hannah pulled the circuit cord from her board and moved the plug at the end toward the designated jack.

Miss Frogge pushed her hand away. "He said three-three-nine, not three-three-five."

"No he didn't. If he did—" Hannah wished the words back immediately.

Yanking the plug from Hannah's hand, Miss Frogge inserted the plug into the jack for 339. "Ring the call through, Miss Gregory."

When a sweet woman's voice came on the line, Hannah flipped her switch.

Seconds later, the light went out, indicating the call was already over.

The customer called back. "What is your problem, girl? You got wax in your ears. I said three-three-five."

"I apologize." She pulled out the circuit cord. "Ringing three-three-five. Thank you."

She glanced up at Miss Frogge, expecting the woman to say she was sorry for her mistake. Instead, she received a scowl. "Eyes back on your board, Miss Gregory." She adjusted her headset. "And there's no need to say the word *ringing*. Unnecessary words simply slow the caller's service."

Was an apology unnecessary? And what about unnecessary interventions by the supervisor? Hannah was saved from uttering the retort by another call. "Hello, Main. Number, please."

Nearly an hour later, Miss Frogge finally stepped away. Hannah lifted her shoulders, trying to ease the tension in them. Her nose itched, but she didn't dare rub it. Wiggling it, she answered her next call. The frantic caller on the other end made her heart race.

An elderly woman with chest pains needed her doctor.

An emergency call. She could do this. As she'd been trained, she raised her hand and then placed the call to the doctor. The doctor's nurse answered. He was at another home, and she didn't know their number. Hannah put a call through to the information operators. They would ring her as soon as the number was found.

"Ma'am?" Hannah tried to raise the caller again. "Ma'am, are you there?"

The elderly woman coughed. "Is the doctor coming?"

"We're trying to reach him, ma'am." She glanced at the list of the patrons on her registry and the numbers assigned to them. "I need to confirm you're Mrs. Ellerbeck."

"Yes, I'm Katherine." Her words were weak, strained.

The light indicating the information operator was calling her back lit, and Hannah jumped. "Mrs. Ellerbeck, hold on. I'll be right back."

Seconds later, she reached the doctor, who promised to go directly to Mrs. Ellerbeck's home on Twelfth Street.

"Mrs. Ellerbeck, are you there?"

A moan, but no answer. Hannah's stomach lurched.

Hannah risked looking at her supervisor, who stood ready to step in and assist if necessary. Surely under these circumstances a little eye-to-eye contact wouldn't get her in trouble. Miss Frogge motioned with her hand for Hannah to continue.

"Mrs. Ellerbeck, the doctor is on his way. Can you hear me? The doctor is coming."

The moaning grew fainter and fainter, and Hannah prayed the doctor would make it in time. She started to disconnect the call, but Miss Frogge stopped her.

"Stay on the line until you hear him enter. The operators on each side of you will handle your calls."

It seemed like an eternity before she heard the sound of the doctor's voice from inside the home. Her fingers trembling, she disconnected the call. Was the elderly woman all right? How could she have made the connection more quickly? Had she said and done the right things?

Apparently not. Miss Frogge pointed to the door. A relief operator laid her hand on Hannah's shoulder, and they switched places. Tears formed in the edges of Hannah's eyes. She'd tried to comfort the woman, and she'd raced to get her help. What else could she have done?

Miss Frogge joined her in the hall and shut the door. "You did well, Miss Gregory. You deserve an extra fifteen minutes after a call like that. Take heart in knowing you quite possibly saved that woman's life today."

Quite possibly? The woman had survived, hadn't she? Hannah sucked in a shaky breath. She would never know the truth.

✤✦✤

"The truth is I could use your help." Lincoln laid a hand on the hood of his Reo Roadster and smiled at Tessa seated behind the steering wheel. If he could secure her and Charlotte's assistance, courting Hannah might become a reality.

149

Tessa cocked her head to the side. "Why should I help you? Can't you get Hannah to like you on your own?"

His brilliant idea of making an alliance with the sisters was beginning to tarnish, and Tessa didn't appear to want to make this easy. Did obstinacy run in the Gregory family? Negotiating with a roomful of lawyers was easier than this.

"I simply thought we could all help each other." He flicked a bud casing from the automobile's windshield. "Hannah doesn't seem to like leaving you and your sister home alone, and I'd like to spend some time with her, so going on a picnic together works for all of us."

Tessa caressed the steering wheel. "Except for Hannah if she doesn't want to be around you."

He shoved his hands into his pockets. "Did she say that?"

"Naw, she's almost as moony-eyed about you as Charlotte is about George—but she'd skin me alive if she knew I told you that." Tessa pretended to make a turn. "But something must be wrong, or you wouldn't be here trying to get Charlotte and me on your side."

"I think you're too smart for your own good." Lincoln glanced down the sidewalk. "Speaking of Charlotte, where is she? Shouldn't she be home by now?"

"She's with Georgie Porgie."

Lincoln frowned and pulled out his pocket watch. It didn't take forty-five minutes to walk home from the high school. And didn't the fictitious Georgie Porgie always kiss the girls and make them cry?

Perhaps he should go check on Hannah's sister.

"If we help you get Hannah to join us on the picnic, will you let me drive it?"

He gulped. "My automobile?"

"No." Sarcasm laced her voice. "Your team of six white horses." She rolled her eyes. "Of course I'm talking about the automobile."

"Do you honestly think I'll say yes?"

She shrugged and grinned, her smile a replica of Hannah's. "I'd settle for a 'maybe' or even a 'someday.'"

His chest rumbled with laughter. "Someday, then."

She stuck out her hand. "Then you've got a deal. I'll do my best to help you win over Hannah. But just so you know, she's not that great a prize."

⁂

A picnic?

Hannah still couldn't believe Lincoln had shown up at the telephone company with a picnic basket in hand and her sisters perched on the extra seat of his Reo. If both sisters hadn't been so excited about the adventure he had planned, she might have been able to turn him down.

She stepped out of the automobile, accepted a quilt from Lincoln, and draped it over her arm. A strand of windblown hair tickled her cheek. She shoved it behind her ear as she surveyed Union Park. Tucked against the bank of the Des Moines River, the park sported rolling hills, open spaces, and plenty of oaks, cottonwoods, elms, and maples.

She risked a glance at Lincoln. Dressed in a lightweight suit and straw hat, he seemed ready to enjoy himself, oblivious to the turmoil inside her. He swung the basket as he walked and encouraged Charlotte and Tessa to run ahead and pick out a location for their picnic.

"Lincoln, I meant what I said yesterday." It wouldn't be fair to let him have any illusions about today.

"I know you did." He turned and flashed her a dangerously handsome smile. "But your sisters and I want to celebrate your first day. Don't spoil this for them, Hannah. And can there be any harm in a little picnic?"

Any harm? From the way her pulse quickened under his gaze, there most certainly could be, but how could she tell him that? Being near him made her palms sweat and her mind grow fuzzy. She yearned to tell him about her day, about the rules, and about Miss Frogge and the emergency, but she mustn't let herself turn to him. They were in different social classes, but it was more than that. She'd given this matter a great deal of thought last night—nearly half a night's worth of thinking. Leaning on Lincoln for support would be too easy. He was physically, intellectually, and spiritually strong, and she was so weary of carrying the load of responsibility alone. If she turned to him one more time, she might not be able to stop—ever.

Besides, it was Hannah's responsibility to take care of her family, and hers alone. It was what her father had asked of her, and it was the least she could do for her parents. If only Lincoln wasn't making it so hard to send him away.

"This is the perfect spot!" Beneath a large oak, Charlotte spun in a circle with her arms outstretched. "Isn't it beautiful?"

Quite a distance to the south, Tessa leaned over the edge of the riverbank. "But there's no view. My spot is a hundred times better."

Hannah cocked her head in a dare. "Negotiate this, counselor."

Lincoln looked from sister to sister and scratched his chin. "What do I do?"

Cupping her hand to her mouth, Hannah shouted, "We'll picnic right here in the middle!" She stopped and shook out the quilt.

Lincoln chuckled. "Just like that?"

"It's the only way to keep the peace. Besides, dictatorship is the oldest sister's prerogative."

"Is it now?" He grinned and set down the basket on the edge of the quilt. "In that case, I'll have to remember to follow your orders."

"You're learning."

As soon as they'd finished their supper and the empty plates had been gathered, Lincoln stood and held out his hand to Hannah. "Now it's time for some fun. Have you ever seen the park's aviary?"

"That's for the birds." Hannah giggled. "And how did you know I like birds?"

"The books, remember? Anything that flies." He grinned. "And I had a little help." Hannah glanced at Charlotte, and from the guilty look on her sister's face, she had a good idea who'd provided that little piece of information.

"You can't take only her." Tessa poked out her bottom lip.

Lincoln chuckled. "No, we're all going. Right, Hannah?"

"Absolutely." She shook out the folds of her skirt. "I wouldn't have it any other way."

The aviary wasn't far from their picnic site. Set on a hill and nestled beneath a heavy canopy of trees, the flight cage appeared to be about as long as four boxcars.

"There are so many." Hannah placed her hand on the wire mesh of the structure. Inside it, a wild turkey waddled across the length of the yard. Small trees offered a place for the birds to light and nest. A few other wooden A-frames provided excellent opportunities to view the birds. A miniature pond gave the ducks a place to swim, and crates made secure homes for the waterfowl. Never had Hannah seen so many species in one place. She'd spent many hours bird watching, but this aviary gave an individual the opportunity to study many birds at one time.

Charlotte pointed to a sleeping barn owl on an upper branch. "This is lovely, but it's kind of sad too. All these birds can only fly as far as the net allows."

"But this is a wonderful habitat."

Charlotte shrugged. "I'm not sure I'd want to be caged, no matter how nice the cage was."

Hannah moved down the length of the aviary, away from her sisters, scanning the area for feathered treasures. "Look, Lincoln, there's a ruffed grouse, and that one is a sharp-tailed one."

Lincoln trailed behind her. "What's the difference?"

"The ruffed grouse is usually referred to as a partridge. The sharp-tailed grouse has a longer, pointier tail. Grouses have elaborate courtship displays, and they're a precocial species."

"They're what?"

Hannah turned toward him and smiled. "They hatch with their eyes open. They're self-reliant from birth. They don't even need their mother to feed them."

"Self-reliant, huh? I suppose they're a favorite of yours."

"As a matter of fact, yes." She moved a few feet farther down and climbed onto a log to see into a nest. The log began to wobble.

Lincoln caught her waist. "So tell me about those courtship displays."

Did he honestly expect her to share that? With his hands splayed across her waist, sending a current through her entire body?

He helped her down, stepped away, and motioned with his hand for her to continue. "Go on. I'm listening."

Could he see the flush of her cheeks? Her discomfort at the subject? He cocked an eyebrow at her, making it clear he didn't plan to let this go and that he enjoyed making her squirm.

She could do this. It was factual information. She cleared her throat and met his eye. "The birds show off at dawn and dusk. The males display their plumage and call out to the females. They may drum their wings or rattle their tails, and occasionally they may fight with other males."

Lincoln held her gaze. "If he's willing to fight for her, then the female he's interested in must really be a prize."

Hannah's heart fluttered like the wings of a bird. She looked away. She had to find something to distract him from this present course of discussion. "Hey, look, that's a prairie chicken."

"I suppose you even know its Latin name."

"*Tympanuchus cupido.*"

"Did you say something about Cupid?"

Her mouth opened, but no words formed.

Good grief. This was going from bad to worse.

20

Had Lincoln just made the situation worse?

Hannah scurried around the end of the aviary and away from him as fast as she could. Right after she had reiterated her standings on a relationship with him, he'd gone and made romantic inferences. Now she'd done an about-face and not spoken to him since. When would he learn some verbal restraint and not push too hard?

From the look on Hannah's face, he'd scared the wits out of her. She wasn't some young lady given to a casual infatuation. She probably sensed, as surely as he did, that he was playing for keeps this time, and this was no game at all. He couldn't push her into that. She had to choose it for herself. But what if he'd ruined that chance?

Tessa grabbed Hannah's hand and pulled her toward the path. "Enough of the squawking birds. Let's go fly like one on the circle swings."

Hannah glanced back at Lincoln and shrugged, surrendering to Tessa's insistence.

"Well, Charlotte." Lincoln swept his arm toward the path. "It looks like we're headed to the circle swings too."

The winding path led to the American Circle Swing Company's creation situated in an open area. Unlike the large, free-flying swings at the World's Fair, these eight narrow porch-like swings were mounted on horizontal rods extending from a center pole. Above each chair, an arched piece of metal was attached to a rope that was connected to the top of the pole. Riders could then rock the swing back and forth, but in reality, the swing didn't truly swing or fly anywhere.

To propel the circle swing, a person would push a beam that extended from the main pole. Like the playground merry-go-round, the faster the pusher walked or ran, the faster the swings could go. On special park days, sometimes a horse would be hooked up to the beam, but most days, a local youth would be on hand to provide the service for a coin or two.

Lincoln smiled when he spotted a sturdy young man working the swings. Perfect. This strapping young fellow would be able to provide an excellent whirl.

Charlotte touched his arm. "I'll get Tessa to go with me so you can ride with Hannah."

"Thanks for your help, but I'm not sure she wants to ride with me."

"Trust me, she does, but she doesn't want to admit it to herself." With that, Charlotte hurried to join her sisters.

Lincoln quickened his pace and pressed a few coins into the young man's outstretched hand. "Give us a good go, okay?"

The youth looked at the money, closed his fist, and nodded enthusiastically. "Yes, sir. I will."

"Come on, Tessa." Charlotte linked her arm in her younger sister's. "You can have the inside."

They scrambled away, and Lincoln smiled at Hannah, hoping to ease her concerns. Her auburn-colored hair had blown loose and whipped around the high collar of her ruffled shirtwaist, but it was her hazel eyes that captured him. Filled with fiery amber flecks, they matched her personality all too well. Fire right down to her soul.

Hmm. Fire could be a beautiful thing to watch, but it could certainly destroy too. Was he setting himself up to be burned by a lady who'd already made up her mind about him? Perhaps he should be careful.

He sighed. Who was he kidding? The spark she'd planted had already begun to smolder, and it was up to Hannah to fan the flame or extinguish it altogether. He wouldn't push, but he was certainly going to do his best to provide excellent kindling.

He motioned toward the swing opposite her sisters. "I guess that leaves us. You can have the inside too."

"Lincoln . . ." Her voice held a note of longing and a touch of censure.

"Hannah, it's just a ride on a swing. I'm sure you'll love the thrill of the wind in your face." He swallowed. "But it's your decision."

Her sisters called for her to hurry, and she looked from him to the swing. Her teeth grazed her lower lip. "I guess one ride couldn't hurt."

<hr />

Hannah dug her fingers into the armrest of the swing until they hurt. The faster the young man ran, the harder it became for Hannah to remain fixed to her half. She slid toward Lincoln and pulled herself back. With Lincoln's arm draped casually across the back of the seat, if she let go she'd have no choice but to lean into his chest. Her cheeks warmed at the thought.

"Ready?" the youth called, picking up his pace.

Tessa whooped and Charlotte squealed as the swing spun faster. The centrifugal force weakened Hannah's tenuous hold. Her fingers slipped, and she slid across the seat—and into Lincoln's open arms.

Immediately, he pulled her tight against him as if he'd been waiting for the moment.

That figured.

She felt the hardness of his chest against her back and started to pull away. His hand came to rest protectively over her midsection, searing her flesh through her shirtwaist.

He pressed his lips to her ear. "Can't let you go flying off like some *Tympanuchus cupido.*"

She swallowed hard as her heart drummed against her rib cage. Could he feel the pounding beneath his large hand?

This was all so wrong. She couldn't let herself lean on him here—or in life. She had to stand on her own. The only one she could count on was herself. She should find some resolve and regain her rightful place.

But even as the swing slowed, not one muscle would heed her command to move away. What was it about this man's touch that paralyzed her and made her heart nearly dance?

"I guess one ride couldn't hurt." Her own words taunted her. Couldn't hurt? Boy, had she been wrong.

Finding the last remnant of her resolve, she wiggled away and hooked her hand around the armrest. Safe. At last.

If she could only manage to avoid his touch until they got home, she'd be fine. At least that's what she told herself.

∾∾∾

Hannah adjusted the pins in her hat after the swing ride. "Charlotte, would you please gather the picnic basket? We've taken up enough of Mr. Cole's time."

"We're not going already. Mr. Cole promised me I could fish." Tessa whipped around toward Lincoln. "Didn't you?"

"That I did, and I'm a man of my word."

"It's getting late, Tessa. I can take you fishing another time. Besides, you don't have a pole or any bait."

"Actually, Hannah, it's in the Reo." Lincoln relieved Charlotte of the basket.

Charlotte flanked Lincoln on the other side, her not-so-innocent face framed by a halo of waves. Traitor. She was making it obvious it was three against one.

Hannah huffed out a breath. "Oh, all right. A short excursion. The sun will be setting soon."

They drove to the edge of Union Park's lake, where Lincoln

rented two rowboats. Charlotte and Tessa hurried off with fishing tackle in hand to claim the first rowboat, leaving Hannah and Lincoln the other.

Lincoln flicked his wrist toward the dock. "After you."

The dock bobbed beneath the pressure of their footfalls, and a cool breeze filled the air with the lake's tangy, spring scent. Tied at the end of the dock was the rowboat.

Their farm pond had had a boat, and she'd climbed in and out of it plenty of times without assistance. If she hurried, she could get into the boat before Lincoln could insist on helping her—and touching her.

She reached the edge and placed a hand on the dock support. "Hannah, wait. Let me—"

"I can manage by myself." She hiked up her skirt and lowered her foot. The distance to the rowboat was farther than she'd anticipated, but at last her shoe found solid wood.

She let go of the support to lower her other foot, but her balance shifted. The boat tilted and pitched her into the chilly lake.

Sputtering, she stood up in the shallow water only to hear the sound of Lincoln's roaring laughter echoing off the glassy surface of the water.

She glared at him. How dare he? "Are you going to stand there? Aren't you going to help me out?"

"Well, Miss Independent, you said you could do it yourself." In four long strides, he left the dock and sat down in the grass on the shore.

She gaped at him. Despite the shivers wracking her body, coal-hot anger gnawed at the pit of her stomach. Was he honestly going to leave her to slog out of this lake alone?

The smirk on his face said he most certainly was.

She sloshed through the weeds to the edge of the shore. Her heavy, water-soaked clothes weighted down each step. Her foot sank into the mire at the bottom, and the mud sucked her shoe off. She bent, dug in the slimy goo, and fished out the shoe with her hands. She heaved it toward the shore, where it missed Lincoln by an inch. Too bad. Maybe her aim would be better with the other shoe. She removed it and heaved it toward him.

He caught it in his right hand. "Want help now?"

"No!"

"Good." He leaned back and rested on his elbows. "Nice sunset, isn't it?"

Oooh, that man. When she got out of here, she was going to give him a tongue-lashing he'd never forget.

Propping her hands on her hips, she determined the best way to climb out. Unfortunately, this was not a gradual-sloping sand beach. No, she had to fall in a lake where the water had eroded the shore and created a ninety-degree angle of dirt and weeds.

Gripping a clump of dry weeds in her numb hands, she pulled herself halfway up the embankment. Then the weeds broke free, and she tumbled backward into the chilly water and landed in a most unladylike position.

After shoving a clump of weeds off her face, she clambered to her feet. When she looked at the bank, there stood Lincoln, now in shirtsleeves and barefoot. He stretched out his hand toward her.

She crossed her arms over her chest and shook her head.

"I know you could get out all on your own." His voice was tender, and the mirth was gone from his face. "But you don't have to."

Her anger blew away like the down of a dandelion, and her insides swirled. He was making a point, and he was offering her much more than assistance in getting out of this lake. But did he realize what he was asking her to do?

She was the oldest sister. She took responsibility. She handled everything life threw at her, and she didn't count on anyone's help. *Not even the Lord's*, a small voice whispered inside her.

Rubbing her chilled arms, she took one step closer and stopped.

"Hannah, I'm giving you the freedom to choose." His dove-blue eyes were filled with hope. "I won't push you, but I thought you liked taking risks."

"I do."

"Then take a risk on me."

Hannah stared at Lincoln's outstretched hand and smiled. She'd take a risk, all right.

As soon as his hand clasped around her own, she yanked him with all her might toward the water.

21

Arms flailing, Lincoln fought his rapid descent. Mud gave way beneath his feet, and he landed with a splash in Union Park's lake.

Shocked to his core, he looked up into Hannah's laughing face. "W-why did you do that?"

"I decided to take a risk." She giggled, backing away, almost daring him to retaliate. "And if you're going to spend time with me, you might as well learn there are going to be some surprises."

"Is that so?" A smile tugged at the corners of his lips, and his chest warmed. So, she was accepting his offer. "Well, Miss Gregory, you'd better expect some surprises as well." He rushed toward her, creating a spray in his wake.

She squealed and dove out of his reach. He caught her waist and pulled the laughing woman into his arms.

With her hair hanging in damp rivulets around her face and her eyes alight with anticipation, she took his breath away. She shivered against his chest.

"Lincoln Cole, if you douse me again—" She squirmed in his arms, then looked into his eyes and stilled. She licked her lips. "What are you doing?"

He raised his hand, removed soggy weed from her hair, and cupped her cheek.

"Giving you the surprise you deserve."

She shivered again, and he noticed a bluish tinge to her lips.

Good grief. She was freezing, and even if he wanted to warm her up as only he could, standing in a lake was hardly the place for a first kiss. Before desire won over practicality, he bent and tossed her over his shoulder.

"Put me down!" She squirmed and pounded on his back with her fists.

"It would serve you right if I did toss you back in." He reached the dock and lifted her onto its dry wood surface. Using his upper body strength, he then pulled himself out.

Teeth chattering like the clacking of a spinning windmill, Hannah scrambled to her feet and wrapped her arms around herself.

"Stay here." He grabbed his suit coat from the grass, returned to her, and attempted to wrap her in it.

She stopped him. "I don't want to ruin it. I'll go get the quilt from the automobile."

"Put this on." He pushed the coat into her hands. "*I'll* go get the quilt because you're going to need all the warmth you can get."

"What about you?"

"So you'd like me to warm you up too?"

Her face bloomed crimson.

He grinned. "I'd love to warm you up, but your sisters are watching."

"Th-that's not what I meant. I was worried about you being cold."

"It's nice to know you care." He pulled the coat from her hands and draped it around her shoulders.

"I didn't say that." She hugged the coat close and lifted her eyebrows. "We simply need you warm enough to drive us home."

~~~♦~~~

"You should have seen her, Rosie." Charlotte leaned on the rake handle. Already, even with only an hour's worth of work, the front yard of their rented home looked better.

Hannah, who'd changed out of her work clothes for the evening

163

and donned a split skirt, placed her boot on the spade and forced it through the crust of the earth.

Charlotte took a deep breath. The scent of freshly turned soil rose up from the ground, and a worm wriggled from the rich, dark clod.

"I didn't look that bad," Hannah insisted.

Flicking the ribbon on Hannah's sunbonnet, Tessa giggled. "You looked like a drowned rat."

Charlotte smiled and sighed. It was true. Yesterday Hannah had emerged from the lake looking like a sopping piece of laundry in need of a good wringing, but Mr. Cole still gazed at her as if she were the most beautiful woman in the world.

Would George ever admire Charlotte like that? Maybe tomorrow night at the box social he'd tell her that she took his breath away.

"And then"—Tessa knelt and carefully placed the dormant rosebush in the hole Hannah had made—"when Mr. Cole went to help her get out, she pulled him right in the lake with her."

Rosie gasped. "Hannah, you didn't!"

"I couldn't let him get away with laughing at me, now could I?" Hannah dug another hole. "He had the nerve to stand there and laugh at me."

The pink tinge in Hannah's cheeks said there was more to the story. From the subtle change in the way she and Mr. Cole interacted after the boating incident, some sort of understanding must have passed between them—at least on Mr. Cole's part. While Hannah didn't rebuff his attention, she didn't encourage it either. At the rate Hannah was going, Mr. Cole would be old and gray before he even got a first kiss. But Charlotte had a sneaking suspicion he would wait no matter how long it took.

She scooped up the dried leaves and branches in her pile and deposited them in the wheelbarrow they'd borrowed from Rosie. How long would George wait for a kiss? Impatience oozed from him. He didn't like to wait too long for her after school, so she always hurried, and he didn't like to wait for her to come out to the porch in the evenings, so she tried to finish her chores quickly.

Even though he'd made his intentions to steal a kiss clear, so far he'd been willing to wait for that. Charlotte didn't know when was the right time to let a fellow kiss her. She could ask Hannah, but Charlotte probably wouldn't like the answer. She could ask Rosie, but she'd most likely tell Hannah. If only her mother was still alive, she'd be able to answer all her questions.

Charlotte wiped her sleeve over her damp eyes and returned to her sisters.

"It's only your second day," Tessa was saying. She stood up and wiped her hands together. The soil sprinkled to the ground. "You're worse than me. At least I can go more than a day without getting in trouble."

Rosie smiled. "So, Hannah, how many marks do you have on your deportment card?"

"Just the two from today. I'm telling you, Rosie, it's much harder than it was in operators' class. I tried not to look around, but everything is so new and fascinating."

"I bet Miss Frogge almost croaked." Tessa giggled and patted the earth around the second rosebush.

"You're incorrigible, Tessa." Hannah dug the final hole for their mother's yellow tea roses.

Tessa moved to Hannah's side and loosened the soil in the bottom with her gloved fingers. Charlotte handed her the burlap-wrapped plant. After removing the string securing the burlap, Tessa examined the plant.

Rosie leaned down for a closer look. "That one looks dead."

"It's not dead. It's dormant, and early spring is the best time to transplant them." Tessa tucked the plant in the opening and filled the hole with water. "After this water soaks in, we'll fill the hole again before we add the soil. The extra moisture will give it a good chance at taking root."

When the water had seeped into the dirt, Tessa refilled the hole. Charlotte fought the urge to laugh. How odd it was to see four people standing around a hole watching the water soak in. After Tessa added soil to the hole, she created a mound, shielding the young plant from drying out. She then took out a pair of sharp scissors.

"Why are you cutting the branches?" Rosie asked.

Tessa made an angled snip above a bud. "They're canes, not branches, and the plant will do better if they're only about eight inches long."

"Tessa is our plant girl." Hannah tapped the shovel against the ground to remove the dirt.

"And Charlotte cooks." Rosie collected her mother's shovel and rake. "So, Hannah, what's your specialty?"

Charlotte giggled. "Bossing us around."

"Speaking of bossy, look who's coming." Tessa tipped her head toward the sidewalk. "Georgie Porgie."

"Don't call him that." Charlotte turned to see George sauntering up the sidewalk, wearing his baseball uniform. Charlotte's heart skipped. He looked so handsome!

He glanced at Charlotte and tipped his cap. Did his heart do a jig at the sight of her like hers did when she'd spotted him?

"Hey, Lottie, come to my game." He leaned over the fence. "I want you there to cheer for me."

Charlotte turned to Hannah but found a frown marring her sister's face.

Please, please, please, Lord, let her say yes.

"Oh, go on and have fun." Hannah made a shooing motion with her hand. "We'll finish up here." She leaned closer and whispered in Charlotte's ear, "But remember how special you are, and make sure he's worthy of you."

Charlotte's face heated. Anger, pleasure, and confusion mingled inside her. Having Hannah remind her she was special was sweet, but why did she say the rest? George was worthy. He was handsome and athletic. Why did it feel like Hannah was implying George wasn't good enough?

With a wave of her hand, she hurried to join George.

After all, he didn't like to wait.

On her third day at the Iowa Telephone Company, Hannah stepped off the elevator with confidence and went to gather her headset. The assurance in her steps contrasted with the turmoil in her thoughts.

Charlotte had come home after the ball game full of "George did this" and "George did that." After the game, he'd officially asked her to be his girl, but he hadn't even taken the time to walk her home. How long would it take Charlotte to see George the way Hannah did?

If Hannah was honest with herself, she'd admit Charlotte wasn't the only person creating turmoil inside her. Ever since the lake experience with Lincoln, she couldn't get his words off her mind. He'd asked her to take a risk on him. Had she agreed? Perhaps she had—sort of.

But there was nothing solid. She could easily explain it was a misunderstanding, but did she want to? If she could only get him to stay out of her thoughts, she could truly think this through. He had a way of sticking his nose into everything. And to make matters worse, her sisters had become his greatest champions. Was she the only person with enough sense to see that she and Lincoln were from two different worlds?

Hannah glanced at the clock. Good. She'd arrived early enough to make a quick stop in the reading room. Maybe that would help turn her thoughts toward something other than a certain attorney. A strong, handsome, thoughtful attorney.

Stop that. Think about something else. Airplanes, laws, Walt—anything except Lincoln Cole.

In the operators' parlor, she avoided the scrapbookers and slipped into the reading room. After reading the spine of each book on the maple shelves, her gaze rested on a set of three blue volumes. Her pulse raced.

She eased them from the shelf and set them on the table. *A History of North American Birds.* Opening the first book, she noted it was first published in 1874. What a treasure! How had this set ended up here in the telephone company's book room? If it were hers, she would never have parted with it.

Scanning the book, she was amazed at the intricate drawings. She paused when she came to the sparrows. Her Bible reading that morning had reminded her that not one sparrow falls without God caring. How much more did God care about her? A sense of awe captured her as she considered the concept again. In view of the size of the earth and the vast number of common sparrows, it was hard to fathom God would even know when one fell to the earth, let alone care.

And God cared much more for her. Even though she struggled with believing this, especially now that her parents had been taken, she knew it was true. God saw her confusion about Lincoln, and he cared. Now if only he'd give her some answers.

Hannah flipped the page and gasped. It couldn't be. A Lincoln's sparrow? She'd never heard of such a bird. It figured he'd be a sparrow. Troublesome birds that nested in places no one wanted them.

But she'd always liked the protective little bird. Once, she had accompanied her father while he was doing his chores. When they neared the barn, a sparrow dove at them, snapping its beak at her and her father. The bird pulled away just inches above her father's head. Her father told her the sparrow would settle down in a few days. He guessed they had young ones in their nests. He also said he had to admire the little bird's willingness to go up against a man in order to protect his wife and babies.

She closed the book and sighed. Was God trying to tell her something now by pointing her to Lincoln's sparrow?

The wall clock in the parlor chimed. She placed the books on the shelf and hurried to join the other women. After lifting her headset from its hook, she strapped the speaker in place around her neck. Over the last few weeks, she'd grown used to its heavy weight resting against her chest, both at the exchange and at the operators' school.

She eased the headset over her wide pompadour and adjusted

the receiver over her ear. Now, if she could just get her stomach to settle.

A few minutes later, the women filed into the main operating room like soldiers and assumed their stations.

All business, Miss Frogge was waiting for her without so much as a smile of greeting. "Remember, Miss Gregory, every morning the operator must ring up all of her subscribers and make sure their lines are in good working order." Miss Frogge waved her hand in a circular motion. "Go ahead. It won't get done with you sitting there."

Hannah sat up straight and touched the jack to the rim of the first plug on her list of subscribers. She heard a sharp click. Knowing that meant the line was busy, she moved on to the next. "Good morning, Mrs. Wallace. Excuse me for troubling you, but I wanted to know if your telephone is working nicely this morning."

Miss Frogge nodded approval and stepped away. Hannah relaxed and thanked Mrs. Wallace. In no time, she had her subscribers called. Thankfully, no one was having line trouble.

Telephone traffic surged by ten o'clock, when wives began to place their orders with the butcher, druggist, or grocer, but eased as the clock neared noon.

"Hello, Main. Number, please." She prayed the callers could hear the smile in her voice.

"Can I have the butcher?"

Hannah recognized Mrs. Connor's sweet voice and smiled. "One-nine-eight. Thank you."

After answering several more calls, Hannah noted that Mrs. Connor's light on the panel again flickered.

"Main?" Mrs. Connor asked. "Do you realize you connected me to the mortician and not the butcher?"

Lowering her voice so Miss Frogge didn't hear, Hannah said, "I apologize, ma'am. I'll connect you now."

"No, wait." The woman laughed. "You should enjoy this as much as I did. Before I realized the mix-up, I asked him if he had any nice soup bones. He said he had several bones but could not recommend the ones he had for soup. My dear Hello Girl, I want to thank you. I haven't had such a good laugh before noon in ages."

Hannah swallowed a giggle. "You're welcome, ma'am."

"Miss Gregory, why is that call taking so long?" Miss Frogge again hovered over her shoulder.

"Ringing one-nine-seven. Thank you." Hannah jabbed the jack into the plug and sighed.

"How many times do I have to tell you not to say the word *ringing*? All you need to say is *thank you*. Anything else wastes valuable time."

"Yes, Miss Frogge."

Lunch was over all too soon, and Hannah hurried back to her switchboard. Unlike the rushed morning, the afternoon seemed to drag. Fighting the urge to look around lest she be reprimanded, Hannah picked up her pencil and began to make a few notes on her notebook of things she needed to take care of before Charlotte's box social tonight.

She connected a call, then leaned back in her chair and smiled. Charlotte had worked past dark on decorating her box with snippets of lace and ribbons. She'd outlined her menu and planned to make everything as soon as she got home from school. If George didn't rave about Charlotte's cooking, her sister would be crushed.

A knot tightened in her stomach whenever she thought of George. Maybe she was simply too protective of her sister. Too bad Lincoln wasn't going to be at the social. She could ask him for his opinion of Charlotte's suitor. As a man, perhaps he'd have a different perspective.

"Miss Gregory!"

Hannah jumped and sat ramrod straight.

"What is the meaning of this?" Miss Frogge thrust her finger at the tablet beside her board.

Hannah glanced at the tablet, and her cheeks warmed. When had she drawn the sparrow? And worse, how did the heart get drawn around it?

"We do not doodle at the switchboard."

"Yes, ma'am. I apologize."

"Apologies will not make up for the lost time. That, you'll have to do by staying later."

"But—" She couldn't stay late. She had planned to see Walt and then get home to help Charlotte.

Miss Frogge hiked an eyebrow, daring Hannah to continue.

Hannah clenched her fists. This wasn't fair. With her lips pressed together, she lowered her gaze. "I understand."

How could she have let her mind wander? This job demanded her complete attention. Why couldn't she have simply followed the rules? Now she'd have to skip seeing Walt, and she hadn't visited him in days. Would he think she'd abandoned him?

She glanced at the tablet and bit her lip. Maybe she already had—in more ways than one.

22

Where was Hannah? Charlotte held the mint dress to her body and looked in the mirror. Yesterday she'd chosen this dress to wear, but perhaps her other Sunday dress would be a better choice. The burnt-orange color might complement her hair, although the mint-green dress was newer. If Hannah was here, she'd help her decide. Hannah never had trouble making a decision.

Charlotte glanced at the wall clock. How odd. Hannah should have been home half an hour ago. Rubbing her chin, Charlotte again glanced between the two dresses. She couldn't wait any longer to decide. Before she could change her mind again, she grabbed the burnt-orange dress and shimmied into it.

It took several minutes to do up the long line of buttons on the cedar-brown voile trim running down the length of the dress's front. She carried her hat downstairs, set it on a table in the parlor, and hurried to the kitchen to pack the food.

With the fried chicken wrapped in brown paper, she hoped it would stay warm and crispy. She added a jar of peaches to each box, then her fresh biscuits and some of the crab apple jelly she and her mother had made last year. The crowning glory was the dessert. No one could resist her warm apple charlotte smothered in velvety vanilla cream sauce. Her mouth watered thinking about it. Surely George would love it as much as she did.

She set the lid on the lace-trimmed box and tied it with a brown velvet ribbon that matched the one on her hat. George knew to be looking for that particular ribbon. She slipped knives, forks, and spoons beneath the ribbon's bow, then did the same for the other box on the table.

"Tessa, do you see any sign of Hannah?"

The screen door banged open and shut before Tessa hurried into the room. "Not yet. I'm heading on over to Betty's, okay?"

"Maybe you should wait for Hannah to get here. She might want to speak with you before you go."

Tessa rolled her eyes. "She'd tell me to listen to Betty's parents and not to get into any trouble."

"And to not shock them with that scrapbook of yours." Charlotte opened the cookie jar and removed two gingerbread wafers. She passed one to Tessa and ate the other.

Tessa took a bite. "They're just headlines. They probably read them in the paper all the time."

"But you have a way of finding the ones that give people nightmares."

Tessa shrugged. "Those are the good ones. Speaking of headlines, do you want to hear my new favorite?"

"If I say no, you're going to tell me anyway."

"Probably." Tessa took a glass from the cupboard and filled it with water. "I'd hate for you to miss it. It's such a good one."

Charlotte sighed. "Oh, all right, tell me."

"'Surgeon cuts arm during autopsy on rabies victim.'"

"Tessa! That's awful."

"I know. Isn't it great?" Tessa downed her water. "No one could keep from reading that story, could they?"

Charlotte sighed. "Please don't tell Betty's parents about your hobby. They're going to think you're some kind of ill-bred heathen."

"I promise to be a perfect lady." Tessa curtsied and crossed her heart. "Have fun with Georgie Porgie—if that's even possible." She giggled and scurried out of the room.

"If you see Han—"

"She's here," Tessa called. "Finally. See you both tomorrow."

Shoes pounded against the hardwood in the parlor before Hannah burst into the kitchen. "I'm so sorry. I got in trouble and had to stay late at work."

"What happened? Did you look at your neighbor again?"

"I drew something on my notepad."

"What was it? A heart?" She giggled. Like Hannah would ever do something like that.

Hannah's cheeks pinked, and Charlotte's mouth dropped open. "You did draw a heart? You were thinking of Lincoln?"

"I never said that."

"You didn't need to. Your face says it all." She pointed to the table. "The boxes are packed and everything is ready, except you."

"Why are there two boxes for the social?"

"Oh, did I forget to tell you?" Charlotte removed her apron and hung it on the hook. "Lincoln offered to help you chaperone, so I made you a box too. Since they're being auctioned for the school's library, I thought you'd want to do your part. I already told him yours will be tied with the dotted yellow ribbon."

"Lincoln's coming? When?"

"He'll be here any time to pick you up."

Hannah held out her gored skirt. "Look at me, Charlotte! How will I ever get ready in time?"

Charlotte tsked. "You are a sorry sight." She picked up the yellow-decked box. "I guess I could give this box to Louisa Jane. I'm sure she'd be happy to share it with Lincoln."

"That flirt? Don't you dare. I'll be ready in twenty minutes."

"Better make it fifteen." She giggled. "Or I might have to tell Lincoln exactly why you're late."

❧◈❧

George was late.

Hannah glanced at Charlotte. She fiddled with the buttons on her dress, nervously watching the street in front of the high school. Decorated boxes lined a table the teachers had set up in the school yard, and young men stood before them doing their best to decide which to purchase. Lincoln walked over to survey the wares. Like Charlotte had done, a girl could give the young fellow she wanted to bid on her box a clue to its identity. Still, they'd have to win the bid in order to have the opportunity to eat with that young lady. If George didn't hurry, he might miss the chance to purchase Charlotte's box.

Excusing herself, Charlotte said she wanted to see if she could spot George coming.

Lincoln ambled back to Hannah's side. "Any sign of him?"

"Not yet. If he doesn't show—"

"He will." He glanced over her shoulder. "Look, here comes Charlotte, and I'm guessing the fellow must be George." He took Hannah's hand in his. "Listen, before they get back, I want to ask you to join me for a show tomorrow."

Her body tingled at the thought. "I really need to go visit Walt. I haven't seen him for days."

"Then we'll go see him first, and if you don't say yes, I may let one of these other young fellows buy your box." Lincoln sucked in his cheeks to keep from laughing. "I think I saw that pimple-faced boy in the checkered shirt eyeing it."

"You wouldn't dare."

"Say yes, or I just might."

"Do you play this unfair in a courtroom?"

"Me?" He pressed his hand to his heart, feigning innocence.

She rolled her eyes. "All right then, yes."

Hannah caught sight of Charlotte leading George in their direction. As they approached, Hannah overheard the young man telling Charlotte she should be glad he was here and not pester him about why he was late.

Her sister forced a smile when she joined them. "George, you remember my sister Hannah."

"Ma'am." He dipped his head.

"And this is Lincoln Cole. Mr. Cole, may I introduce George Donnelly."

"Sir." He nodded.

Hannah fought the urge to frown. Why didn't he offer Lincoln his hand?

The auctioneer stepped to the table and shouted for all the young men to circle around.

Lincoln laid his hand on the young man's shoulder. "Come on, George. We've got some boxes to purchase."

As soon as Lincoln and George left, Hannah turned to her sister. Charlotte's face, so joyful an hour ago, was now lined with concern.

"Are you okay, Charlotte?"

She gave a weak smile. "Yes. I'm just glad George is here."

"And soon you and he will be enjoying your delicious fare. Did you make your apple charlotte?"

"Naturally." Her smile returned. "I sure hope George likes it."

"He'd be a fool not to." She linked her arm in Charlotte's. "Come on. Let's go see who gets stuck with Louisa Jane's hard-as-a-brick biscuits."

❧❦❧

The first boxes sold for a quarter each. Not a bad start, but Lincoln planned on bidding more for Hannah's right from the start. He wasn't taking any chances on someone else trying to steal the yellow beribboned box with its delicious, Charlotte-made contents. If Charlotte was half the cook Hannah claimed, they were in for a treat.

A young man whooped after paying forty cents for his box. He scampered off to claim the box and the girl to go with it. She didn't look half as pleased, but perhaps God had other plans for them. Lincoln had a greater appreciation for God's timing than ever before.

He glanced at George. The young man had his hand held out with a splattering of coins on his palm. Fifty-two cents total. What if Charlotte's box went over that? With all the fanciful decorations she'd put on it, it might.

Nudged by generosity, Lincoln leaned close to the boy's ear. "If you need any extra money, I'll be glad to give you some."

The young man glared at him. "I don't take charity."

"It can be a loan—and only if Charlotte's box goes over what you brought. She's really looking forward to dinner with you tonight. I'd hate for her to be disappointed." He glanced toward the two sisters and smiled at Hannah. Charlotte wasn't the only one looking forward to dinner. He couldn't wait to have a few minutes with Hannah all to himself.

"If her box is more than this, she'll be eating with someone else." George jammed his fist back in his pocket.

This young fellow had a lot to learn, but Lincoln tried to give him the benefit of the doubt. A lot of boys were taught not to accept charity, so he could offer to hire George for something if it seemed necessary when the time came.

"Well, look here, fellows!" The auctioneer's voice boomed as he held up Charlotte's box. "Isn't this about the prettiest package up here? We'd better start it at fifteen cents."

George let someone else have the first bid. Lincoln turned to see Charlotte with her knuckle pressed against her lips. Jumping into the action, George accepted the volley of bids. It appeared he won the box at fifty cents.

"Going once. Going twice."

Another fellow raised his hand.

George glanced at Charlotte and shrugged. Even from a distance, Lincoln could see she was crestfallen.

"Don't be a fool, George. Raise the bid."

"I told you—"

"Going once."

Lincoln positioned himself so Charlotte couldn't see her beau, grabbed George's arm, and thrust it in the air.

"Sixty cents." The auctioneer grinned. "Going once. Going twice. Sold to the young man in the middle."

"You can work it off." Lincoln handed him a dime and nudged him toward the picnic area. "And you can thank me later."

George stomped to the front and claimed the box. Charlotte threw her arms around him and kissed his cheek.

Yep, the boy could thank him later.

Hannah's box, similar to Charlotte's but bearing the dotted yellow ribbon, came up five boxes later. The auctioneer again started it at fifteen cents. However, Lincoln shot his hand into the air and offered three dollars. Girls gasped and some of the men chuckled, but no one bid against him.

When he went to claim his dinner and his date, he had to grin. Hannah's cheeks bloomed like the spring blossoms on the trees. He accepted his box and offered her his arm.

She slipped her hand in place and waited to speak until he'd led them to a secluded spot. "We're supposed to be chaperoning."

"Look who's over there." He nodded toward Charlotte and George. "Besides, I think it's our duty to make sure no other young couples find this place, don't you?"

A smile reached her hazel eyes. "Hmm. Perhaps that is a good idea."

⟿⟾⟿⟾

Every moment Hannah spent with Lincoln chipped away at her doubts and concerns.

Lincoln removed his coat, spread it on the grass, and held out his hand. "For you, my lady."

Hannah took his hand, and his touch sent currents through her once again. Would she ever be able to be in this man's presence without it undoing her? She allowed him to help her settle on the coat.

He placed the box in front of her. "Will you do the honors?"

She tugged the ribbon free and lifted the lid off the box. The scent of fried chicken and cinnamon blended in the air. Charlotte had outdone herself. Hannah withdrew the linen napkins and handed one to Lincoln. Within minutes, Lincoln had blessed the food and they were enjoying the crunch of Charlotte's chicken and her flaky biscuits. Lincoln loved her mother's crab apple jelly and said he hoped Hannah, too, had learned to make the concoction. She assured him she had, but hers never gelled quite as well as Charlotte's or her mother's.

Hannah marveled at how easily conversation with Lincoln came. After hearing a few stories about his independent, fun-loving aunt, Hannah felt like she knew the woman. In turn, he pried information out of her about college. Soon they were sharing Drake stories, everything from difficult courses to influential professors to favorite locations on the campus. She learned they both enjoyed tennis, had served on the staff for the Quax yearbook, and had been in the Latin club. They'd also both fallen asleep in a few of their law lectures in Cole Hall.

"If only we could have been fellows at the same time." Lincoln accepted a plate of apple charlotte drenched in vanilla cream. "On second thought, my marks would have suffered horribly if you had been there to distract me."

"And the dean of women would have called me in." Hannah sat up straight and folded her hands across her chest to appear more like the woman she remembered. "Dr. Mary Craig would have said, 'Miss Gregory, you must put forth more effort. As women, we have much to offer the world, but no one will ever see it if we allow ourselves to be distracted.'"

He took a bite of his dessert and moaned. "This is incredible. What is it?"

"Apple charlotte."

"She named it after herself?"

"No, silly." Hannah forked her own bite. "That's the recipe's name, and Charlotte's apple charlotte is the best."

Lincoln glanced at the other couple. "And it looks like George is about to get his first taste."

George said something as Charlotte handed him a piece of the dessert, and Charlotte didn't look happy. What had he done to upset her sister now?

Lincoln frowned. "Hannah, what's wrong?"

"Charlotte is near tears."

Repositioning himself, Lincoln studied the other couple. "How can you tell?"

"We're sisters. I can tell." He probably wouldn't understand, but it was the truth. "I can't believe he upset her. I should march over there and—"

"And what?" Lincoln took her hand in his, caressing it with the pad of his thumb.

"Are you comforting me or holding me back?"

He grinned. "A little of both."

23

"So what upset Charlotte earlier?" Lincoln offered Hannah his hand and helped her out of the Reo. "They seemed all right when we left the box social."

Even though he'd offered to give George and Charlotte a ride home too, the young man had insisted on walking Charlotte home himself. The more Lincoln thought about it, the more that fact bothered him.

Hannah propped her hands on her hips. "George said for as much as he paid for her box, he thought he'd at least get a pie."

"You mean when Charlotte presented him with that delicious dessert bearing her name, he had the nerve to say it wasn't what he wanted?"

"Apparently." She leaned against the automobile's fender and removed the silk scarf he'd made sure was waiting for her.

"The cad. No wonder she was upset." He smiled when Hannah folded the scarf and slipped it in her pocket. Maybe she was simply distracted, but he'd take any headway he could get.

"Charlotte said it was her fault, and she should've remembered apple pie is his favorite." Hannah shrugged. "I don't understand it. The Charlotte I know would have dumped that dessert on his head, not apologized. Why is she so different with him?"

"I'll be happy to speak to him for you. I can tell him you'd rather he not see her anymore."

"If someone told me that, I'd want to see him all the more."
Hannah smiled. "Thank you, but I can handle it. I'll speak with
Charlotte and voice my concerns."

"Then I'll pray for you to find the right words."

"Is that what you do when you're in the courtroom? Pray?"

He nodded. "I do, and sometimes words and thoughts come that
I've never considered before. That's when I know I'm doing the job
God wants me to do. I love helping people in trouble. Cases like
Walt's—the ones that look hopeless—are my favorite."

Hannah cocked her head to the side. "Then why do you want
to go into politics?"

He shrugged. "It's what I'm supposed to do."

"Says who?"

"You're good at cross-examining, counselor." He squeezed her
hands. "I've been groomed to follow in my father's footsteps."

"But is it what you want?"

"Honestly? Until this moment, I've never considered it." He
whistled. "Do you realize the kind of stir I'd cause if I changed
my mind?"

Her eyes flashed with amusement. "Take it from someone who
knows a lot about causing stirs—it's not so bad." She pulled her
hands free. "Sorry, the prodigals are returning, and I don't want
to set a bad example."

Lincoln sighed. So much for his plan to kiss her good night.

⌘

"Don't be nervous. You're going to do great. After all, you're the
second one in our class to advance. I bet Ginger was livid." With
her arm linked in Rosie's, Hannah stepped off the telephone company's elevator. "We're here plenty early, so I'll show you around,
but your supervisor will give you a longer tour later and explain
all the details."

"You can skip giving me the tour and tell me what's been going
on with you and Lincoln Cole. I saw him at your house on Friday,

Saturday, and Sunday. Is there somewhere we can sneak away so you can fill me in?"

"Wouldn't you rather get settled?"

"No, my friend. I need details. How can I live vicariously through your experiences if you don't fess up?"

Hannah giggled and pulled Rosie into the operators' parlor. They secluded themselves in the library area, where Hannah proceeded to tell Rosie about the box social.

"We went to Fosters Theater on Saturday, and afterward we went to visit Walt." Hannah's chest tightened. "Oh, Rosie, Walt's spirits were so low."

"What are his chances at today's hearing?"

Hannah shook her head, and her stomach knotted. Lincoln had been honest with her again yesterday. He wanted her to be prepared for Walt to be handed over for trial. "I'm praying things go better than Lincoln thinks they will."

"I'm so sorry." Rosie patted her arm. "Now, on to happier subjects. What show did you see? Did Lincoln hold your hand?"

"Rosie!" Hannah covered her wide smile with her hand. "We saw Mary Mannering in *Glorious Betsy*. It's a romantic comedy about Napoleon's brother Jérôme and a woman from America he falls in love with. It's roughly based on a true story."

"Does it end happily ever after?"

"In the play it does. Napoleon persuades Betsy that it's in his brother's best interest to return to France. He does, but then he goes back to America and chooses to stay with Betsy."

"And in real life?"

"Elizabeth Patterson married Jérôme Bonaparte, but Napoleon refused to recognize the match. She was given sixty thousand francs a year, while her husband returned to France and married the woman Napoleon deemed a proper fit—of the right class and social standing."

"Hannah, you're not thinking what I think you're thinking, are you? Emperor of France and attorney in Iowa are two very different things."

"But Lincoln wants to be in politics. How could I further his ambitions? I'm a Hello Girl. I didn't even finish college. He needs a wife who can throw parties and impress male voters—not a wife who would rather argue with them about why a woman should have the right to vote."

A broad grin creased Rosie's face.

"What?"

"You're already thinking of marrying him."

Hannah stood up. "Of course not, but it's prudent to consider the possibilities."

"Prudent, huh?" Rosie followed Hannah out of the parlor. "Just remember, there's no Napoleon in Lincoln's life. I believe he's quite capable of making his own choices, and right now, that choice appears to be you."

In the central exchange, Hannah snuck a glance in Rosie's direction. Her friend was assigned to station number ten, so her supervisor would be Miss Hathaway. Miss Frogge oversaw the operators at stations eleven to twenty, so at least Rosie would be spared some of the first day's stress Hannah had endured.

During the early morning, Miss Frogge took several opportunities to insert the plug of her headset into the special jack at the top of Hannah's station. This allowed her supervisor to listen in on all of her calls. But why was Miss Frogge so focused on her today?

The supervisor's presence created so much tension, Hannah developed a crick in her neck. It throbbed through several calls, but Hannah dared not rub it. Finally, Miss Frogge withdrew her jack and stepped back. Footfalls on the tiled floor indicated she'd headed toward the stations on Hannah's left. Hannah risked a glance to her right to see how Rosie was faring. The knot in her neck kinked, and she grabbed the spot.

"Miss Gregory." Miss Frogge was beside her. "Eyes on your board. Hands at the ready. Must I watch you every second?"

Hannah's anger burned, and she had to clamp her mouth shut

to keep from speaking. If Miss Frogge wasn't constantly watching her, she wouldn't have needed to rub her neck in the first place.

Please, Lord, can you help me get a few Frogge-free moments? I'm afraid I may say something I shouldn't soon.

Out of her peripheral vision, Hannah saw a hand shoot up down the line. Miss Frogge darted away, and Hannah let out a long sigh. Finally. Frogge-free.

The volume of calls had yet to pick up, and her supervisor was occupied. She thanked God for the reprieve as a light on her board lit. The number belonged to hard-of-hearing Mr. Green, and as far as Hannah remembered, he'd not made a single call since she started working there.

Hannah inserted the jack and spoke more loudly than normal. "Hello, Main. Number, please."

"Hello, Main. You've got a lovely voice. Has anyone ever told you that?"

"Yes, sir. Number, please."

"A clear voice too. It's easy for my old ears to hear. I don't know if you realize this, but I'm an invalid." Mr. Green cleared his throat. "It's been over a week since I talked to another human being, and I thought maybe you could chat for a few minutes."

Hannah's heart ached for the man. How could she tell a lonely invalid she didn't have time to speak with him? She hadn't had a call in several minutes, so what would it hurt?

She cupped her speaker and leaned close to it. "What would you like to talk about, Mr. Green?"

"What's the weather like today?"

"It's a gorgeous day. Bright and sunny. The crab apple trees are almost finished blossoming, and everything has greened up nicely."

"Thank you, my dear."

"You're welcome. Goodbye."

She disconnected the call and leaned back in her chair. A tingly feeling surged through her. It was a small thing, but she'd made a difference in Mr. Green's day.

"Miss Gregory."

185

Her heart plunged. The voice behind her was deep. Oh no. It had to be the chief operator, Mr. Cayhill.

She turned. "Yes, sir."

"May I see you for a moment? The other girls can handle your calls."

24

With her hands clasped in front of her, Hannah faced Mr. Cayhill. She stared at the puce-colored walls, choosing to focus on a spot where the paint had chipped away rather than on Mr. Cayhill's solemn face. He didn't indicate she should sit down, so she remained standing. Was she going to be fired over her phone call with Mr. Green?

He placed her deportment card on the desk in front of her. "Have you seen this?"

She glanced downward. "No, sir."

"Take a look now, then." He leaned back in his chair and steepled his fingers.

Hannah picked up the card and studied the comments on it. At the top of the card, her name was written in a scrolling script. Beneath it, every glance at her neighbor, every call that took too long, and every reprimand was recorded.

"From time to time, we see a young woman who has difficulty conforming to our rules. Miss Frogge feels you are such an operator."

"Sir, I will do better. I promise."

"Yes, I'm sure you will." He leaned forward. "You're a very fast learner. That's why when I was told they needed an operator to fill in on evenings for a week or so, I decided you would be the perfect choice. The pace is slower, and the supervisor is a little more lenient. You may actually find you enjoy working as a Hello Girl during the evening shift."

"Evenings, sir?" Her voice warbled, and she swallowed hard.

"Yes, you'll work three thirty in the afternoon until midnight."

Hannah's heart grabbed. How would she take care of her sisters? If she left for work at three, she'd not even see them after school. And what about Lincoln?

Mr. Cayhill picked up a stack of papers and began to thumb through them. "Go home now. Come back this afternoon at three thirty and report to Mr. Grabowski. He'll be your new supervisor."

"My temporary supervisor, sir?"

"Yes. Yes, of course." He waved his hand in dismissal. "Three thirty, Miss Gregory. Don't be late."

And what if she was? Would they move her to nights? Maybe Charlotte was right. This job was not for her, but it was too late now.

After grabbing her wrap from the cloakroom, Hannah hurried to the elevator before anyone could ask her where she was going. Even though Mr. Cayhill hadn't said she was being demoted to the evening shift, Hannah couldn't figure out another reason for it—especially when he coupled the news with showing her the rather full deportment card.

One good thing could come of this. She could make Walt's hearing. But how would she explain her presence to Lincoln? Pride alone wouldn't let her tell him the real reason why she'd been reassigned. Since she also refused to lie, she'd have to do her best to change the subject whenever it came up.

On a few occasions, Hannah had visited the Polk County Courthouse simply to walk around and imagine herself presenting a case there. A few times she'd snuck into the galley of the court to watch the proceedings. But today her pulse raced. Back then, court seemed more like a game, but what was happening to Walt was far from any game.

On her way inside, she glanced at the courthouse's clock tower. Walt's hearing was scheduled for eleven, and it was only ten thirty now. She took a deep breath. She didn't need to rush, but she could use the extra time to pray. Her shoes clicked against the polished marble as she climbed the stairs to the second floor, marveling at the pristine sheen on the brass handrails. She paused beneath the rotunda and glanced upward. It was the perfect spot to petition the Father on Walt's behalf. She imagined her prayer rising through the ornate stained-glass window.

She glanced around the rest of the rotunda. In one high alcove, golden goddesses bearing trumpets stood guard over the words of Abraham Lincoln: "Let us have faith that right makes might, and in that faith, let us, to the end, dare to do our duty."

Right makes might? She liked the thought and prayed it was true, but already she'd seen the opposite happen so many times she had difficulty putting her faith in the thought.

"Hannah?"

She turned at the sound of Lincoln's voice.

"What are you doing here?"

She paused and licked her lips. "I was able to get away after all." She looked down the hall. "Where's Walt? Can I see him before the hearing?"

"I'm afraid not." He directed her toward the courtroom door. "They'll bring him over and straight into the courtroom." He paused as if he were gauging her reaction.

She gave him a weak smile. "I'll be fine."

"Then let's get inside. I believe his parents are already there." He took her elbow. "They'll be glad to see you."

Lincoln spoke to all three of them, reminding them this was a hearing to see if there was enough evidence to bind Walt over for trial. He explained that although all the prosecution's evidence was circumstantial, it would probably be enough for his case to go to trial. "Remember, that doesn't mean the judge thinks he's guilty. It simply means they expect me to prove he's not."

"We appreciate everything you've done for our son." Mr. Calloway's voice cracked with emotion.

Lincoln brushed Hannah's arm as he strode to his place in the front of the courtroom. The tender gesture made her smile.

Minutes later, Walt was brought in, bound and shackled. Mrs. Calloway clung to Hannah like a lifeline. Tears pricked Hannah's eyes. Why hadn't she remembered prisoners were treated this way from her earlier visits? As hard as it was for her to see her friend treated like a common criminal, how much harder was it for his mother?

Glancing at the three of them, Walt smiled. He then mouthed the words, "I love you," to his mother. The woman sniffed, and Hannah patted her hand.

Walt seemed pale and gaunt. They needed to get him out of jail before he became seriously ill.

The judge entered and sat down behind the mammoth mahogany bench. The hearing began, and Hannah's resolve to see Walt acquitted strengthened with each piece of circumstantial evidence the prosecuting attorney presented.

Yes, Walt had publicly spoken against the company. Yes, he was upset by the company's blacklisting the former employees, and yes, he had no alibi for the times the fires were set.

Guilt kicked Hannah hard. No alibi except for her. She should stand up and say something. As if he sensed her thoughts, Lincoln turned and pinned her in place with a don't-you-dare stare. His eyes demanded she trust him. But didn't he see how hard all of this was on Walt?

In less than twenty minutes, the hearing was over, and all had gone as Lincoln predicted. Walt would be bound over for trial, but when the judge set the date, Hannah gasped. So quickly? Could they prove Walt's innocence in such a short time?

Lincoln spoke privately with Walt for a few minutes before Walt was taken away, then he joined Hannah and Mr. and Mrs. Calloway.

"It's what we expected." Lincoln placed his hand on Mr. Calloway's shoulder. "So don't lose heart."

"How's Walt?" Hannah glanced at the door he'd disappeared through.

"He's doing well, considering." He looked at Mrs. Calloway. "He'd like you and your husband to visit him. He's missing his family."

"We'll go over right now." She linked her arm in her husband's.

"Yes, ma'am." Mr. Calloway grinned and squeezed her hand. "You're the boss." He turned to Lincoln. "I feel so bad about not being able to post his bail and get him out, so I want to thank you again, Mr. Cole, for helping our boy."

They started for the door, and Mrs. Calloway turned back. "Hannah, aren't you coming?"

She glanced at Lincoln, who had crossed the room to hand some papers to a clerk. Spending some time with him would be delightful, but if she went with the Calloways, not only would she get to see Walt, but she could also avoid telling Lincoln about the change in her hours.

"Uh, yes." She paused. "That is, unless Mr. Cole needs to speak with me."

He didn't meet her gaze. "No, go ahead. I'll catch you later."

Hurt pricked her heart. Didn't he want to spend time together now that they had this chance? Maybe she shouldn't have said yes to the Calloways.

One look back at Lincoln and Hannah almost changed her mind. If he was okay with her leaving, why did he look so disappointed?

❧

Sometimes he was a fool.

Lincoln walked into his office and slammed the file in his hands onto the desk. A pile of papers ruffled from the breeze he created. Why hadn't he asked Hannah to lunch?

Because he'd let her down. Even though the case had gone as

he expected, he would have done anything to get Hannah's friend off. He wanted to prove to her that she could count on him and lean on him, and he didn't want her risking her job for the slim chance it would make a difference for Walt.

Who was he kidding? That wasn't the only reason he'd not asked her. He'd seen the way Hannah looked at Walt Calloway when he came into the room. He'd witnessed her concern for Walt's parents, and he'd sensed her worry when the judge announced the trial date. Deep inside, the truth sat like a stone in his gut. He was jealous of a man in jail.

"Well, well, well." Cedric Knox swaggered toward Lincoln's desk. "I heard your arsonist is headed for trial."

"I'm not in the mood, Cedric." Lincoln flipped open the file. No time like the present to start planning Walt's defense. He'd get Walt off for Hannah.

"Too bad your firebug will have to find someone else to represent him."

Lincoln looked up. "What are you talking about?"

"Pete and Charles allowed you to continue to represent him because you'd already received some press in regard to the case." Cedric crossed his arms over his chest. "But do you think they'll be nearly so agreeable if I happen to have not one but two insurance companies ready to sign with this firm tomorrow if we refuse to represent an accused arsonist?"

Lincoln's temples throbbed, but he refused to react to Cedric's taunting. Two large clients? Would Pete continue to support him against Charles in view of that?

But he couldn't let down Walt, or especially Hannah, now. If he quit this case, Walt would never find anyone willing to fight for him as hard as Lincoln.

Lincoln leaned back in his chair and peaked his fingers. "Cedric, are you finished?"

"Didn't you hear me? There's no way Pete and Charles will let you continue."

"I heard you. I simply don't believe you." He picked up his

fountain pen. "Now, if you'll kindly remove yourself from my work area, I've got a defense to prepare."

Cedric sauntered away, and Lincoln rubbed his left temple. How could he convince Pete and Charles to let him see Walt's case through?

25

"When I get out of here . . ."

Walt's breath tickled Hannah's ear. She pulled away from the goodbye hug inside his jail cell. He didn't finish the sentence, and for that she was grateful. She should probably set him straight, but right now he needed all the hope he could muster—even if it was misplaced hope.

She laid her hand on Walt's whiskered cheek. The beard growth made him look much less like her oldest and dearest friend and more like a man capable of committing a horrible crime. Before his trial, he'd need a shave. She'd have to speak to Lincoln about arranging that.

"Take care, Walt. Lincoln and I won't stop until we prove you're innocent."

"And your father and I pray for you constantly," Mrs. Calloway said.

Walt turned from Hannah and enveloped his mother in a hug. "Don't worry about me. I'll be fine. This will all be over soon."

His father clapped his shoulder. "We believe in you, son. Remember that."

They departed, and the cell door clanged shut behind them, sealing Walt in once again. Guilt nudged Hannah. She'd been spending far too much time at picnics and socials when she should have been addressing Walt's case.

Starting today, she'd work harder. With her days free, she could do more research, and if she kept Lincoln at bay, she wouldn't be distracted. It couldn't be any other way. Her friend needed her. Lincoln would simply have to understand that any relationship between the two of them would have to come second to Walt's case right now.

Now she only needed to get Lincoln to see things her way.

After saying goodbye to the Calloways, Hannah hurried home. She stopped at Rosie's mother's, explained the change in her schedule, and asked her to keep an eye on her sisters, including chaperoning George and Charlotte if necessary.

"It'd be me pleasure," Mrs. Murphy said in her lilting brogue. She wiped her hands on her apron. "We'll have a grand time, pet. And you write those sisters of yours a note that says they should come over here for supper. If that lad comes around, I'll make it clear to your sister that any sparkin' better be happenin' with fireflies and not with the lad."

Hannah chuckled, thanked the kind woman, and went home to write the missive. She added she'd be home after midnight, so they should not wait up for her. After placing the note on the kitchen table, she made herself a sandwich and put on a small pot of coffee. She'd earned the second pot after all that occurred this morning, and nothing eased the tension like a warm cup of her favorite brew.

While it was heating, she located one of her law texts and carried it back to the kitchen. Three cups of coffee and one egg salad sandwich later, she had a better understanding of how most defense attorneys refuted circumstantial evidence. The prosecuting attorney would try to create his case on the basis that it was reasonable to suspect Walt had set the fires. Lincoln would need to show that while it might be reasonable for Walt to be the arsonist, it could just as reasonably be someone else. That was why Lincoln had tried so hard to get Walt to divulge the name of who he thought started the fires.

Well, if Lincoln couldn't get the name out of Walt, she'd have to do it. And one thing she knew for certain—Walt Calloway had a very hard time saying no to her.

The wall clock in the parlor gonged, signaling it was time for Hannah to leave. She arrived at the Iowa Telephone Company early enough not to feel rushed. She secured her headset and was introduced to her new supervisor. Wiry white hair ringed Mr. Grabowski's bald head like a victor's crown. His saggy eyes bespoke of too many years with little happiness.

"You'll do." He sighed, as if the effort to speak took all his energy. "One of the regular girls will be out for a while. Her mother died." His tone was flat, without an ounce of compassion. "She's at station thirteen. Are you familiar with the subscribers?"

Hannah could scarcely believe her luck. "Yes, sir. That's where I work during the day."

He sat down behind one of the desks. "Good. Follow the rules, and don't make me have to come over there."

Was the day shift that different? She couldn't imagine Miss Frogge ever sitting down. She flitted from one station to another like a hummingbird, slipping her supervisor's plug into the special jack to monitor the sweet nectar of the operator's errors.

During her shift, Hannah discovered it was easy to keep from getting reprimanded by Mr. Grabowski. Once an hour, he made rounds, briefly stopping behind each operator. Not once did he intervene or correct Hannah in any way.

After her dinner break, she heard a soft snoring noise behind her. She dared look back and smiled. Mr. Grabowski, head propped on his fisted hand, was asleep.

A light flickered on her panel. She slipped the plug into the jack. "Hello, Main. Number, please."

"I wanna lull-by," a child's voice responded.

"Sweetie, you should hang up the telephone. Telephones are for grown-ups."

"Sing me."

Hannah smiled. The child was very young. If she had to guess, she'd say he was about two. Where was his mother?

She recalled Mrs. Reuff at the operators' school telling them that some parents gave the phone to their children as a toy to entertain them. Perhaps this was one such occasion. Mrs. Reuff had insisted the best way to handle the situation was not to encourage the child by interacting with him or her. Should she disconnect this call?

"Sing me. Pweeese."

Such a sweet little voice. Jesus never refused the children. Why should she? One song wouldn't hurt.

The only song she could recall at the moment was one she'd learned in Sunday school. She wrapped her hand around the cold metal of the speaker and held it close to her lips. "Thy little ones, dear Lord, are we, and come thy lowly bed to see. Enlighten every soul and mind, that we the way to thee may find."

"More!" the toddler squealed.

She smiled, imagining a cherubic face with dove-blue eyes like Lincoln's.

"Miss Gregory!"

"Sir?" She jumped but didn't dare turn her head to face the man now looming over her.

"Please tell me I did not hear singing."

How was she to answer him?

"If I hear any melodies from this area again, I'll assume you'd like to see if the night shift's supervisor would enjoy being serenaded, because I, Miss Gregory, do not."

"Yes, sir."

Night shift? Good grief. What had she done? She'd never be able to help Lincoln clear Walt if she was moved to that. Instead of doing research during the day, she'd have to sleep.

Until the clock struck midnight, Hannah made certain she was the perfect switchboard operator. Every call was completed in seconds, and not one word was uttered other than those deemed acceptable by the Iowa Telephone Company. Even when thunder rumbled outside, she kept her eyes on her switchboard, not glancing up at the overhead windows once.

When the time came for the night shift to take over, the fresh operator appeared behind her and laid a hand on her shoulder. The switch was made flawlessly, and Mr. Grabowski nodded his approval at her. Perhaps she'd redeemed herself.

She stepped out of the building into the dark of the night and shivered in the chill of the air. The brief thunderstorm had left the air scented with rain, and clouds still shrouded the moon and stars. Even though she already knew no cars would clang along, she glanced at the streetcar line. Buggies lined the curb, driven by husbands, fathers, and brothers to pick up the other operators. Only she had no ride home.

Mr. Grabowski glanced back at her from the bottom of the stairs. "Miss Gregory, you do have a ride home, don't you?"

What would he think of her if he knew the truth? After tonight's faux pas, she didn't dare disappoint the man further.

"I'll be fine, sir," she said. "Thank you for your concern."

He nodded and started walking in the opposite direction of her home.

Slipping her hands beneath her spring cloak, she started down the stairs. Solitude descended on her like a fog. Shadows seemed to arch and grin at her cowardice.

A cat yowled and darted across her path. She gasped and pressed a hand to her throat. Beneath her palm, her pulse raced. Why was she acting like a silly schoolgirl? It would take less than half an hour to walk the few blocks home. So what if it was past midnight? It wasn't like she was walking in a bad area of town.

She squared her shoulders, took a deep breath, and plunged down the dark, empty street.

⁂

Lincoln punched his pillow and jammed it beneath his head. When sleep failed to claim him, he rolled onto his back and stared at the ceiling of his bedroom. What was his problem?

He already knew the answer.

Hannah Gregory.

Maybe some fresh air would settle his thoughts. He crawled

out of bed, went to the window, and lifted the sash. A cool breeze drifted inside the stuffy room. He drank in the clean scent. Was Hannah sleeping any better than he was?

Obviously, she was upset with the way he'd acted earlier today. When he'd called her this evening, Charlotte said she wasn't home. He wasn't a fool. He recognized her sister's answer for what it was—an excuse for Hannah not to speak to him. Still, it seemed so unlike Hannah to lie to him and especially to ask her sister to lie on her behalf.

He sat down in the overstuffed chair and ran his hand through his hair. Something felt off. Wrong. God kept pointing him to Hannah and that call. Why?

When she'd come to the hearing—

Wait. She should have been working, but what had she told him? She'd been able to get away. He pictured her face and remembered catching the way she'd paused and licked her lips before answering. She changed the subject as soon as she answered too. Usually, all those things would tell him a client was hiding something. But what would Hannah be hiding about her presence there? Had she lost her job?

No. She wasn't in poor spirits, and he'd seen few signs of stress on her face.

But the telephone company wouldn't let her off to come to the hearing in the middle of the day . . .

Unless she really wasn't home when he called.

Was Hannah working evenings or nights now?

The clock downstairs gonged twelve times. Midnight was much too late to telephone her home, but he'd never get any sleep unless he knew where she was. His stomach fisted. Even with all the courtroom trials he'd faced, nothing had demanded an answer like this did.

It felt improper to ring her wearing his pajamas, so he threw on a pair of trousers and a shirt before rushing downstairs.

He glanced at her number jotted on a pad by his candlestick telephone and picked up the receiver. In seconds, the switchboard operator was ringing the Gregory house, but it took several rings before anyone came on the line.

A sleepy voice answered.

"Tessa?"

"Mr. Cole?"

"May I speak to Hannah?"

"Uh, she's not home from work yet."

So he was right. She was now working nights. Poor thing probably wouldn't get off until morning. Maybe he could take her to breakfast. "When will she get home?"

"Probably half past midnight or so."

"Tonight?" His chest squeezed tight. "Who's bringing her home?"

"I dunno." Tessa's voice cracked. "No one, I guess, if you aren't. Can I go back to bed now?"

"Sure, Tessa. Good night."

He slammed the phone back on the hook. Surely Hannah wouldn't take a chance like walking home in the dark alone.

Or would she?

❧

A dog growled.

Hannah halted and scanned the street for the animal. Her gaze fell on the massive beast lurking half a block before her.

Fingers of fear spread down her neck.

Don't be silly. You've dealt with dogs before. Show him who is boss.

She took a step forward.

Another low, menacing growl.

Maybe this dog already knew who was boss—him.

Perhaps she could retrace her steps and go around the block. It would take longer, but she'd get home with all her parts intact.

Backing away from the dog, she sent a prayer heavenward, asking God to clamp the mouth of the dog like he had those of the lions for Daniel.

The dog rumbled another threat and advanced. She froze. What was she going to do? She couldn't stand here until daybreak.

The sound of an automobile nearing made her pulse thunder. She swallowed. Who would be out driving this late at night? She'd heard about dandy young men out and about, up to no good. What if the driver was one of them? Which was a worse threat? The dog or the driver?

The dog charged forward. Her blood ran cold. She fisted her skirt and turned to run. Feet pounding against the street, she raced toward the gas lamps of the oncoming automobile. Her foot slipped on the wet paving bricks, and she stumbled. The automobile swerved and stopped.

"Hannah!"

Lincoln? She whirled and bolted for the Reo. She jumped onto the running board, but the forward momentum thrust her over the side of the seat and halfway into the automobile. Her hands met the leather seat. The dog yanked on her skirt, and she cringed at the sound of ripping fabric. Lincoln hurled something at the dog, and it yelped and ran away.

Safe at last, she released a puff of breath, but her heart continued to hammer beneath her corset. With her backside pointed toward the moon, she looked up at him. "Would you mind helping me right myself?"

"Actually, I've a good mind to take advantage of your current position and give you the paddling you deserve."

She squirmed, trying to get up on her own. "You wouldn't dare."

He exited the Reo, rounded the back, and placed his hands on her waist. "Are you sure about that, Miss Risk Taker?"

26

Hannah tensed, but Lincoln didn't throttle her. Instead he drew her waist toward him until she could feel her backside against his body. Once she was upright, he stepped back and let her climb down from the running board on her own.

Anger poured off him like steam from a teakettle. Why would he be mad? Was he worried about her ungraceful arrival scratching his precious automobile?

She adjusted her shirtwaist and skirt. "Are you upset with me?"

"Get in."

When she was properly seated in the Reo, she stuck her finger through the slobber-covered hole in her skirt. Would a patch be noticeable?

"It was a good thing you showed up when you did. For some reason, that dog considered me his midnight snack." She laughed, but it came out forced and nervous.

"It's not funny, Hannah." Lincoln shifted the foot pedal, then jammed the throttle lever upward. The automobile roared to life and took off.

When he turned toward her home, she gasped. "Where do you think you're going?"

"I'm taking you home."

"You can't do that!"

"You'd prefer to be escorted by Fido?"

"But Lincoln, it's not proper. Our neighbors will hear the automobile, and they won't understand why I'm out in the middle of the night with you."

He pulled the car to the side of the street, beside an empty lot, and shut it off. He gripped the steering wheel with both gloved hands. "Why?"

"I told you. It's not proper. What would people think?"

"No." He turned toward her. "I mean why didn't you tell me your hours changed? Why didn't you tell me you needed someone to take you home? Why didn't you ask me for help?"

"I couldn't."

"No, Hannah. You could, but you wouldn't." His chest heaved. "Get out."

Her heart thudded to a stop. Was it over between them? "I'm sorry. I just didn't see a way you could help."

He marched to her side of the Reo. "I said get out."

Easing off the seat, she stepped onto the running board. He placed his hands on her waist and lifted her to the ground but didn't release her. "You didn't think I could figure something out so the woman I care about doesn't have to walk home in the dark, running from wild dogs? You didn't think I could manage to arrange that and still maintain your honor?"

He smelled like Diamond C soap and something woodsy, and his nearness was intoxicating. She splayed her hands on his chest and could feel it heave beneath her palms. "I'm sorry. I didn't mean to offend you."

"Hannah, I'm not offended." He cupped her cheek with one hand. "You scared me senseless."

"I scared you?"

"Yes, and I'd tell you never to do it again, but I think that would be a wasted effort." He traced her lips with the pad of his thumb. "And right now, I have something else I'd much rather put my effort into."

His hand slipped around the back of her neck, sending shivers coursing through her. She held her breath as he lowered his head until his lips touched hers in the sweetest of kisses.

As if he'd struck a match within her, warmth spread in her soul like wildfire. Never before had she felt a rush like this. She leaned into his touch, savoring the moment. All too quickly the kiss was over, and disappointment flooded through her.

"Now, I'm going to walk you home, and you're going to let me. And tomorrow night I'll make sure you're not walking home alone, and you're going to trust me to take care of that. Understand?"

She simply nodded, because for the first time in her life, she was speechless.

❧◦⟡◦❧

Wearing a snow-white muslin dress remade from one of their mother's, Charlotte walked down the aisle toward the front of the auditorium, and Hannah's heart swelled with pride. As one of the nearly 250 greater Des Moines graduates in the auditorium, Charlotte might have been easy to lose in the crowd if not for her maple-syrup-colored hair set off by a white silk ribbon.

"Charlotte Gregory." The school superintendent's voice rang out.

With great poise, she crossed the stage, and the school board president presented her with a diploma. Hannah swiped a tear from the corner of her eye, and Lincoln squeezed her hand. Thank goodness she'd been able to change with one of the other Hello Girls, or she would have missed this. She'd never have forgiven herself if that had happened. This graduation had stirred everyone's grief, but especially Charlotte's.

It was at times like this that Hannah struggled the most. It never seemed fair. Their parents should have been present for this day.

After the ceremony, Charlotte hurried over to them, and after a round of congratulatory hugs, Lincoln announced they were going to his home to celebrate.

"Your place?" Charlotte's eyes widened.

"I asked my housekeeper to prepare a special dinner. She's an excellent cook." He tapped Charlotte's nose. "Not as good as you, but I think you'll find her food more than palatable."

Charlotte looked at Hannah for confirmation, and Hannah laughed. "Don't look so shocked. He asked if he could do this for you, and I agreed."

"Do I get to go too?" Tessa asked.

Lincoln's eyes crinkled. "I don't know, Hannah. What do you think?"

"Hmm. Maybe we could squeeze her in if she promises to keep her headlines to herself."

"I will. I promise." She whipped off her gloves and fell in step beside them. "But I have to tell you all about the earthworms I've been reading about. They're amazing. Did you know—"

Hannah moaned.

"She's your sister." Charlotte laughed. "As the eldest, it's your job to educate her."

"Uh-uh-uh." Hannah wagged her finger. "Now that you're a graduate, I think we should share the burden equally. It's going to take both of us to make Tessa into a lady."

"A lady?" Tessa ran ahead, then turned and walked backward so she could face them. "I want to be a newspaperwoman or a horticulturalist, or maybe I'll race cars like Mr. Vanderbilt."

Hannah shot a mock glare at Lincoln as if the last part was his fault, then hooked her arm with Charlotte's. "On second thought, Charlotte, she's all yours."

27

Lincoln stared at Pete. How could the man let his wife use one of those electrical home treatment machines for her melancholy? Sure, the makers claimed it was a safe curative, but Lincoln found that hard to imagine.

Leaning forward, Pete placed his folded hands on top of his desk. "Elise has used it for three days now and says it's helping."

"I'm shocked."

Pete chuckled. "So is she—literally—twice a day."

"May I ask how much the little apparatus cost you?"

"Five whole dollars. I know it's probably quackery, but if it helps her spirits, it's worth every penny." He leaned back in his chair, and it squeaked beneath his weight. "The worst part is she wants me to use the special electrical comb attachment. It's supposed to stimulate hair follicles."

"You are getting a little thin up top." Lincoln patted the top of his own head to indicate Pete's thinning area.

He frowned. "Your day will come soon enough."

"Not for a long time." He chuckled. "So what does this contraption look like?"

"You can see it for yourself on Friday. She's feeling so well she's having a dinner party, and she wants you and Miss Gregory to come."

Lincoln rubbed the back of his neck. "I'm not sure if Hannah can make it. Her hours have changed at the telephone company."

It had been two weeks since she'd been transferred, and Hannah's supervisor had yet to tell her she was going back to days. Although Lincoln had made arrangements for a hansom cab to bring her home each night, he still worried about her being out so late. Not only were these hours difficult on her physically and emotionally, they were also hard on her sisters. Tessa and Charlotte needed her, and they'd already grown tired of her absence.

Most of all, the evening shift was hard on the time he and Hannah had together. In order to see one another, it had to be during the daytime, and most of his days were filled with work at the law practice. Sneaking in a research trip or a quick lunch was not giving him the quality time with Hannah he so wanted to have during the week. Although he'd prayed for a solution to the problem, so far none had come his way, and he wasn't sure she'd let him help out even if he discovered the perfect answer.

"Well, I hope you can persuade her to come Friday," Pete said. "I thought that meeting her might convince Charles to let you continue the pro bono case with the Calloway fellow."

Lincoln stiffened. "Has he been fighting you about that again?"

"He has a point, Lincoln. Two fire insurance companies are interested in retaining us, but they won't if we're representing an arsonist. I understand your position, so I've been able to keep Charles from doing anything rash." Pete rapped on his desk. "But I can assure you Cedric is doing everything he can to stir things up. I believe it would be harder for Charles to force the point if he met Miss Gregory, so I do hope you'll try to persuade her."

"I'll certainly do my best." He pushed to his feet. "I'm off to meet her now. We're headed to the state law library."

"Ah, a research trip with a pretty lady."

"We will be working," Lincoln assured him.

"Well, I certainly hope it won't be all work, or I'll have to admit failure as a mentor."

Lincoln bid Pete goodbye and headed for the courthouse. After delivering the affidavit he needed filed, he hurried down the marble steps toward the door. He glanced toward his right and paused. The door to the building's switchboard was open, and Josephina Beecher, the operator, sat inside. He'd never given her much thought before, but could she be the answer to his prayers?

⁓⤳⟣⤲⁓

Charlotte thrust pancakes in Hannah's direction. "It's not fair. You think it's fine for Lincoln to bring you home in the middle of the night, and yet you won't let me see George without Rosie's mother hovering over us."

Using the edge of her fork, Hannah cut off a bite of pancake. How could she make Charlotte understand? "I explained to you what happened with Lincoln that first night, and since then, he's sent a hansom cab to pick me up instead of coming himself. Besides, Lincoln and I are much older than you and George."

Tessa bounced into the room. "Morning glories."

"Good morning, Tessa." Hannah patted the chair next to her. "Come tell me your plans for the day."

Tessa slid into place and drenched her pancakes with syrup.

"Don't you dare change the subject." Charlotte sat down in her chair and glared at Hannah. "What do George and I have to do in order for you to trust us?"

"I trust you. It's George I don't trust."

"You don't even know him."

Hannah bit back the words forming in her mind and prayed for wisdom. She took a sip of hot coffee and let it help settle her. "You're right, Charlotte. We don't know him. Why don't you invite him over next Sunday? I'll invite Lincoln too, so George doesn't feel surrounded by women."

Charlotte grinned. "Really? You'll give him a chance?"

Hannah nodded.

"Well, that's proof." Tessa waved a forked bite of pancake in the air.

"Proof of what?" Hannah took a sip of coffee.

"That love makes you stupid." Tessa shook her head. "First Charlotte, and now you."

Hannah sputtered coffee across the table. "I'm not in—we're not in—"

Tessa rolled her eyes and stood up. "Like I said, love makes you stupid."

By the time Tessa and Charlotte left for the local girls' club, Hannah needed a second cup of coffee. She hastily downed it and washed the grounds out of the bottom of the cup.

Lincoln arrived on time and greeted her with a smile at the door. "Ready?"

"I am." She pulled the door shut behind her. "I was just praying we'd find something we can use on Walt's defense."

"If we can't find something at the state law library, then we won't find it anywhere."

The drive to the Iowa State Capitol seemed much shorter than Hannah expected. She caught the glint of the morning sun off the gold-leaf dome when they turned the corner, and her pulse quickened. Of course she'd seen the exterior of the ornate capitol building often, but she'd never ventured beyond the doors.

"I can't wait to show you the law library." Lincoln pulled his car to the side of the street and parked. "And even though we're here to work, I think we can take a peek into the other wings as well. I want to show you where my dad once worked."

After Lincoln helped her from the Reo, Hannah fell in step beside him. They mounted the numerous steps leading to the front door and finally entered. Hannah stepped inside the rotunda and gasped. A plethora of marble, wood, tile, and stencil patterns greeted her. "It's stunning."

"Most of the artwork in here is new, and some is still being added." He took her hand. "Come on. Let me show you my favorite."

They climbed the grand staircase, and he pointed to a mural depicting settlers on the third floor. "It's called *Westward*. The mosaics above are from Italy, and they're made of glass tiles."

Hannah itched to touch the lifelike figures.

He led her to the circular railing and held her shoulders. "Look up."

Gilded trim work surrounded fluffy clouds painted on a blue sky. "Is that the inside of the dome?"

"Sort of. It's the dome inside the dome."

She turned to face him. "Where did your father work?"

"The senate. It's in the south wing."

Several minutes later, Lincoln eased open heavy doors. Hannah put her hand on his arm to stop him. "What if we're interrupting?"

"The session concluded in April."

They stepped inside the enormous chamber, and instantly Hannah felt small. A couple of workers looked up, smiled, and continued to polish the marble wainscot.

Brass chandeliers sparkled overhead, and Lincoln told her each weighed over five hundred pounds. She touched a rose-colored marble pillar. "I've never seen marble like this."

"My father told me it's scagliola, an imitation marble made of finely ground gypsum and glue."

"Remarkable." She approached the mahogany desks and pressed her hand to the leather blotter. "You can almost feel the history made here in the last twenty years. I can understand why you want to be in politics."

"It's what I've thought about for years, but it'll be a while before I can run for a senate seat."

"But you're twenty-five. Isn't that old enough?"

"Legally, yes." He grinned. "But most senators are a bit more mature. Let me show you where my father sat."

Lincoln led her to the spot, and she didn't miss the way he trailed his hand along the back of the chair as if he could sense his father's presence.

"When I'm here," Lincoln said, "it doesn't feel like he's been gone so long."

"How often did he bring you to the capitol with him?"

"At least once a week starting when I was ten or so." He approached the front of the room and turned to face her. "I'd sit in the gallery and watch him speak to the other senators. When he spoke, everyone listened. He just had a way about him."

"And you do too." Her chest warmed at the sight of him, so poised and comfortable in this austere room. How easily Lincoln could slip into this world. It was a second home to him, and if she allowed this relationship to continue, she needed to understand she was possibly agreeing to life as a politician's wife.

He returned to her and offered his elbow. "Ready to see the law library?"

She slipped her hand into the crook of his arm. "If it's as beautiful as this, I might faint."

"Then I guess I'll simply have to enjoy catching you."

28

Covering Hannah's hand, Lincoln squeezed gently as they approached the library. It covered the entire second and third floors of the west wing, and even though he'd been there dozens of times, the library never failed to rob him of his breath.

She touched her lips with her hand, and tears filled her eyes. "I feel like I've stepped into a fairy tale."

"That makes me the handsome prince, right?"

Still under the library's spell, she didn't answer.

Lincoln tried to imagine what she was thinking. While most libraries were dark, enclosed places, the Iowa law library was bright and open. From its tiled floor to its skylight, everything about the area begged a visitor to step inside. Five levels of books, guarded by white filigree iron railings, rose to the height of the hall, and the same type of scagliola columns gracing the senate stood sentry here too.

"Look at the stairs!" Hannah pulled him toward the nearest of two matching spiral staircases. She leaned close to him and whispered, "Do you think anyone's ever tried riding down the banister?"

"Leave it to you to think of something dangerous in the library." He chuckled. "You go ahead and look around while I get started."

"No, I want to help. Show me what to do."

As they gathered the law books he wanted to examine, he explained the case. "The prosecution must prove three things. First, they have to prove the fire was not an accident of any kind. Second, they must prove Walt was the man responsible for the fire. And third, they must prove it was a willful act. So far, every case I've found that ended with a conviction was based on circumstantial evidence—like they have on Walt."

"But they can't prove it's him."

"That's their greatest weakness so far, but we need a previous case on which to build our defense." He handed her a large volume. "And we're going to find it."

A short time later, Lincoln sat beside her at one of the library tables with tomes piled high before them. Given her law school experience, he hadn't been surprised she took to the research so easily, but he had been amazed at how absorbed she'd become in the cases she studied.

"There are a lot of arson cases." He sighed. "So we need to focus on cases where the circumstantial evidence was ruled inadmissible or insufficient to use in building our defense."

"Lincoln, do you think I should come forward?"

"It wouldn't be enough to clear him. He might have been at your house the afternoon of that second fire, but there still would have been time to set it." He squeezed her hand. "We'll find something. Trust me."

As they worked side by side, an odd sense of satisfaction washed over him. Would a life with Hannah include days like this—both focused on a case but in tune with each other?

For over an hour he heard only the occasional whispered voices of other patrons and the gentle swish of turning pages. Then Hannah placed her hand on his arm. "Lincoln, I think I found something."

Lincoln read the area Hannah's slender finger indicated. In the arson case of *Decatur v. Long*, the court stated that facts, rather than suspicions or speculations, must be substantial enough to support a verdict.

"This is perfect!" He kissed her cheek. "We're going to do this, Hannah. Together."

Hannah jotted the reference down on the tablet Lincoln had brought. "How many more do we need?"

"As many as we can get. It will all help when I prepare the brief."

An hour later, he reached for the cover of Hannah's book and closed it. "Let's call it quits for the day."

She frowned. "But it's not even lunchtime."

"I know, but there's something I want to show you." He stood and pulled out her chair. "Trust me. I think you'll like it."

"But—"

"The books will be here tomorrow too." He pressed his hand to the small of her back and urged her toward the rotunda.

"Can I come back without you, or is this only open to attorneys?"

He grabbed his heart, feigning a fatal wound. "Without me? I thought we were partners."

"Partners." Her warm hazel eyes lit with teasing. "Not Siamese twins."

He chuckled. "To answer your question, yes, you can come without me. This is a public library. It's open to all."

"Then I shall arrive early and not stop until I have to go to work."

"Don't forget you need to eat." They weaved through the hallways, and he stopped in front of a door. "Or maybe I will have to come whisk you away for lunch."

She tipped her face up toward his. "And if you're lucky, I might even let you."

❧⤜⤚❧⤚⤜❧

When Lincoln opened the door in the third-story hall, Hannah expected to find an office or another room. Instead, he pointed to a steep, spiral staircase.

"Where are we going?" she asked.

"Up."

Curiosity pulled her forward. She grasped the wooden banister and began her ascent. Lincoln followed behind. Her breathing became heavier the higher they climbed.

214

"We're almost to the first stop. We can take a breather there." Lincoln sounded a bit winded as well.

They stepped onto a brightly tiled floor, and Hannah scanned the area. When she looked up, she could again see the gilded woodwork, small windows, and painted clouds, but they were much clearer than before. "We're just below the dome." She leaned over the railing and saw the circular railings marking the rotunda of each floor all the way down to the first floor below. "And we're up very high."

"We're below the interior dome, and we're about a third of the way to the top."

Excitement bubbled inside her. "Are we going all the way up?"

"Thought you'd like that." He flashed her a roguish grin. "Stay here."

Lincoln rounded the circle and stood opposite her, over sixty feet away on the other side of the dome. "Can you hear me?" he asked in a whisper.

She blinked. Why did it sound like he was next to her?

"Yes, I can hear you."

"I have something important to tell you." He leaned against a rose-colored scagliola column. "Hannah Gregory, I think I'm falling in love with you."

Her heart drummed against her chest as his words took seed. Vulnerability, fresh and raw, fought with delight for control of her heart. This man—this wonderful man—loved her, but could she let go and love him in return?

The truth hit her hard. She already did.

Taking a deep breath, she whispered, "I think I'm falling in love with you too."

✦

Had Lincoln truly heard Hannah, or had he just imagined she'd responded to his words?

Warmth spread through him. He'd not planned on falling for someone like Hannah—vivacious, honest, devoted, and stubborn—but he certainly had. Did she have any idea what she'd done to him?

Because of the sound tricks played by the dome, it seemed as if she'd whispered the words into his ear. Maybe he'd simply wanted to hear them.

He looked across the expanse separating them. She smiled and dropped her gaze. His Hannah—shy? If only he could capture the demure expression on her face and save it for a time when she was riding down banisters or walking home in the dark.

Wasting no time, he hurried to reconnect with her. He extended his hand and waited until she clasped it before leading her to the next set of stairs.

"Careful." He watched her climb, enjoying his view from behind more than he ought.

"Lincoln, this spiral staircase is so tight, I feel like I'm inside a conch shell. How many more steps are there?"

He chuckled. "About two hundred."

"Honestly?" She stared at him. "For once I'm glad I'll be sitting at a switchboard all evening."

"That's the spirit."

They didn't rest until they had climbed into the windowed cupola. He entered first and offered her his hand. It was a long way down if one of them slipped.

Hannah sucked in a breath of the stale, dusty air. "We're above the gold dome!"

He chuckled. When he was about twelve, one of the groundskeepers had shown him the staircases that led up here. He still recalled the first time he'd stepped into the cupola and looked out over the city. He'd been gobsmacked.

She pressed her hands to the glass windows. "We're on top of the world."

"Well, at least Iowa."

"You can see for miles." She moved around the circular area. "There's downtown, and I think that's the state fairgrounds. How high are we?"

"One of the groundskeepers once told me this is about 260 feet up."

"Lincoln, look! There's a door so you can go outside. Can we go?"

"I don't know about that, Hannah."

"Why not? There's a railing out there to keep us from falling." She tried the door and it opened. "See? It's not locked."

"But Hannah, we don't know if the railing is secure."

Before he could stop her, she stepped onto the ledge.

29

Having no choice, Lincoln followed Hannah outside the cupola. The wind immediately whipped at his face. He barely caught his hat before it went swooping down to the ground like a plummeting kite. He tossed the hat inside the cupola and noticed Hannah, too, had her hat in hand. He took it from her and set it inside with his own.

When he turned back, his stomach somersaulted. Heights had never bothered him before, but then again, he'd never been outside the protection of the cupola. As many times as he'd snuck up here over the years, he'd never considered venturing beyond the protective windows. Of course, it had taken Hannah less than five minutes to breach that barrier.

"There's your Reo. Look how small it is!" Hannah leaned over the railing and pointed.

"Whoa!" His chest squeezed at the sight of her so close to the edge. Placing his hands on her waist, he pulled her back. "Let's not give me heart failure."

She leaned against his chest. "I'm sorry. I'm simply overwhelmed. I've never seen anything like this."

Her hair broke loose from its pins and flew about her head. He smoothed it down and sighed. It was even silkier than he'd imagined.

"Oh, Lincoln." She pulled away and spun to face him, arms outstretched. "From up here, I can almost imagine what it's like to fly."

"Well, I hope the birds are warmer than we are."

She folded her arms across her chest and rubbed them. "It is a bit chilly."

When he suggested they go in, she pleaded for a few more minutes. She tipped her face to the sky, and the sun seemed to kiss her cheeks.

Lincoln rubbed her arms. Could anyone look more beautiful?

The clock on "Old Fed," the Federal Courthouse, chimed one o'clock faintly, and she turned to him. "I guess you need to be getting back to the office."

He took her hand. "After I take you to lunch."

They slipped back inside, and she started to rearrange her hair. He stilled her hands. "Not yet. Please."

She looked up at him. "Thank you for today. I feel like I'm on top of the world, or maybe I should say on top of *your* world."

He curled a strand of her hair around his finger. "What do you mean by that?"

"This whole capitol is like a second home to you. You belong here."

"And you don't?" He laughed. "Iowa's capitol belongs to all of her citizens, and now you've certainly claimed this little spot."

She looked down, her lashes resting against her creamy cheeks. "Lincoln, I'm scared."

He took hold of her hand and pressed a kiss to her fingers. "Of what?"

"You. Your world." Lifting her gaze to his, she sucked in a breath. "How I feel about all this."

"There's nothing to be afraid of."

"Isn't there? It may not be tomorrow or even next week, but at some point you're going to take me to some suave function, and I'll commit a grave social error. I'll speak what I'm thinking or I'll do something no lady would, and you'll see I'm right. That's what I do. I can't follow conventions. If there's a rule, it's like I have to break it."

"And I love that about you." He chuckled. "Listen, society needs more young ladies who will say what they're thinking. God gave you a mind, and you have every right to use it."

She started to protest, and he placed his finger against her lips. "And I think you'll do much better at suave social functions than you think. In fact, you're going to get a chance to prove it on Friday if you say yes."

Her lips turned downward. "Yes to what?"

"Pete's wife is hosting a dinner party for the members of the firm, and they expressly requested you attend."

"Me?"

He nodded. "And if you won't do it for me, do it for Walt."

"What could he possibly have to do with Mrs. Williams's dinner party?"

Lincoln tried to keep his voice casual, but a nervous edge crept in. "Do you remember Cedric Knox? He's stirred up some problems with Charles, the other senior partner. Pete seems to think once Charles meets you, he'll realize why it's so important to continue with Walt's case."

Her face paled. "He's going to make you give up Walt's case?"

"Charles might encourage me to, but I'd refuse."

"Then what would happen?"

Lincoln shrugged. "It won't come that far. Once Charles meets you, he'll be as taken with you as I am."

"I highly doubt that." She rolled her eyes. "Remember, I reserve the right to say 'I told you so' after this dinner."

"You'll be stellar. Besides, have you forgotten what I told you in the dome?"

A blush crept into her cheeks, followed by a smile that brought out the caramel color in her hazel eyes.

"I meant every word." He cupped her cheek. "You know what? I've never kissed anyone on top of the world."

"I'm sure there are rules against that kind of thing up here."

"You're going to start following the rules now?"

"I'm trying to be a proper lady." She licked her lips. "But alas, I fear I'm hopeless."

Needing no further invitation, he dipped his head and kissed her thoroughly. Every sense came alive, and he pulled her closer, tangling his hand in her silky tresses.

If anyone was hopeless, it was him. Hopelessly in love with Hannah Gregory and on top of the world.

❧❧❧❧❧

The letter Charlotte held would decide her future. If Fannie Farmer's School of Cookery accepted her, her dreams would come true. If they didn't, she'd have to reapply later or to a different school. But this was the one she most wanted to attend. If only Hannah were here to share the news.

"If you don't open that thing, I'm going to rip it out of your hands and do it myself." Tessa lunged for the envelope.

Charlotte yanked it out of her reach. "I'll open it when I'm good and ready."

"Are you ready now?"

"No, I'm not." She held the letter to her chest.

"Now?"

"Not quite."

Tessa tapped her foot against the hardwood floor. "How about now?"

Charlotte giggled. "Yes!" She ripped the seal and withdrew the letter inside.

"What does it say?"

"'Dear Miss Gregory, we are pleased to accept you—'"

Tessa threw her arms around Charlotte's neck and let out a whoop. "You did it! You got in! You're going to own your own restaurant."

"I'm a long way from that." Charlotte grinned so wide it felt as if her face might split. "I can't believe it."

"Go on. Read the rest."

"'We are pleased to accept you into the spring class of 1909.'" Charlotte stopped. That was a year from now. What would she do for a year?

Tessa frowned. "Not this summer?"

Charlotte swallowed and continued, "'As you know, we have many applicants and select only the best and brightest to participate in our school. We look forward to your attendance next spring.'"

"Oh well." Tessa flopped down on one of the chairs in the parlor. "I guess I can put up with you for a little while longer."

"At least George will be happy." She folded the letter and placed it back in the envelope. "He didn't want me to leave this summer."

"Who cares what he thinks?"

Charlotte slipped the letter in her apron pocket. "I do, Tessa, but you're too young to understand."

"Really?" Tessa picked up a newspaper off the end table. "I think if a fellow really cares about you, he'll want you to be happy doing what God made you to do."

"It's not that simple, Tessa."

"It's not that hard, either."

What did Tessa know? She'd not looked into George's green eyes when he said how much he liked being with her. She'd not held his hand on the way home, and she'd not lain awake at night dreaming about a future with a little house and a baby to hold.

No, Tessa was far too young to understand anything.

❧⁓⟡⁓❧

A glance toward the clock tower on top of the Polk County Courthouse told Lincoln he'd arrived early enough to check out his idea. His meeting with an opposing attorney wasn't scheduled for forty-five minutes.

Lincoln approached the switchboard area. It had a Dutch door, so the top half of the door was open, but the bottom half barred entrance. He knocked on the doorjamb. Mrs. Beecher, a matronly woman with kind blue eyes the color of forget-me-nots, looked up at him. "Mr. Cole, what a pleasant surprise. What can I do for you?"

"Ma'am." He placed his hands on the bottom half of the door. "I was wondering if you happen to need another switchboard operator around here."

She quirked an eyebrow at him. "Are you applying?"

"No, ma'am." He chuckled. "But I know of a young woman who I believe would be a good fit if you're in need of another operator."

"Funny you should ask." She adjusted her headset. "My fellow operator quit three days ago, but the telephone company has yet to fill her vacancy. I fear they're not in any hurry. They simply don't understand I can't manage this exchange by myself. When am I supposed to have a break or eat my lunch?"

His hopes nose-dived. "The telephone company chooses who works here?"

"Of course. It's their exchange." She glanced at the board and saw a light lit. "If you'll excuse me for a minute." After she connected the call, she faced him again. "It's a handful to work alone. I do hope they'll select a new girl soon, but it's hard to find the right girl. She must be a quick study and able to work with judges, attorneys, and clerks, as well as the public. You professional men unnerve some of the timid girls, and sometimes the men can be quite demanding."

"I apologize on behalf of my part of the populace." He flashed the woman a genuine smile, then waited while she connected another call. Maybe, if he spoke to the telephone company, he could point them toward the value of placing Hannah in this position. But he'd need a valid reason to suggest her.

Mrs. Beecher glanced at him. "Is there anything else I can do for you?"

"One more thing. Would it help if the young lady had knowledge of the law?"

"Oh yes. Very much so."

"Thank you for the information." He touched the brim of his hat. "I hope they find you additional help soon."

If he had his way, "soon" would be today. But how would Hannah feel if he interfered with her job?

30

God was smiling on Lincoln's plan. He read the gold-lettered name on the door again and smiled. Iowa Telephone Company's vice president, Victor Bradford, had attended Drake College with him. They'd been on the same rowing team. From the time he'd looked up the information back in his office, he'd taken this as a good sign.

He patted his pocket, armed with Vic's favorite item, and entered the office. Vic's stenographer took his name. A few minutes later, he entered his alum's office and shook the man's hand.

"Linc, it's been too long." Vic motioned to a chair. "I hope you're not here for legal reasons?"

"No, not at all." He sat down in the leather chair and crossed his ankle over his knee. "I was hoping you could help me with something."

Vic nodded. "Anything for the man who led our rowing team to victory."

"This is concerning the switchboard operator's vacancy at the courthouse."

"Linc, is that all? I'll have that filled by day's end."

"You've already selected the new Hello Girl?"

"Not actually." Vic sighed. "I have a feeling you have a suggestion."

"I do. She's intelligent, a quick learner, not afraid of judges and attorneys." He pulled a cigar from his pocket. "And best of all, she's had training in law school at Drake."

"You must be speaking of Miss Gregory." His old friend eyed the cigar.

"I am."

Lincoln offered Vic the smoke. He took it and sniffed his prize. "She's not had the best success following the rules here, but that might be an ideal position for her. Let me send for her supervisor and see what she thinks."

"Former supervisor?" Lincoln took a deep breath. "I believe she's been temporarily reassigned."

"Why, yes, she has." Vic scowled. He went to his door and summoned the supervisor. When he returned, he sat on the corner of his desk. "To tell you the truth, I've been considering what to do with Miss Gregory next. The girl she was covering for is set to return tomorrow, and I'm not sure Miss Frogge wants her back."

Releasing a slow breath, Lincoln fought the urge to defend Hannah. But if Vic intended to put her with Miss Frogge again, Hannah was doomed.

"Linc, you seem to know a great deal about Miss Gregory." Vic adjusted his tie. "You know, 90 percent of the telephone girls we have today will be gone in three years because they've chosen to marry. You aren't planning to steal one of my Hello Girls, are you?"

A knock at the door came before Lincoln had the chance to answer.

When the woman entered the room, Lincoln had to clamp his mouth shut to keep from laughing at Hannah's accurate description of the woman with the bulging eyes. He half expected Miss Frogge's tongue to dart out and snatch the fly buzzing about the room.

She stood to the side of Vic's desk and gave the two men a brief nod. "Mr. Bradford, you sent for me."

"Yes, I did." He leaned forward. "It's come time for me to reassign Miss Gregory."

The woman's nose wrinkled slightly.

"I have two choices. Either I can return her to her previous post under your direction, or I can reassign her to work at the county courthouse's exchange. Which do you think best suits her?"

"Sir, Miss Gregory is indeed a quick learner. I've not seen anyone catch on as quickly." She paused and cleared her throat. "However, I believe it would be in the Iowa Telephone Company's best interest to send her to the courthouse. But may I suggest Mrs. Beecher be made aware of Miss Gregory's lack of decorum and her propensity for rule breaking? In a place such as the courthouse, adherence to the rules is vital. She'll require close supervision."

"Thank you, Miss Frogge. That's an excellent point." He nodded his dismissal. "You may go."

Lincoln waited until the woman departed before he met Vic's gaze. "Well?"

Vic rubbed his chin. "We'll give her a try at the courthouse. Just don't marry her and steal her away."

A laugh bubbled in Lincoln's chest. "I'm not making any promises."

⁓⁓⁕⁓⁓

As Hannah hopped on the streetcar, her temples throbbed. Running late always unnerved her. She dropped in her token and claimed a seat toward the back. Most of the time, she walked the blocks from her home to the telephone company to save money, but today was different. She had been doing research at the state law library and had lost track of time. The only way she could possibly arrive on time was to take the streetcar.

She glanced behind her and saw a young man on a bicycle reach his hand out and clamp on to the bumper of the streetcar. The newspapers had contained several recent articles disapproving of the dangerous activity, but she could understand why a cyclist would "hitch a ride." If she were in their place, she'd probably do the same.

The lady across the aisle gasped when she spotted the young man and proceeded to tell the driver. But it was too late. The streetcar rounded the corner and the bicyclist safely road away, despite all the newspapers' dire predictions. Hannah shook her head. So many unnecessary rules. So many people intent on rule keeping.

Guilt tugged at her. Why was she being so unkind? Her mother would be ashamed. She'd often reminded her that God made the rule keepers just like he made the rule breakers. "Your independent spirit can be a blessing or a curse," her mother had said. "And so can being a rule keeper. Each can be used to God's glory, and each needs the other. God is perfect in both justice and mercy. We, my dear, are not."

When the streetcar reached her block, she made her way down the aisle and stepped off. Hiking up her skirt, she hurried up the stairs and inside the telephone company.

"Hold the elevator, please!" She pressed a hand to her hat and stepped as fast as she dared. Once inside, she heaved a sigh. "Thank you."

After a quick straightening of her hat, she glanced around at her fellow operators. One frowned at her.

"Sorry," Hannah said. "I don't want to be late."

"Then maybe you should start earlier so you don't make the rest of us late."

To Hannah's great relief, the elevator stopped and the operator slid the cage back. She hurried off.

Smack into a man's solid chest.

The familiar scent of Diamond C soap touched her, and she looked up.

"Hello, Hannah."

"Lincoln, what are you doing here?"

He gave her a lilting grin, but no answer.

Mr. Bradford stepped from behind Lincoln. "Miss Gregory, there you are. May I see you for a moment?" He turned to Lincoln. "And Linc, let's get together soon."

"Sounds good, Vic." He shook her boss's hand. "And thanks." He nodded to Hannah and entered the elevator.

Hannah gaped at him as the elevator operator drew the cage door closed.

"Miss Gregory?"

Oh dear, what had Lincoln done?

Leaning against the fender of his Reo, Lincoln waited. He kept an eye on the front door of the tall brick building. Hannah should get her great news and be out in a few minutes.

He chuckled as he remembered Miss Frogge's reaction to the idea of Hannah's return. Had Hannah truly given the woman that much grief? He found it hard to believe, as Hannah had been honest about her indiscretions with him. On the way back from the state capitol the other day, they'd laughed together about the lullaby, the invalid, and the mix-up with the undertaker. She stopped short when he asked her what finally got her moved to the evening shift, and her face took on a most becoming hue of pink.

A sparrow swooped through the air, and Lincoln smiled. How like a bird his Hannah was—God's most beautiful creation. No wonder she liked the idea of flying. Her mere presence brought a song to his day, and the last place she belonged was in this cage.

She appeared at the top of the building's stairs, and his chest warmed. Most of the women who worked in the city wore similar white shirtwaists and black skirts, but somehow they looked so much better on Hannah. Catching sight of him, she tipped her head, and her ribbon tails fluttered in the wind. He waved. Maybe they could go get her sisters and all go out for dinner tonight to celebrate the new position.

Striding toward him, she appeared upset. His chest clenched. Had things not gone as he thought they would? Surely Vic didn't let her go.

She jammed her fists onto her narrow hips. "Lincoln Cole, why did you think I needed you to interfere with my job?"

31

"I—I—just wanted to help," Lincoln sputtered. Good grief. What was she doing to him? He hadn't jumbled his words since his first court trial. "I heard about the opening at the courthouse and knew you'd be a perfect fit, so I came here to suggest it."

He glanced around the telephone company and saw a few on-lookers. Great. An audience.

"If"—she jabbed her finger at his chest—"you thought I was such a 'perfect fit,' why did you think you needed to come throw your college chum weight around?" She poked his chest again. "If I was such a 'perfect fit,' why didn't you let me go to Mr. Bradford myself and inquire about the position?"

His back stiffened and his jaw ticked. Irritation burred under his skin. She should be lavishing appreciation on him, not pecking at him. "I got you out of that horrendous evening shift. I thought you'd be pleased. Grateful, even."

"Well, you thought wrong." She turned from him, arms crossed over her chest.

Lincoln rubbed his neck, tempering his building anger. This was not going well. Should he apologize? But for what? He hadn't done anything wrong.

Father, why is Hannah acting . . . threatened? What should I do?

Had he threatened her in some way? Birds do one of two things when they are threatened—they fight back or fly away. Hannah, of course, would peck, bite, and claw like her life depended on it, but how had he made her feel threatened?

Love is patient. He felt the words press on his heart. But he didn't want to be patient. He wanted to demand an answer right now.

Love is kind.

Kind? Now? Did God really expect that?

Drawing in a long breath, he spread out his hands in an open gesture and softened his tone. "What's the real problem?"

She whirled toward him, her eyes bright with unshed tears. "You didn't trust me to try to do it myself. If you really believed I was the best candidate, you would have let me handle it." She jabbed her thumb at her chest. "I could have taken care of it without you."

"So you feel like I don't believe in you?" The realization kicked him in the gut.

A tear slithered down her cheek.

He thumbed it away. "Nothing could be further from the truth. I promise you." Easing his arms around her, he pulled her close.

How was he ever going to negotiate this? How was he going to make her see he wanted to take care of her, not cage her?

Love is patient. He had to remember that. One couldn't grab a bird, or he might end up with a handful of feathers.

❦

Rosie's mother appeared more often than the cuckoo on a cuckoo clock. Charlotte almost laughed when the kind woman popped out her door the third time, smiled, and pulled her head back in.

"She's worse than your sister," George said from his chair.

According to Mrs. Murphy's mandates, Charlotte had to sit on the swing alone. George had groused, but so far he hadn't tried to break the rule.

Charlotte pulled an envelope from her apron pocket and waved it in the air. "I've got some good news to share."

"Someone leave you money?"

"No." She pressed the letter to her chest. "Better."

"Are you going to sit there all day keeping me in suspense?" He held out his hand.

Charlotte hurried to hand over the letter. The last thing she wanted was for Mrs. Murphy to hear George get upset. She should have known better. After all, George hated to wait.

He opened the letter, read the contents, and frowned. "So you want to do this?"

"Yes!" She couldn't keep a smile from exploding on her face. "I want to learn Fannie Farmer's scientific cookery more than anything."

"You're a good cook already. Why do you need to go to some fancy school?"

"I'm a good cook, but I want to know more. I want to own a fine restaurant." When his frown didn't disappear, she went on. "It's a dream. Like you playing baseball."

"I'm smart enough to know that baseball is only a dream, and I'm not fool enough to think I could actually play in the majors."

"You think my dream is foolish?"

"Come on, Charlotte. How many women restaurant owners do you know?" He chuckled, then reached for her hand. "And why do you want to leave me? I thought we had something special."

"We do, but—"

Mrs. Murphy opened the door. "George, I think it's time you best said your goodbyes."

"Yes, ma'am," he mumbled. He pulled Charlotte to her feet and kissed her hand. "Walk me to the end of the block?"

"I shouldn't."

"What could a few steps off the porch hurt?"

"Please, George, that's her rule. Mrs. Murphy is a family friend. I don't want to hurt her feelings."

"What about my feelings?" He wrapped her in a hug and held her tight.

She squirmed free but offered him her right cheek.

He sighed and placed a quick peck on it. "Good night, Charlotte."

"Good night, George." She waved to him when he reached the

curb. "Oh, wait! I almost forgot." She raced down the steps and grabbed his arm. "Hannah wants you to join us for Sunday dinner."

"I dunno. I'm not sure I want to spend the afternoon with your bossy sister."

She bit her lip. "But you'll come?"

"Sure. Anything for you." He laughed. Then, before she realized what was happening, he drew her into the bushes and pressed his lips to hers.

"Charlotte?" Mrs. Murphy called from the porch door.

Not daring to cry out, she jerked away and covered her mouth.

Hot tears pricked her eyes as disappointment flooded over her. This was not the magical moment she'd expected a first kiss to be.

❧◈❧

"But Charlotte was off the porch with George."

Hannah glared at her protesting little sister. Then looked up at the parlor's ceiling and prayed for God to help her to keep from throttling Tessa. "Pointing fingers at Charlotte doesn't make you any less guilty." She read the note from Tessa's teacher again. What was Tessa thinking?

Setting the note on the table, she turned to her sister seated on the couch. "So, tell me. Why did you cheat on the exam at girls' club?"

"It wasn't my fault. Ingrid had her paper out so everyone could see it."

"Is that so?" This was not going to be easy. Then again, was anything ever easy with Tessa?

Tessa nodded. "Yes, she had her paper right out on her desk."

"Quite possibly because she was taking an exam!" Hannah crossed her arms over her chest. "Why did you do it, Tessa? Do you realize you cheated on a *Bible* exam?"

"I wanted my ribbon. Mrs. Devorak said everyone who passed the Bible test got a ribbon to wear, and I didn't want to be the only girl without one."

"That's what Mrs. Devorak thought. She said she'll give you

an alternate, more difficult oral exam tomorrow, so I suggest you start studying."

"Is that all?" Too late, Tessa sucked in her cheeks to cover the smile erupting on her face.

Charlotte bounced down the stairs, and Hannah glanced at her before pinning Tessa with a glare. "No, that is not all. For the next two weeks, you will be restricted to this house. You'll have extra chores every day, and you'll be writing a letter of apology to both Mrs. Devorak and Ingrid."

Tessa's eyes widened. "Ingrid? Why her?"

"You stole from her."

"I didn't take anything."

"You took her intellectual property." Hannah softened her voice. "And I think you already know what you did was wrong. Don't you?"

Tessa gave a defeated sigh. "Guess I'd better go study."

"Good idea."

Tessa jutted out her lip. "And what are you going to do about Charlotte?"

Hannah thrust a finger toward the kitchen. "Go!"

After Tessa slinked away, Hannah dropped to the couch. "That girl."

"Maybe it will be easier on all of us for you to be home in the evenings again." Charlotte pulled out the checkerboard. "I've missed you."

"I've missed you too." Hannah studied her sister as she lined up the checkers on the board. Sneaking off the porch for a few stolen moments with George wasn't a crime worth addressing, but the subtle changes in Charlotte's demeanor certainly were. Tonight Charlotte seemed especially quiet, and Hannah thought she'd heard her crying earlier. Still, Hannah's first night back home hardly seemed the appropriate time for a conversation about George. Maybe, once they'd had a chance to reconnect, she could have a heart-to-heart with her sister and settle this George situation once and for all.

She glanced at the oval frame on the wall. Beneath the curved glass of the photograph, her parents smiled at her. The familiar ache in her chest throbbed. Were they watching her? What would her mother say to Charlotte about George? For that matter, what would she say about Lincoln? Could her mother have helped her make sense of Lincoln's actions today? Try as she might, Hannah still had difficulty understanding why he felt the need to interfere.

"Hannah? Are you going to play or not?" Charlotte asked.

"Yes, sorry."

Three games of checkers later, Charlotte leaned back in her chair. "Your mind is not in the game tonight. I don't remember the last time I beat you three times in a row."

Tessa returned from the kitchen. "Can I play?"

"Are you ready for your exam?" Hannah looked up and stretched the kink in her neck.

Tessa nodded. "Ask me anything."

"I will." Hannah stood up. "But first I need a little break. You may play one game, and then I'll quiz you."

With a grin, Tessa flopped down on the couch and snapped each checker on its place. "Dear sister, prepare to meet thy doom."

Charlotte rolled her eyes and made the first move.

Hannah watched her sisters' calculated moves. Tessa, the more offensive player, took control of the center of the board, while Charlotte played more defensively. Tessa jumped two of Charlotte's black men, and Charlotte returned the effort in kind. Since Tessa was never one to take time to think through any strategy, the game was over in less than ten minutes.

"I won!" Tessa clapped her hands.

Charlotte laughed. "If you skip the part about being restricted to the house, doing extra chores, and writing apologies—then yes, you are absolutely a winner tonight."

A laugh exploded from Hannah's lips. Oh, how she'd missed her sisters.

"Did you write the apology notes?" Hannah asked Tessa.

"Do I really have to do that?"

"What do you think?"

Tessa stomped away, and Hannah sighed. Had she been too hard on the girl? But Tessa needed to learn there were boundaries—and so did Lincoln.

His downcast face came to the forefront of her thoughts. Had she been too rough on him? He'd only been trying to help, and it was thanks to him she was now able to be home again.

Maybe Tessa wasn't the only one who needed to write an apology note.

32

After rapping on the doorjamb, Hannah waited for her new supervisor to turn toward her. "Mrs. Beecher, I'm Hannah Gregory."

Squeezed into what was once the handyman's workroom, the courthouse switchboard was a far cry from the central exchange. Hannah eyed the two panels, which served 140 phone lines on the exchange.

Mrs. Beecher smiled broadly. "Do come in, dear."

Hannah turned the knob on the lower half of the Dutch door and entered. She closed the door behind her and waited until Mrs. Beecher completed the call she was connecting.

Mrs. Beecher stood and gripped Hannah's hands. "Dear, you are an answer to my prayers. Mr. Bradford telephoned me late yesterday to say you'd be here in the morning."

Hannah's mouth gaped. Miss Frogge would never greet anyone in such a familiar manner.

"Come, let's get you settled."

"What about the callers?" Hannah asked.

"They can wait a few minutes." Mrs. Beecher led her to the adjacent smaller room. It had been fitted with a small table and two straight-back chairs. "You may hang your wraps on the hooks there. It isn't much compared to the parlor at the telephone company, but it's a nice place to relax if you get a moment or two to eat your lunch." She moved to the other side of the room and placed

236

her hand on a tall brass item with a glass globe. "And this is our fountain of joy."

Hannah eyed the brass pot mounted on a solid base. It had a metal tube that appeared to come through its center. Beneath the pot, a tiny flame flickered over an alcohol burner. The glass contained a familiar dark liquid. Realization brought a smile to Hannah's face. A table coffee machine. Could she really be this lucky? She'd heard of these but hadn't seen one in person.

"If you tell me that's a Sternau coffee percolator, I just might kiss you."

"I knew I liked you." Mrs. Beecher poured a cup from the spigot and passed it to Hannah, then she poured one for herself. "I guess we'd better get to work. I'll explain everything as we go. If I go too fast, please tell me to slow down. I don't want you to be uncomfortable in any way. We're going to have great fun."

From that moment on, Hannah couldn't stop smiling. She might have to consider forgiving Lincoln for his interference. While Miss Frogge made Hannah feel ill at ease, Mrs. Beecher's inherent warmth welcomed Hannah as if she were at home.

When they returned to the board, the lights were lit up like fireflies on a dark night. Mrs. Beecher's fingers flew as she made the connections. Hannah could scarcely believe the older woman's speed. In minutes the switchboard's front was crisscrossed with red cords.

After Mrs. Beecher had caught up on her connections, she turned to introduce all of the numbers and the area or patrons they represented. The exchange served not only the Polk County Courthouse but also the Federal Courthouse across the street. Mrs. Beecher passed Hannah a simple listing she'd made for easy reference until she could memorize all of the connections.

"I don't know if Mr. Bradford told you, but the hours here are a bit different than the regular switchboard. You'll arrive at seven thirty and leave at four. You'll have an hour lunch and a half-hour break. We'll have to adjust our lunches so the board is covered, but that shouldn't be too hard. You can either stay here and eat . . ."

Her blue eyes crinkled. "Or you might choose to take your lunch with a certain attorney who spoke to me yesterday."

Hannah stiffened. "I am qualified. I was in law school before my parents passed, so I'm familiar with the work done here."

Mrs. Beecher held up her hand to silence Hannah. "Dear, I have no doubt you're qualified, and I also have no doubt Mr. Cole is smitten with you. Both are fine with me." She paused and answered a call from the Federal Courthouse, immediately followed by one to the court recorder. She turned to Hannah. "Now, where was I?"

"The rules, perhaps?"

She waved her hand in a dismissive gesture. "I'm not a stickler for all those silly rules like never crossing your legs or blowing your nose, but I am a stickler about one thing." Mrs. Beecher looked Hannah straight in the eye. "You will hear a great deal of information here—by accident, of course, but you'll hear it all the same. It's important you keep it in the strictest confidence. Don't even share it with me. Is that clear?"

"Yes, ma'am."

Mrs. Beecher pointed to the other headset and smiled. "Then let's get started, shall we?"

By midmorning things began to slow down a bit. Hannah rubbed a spot beneath her ear where the receiver irritated the skin, then offered to refill Mrs. Beecher's cup. After she returned, she pulled the apology note out of her pocket and fingered it absently while staring at her board.

"Something on your mind?" Mrs. Beecher asked.

Hannah turned, surprised her supervisor initiated conversation.

Mrs. Beecher laughed. "Dear, I told you I'm not a stickler for the rules. There's no harm in the two of us talking between calls. This room is so small, we can't possibly miss a light on our board." She pointed to the envelope. "Did you need to go post that?"

"No." Hannah shook her head. "It's for—"

"A sweet note for your fellow, Mr. Cole."

"An apology, actually."

Mrs. Beecher connected another call and turned back to Hannah.

She didn't ask about the note again, but in between calls, she did ask Hannah other questions. They weren't nosy ones but were filled with genuine interest. Before long, Hannah had told Mrs. Beecher about the death of her parents from influenza, how she'd dropped out of law school to raise her sisters, and even how Mr. Cole had come to take their farm.

"And then he came to help us move." Hannah's insides seemed to glow as she remembered him with his sleeves rolled up, carrying boxes and taking down the beds. "He was a hard man to shake."

Mrs. Beecher chuckled. "From what I've seen, I don't know why you'd even want to."

Hannah grinned, and they shared a laugh. "I know I just met you, Mrs. Beecher, but it's odd, I feel like I've known you for years."

"Dear, call me Jo, and I feel the same way." She squeezed Hannah's arm. "The Lord heard my prayers and sent me a friend."

"Then you must call me Hannah."

"All right, Hannah, my new friend, why don't you tell me why you've been holding that envelope for the last half hour?" Her gaze settled on the sealed envelope.

Hannah sighed. She needed to talk to someone about Lincoln, and right now, Jo seemed like the best option. But what would her new supervisor think if she knew the whole story?

Drawing in a deep breath, Hannah plunged in. Jo deserved to know how she came to get this job. In between calls, she told the whole story from her miserable failure at the main exchange, to her move to the evening shift, to Lincoln's visit to Mr. Bradford. She even added her own frustration over the matter.

"Are you a Christian, Hannah?" Jo sipped from her cup.

"Yes, ma'am."

"Good, then you're probably familiar with the story of Ruth and Naomi."

Hannah nodded. "After her husband died, Ruth left her homeland and went with her mother-in-law, Naomi, to her country. She gleaned from the fields there and finally met Boaz."

"That's the gist of it." Jo smiled. "Have you ever thought about how much you're like Ruth?"

"Me?" Hannah hated to wait for the answer, but she had to connect a call. When she turned back to Jo, the woman appeared to have forgotten the conversation. "You were saying?"

"Oh yes. Ruth left what she loved to care for her family. You left law school and the farm to come into town and care for your sisters. You might not have gleaned in a field, but you took a job beneath you in order to meet their needs. And then your Boaz noticed the love and kindness you showed your sisters."

"My Boaz?"

Jo nodded. "He couldn't tell the workers to leave you extra grain, but he came to me, and then he spoke to Mr. Bradford. He saw how hard you worked and wanted to make your life easier."

Lincoln was her Boaz? She'd never considered him going to Mr. Bradford as an act of kindness. Had she read the situation entirely wrong?

After answering a few more calls, Jo touched Hannah's hand. "Do you remember what Ruth did next?"

Hannah held up both hands. "I'm not going to lie at his feet, if that's what you're suggesting."

Jo laughed. "No, but Ruth asked Boaz to cover her. A godly man who loves a woman will want to cover her, protect her, and provide for her, but dear, you first have to accept the edge of his robe."

"First of all, I didn't ask, and second, he doesn't cover. He smothers."

"Therein lies the age-old problem."

"What? No advice?"

Jo glanced over her head. "Why, Mr. Cole, you're just in time to take Ruth to lunch."

Hannah whirled toward the door to see Lincoln quirking an eyebrow at her. "Ruth?"

"Oh, did I say Ruth?" Jo grinned knowingly at Hannah. "I meant Hannah. Have a good lunch, dear."

33

Every time Lincoln came to Hannah's home, neighbors poured out of their houses like bees from a hive to ogle Lincoln's automobile. This evening, while he spoke to them, she remained inside, delighted Rosie had arrived to help her get ready for the dinner at the Williamses'.

Since they'd worked out their differences earlier in the week, she and Lincoln had come to an understanding, and Hannah was beginning to consider what a future with Lincoln could hold. Tonight, the dinner at Pete and Elise's house would be a test. But why Lincoln had arrived so early puzzled her.

"That's him?" Rosie pushed aside the curtains at the bedroom window and whistled. "I don't think your description did the man justice."

Hannah grinned and laid her ivy-green tailored suit on her bed. She then placed her rose evening gown beside it. She'd remade the rose gown this winter with a higher waist and narrower skirt. It was now fashionable and appropriate for evening, but it also had a lower neckline. She reached for the suit.

Rosie relieved her of the suit and pointed to the rose gown. "This is a special night. You have to wear that one. You'll be stunning with all the ivory lace on the bodice. Hurry and dress, and I'll do your hair."

With expert precision, Rosie swept part of Hannah's hair on top of her head but let the rest remain loose. "Your hair is like the color of honey with a mere hint of cherries, and with all these perfect waves, Lincoln won't be able to take his eyes off you."

Hannah pulled on her gloves. "Let's pray I don't make him regret inviting me."

"You'll be great." Rosie grinned and passed Hannah her layered cloak. "I'll go tell him you're ready, and I'll drag Tessa away from him if I have to." She patted Hannah's arm. "No frowning. Enjoy yourself. Try not to act like an old lady in need of some prune juice."

Hannah laughed and watched her friend leave the room. She pressed a gloved hand to her exposed neck. Maybe she should slip into the ready-made suit after all.

The door flew open, and Tessa stuck her head in. "Come on, Hannah banana! Mr. Cole is waiting."

Charlotte entered and sighed. "You look lovely."

"Thank you." Hannah adjusted the pins in her hair.

"Lincoln's been waiting a while. Don't you need to hurry? What if you upset him?"

"He'll be fine." Hannah pinched her cheeks and flashed her sisters a cheeky grin. "And a girl should realize she's worth waiting for."

She descended the stairs, and Lincoln turned. A smile lit his eyes, but he said nothing. For a moment, a surge of panic threatened. Was she overdressed or underdressed?

His Adam's apple bobbed. "You take my breath away."

Heat pooled in her stomach. "Thank you."

"Shall we?" He offered her his arm, and she slipped her hand in place. "Ladies, I promise to bring her home before midnight, because we all have a big day tomorrow."

To her delight, Lincoln had the top up on the Reo. Once she was seated, she adjusted her skirt about her ankles and looked over the hood at Lincoln. "Tomorrow?"

"I thought maybe you and the girls would like to take in the Memorial Day celebration at the state fairgrounds." He cranked the engine and got in. "I hope it's okay, but I told Charlotte to invite George to come along with us instead of coming for dinner on Sunday. I thought he might be more at ease doing something rather than simply sitting at the table with all of us staring at him."

"That's very thoughtful. Thank you."

He grinned and began to drive. "My pleasure."

On the way, Hannah persuaded Lincoln to tell her more about Pete and Elise. She learned Elise sometimes suffered from bouts of melancholy, but Pete was one of the jolliest men on the planet. Lincoln told her how Pete had helped him stick it out when he lost his first three court cases and wanted to quit. In many ways, Pete had become the father Lincoln needed, and his admiration for the man was boundless.

Hannah gasped when they pulled up in front of the Williamses' home, but Lincoln allayed her fears. "They're going to love you as much as I do."

Inside, she tried not to gawk at the shimmering crystal chandelier in the foyer.

"Lincoln, this must be your Miss Gregory." Elise grasped Hannah's hands. "She's a beauty. Shame on you for not bringing her over sooner."

Pete joined his wife. "Miss Gregory, our boy here is quite smitten with you. You aren't planning on breaking his heart, are you?"

"Peter, behave yourself." Elise fired a mock glare at her husband. "Come, now. Let's introduce Miss Gregory to our other guests."

After insisting they all call her Hannah, she was swept away into the front parlor, where Pete made the introductions. "Miss Gregory, may I present our son, Albert."

About the same age as she, Albert had neither his father's obvious zest for life nor his mother's outgoing personality. He pushed up his wire-rimmed spectacles and nodded first to Lincoln, then to her.

Lincoln greeted the young man warmly. If Pete was like a father to Lincoln, then Albert must be like a brother.

"And Miss Gregory, this is the other senior partner in the law firm, Mr. Charles Harlington, and his lovely wife, Susan."

She nodded to them. "A pleasure to meet you both."

"And to your right is our other junior partner, Cedric Knox."

"We've already met, but under decidedly different circumstances," Cedric said. "Right, Miss Gregory?"

Before she had a chance to answer, Elise linked their arms and announced, "Now, before any of you can start a barrage of questions for Hannah, let's feed the poor girl."

Beside her, Charles clamped a hand on Lincoln's shoulder. "I can see why you want to make her happy."

"That I do, Charles. In every way."

⚜

When in good spirits, Elise never failed to set a fine table. Lincoln discovered today was no exception. Despite Hannah's claims of being unfamiliar in these types of social settings, she handled everything from the four different forks to the collection of stemware to the right of her plate with grace and proficiency. Someone at Drake had taught her well.

He caught a whiff of mint as the lamb was passed. The creamed carrots were more to his liking, but he found Elise's asparagus salad with champagne-saffron vinaigrette something delightfully new. Hannah seemed to enjoy every bite.

They hadn't finished their first course before Susan asked Albert about his plans to return to Yale. The brilliant young man explained that his vacation in Germany had done him wonders, and he was looking forward to tackling his rigorous course work this fall.

"What are you studying?" Hannah asked.

"Science," Albert answered. "I'm interested in electrical research."

As the conversation turned to current topics like prohibition, Hannah leaned close to tell Lincoln how much Charlotte would enjoy this dinner, and an odd empty feeling came over him. Why did he suddenly miss Hannah's two sisters?

Lost in his own thoughts, he missed Cedric addressing Hannah until she stiffened beside him. When had the topic shifted to suffrage?

Cedric's voice rose. "All this whining from women first about prohibition and then about suffrage is annoying. What's the big deal?"

Lincoln cleared his throat, trying to warn Hannah that Cedric was goading her.

"So, you believe half the population should be without representation, Mr. Knox?" Her tone was sweet, but Lincoln could hear the annoyance lacing it. "I believe our own constitution says there should be no taxation without representation. If that is the case, then women should not have to pay taxes."

Lincoln caught the amused glances of Pete and Charles. Their wives, however, shifted uncomfortably, frowns marring their faces. Whether they were upset with Cedric for his questions or Hannah for her answers, he didn't know.

Cedric pointed at her with his fork. "But even you must admit, women are simply too emotional for the responsibility of voting for our elected offices."

"There are some who would agree with you." She cut a piece of asparagus with her knife. "They say men are the superior species because of their ability to not respond emotionally to stimulus."

She dropped her gaze to her plate, ending the subject.

"That's all?" Cedric pushed. "What about you? Don't you have a thought of your own on the matter? Don't you want to give us your opinion?"

She met his gaze and held it. "If you honestly cared about my opinion, I would express it."

Smiles broke on Elise's and Susan's faces.

Hannah sipped from her water goblet but said nothing more.

Cedric's face reddened. "So now you're going to sulk and give me the silent treatment? You make my point, Miss Gregory. Women are too emotional."

"That's enough, Cedric." Lincoln balled up his napkin and tossed it beside his plate. "I'll not have you badgering her."

"Gentlemen." Charles eyed Hannah and chuckled. "And who is acting emotional now?" He turned to Hannah. "You, Miss Gregory, are a genius. I believe you made your point without even opening your mouth." He lifted his glass. "A toast to Miss Gregory, whose courtroom skills appear to outshine even those of our very own Cedric."

Pushing away from the table, Cedric placed his napkin beside his plate. "I think I shall take my leave early. Dinner is not sitting well with me."

"Oh, don't be such a spoilsport. Sit down and eat dessert." Pete patted his belly.

Obliging his host, Cedric sat back down, but his glare cut right to Hannah.

Lincoln's jaw muscles clenched. Apparently, he was no longer alone on Cedric's "least favorite people" list.

Catching Hannah's hand beneath the table, Lincoln pressed his lips to her ear. "Well done, counselor. Well done."

⚜

Seated in the Williamses' front parlor, Hannah tried not to stare at the pieces of artwork and the Tiffany lamp. She guessed Pete spared no expense in making his wife happy.

The men returned from their after-dinner reprieve to the study, and to Hannah's relief, she noticed Cedric had departed.

"I have something I must show you all." Elise clasped her hands together, then beckoned a servant to fetch the electrical home machine.

While Lincoln took his place behind Hannah, the servant set the wooden case on the table.

"You may have seen the old magnetoelectric machines, but this one is a scientific breakthrough and a miracle cure." Elise undid the latch and opened the box. "All you have to do is press one of these brass electrodes to the part of the body you need healed and hold the other in your hand while someone else turns this crank." She pointed to the writing inside the lid. "It says right here it treats rheumatism, poor circulation, headaches, tonsillitis, catarrh, asthma, earaches, lumbago, aches, and nervousness." She looked at her husband. "There's even a special comb to use to treat dandruff and stimulate hair follicles."

"Mother, I've told you before that machine is ridiculous." Albert leaned against the fireplace. "I don't know why you insist on using that dangerous contraption."

"It's dangerous?" Susan asked.

"Nonsense." Elise poured water into the battery. "Look at me. I've used it twice a day for days now, and I've never felt better."

"I'm leaving. I want no part in this quackery." Albert marched from the room.

"Enough of your new toy, my dear. I think a little music is in order." Pete turned to Susan. "Will you play the piano for us?"

Susan agreed and played several pieces. In the middle of a lovely sonata, an explosion shook the house.

Elise shrieked.

Hannah turned to Lincoln. "What was that?"

"I don't know. Stay here." He rushed to the window.

A servant ran into the room. "Mr. Williams! It's the Grennen place."

Pete paled. "Their carriage house?"

"No!" Lincoln ran toward the door. "This time I think it's their home!"

34

It was well after midnight by the time the fire was under control. Lincoln stood by, helpless to stop the flames from destroying the stately home. He kept his arm anchored around Hannah. The Grennens had lost everything, but at least they still had each other. Thankfully, the daughter of Western Union's manager and her family had not been home at the time of the explosion, but now they stood watching their home consumed by flames.

Pete and Elise offered to take in the family, but they insisted on going to the home of their parents. Charles and Susan finally persuaded them to leave and took them in their carriage.

When the young family had departed, Elise burst into tears. Pete held her. One look at Hannah told Lincoln she was close to following suit. He thumbed a tear from her cheek. "We'll leave as soon as I speak to the fire marshal."

"Mother." Albert laid his hand on his mother's shoulder. "Let's get you home. You need your rest."

"Let me take her," Hannah offered.

Albert and Pete slowly agreed and relinquished Elise to Hannah, who draped her arm around Elise's shoulders and led her toward the house, murmuring words of comfort.

Lincoln marveled at how gentle Hannah was with the woman she'd only just met. She seemed to sense how mentally frail Elise was, and yet she didn't treat the condition with disdain like so many other women would.

Once the two women had disappeared into the house, he sought out the fire marshal. The man recognized him but was far from thrilled to see him present at the scene.

Lincoln fell in step beside him. "Was it caused by a gas explosion?"

"Nope."

"You're sure?"

The fire marshal glared, his position unyielding. "Dynamite."

"How can you tell?"

The fire marshal pointed to the crater in the ground. "The gas line is over there. Only one other thing makes a porch go up like that. All I can say is they're lucky they weren't home." He leaned back. "Guess you're happy. Your firebug should get out of jail now."

❧◦◦◦◦◦❧

After turning Elise over to her maid, Hannah stepped into the hallway outside the woman's room. While the main floor had gas lights, the upstairs did not, so she took the oil lamp from the room to light her way. Bone weary and reeking of smoke, she searched for the washroom. If she could find it, perhaps she could at least wash the ash from her face before going home.

Turning to the right, she tried two doors and found only additional bedrooms. A third door was ajar, and she nudged it with the toe of her shoe. Her lamplight flickered off bottles, wires, coils, and all sorts of unfamiliar objects.

"Can I help you find something?"

She jumped and whirled at the sound of a voice behind her. "Albert." Relief flooded over her. "I was looking for the washroom."

"I'm afraid you found my laboratory instead. The washroom is at the end of the hall. And Lincoln is waiting for you downstairs."

"Thank you." She turned toward the direction he indicated.

Albert clamped his hand on her arm. "Miss Gregory, is my mother all right?"

"Yes, she's sleeping now."

"Good." He stared at Elise's door. "I'd hate for this to send her into a downward spiral."

Hannah saw the worry in his eyes, and for a brief moment, Albert reminded her of his father. "I'll say a prayer for her."

"Prayers. Yes. That would be good." He didn't take his eyes off the bedroom's entrance.

Albert was certainly an odd duck, and he sounded as tired as she felt. "Good night. Please thank your mother for Lincoln and me."

She hurried down the hall but swore she heard Albert talking to himself. Hannah's lips curled. His concern for his mother was admirable, but if her father were there, he would probably have said the young man was a few sandwiches short of a picnic.

❧❦❧

Using this arena for the Memorial Day celebration was brilliant. Lincoln helped Hannah take a seat in the Monster Grand Stands at the Iowa State Fair grounds. With lots of room for both the participants and the spectators, and at only ten cents a seat, it was an easy way for him to treat the whole family.

He swallowed hard as a warm yet strange sensation settled over him. Family. How odd he kept thinking of Hannah and her sisters that way.

Hannah tucked her ivy-green suit out of the way and smiled at him. "Thank you for bringing us all here. What a special day."

She stifled a yawn with her gloved hand, and guilt nudged him. Maybe he should have canceled their planned outing after last night's events. But when he'd mentioned that option to Hannah, she'd insisted she didn't want to disappoint her sisters.

Tessa, her copper braid shining in the sun, scooted in next to Hannah. Charlotte and George eased into the seats in front of them. From what Lincoln could tell, George must be quite the witty young man to elicit scores of giggles from Charlotte. But if he didn't put some space between himself and Charlotte, Lincoln was going to have to volunteer young George to be the target in the upcoming military drill.

"Look! Here they come." Tessa clapped her hands.

Two of the Des Moines fire department's crack horse teams took their places on the field.

"Which team is which?" Hannah asked.

Lincoln pointed to the pair on the right. "That one is Jack and Jack. They won the state competition last year. The other team is Black and Tan. They're younger but great too." Two teams of firemen drew their hose carts onto the field and lined up at the starting line. "The first one is the hub-and-hub competition."

At the pop of a pistol, the two teams raced down the length of the field with two team members pulling the hose cart. Every fifty yards, they exchanged places with other members. The crowd cheered the teams as those from station number two, Jack and Jack's station, captured top honors.

"Next up are the bunk hitches!" the announcer decreed.

"This one is Jack and Jack's specialty." Lincoln eyed the horses as they took their places. "The firemen have to hitch their team to the steam engine. Then one man will climb on the cart and race it around to the finish line."

Charlotte turned back toward Hannah and him. "How far do they have to run?"

"Around the arena twice, right, Lincoln?"

"That's right, Tessa."

George shielded his eyes against the morning sun. "Looks like about six or seven hundred yards."

"Close. It's eight hundred eighty," Lincoln answered. "It's a half mile."

George scowled, and Lincoln winced. He should have known better than to correct George in front of his girl.

He jolted at the crack of the pistol. Both teams had their horses hitched and coupled to the engine cart faster than Lincoln thought possible. Neck and neck, the two teams raced like lightning. In just over a minute, the race was over. The announcer proclaimed Jack and Jack the winner at one minute, fourteen seconds.

"Black and Tan lost by only four seconds, folks. Let's give both teams a round of applause," the announcer said. "Next up is the contest for hose laying and coupling."

By the end of the fire drills, Tessa announced she wanted to become a fireman.

"There's only one problem." George looked at her and laughed. "They're fire*men*, not fire*women*."

Tessa's eyes narrowed. "Women have been putting out all kinds of fires for centuries. I don't see why they can't put out real ones too. What do you think, Charlotte?"

Charlotte looked from Tessa to George, clearly nervous about answering. She glanced at Hannah, perhaps hoping for a reprieve.

"Yes, Charlotte, what do you think?" Hannah smiled sweetly.

"I . . . uh . . ."

"Go ahead and tell us what you think. You're allowed your own opinions." Lincoln held out his hands, hoping to encourage her. If she gave an answer contrary to George's, his reaction would tell a lot about his character. How would George handle it?

She swallowed. "I think it's a very difficult job, but there's no reason a woman couldn't do it if she can manage the lifting and such. If a lady's house was on fire and her children were inside, none of us would think twice about her fighting a fire to save them. Yet, when it's someone else's home, we wonder if she could do it." She glanced at George. "I don't think it's a question of if a woman is able, but if men are willing to let her join their ranks."

While he wouldn't want Hannah or her sisters ever to take up such a cause, Lincoln wanted to cheer. Apparently, Hannah wasn't the only one who could present a decent argument. The Gregory sisters knew how to use their beautiful brains.

George vaulted to his feet.

"Where are you going?" Charlotte grabbed his arm.

"For a walk." He jerked free of her grasp and stalked out of the stands.

Charlotte looked at her sisters, eyes filled with tears. "I shouldn't have said anything."

"Are you serious?" Lincoln laid a hand on Charlotte's shoulder. "You made an excellent point. Give him a few minutes to cool off."

George didn't return until after the fire drill competition had concluded and the bugle had sounded for the military review and dress parade to begin. He took his place beside Charlotte but didn't say anything as the entire regiment of the second cavalry marched into the arena. It wasn't until they began their elaborate drills that George seemed to get over his snit.

"George." Lincoln touched his shoulder. "Why don't you and I go get the ladies some Coca-Colas?"

"Sure. I guess."

Once they'd left the arena, Lincoln directed George toward a refreshment stand. He asked the clerk for five bottles and waited. "So, George, what does your father do for a living?"

"Right now, he's working at the quarry. He lost his other job in some mess."

"The quarry? How far is that away from your home?" He handed the clerk a quarter for the Coca-Colas and handed two to George.

"About twenty miles out of town."

Lincoln tucked one bottle in the crook of his arm and grasped the other two in his hands. "That's a long way to travel every day."

George shrugged. "Sometimes he stays there for a couple of days at a time. It just depends."

"So you're home alone with your mother?" Lincoln motioned for them to head back.

"My ma's dead. Died giving birth." He looked down at the ground as he walked. "And I don't mind being home alone. I'm not a kid anymore."

"No, you aren't." Lincoln laughed. "What do you do with your time?"

"I have baseball practice every day after school. Then I see Charlotte for a while if her sister lets me. Finally, I go to the Opera

House Pharmacy and sweep up. It earns me a little so I can help out my dad."

Lincoln's heart softened toward the young man. No mother. His father gone all the time. Working into the night to help out his dad with expenses. With Charlotte's big heart, no wonder she was so willing to overlook some of the boy's obvious flaws. Did Hannah know about any of this, and if so, what did she think? More so, what did he think of this young man dating Hannah's sister—problems or not?

35

Lincoln and George climbed back into the stands and handed the girls their bottles of soda.

"Thank you." Hannah pressed the bottle to her lips and drew in a long swallow. Her eyes closed with apparent pleasure.

"You're certainly welcome." Sitting down beside her, he forced his gaze away from her face and back toward the arena.

The entire Fort Des Moines army regiment in full dress, including two all-Negro infantry companies, stood at the field entrance. To the patriotic tunes of the second cavalry's mounted band, each infantry company took its turn marching in front of the military reviewing party made up of the regiment's officers.

"Ladies and gentlemen, you're in for a treat now!" the announcer's voice boomed. "Let's hear it for the infantry drill team."

Even George seemed to sit up and take notice when the all-Negro drill team marched forward and dazzled the crowd by spinning, turning, and flipping their Smithfield rifles in synchronized movements without a single slip. Their unflinching drillmaster, a sergeant, never said a word.

The crowd roared when the pounding of horses' hooves announced the arrival of the cavalry. At the front of the line, the first two mounts carried both the United States flag and the flag representing the second cavalry. The crowd stood in honor of the flag as it passed their position. The horses circled the arena before coming to a stop at one end.

Hannah leaned close to Lincoln. "What do you think of George?"

"I'm not ready to render a verdict yet."

"I want to like him for Charlotte's sake."

"I know, so do I."

"But—"

He covered her hand. "I know. I'll keep an eye on him."

The announcer explained the cavalry would now commence their daring drills, starting with the Roman standing race. Two riders and four horses took to the field. Each rider then took off on one horse with an additional horse riding alongside.

Hannah gasped and grabbed Lincoln's arm when the two soldiers stood up in their saddles. They then placed a foot on the second horse's saddle and drove the two mounts Roman style around the arena. They crossed the finish line almost neck and neck.

"That was amazing." Hannah let out a wistful sigh.

Lincoln chuckled. "You'd love to try that, wouldn't you?"

"I would. It's almost like—"

"Flying?" Lincoln kissed her cheek, and his heart swelled. He loved this woman and he loved her sisters. He'd do anything to make them all happy. "We'll get you in the air someday, Hannah. I don't know how, but we will."

❧

Hannah spread out the blanket they'd brought to Ingersoll Park. A picnic seemed like the perfect end to a perfect day. While George and Charlotte went for a walk and Tessa was off examining a flower garden, she and Lincoln had a few minutes alone.

"Mind if I take my coat off? It's getting downright balmy."

"Not at all."

After shrugging out of it, he rolled up his shirtsleeves and lay down on the blanket. "I think I'll rest my eyes for a minute." He covered his eyes with his straw hat, and within minutes the steady rise and fall of his chest told her sleep had claimed him.

Poor man. He had to be even more tired than she. After all, he wouldn't have gotten to bed until after he'd seen her home last night.

She reached into the picnic basket and withdrew the plates with as little noise as possible. She set them on the blanket and smiled at the man who'd captured her heart. Beneath his tipped hat, his lips pursed as he dozed.

Her gaze settled on his soft, full lips.

Heat tinged her cheeks. What was she doing? She shouldn't be watching him sleep, and she certainly shouldn't be thinking about his kisses while they were sitting on the same blanket. There was something so intimate about being near him as he slept. It was almost as if it made her extra aware of him as a man. Or maybe it was because she'd begun to picture a future with Lincoln, and this scene fit right into her mental photograph.

She reached into the basket and withdrew an apple pie. Naturally, Charlotte would make that, after George's little fit about Charlotte not packing pie for the box social. Well, she certainly hoped he was pleased this time.

Glancing at Lincoln again, she sighed. George was a far cry from Lincoln Cole. Maybe the boy was simply young and immature, but Hannah feared he had a lot to learn about truly loving someone. She imagined his father, like so many men, hadn't provided the best example.

Hannah recalled Lincoln's promise about finding a way for her to someday fly. The idea warmed her deep in her heart. How did she get so lucky? It wasn't that she truly expected to ride in an airplane someday or float in the clouds. It was that he cared that she wanted to. While he might be quite content to live life with his feet firmly planted on solid ground, he knew she wanted something else, and he was willing to promise her he'd find a way to make that happen.

She removed a box of sandwiches from the basket and poured glasses of lemonade for each of them from a Mason jar.

Lincoln pushed the hat off his eyes. "Were you going to let me sleep all day?"

"I figured you needed it."

"But I'd rather spend my time with you." He rubbed his eyes and sat up. He yawned and accepted the glass she offered. "Is that an apple pie?"

"George's favorite."

They shared a laugh.

"Did you know his mother is dead?" Lincoln sipped from his glass. "And his dad is gone a lot. The boy has a job too. He sweeps up in the evenings at a pharmacy."

"You learned all that when you were getting the Cokes?"

He nodded. "Kind of makes me want to give him the benefit of the doubt."

"I do too, for Charlotte's sake and for his, but she's simply not herself when she's with him." She sighed. "No, it's more than that. She hides her true self."

"Well, you're in no danger of hiding your true self from me." Lincoln chuckled, then took her hand. "However, I do worry you're hiding some of your true self from the world."

She stiffened. What was Lincoln talking about? "Pardon me?"

"You're not a switchboard operator. There's nothing wrong with being one, but that's not what you were meant to be."

The tender look in his eyes made her relax a bit. "And what exactly was I meant to be?"

"What do you think?" He drew circles on the soft flesh of her palm.

"None of us knows for certain. Just because I like to argue doesn't mean I'd make a good attorney. In fact, maybe I'd be an awful one. Then what would you think?"

He grinned. "You'd be outstanding. Charlotte is passionate about pies, and you're passionate about right and wrong."

She pulled her hand free and grabbed the box of sandwiches. "Well, that dream has to die."

"For now, but not forever."

"Lincoln, please don't make me want it more than I already do."

George and Charlotte walked up, followed by Tessa. All three sat down on the quilt, Hannah disbursed the sandwiches, and Lincoln offered a blessing.

After one bite of the succulent roast beef in between two slices of soft bread, Hannah complimented her sister. No one else could make a sandwich turn out so delicious.

When they'd finished their sandwiches, Charlotte cut the pie and loaded slices onto their plates. Hannah smiled as Charlotte scooped an extra-large piece onto George's plate, and he thanked her.

Lincoln forked a bite and moaned. "This is amazing." He raised his glass. "A toast to Charlotte and her culinary skills. Fannie Farmer's School will be lucky to get you."

Charlotte looked at George and then at Hannah.

"Tell them." George nudged her arm.

Tessa dropped her sandwich to her lap. "Tell us what?"

"I'm not going to go away to school. George says I already know everything I need to."

"So she's going to stay in Des Moines with me." George puffed out his chest. "Right where she belongs."

"Over my dead body!" Hannah drew back her plate, ready to hurl it in George's face.

"Easy, there." Lincoln grabbed her wrist. "Son, I think you and I should go for a walk."

"But I'm not done with my pie."

Lincoln snagged it out of his hand and passed it to Charlotte. Hooking the boy's arm, he hauled him to his feet. "I think it's in your best interest to come with me."

"Why?" He struggled to get his footing.

"Because Charlotte's switchboard-operating sister may disconnect you for good."

36

Charlotte glared at her older sister sitting across from her on the blanket. For the last five minutes, they'd sat in silence with their gazes locked. As far as she was concerned, they could sit there all day. She was not giving up George, and no one was going to convince her otherwise.

"Okay." Tessa stood up and looked at Hannah. "I'll say it if you won't." She turned to Charlotte. "Sister, you've sniffed one too many sheets of burnt cookies."

Charlotte scowled.

"What are you talking about?" Hannah unfolded her legs and stood.

"I'm talking about Charlotte. Her bread isn't baked. Her pie ain't got all its slices." She held out her hands, palms upward, as if she were offering Hannah the answer.

Hannah held up her hand. "That's enough."

Tessa plunged on. "I think she fell out of the stupid tree and hit every branch on the way down."

"I said stop." But the corner of Hannah's lip lifted ever so slightly.

Charlotte's simmering anger came to a boil. "I think you've made your point, little sister." She grabbed the empty plates and thrust them into the basket. "I don't care what you or Hannah or Lincoln or anyone else thinks."

"No, you only care what George thinks." Hannah's words were laced with sarcasm.

Charlotte tossed the contents of one of the glasses into the grass. "Why can't you let me make my own decisions?"

"Your own decisions?" Hannah picked up the other glasses and stacked them. "You haven't thought for yourself since George walked into your life. The Charlotte I know wouldn't jump when a fellow said boo, wouldn't cry when he didn't like the dessert she made, and would never sell out her dreams for some fellow."

"You're willing to become a politician's wife." Charlotte could tell her words punched hard.

"That's different. Besides, we're talking about you." Hannah handed the stack of glasses to Charlotte. "Why are you doing this? Is this what you really want?"

Without wrapping them, she set the glasses in the basket. They rattled against the plates, but she didn't care. "George says—"

"No! Not George. You. Do you know what you want anymore? Do you even know who you are?"

Charlotte blinked. Did she?

She stood and shook out the blanket. She folded it in half. Again. And again. Then hugged the quilt to her chest. Of course she knew who she was. She was George's girl. He needed her. She belonged with him. Didn't Hannah understand how much she needed George—especially now? Didn't Hannah feel the same grief-weary emptiness that she did? Isn't that why she'd turned to Lincoln?

"Do you think he loves you?" Hannah eased the quilt from her arms, her voice now back to its soothing, velvet sound. "Has he kissed you? Is that why you're willing to do whatever he wants?"

Charlotte's hand shot to her mouth, her stomach roiling at the memory of that awful stolen kiss. But that had been her fault. If she'd let him kiss her willingly, he wouldn't have gone to such extremes.

"Charlotte, honey, how do you know he cares about you?"

Tears flooded Charlotte's eyes. He cared. Couldn't Hannah

at least see that? Hurt and anger exploded inside her. "He's here putting up with you, isn't he?"

Hannah reeled back as if she'd been slapped. "I think we should discuss this more later."

"There's nothing to discuss. It's my life and my choice." She tipped her chin in the air. Her decision was final.

Tessa grabbed Charlotte's arm. "But we promised to support each other's dreams."

"And what if my dream is to marry George? Are you going to support that?"

"No, we aren't." Hannah shook her head. "Not unless you find yourself again. You can't let George or anyone else define you."

"You're not my mother!"

"But I'm your sister." Tears pooled in her hazel eyes. "And I love you enough to tell you the truth, even if it hurts."

Lincoln and George returned, and Charlotte sighed with relief. However, George didn't move to join her. He didn't even meet her gaze.

Had Lincoln and Hannah ruined everything?

∽∽⊙∽∽

Hannah touched the tip of her jack to the rim of the plug. Hearing a sharp click, she let the cord retract and spoke into her receiver. "I'm sorry, sir. That line is busy at the moment."

"Can't you break into their call?"

"Is it an emergency, sir?"

"No, I guess not. I'll ring them in a little while."

"I'll ring you when the line is free." She made a note of the caller's number on her tablet. "Thank you."

She waved goodbye to Jo, who was off for her break, then leaned back in her chair and rubbed the back of her neck. After a nearly silent streetcar ride home on Saturday, tensions remained high into the night and on Sunday.

Before Lincoln left Saturday evening, he explained he'd told George that he and Charlotte needed a little vacation from each other. Lincoln told him not to come around for two weeks, but he could write her. He'd even given George ten cents for postage.

"I know I should have talked it over with you first," Lincoln had told her. "But I thought if she had a little space from him, she might start seeing things clearly. I don't think he's a bad kid, but he's young and selfish."

At first Hannah bristled at his taking control of the situation, but the more she thought about it, the more she admired Lincoln's willingness to do so and his gentle way of dealing with both Charlotte and George.

If only she had been as gentle.

Charlotte had gone to their bedroom and locked the door as soon as they'd gotten home that day. After Tessa threatened to go in the kitchen and rearrange every spice in the cupboard, she had finally let them in to go to bed.

Even Sunday's sermon hadn't helped. The preacher had talked about how often love demands making tough choices, including leaving people and places you care about or risking your heart or your pride. Hannah's thoughts had wandered back to the story of Ruth and Naomi and how Ruth had left her homeland because she loved her mother-in-law. She'd also taken a huge risk. Her chances of finding love in a new country as an outsider were slim, and in that day, no husband meant a life of poverty.

The preacher pointed out the choices Jonathan made to be loyal to David even when his father wanted to kill David, and Queen Esther risking her life by going before the king to save her people.

"At some point," Brother Molden had said, "you will be faced with a choice where there seems no right answer. Love demands you put others' needs before your own. Love demands you make the tough choice, even if it costs you."

Suddenly the light for one of the second-floor courtrooms lit on the switchboard. How strange. The court seldom used the phone when in session. Hannah inserted a jack into the plug. "Number, please."

"We need the police up here now!" Urgency in the caller's voice made Hannah's skin prickle.

A loud bang rang out.

"Hello? Hello?" She tried to raise a response. No one responded, but she heard scuffling and shouting.

Her pulse raced and the room tilted. Where was Lincoln? Didn't he say he had court this morning?

Fighting her panic, she sucked in a breath and jammed the jack into the police department's plug. She rang them hard.

"Sergeant Griffin."

"This is the courthouse switchboard operator, and we have an emergency. There's a dire need for assistance in one of the upstairs courtrooms. They requested I telephone the police, and then I believe I heard a gunshot."

"Miss, could it have been something else? Perhaps a chair falling over?"

"No, it wasn't a chair!" If she could grab the man and pull him through the telephone lines, she would.

"Easy, ma'am. Which courtroom?"

She relayed the data.

"I'll send someone right away."

Cupping her hand over the earpiece, she listened for anything that might indicate if Lincoln was there or even a hint of what was now going on in the courtroom.

Two policemen burst through the front doors. Footsteps pounding, they raced across the first floor and up the marble staircase.

More movement and muffled voices came through the telephone line.

A clatter in her ear told her someone had picked up the earpiece. "Are you still there?" the previous caller asked.

"Yes, this is the operator."

"We need a doctor up here."

"Who's hurt?" Her voice cracked. She prayed it wasn't Lincoln.

"One of the lawyers got a little roughed up while we were wresting the bailiff's gun away from the suspect." He paused.

"How bad is it?"

"Well, he'll probably go away for a long time now."

"No, I mean how badly is the attorney hurt?"

"Nothing too serious."

Click. He hung up his receiver.

Only her training kept Hannah from racing up the stairs and seeing who the injured man was and what the caller had meant by "nothing too serious." Her fingers trembled as she placed a call to the nearest doctor.

She jolted when Jo opened the Dutch door and stepped inside. She carried a bouquet of pink and white peonies that filled the air with their sweet scent.

"Everything all right, Hannah?" Jo eyed her critically. "You look like a ghost."

"There was an emergency upstairs." Hannah quickly covered her mouth. "I shouldn't have told you that, right?"

Jo smiled. "If there's an emergency, I think you should share it with me."

"Someone shot a gun upstairs in one of the courtrooms. I've telephoned the police, but I don't know what's transpired since then."

"And you don't know if your Lincoln is up there?"

Tears pricked Hannah's eyes.

"Then why are you sitting here? Go." Jo made a shooing motion with her hands. "I'll handle things."

Without a second thought, Hannah discarded her headset and hurried out of the tiny room. Once in the foyer, she gathered her skirt in her fist and rushed toward the stairs.

37

"Hey! What's your hurry?"

Hannah stopped and turned at the sound of Lincoln's voice. He jogged up to her, and she wrapped her arms around his neck, hugging him without letting go.

He eased her back but kept his hands on her arms. "What's wrong? You're scaring me."

"Are you really okay?" Emotion thickened her voice.

"I'm a little out of breath from chasing you, but other than that I'm fine." He cocked his head to the side. "Why?"

"Upstairs. A shot was fired in a courtroom."

"Which one?" He glanced upward. "Did you think I was there?" She nodded.

"My case finished early. Listen, I need to go see what happened, but first I want to show you the surprise I picked up for you." He swept his arm toward the front door.

She turned and spotted the surprise—all six foot two of him. Her heart leapt, and she hurried across the marble floor much more quickly than any proper Hello Girl should dare.

But it was worth it.

Walt, freshly shaven and in clean clothes, drew her into his arms and lifted her off the ground.

Free. Walt was free, thank goodness, and freedom smelled like Diamond C soap.

⚜

Jealousy barbed Lincoln as he watched Walt sweep Hannah into his arms, but he shoved the unwelcome feeling aside. In the battle for Hannah's heart, he'd already won, and if he loved her, he needed to accept that Walt would always be a part of her life.

Walt released her, and Lincoln joined them and placed his hand on the small of Hannah's back. She was his, and Walt might as well know that.

Hannah smiled at him. "Why did they release Walt?"

"After the fire the other night, it wasn't hard to convince the detective they had the wrong man in custody. I went to talk to him first thing this morning."

"Thank you." Pure joy radiated from her.

"I want to head upstairs now and see who was hurt," Lincoln said. "Walt, I trust you can find a way home?"

"I'll take the streetcar. It's only a half-mile walk from the end of the line, and I have a new appreciation for being able to walk in open air."

"Then I'd better get going." Lincoln offered Walt his hand.

Walt shook it. "Thank you for everything."

"My pleasure." Lincoln placed a kiss on Hannah's cheek. "And I'll see *you* later."

⚜

Since Walt wanted to walk a bit before he got on the streetcar to head home, Hannah asked him to accompany her on a visit to the open-air market on Locust during lunch. She'd checked with Jo before leaving, filled her in on Lincoln's well-being, and requested an early lunch so she could see Walt off. Jo had told her to enjoy herself.

Walking beside Walt on the Mulberry Street sidewalk seemed strange. His gait was longer than Lincoln's, and when he took her elbow to step off the curb, his touch was foreign. Hannah glanced at her oldest friend. It was probably because he'd been locked in jail for the last month. She'd simply grown unaccustomed to his presence.

Four horse-drawn wagons were lined up in the vacant lot where the open-air market was held. Bushel baskets filled with spring produce lined the wagons.

"Do you know how good all of this looks after the food I had in jail?" Walt held up a handful of spinach. "Even this is tempting, and you know how much I like spinach." He wrinkled his nose.

She laughed. "Well, give it to me. I love it." She paid the farmer and put the fresh greens in her basket.

"What about Lincoln? Does he like spinach?" Walt stuffed his hands in his pockets.

Was Walt digging? She shrugged and added a generous amount of shell peas to her basket. "That hasn't come up."

He removed the basket from her arm. "He took me to his house to get cleaned up. It's really something."

"Yes, he's quite proud of it." How did she get him to end this line of questioning without being rude?

"He has expensive tastes. He's not like you and me." Walt picked up a small head of cauliflower and handed it to Hannah, brushing her hand in the process. "Even his washroom has a china sink, but you probably know that."

"I haven't seen his washroom, only the dining room and parlor for Charlotte's graduation dinner." She moved around to the other side of the wagon and selected a pint basket of strawberries. "He loves these. Maybe I should get two for when he comes over."

"Is he over at your house often?" A note of jealousy rang in his words.

"I guess you could say that."

Walt scowled. "You think that's wise? I mean, is it setting a good example for your sisters?"

Hannah shot him a glare. "We do nothing inappropriate. I thought you knew me better."

"I do know you. Probably better than you know yourself."

She found that hard to believe, but the sentiment brought a smile to her face anyway. Dear Walt. He did want her to be happy. As the awkwardness seemed to melt away between them, she found herself recalling some of her favorite times with Walt. Fishing at the pond. Getting caught stealing apples from the neighbor. Putting on *Romeo and Juliet* in school. Walt had made a horrible Romeo, and he kept complaining about Shakespeare not speaking plain English.

Hannah traced her lips with her finger. What kind of Romeo would Lincoln make? She had no doubt his "she doth teach the torches to burn bright" would make her weak in the knees.

After purchasing a pint of strawberries, she offered them to Walt. He popped a handful in his mouth and moaned. Strawberry juice trickled down his chin.

"You never could eat without making a mess." She laughed and dabbed at the corners of his lips with her handkerchief. "Let's go. That's all I can afford today."

Turning down Locust Street, she looked up at the Observatory Building. With a five-story tower on top of the ten-story building, it was the tallest office building in the city. She wondered if the view from the top was anything like the view from the state capitol.

She grabbed Walt's arm. "Let's go up there to the top."

"Why would we do that?"

"To see the view."

"It's the same view from a different angle."

She sighed and took her basket from him. Once Walt made up his mind about something, he seldom changed it—especially if he thought he was being sensible.

As she and Walt passed beneath the brightly colored storefront awnings, her thoughts wandered. Walt knew her based on who she was. Lincoln knew who she wanted to become. Walt was familiar, safe. Lincoln was fresh, a challenge. As much as she enjoyed spending time with Walt, right now her heart ached for Lincoln.

They crossed the street and stopped in front of the Savory Hotel. With its neoclassical cornices, it was her favorite hotel in the city. She peered in the window to see the hotel's plush lobby. Behind her, the clopping of horses' hooves on the paved brick street blended with the sound of someone's automobile. Would automobiles someday outnumber carriages?

Walt placed his hands on her shoulders. "Hannah, I need to tell you something."

She turned, and the look in his eyes made her nerves tingle. "What is it?"

"I had a lot of time to think in jail, and I hope you know I have your best interests at heart."

Hannah stiffened. Nothing good came from a sentence prefaced by that.

He took her hand. "I think you're making a mistake with Lincoln Cole."

"That's none of your business." She yanked her hand away and marched down the sidewalk.

He fell in step beside her. "I know what you need better than anyone."

"No, I know what I need more than you do." She stopped at the corner where the streetcar would pick him up. "And for your information, he loves me and I love him."

"Then I'd say you have some deciding to do."

The streetcar approached, bell clanging. She held her basket in front of her like a barrier. "And why is that?"

"Because I love you too."

<hr/>

Dropping into a chair in the conference room at the courthouse, Lincoln crossed his ankle over his knee and adjusted his tie.

Pete looked up from the documents before him. "Did you get Cedric home okay? How serious were his injuries?"

"He got a pretty good knock on the head, but I think he'll live. He said his client reached for the bailiff's gun and fired the shot before they could subdue him." Lincoln drummed his fingers on the table. "After I took him home, I went to visit the fire marshal about the Grennen place."

"And?"

"He found something that indicated some sort of an infernal device."

Pete's brows tipped inward. "Consisting of what?"

Lincoln shrugged. "Dynamite, caps, and fuses, I suppose."

"But what triggered it?"

"He wasn't sure how it was triggered. The evidence probably exploded along with the porch." Lincoln leaned forward and placed his elbows on the table, clasping his hands in front of him. "I don't think there's any way this fire is related to the last ones, but the fire marshal feels they are because of the Western Union link."

"It's a pretty weak link this time too, but if you disagree with him and tell the detective, you'll be putting your client back in jail."

Lincoln nodded.

"It's a tough call. Are you going to tell Hannah about this?"

"There's no need, really, and there's nothing she could do except fret about Walt being arrested again."

"And she'll have enough to fret about soon enough." He chuckled. "Don't look so nervous. We got a telegram at the office this morning. Your aunt is coming for a visit."

38

"When will she be here? And did it say why she's coming?" Lincoln tapped a pencil against the tablet in front of him. Excitement rippled through him. Six months was a long time between visits with the woman he held so dear. How much time did he need to make arrangements for her stay?

"She'll be here in less than two weeks." Pete drew his hand down the length of his beard. "As for her reasons, I'm guessing she simply wants to check on you. Have you written to her about Hannah?"

Lincoln nodded. "I learned a long time ago not to keep secrets from Aunt Sam. She has an uncanny sense about such things."

"She's always been quite a character. If I had to hazard a guess, I think she's coming to meet your girl." Pete coughed. "What do you think she'll say about Hannah?"

"She'll probably be thrilled I'm finally interested in someone—even if Hannah doesn't fit the usual mold of a politician's wife."

"About that . . ."

"Listen, Pete, if you're going to try to talk me out of seeing her, then I don't want to hear it."

"No, no. That's not it." Pete waved his hand back and forth. "I've been thinking about your political future."

"And?"

"Are you sure it's what you want to do? I mean, you like to win."

"You think I'll lose?"

"Probably not. Since you're following in your father's footsteps, name recognition alone will most likely earn you the bid."

"I hear a 'but' coming."

Pete chuckled. "Politics isn't about winning. It's most often about compromise and forging relationships with people you may not even like. People like Cedric who have their own agendas for everything they do. You're not like that."

"Was my father?"

Pete nodded. "He played the game well."

"And you don't think I can?"

"Actually, I think you would learn to and do it exceptionally well, but I've been thinking a lot lately about the cost of living a lie—probably because of this fraud case I've been working on. I want you to think about whether this is what you're really meant to do. Maybe we've all pushed you toward it because of your father, but I want you to be true to who God made you to be and not compromise your values for anyone or anything." His eyes took on a far-off quality for a few seconds, then he slapped his hands onto his legs and stood. "End of lecture. Are you heading back to the office?"

Why was Pete bringing up the subject of living a lie? He'd never met a more honest man. But did he have a point? Had they all pushed Lincoln in the direction of politics? Lately he'd been questioning that calling, praying God would lead him to do what he wanted. But surely having a godly man in politics was a good thing.

"Yes, I'm heading back. I have an appeal to work on. You coming?"

"I want to finish up here." He picked up the top paper from the file. "Tell Hannah hi."

"Pete." He pressed his hand to his chest, feigning indignation. "She's working right now. It's impolite to bother a Hello Girl.'"

"But you're going to do it anyway."

He laughed. "Absolutely."

The small pork sandwich Hannah had quickly eaten before returning from her walk sat heavy in her stomach. She still had a few minutes remaining of her lunch break, so she poured herself a cup of coffee and washed down the dry bread. She breathed in the coffee's full-bodied roast and sighed. Should she tell Lincoln what Walt had told her? Since she didn't reciprocate Walt's feelings, did Lincoln even need to know?

She swallowed the last of her coffee and then rinsed the dregs from the bottom of the cup before returning to her station. Since it was now Jo's turn to go eat, she placed a hand on her shoulder. "Anything I should know about?"

"We're having a bit of noise on the lines. I'm wondering if the gunshot hit something upstairs. I'll have to put in a repair call today if there's been damage. Can you be a dear and check the lines when you have the time?"

"Certainly." She slipped into place and adjusted her headset. "Did you hear who was injured?"

Jo chuckled. "Well, if I did, I still couldn't tell you. Confidentiality, remember?"

"Yes, ma'am, of course."

Jo pinned her hat in place. "I'm headed to the café. Would you like me to bring you back a slice of pie?"

"No thanks. Enjoy your lunch." Hannah waved goodbye and turned toward the switchboard to connect a call.

As if he'd been watching, Lincoln appeared at the switchboard office's Dutch door a few minutes after Jo left. His dove-blue eyes twinkled as he threatened to sneak inside and remind Hannah of how much he loved her.

"You do and I'll lock the top half of that door too."

He chuckled. "I've got two surprises for you after work."

She flashed him a smile. "That will make three in one day. I don't know if I can handle so many surprises."

"I'm sure you'll manage." He slapped the doorjamb with his hand. "See you after work."

A steady volume of calls prevented Hannah from doing the line check Jo had requested. Finally, things slowed down. She started at the top of her switchboard, inserted the plug, and listened for any clicking sounds. Hearing none, she rang the number.

"Hello," a deep voice answered on the other end of the line.

"This is the switchboard operator. Is your phone working properly?"

"Can't you tell for yourself?"

She forced a smile into her voice. "Thank you for your time."

After pulling the plug on that call, she made her way down the first row on her switchboard. If a line was in use, she inserted her plug anyway and listened for less than a minute—not to the conversation but for crackling and popping on the line. In between placing other calls, she jotted down a couple of lines that warranted reporting.

She inserted her plug into the first hole on the third row. It belonged to an upstairs conference room—not far from the gunshot-plagued courtroom—where attorneys could meet with their clients or with other lawyers. Already in use, she listened in on the call. Faint static on the line. Was it enough to report?

Covering her earpiece with her hand, she listened harder.

"Elise, sweetheart, please don't trouble yourself about this."

Oh my. She recognized Pete Williams's voice. Should she disconnect the call? But she wanted to get the task completed before Jo returned, and she only needed a few more seconds to determine if repairs might be needed.

"But what if he is involved?" Elise's voice was high-pitched. "I can't stop thinking of that poor family and those flames. You know his history."

Who was she talking about? Did Elise suspect someone of starting the fires?

"He's better now, so put your worries to rest, sweetheart," Pete crooned. "His time in Germany cured him. You said so yourself."

Heart pounding, she pulled the plug. Did Elise suspect her own son? Could Albert have started the fire at the Grennens'?

She shook her head. Surely not. Like Pete said, he'd been healed.

Besides, if Pete suspected his son, as an officer of the court, he'd have to report him. But Pete loved his wife dearly, and Lincoln had said she struggled with melancholy. Would his fear of sending her into a blue period keep him from revealing the truth?

Without thinking, Hannah connected the next call that came in. She needed to finish checking the lines, but she couldn't dismiss what she'd heard. If Pete was hiding Albert's role in the fires, Lincoln would be crushed. Maybe Lincoln could speak to Pete and get a better feeling on the matter.

She sucked in a breath. She couldn't do that. What she happened to overhear was confidential. Even Jo couldn't be told.

But what if Albert was the arsonist and he set another fire?

Her chest felt as if someone had pulled her corset strings taut. She pressed a trembling hand to her middle. Maybe this was one time when that rule should be broken—just in case. But if she said anything, she could lose her position entirely. Could she do that to her sisters?

<hr/>

The Reo rumbled around the corner, and Lincoln cast another glance at Hannah. Unusually quiet since he'd picked her up, she seemed to be lost in thought. Although she claimed nothing was bothering her, he didn't believe her.

Perhaps returning home to a disgruntled Charlotte was troubling her. The three Gregory girls had a bond that defied explanation. Maybe his surprises would take her mind off that whole situation.

They passed Schlampp's Jewelry Store. He pulled to the curb and parked the automobile. Hannah jerked as if she'd awakened from a dream.

He helped her step down onto the curb. "Ready for your first surprise?"

She glanced at the jewelry store, her eyes wide, and he had to bite back a chuckle. With his hands on her shoulders, he turned her toward the store next door. "That's where we're headed."

"Anthony's Cycle Company? Why are we going there?"

"You'll see."

The bell jingled as they entered, and the owner greeted them. "Mr. Cole, glad you made it. I have your purchase all ready to go."

Hannah tipped her head to the side. "You're purchasing a bicycle?"

"I am."

"I didn't know you were a wheelman."

"I'm not."

The owner wheeled out the bicycle and placed it in front of Hannah. "Hope you enjoy it, ma'am."

Her breath caught, and she looked at Lincoln. "You know I can't accept this."

"The fact is you only own one-third of the bicycle, but it will be hard to return your third because your sisters own the other two-thirds. Charlotte's going to need it if she gets a position until she goes away to school, and if I know Tessa, you won't be able to convince her to give her part back, so I guess you're stuck with it."

A low chuckle came from the owner.

Hannah leaned close, and her breath tickled his ear. "It's too much. It isn't proper."

"You need it if you're going to do me the favor I have yet to ask you." He ran his hand down the length of her arm. "Please, Hannah. I want you to have it so you can fly."

39

Hannah blinked and bit her lip. Did Lincoln realize how much she'd wanted to ride a bicycle? She'd never mentioned it before, but she'd longed to try it.

After glancing from him to the bicycle, she ran her hand along the handlebars with a tender caress. The metal was cool beneath her fingertips.

Still, should she accept this gift? Lincoln liked to win, and he made an excellent case with her only owning a third of it.

She glanced into his hopeful eyes and smiled. "Well, if I need it to do you a favor, then I guess it would be all right. How do we get it home?"

The shop owner chuckled again. "Most folks ride it."

Her eyebrows shot up. "I—I've never—I don't think I could—"

"Relax." Lincoln gripped the handlebars. "I think we can rig it onto the Reo."

A half hour later, Lincoln tugged the ropes free and lifted the bike from the back of the Reo. Charlotte and Tessa had joined them as soon as they'd arrived, and both cheered when Lincoln told them the bicycle was a gift for the three of them. She'd never be able to give it back now.

He set it on the ground, keeping a firm grip on the handlebars. "Ready to try this out?"

Hannah pressed her knuckle to her lips. Everything inside her wanted to leap on the bicycle, but it was such a big gift.

He patted the seat. "Afraid?"

"No, of course not." She tried to keep the bravado in her voice. It was mostly true, but an inkling of fear might be making her question the wisdom of this decision. As much as she liked taking chances, the idea of making a fool of herself in front of Lincoln was disconcerting.

"I think you're scared." His eyebrows arched in a dare.

Tessa stepped forward and tipped her chin upward. "I'm not. I'll ride it."

Charlotte tugged her back. "Hannah gets to go first. Then me."

"Why am I last?" A crease formed between Tessa's brows.

"Age order. It's the, uh, bicyclist way." Charlotte gave her a definitive nod, settling the argument.

Tessa turned to Lincoln and held out her palms. "But Hannah's afraid to get on."

"I am not." Hiking up her walking skirt, Hannah slid into place and gripped the handlebars.

"That's my girl." A wide grin split Lincoln's face. "And I'll hold on to the seat until you get going. I wouldn't want you to take a spill."

She nodded. "How do I stop?"

"Put your feet down or pedal backward." He kissed her cheek. "You're going to love this."

After checking the placement of her slick-soled shoes on the pedals, she began to press the pedals downward. Only when she started moving did she become aware of Lincoln gripping the seat behind her. Her cheeks heated, and it wasn't from the effort she was putting forth.

"Concentrate." He ran along beside her.

Did the man realize how hard that was to do, given the placement of his hand? She should ask him to remove it, but if she did, she'd fall for certain.

Focus.

The bicycle wobbled, but he held it steady. "Pedal faster. You need more speed."

She pushed harder and felt the bicycle respond beneath her. She concentrated on her balance and keeping the bicycle steady.

"Hannah, you're doing it!"

Lincoln's voice came from a distance. She was riding it! When had that happened? The wind whipped her hair about her cheeks and filled her skirt, and she didn't want to stop. She wasn't even sure she could.

With her heart pounding against the stays of her corset, she pressed on—in control, free, and breathless. Lincoln was right. She was almost flying.

∽⌒⌒∽

Lincoln's heart swelled as he watched Hannah master the conveyance. He'd stopped holding on when he was certain she had the hang of riding it. Now she giggled like a schoolgirl as she drove down the center of the street.

Her speed slowed, and the two-wheeler wobbled. She lost her balance, and the bicycle toppled to the side.

Jogging down to meet her, he fought his concerns when she didn't try to get up right away. Was she injured?

He stopped in front of her and lifted off the velocipede. "Are you hurt?"

"No." She laughed, her chest heaving. She accepted the hand he offered. "That was amazing!"

"I'm glad you feel that way." He started to walk the two-wheeler back toward her house, and Hannah walked beside him. "It makes it easier to ask my favor."

"You mean you really do have a favor to ask? It wasn't a ruse to get me to try the bicycle?"

"'Fraid not." He paused in front of Rosie's house. Mrs. Murphy waved from the porch, where she sat sipping lemonade. "You see, my Aunt Sam is coming to town, and she's an avid cyclist. I'm hoping you'll accompany her on her rides."

"Your aunt from Saint Paul? The one who raised you?"

Taking her hand, he smiled. "Don't look like a scared bunny ready to bolt for the bushes. She's going to love you."

"I find that quite unlikely. Have you considered that someone of your aunt's social standing may not approve of a young woman like me? Most wealthy ladies don't spend much time with any Hello Girls, and they don't expect their sons—or nephews—to either."

"Aunt Sam isn't like most ladies. You'll see."

"When will she be here?"

He flashed her a roguish grin. "Stop fretting."

"I'm not fretting."

"Tight smile. Worry lines around your eyes. Yes, Hannah, you're fretting." He glanced toward her sisters and chuckled. "And you're so absorbed in your own thoughts, you missed Tessa yelling at us to hurry up. But before we head back to them, I want you to know I'm more worried about what you'll think of her than the other way around."

"Why is that?"

"You'll see soon enough. She'll be here on Friday the twelfth."

⁂

"At least Charlotte's speaking to you again." Seated on the porch swing, Lincoln draped his arm around Hannah and toyed with the hair at the back of her neck. The whiff of peonies from the neighbor's yard floated on the warm breeze, and fireflies flickered in the bushes. Only a dim lamp glowed inside the house.

"If you count 'please pass the butter' as meaningful conversation, then I guess I can agree with you."

"She'll get over it soon. Besides, I'm the one who told him to take the two-week break."

"But she *likes* you."

"Of course she does. I'm a very likable fellow." He drew circles on the back of her neck. She shuddered beneath his caresses, and he smiled. "Don't you agree?"

"Most of the time."

He loved the teasing sound of her chocolaty voice. "So, are you going to tell me what was troubling you earlier today after work? Did something happen with Walt?"

She stiffened beside him ever so slightly. "Lincoln, tell me about Albert."

Changing the subject. Not a good sign, but he'd indulge her. "I've told you about him. Pete and Elise had him later in life, so he's about your age. He's quite intelligent, as you heard, and he plans to return to Yale in the fall."

"But why did he leave there in the first place?"

Lincoln swallowed hard. The last thing he wanted to do was scare Hannah, and Albert was a bit of a frightening character when one knew the whole story. "You remember I told you Elise suffers from melancholy, right?"

"Yes."

"It seems that Albert does as well. Only when he gets down, he sometimes makes poor choices."

"Such as?"

He sighed. Of course Hannah wouldn't let him off that easily, but he didn't have to tell her the whole truth. The two of them would be spending a lot of time at Pete and Elise's, given where their relationship was headed. "He did a little damage at the college and threatened some people." He cupped her shoulder and tucked her close. "So why all the interest in Albert? Do I have competition?"

"No, not in the least." She laughed, and her skirts swished in rhythm with the swing.

"Then, a new subject. Let's talk about your day."

She glanced at him and smiled. "I'd rather talk about you."

"Me?"

"Seeing Tessa and Charlotte both learning to ride the bicycle today was such a joy. I don't know if I've told you how much I appreciate the way you treat them, almost like . . ."

She didn't finish her sentence. Was she afraid to imply too much? Why did she always seem to have doubts or fears in the back of her mind? True, he'd not made any verbal promises or asked for her hand, but sometime between taking their farm and taking them to a Memorial Day outing, Hannah's family had become his own.

"I treat them like family because they are."

He heard a little gasp from Hannah. Unable to keep from taking advantage of her parted lips, he claimed them and kissed her, hoping to chase every doubt, worry, and fear from her heart and mind.

40

After once again checking the cast-iron mailbox in their front yard, Charlotte slammed the tiny door. It had been a week. Why hadn't George written her?

She dropped onto the porch steps, crossed her arms over her knees, and buried her head. It was all Hannah's fault. If she hadn't interfered, then everything with George would be fine. And Lincoln—what right did he have to tell George not to come around for two weeks?

The screen door rattled, and Charlotte heard Tessa step onto the porch.

"Not again." Tessa groaned and plopped onto the swing. The chain rattled, and then the familiar *squeak*, *squeak* of swinging began. "So, what do you want to do today?"

"Nothing."

"You know what I think?" Tessa paused, then continued when Charlotte didn't respond. "I think you're the luckiest girl on earth."

Charlotte lifted her head. "And how do you figure that?"

"Georgie Porgie doesn't care about you as much as he cares about having you. At least you're seeing him for who he is now rather than later."

"Excuse me?"

"Think about it. He likes having you on his arm, but does he care about what makes you *you*?"

Charlotte scowled. What did Tessa know? She was only four-teen years old, and she was hardly an expert on relationships. "He cares."

"How do you know?" Tessa pushed off the porch floorboards and made the swing go higher. "You've seen what real love looks like. It's buying a bicycle so your girl can fly. It's treating her sisters like they're your own. It's not letting a day go by without making her smile. I may be fourteen, but I've got eyes. When has George ever put what you want before what he wants?"

Charlotte's mind whirled, seeking an answer. It was a simple question, so why couldn't she come up with an answer? He walked her home every day. They talked about his day. He told her he wanted her with him, by his side, but none of that answered Tessa's question.

The slow burn at finding the mailbox empty flamed. Why hadn't he written? She could use that as proof he cared. She could show the letter to Tessa and say, "See? This is why."

But she didn't have a letter.

"You're too young to understand. You're just a baby." The words, like acid on her tongue, sliced at her sister.

"I'm not a baby, and at least I can see George for what he is. You're the one who's being a baby. It's like he pulled you in and kept criticizing you and changing you until you didn't know who you were anymore. 'Charlotte, come here.'" Her voice took on a singsong quality to mimic George. "'Charlotte, I hate it when you make me wait.' 'Charlotte, stay. I don't want you to go.'" She jumped off the swing. "And what did you do? Followed along like Georgie Porgie's puppy."

"I am not his puppy."

"Oh really? When was the last time you did what you wanted to do?" She opened the screen door. "Like I said before, love makes you stupid, and you're all the proof I need."

The screen door banged shut, and emotions somersaulted through Charlotte. Anger mixed with pain and humiliation. Tears burned her eyes. Had she been blind to the truth? Had she wanted George's affections so much she'd only seen what she wanted to see?

Lord, please help me see the truth.

⁓⁓◦◯◦⁓⁓

Hannah leaned the bicycle against the rack and hurried inside the courthouse. In the last week, she'd become quite accustomed to using the bicycle instead of walking the short distance to work. When Charlotte secured a position, she'd probably relinquish the two-wheeler to her, but in the meantime, she needed to learn to ride well enough to ride with Lincoln's aunt.

"Good morning, Jo." Hannah removed her hat and placed it on the hook. "Anything new?"

"There was another fire last night."

Hannah gasped. "Where?"

"Outside of town." She paused to connect a call. "Mr. Cole stopped in to tell you about it. He said he'd stop by later."

Hannah took her seat at the switchboard, and her fingers trembled as she adjusted the headset over her ear. What if Albert had been involved? Could she have prevented this fire by saying something? She shook her head. No, Lincoln said he'd done a little damage, not that he'd started any fires. If he were concerned about Albert, he would have said something.

Jo pointed to a light on Hannah's switchboard. "Aren't you going to answer that?"

Hannah startled. "Oh yes. I'm sorry." She inserted the plug into the jack. "Number, please."

The man barked out the number, and Hannah tried to respond as sweetly as possible. "Three-eight-five. Thank you." When she touched the tip of the circuit plug to the jack, she heard a sharp click. She returned to her caller. "I'm sorry, sir, that number is busy. Please try again later."

He let out a string of rude words. Hannah fought to contain herself. "Sir, I'll be forced to report you to my supervisor if you don't calm down."

"I am calm. Just keep your shirt on."

"Well, I never . . ." She disconnected the call and took a deep breath.

Jo touched her arm. "Did you get a rude one? What did he say?"

Doing her best to relay the gist of the conversation without repeating the colorful language, Hannah told Jo what the man had said.

"That young man needs to learn some manners. What caller was it?"

Hannah showed Jo the number and then watched her supervisor insert her seldom-used special plug into the top of Hannah's switchboard and ring up the young man.

"Sir," Jo said, "this is the chief operator at the courthouse. On behalf of my operator, I must demand you apologize to her immediately, or I shall have your telephone removed."

She indicated Hannah should connect to the line. "Hello."

"Are you the girl I told to keep her shirt on?" His voice had softened, and he seemed contrite.

"Yes, sir, I am the one."

"Well, I'm sorry," he mumbled, obviously flustered. "You can take it off now."

Hannah glanced at Jo as they shared a knowing grin. Laughter threatened to explode, so she hurried to disconnect the call. As soon as she had, the two of them collapsed into a fit of giggles.

Hannah wiped the tears from her eyes. "You scared the poor man so badly, I don't think he knew what he was saying."

A rap on the doorjamb drew their attention. Lincoln leaned over the Dutch door. "What's going on in here?"

"Just a man telling Hannah to keep—"

"Jo! You can't tell him that." Hannah's cheeks burned under Lincoln's amused gaze.

"If I need to go defend your honor, I should at least know why."

Jo waved her hand in a dismissive motion and giggled. "You can put your sword away. I took care of the insult." She turned to Hannah. "Go have a word with Boaz. I'll handle the switchboard."

Hannah nodded and moved to meet Lincoln at the Dutch door. "Boaz?"

"It's a long story."

"I think it's one I'd like to hear." His dove-blue eyes bore into hers as if they alone could extract the information.

"And I think I might tell you someday, but not today." She flashed him a cheeky grin before slipping her headset off and setting it on the flat surface of the Dutch door. After patting her hair to make sure she'd not mussed it, she asked, "What brings you here?"

He stared at the headset. "Perhaps what I came to tell you can wait until you get off. You're having such a pleasant day."

"Don't coddle me." She stiffened her backbone. "You came down here for a reason. What is it?"

"There was another fire."

"I know that. Jo told me. She said it was outside of town."

"At a Western Union repair shed." He swallowed. "On Walt's old line."

Her breath caught.

"He's been arrested again."

"Oh, Lincoln, please tell me he has an alibi."

He raked his hand through his hair. "He does. Until his parents went to bed. The trouble is the fire began in the middle of the night."

"You believe him, don't you?"

He nodded. "Yes, but the prosecutor will argue he could have snuck out and tossed the dynamite."

She cocked her head. "Dynamite again? Walt's never used dynamite. His dad doesn't even use it to remove stumps like some farmers. He had a brother who was killed with the explosive and refused to keep it around. So why would Walt have it, and where would he get it?"

Rubbing his jaw, Lincoln smiled. "It bears looking into."

"So you'll do it right away?"

He took her hand. "The senior partners aren't sold on me taking his case again."

"Pete too?"

He nodded. "I'm afraid so."

"Oh."

"Don't worry. I'm going to do it anyway, Hannah, but I won't be able to work on it during the day like I did before. What we need is the name of the person he thinks is doing this." He cupped her cheek, brushing his thumb over her skin. "Try not to worry. We'll go see him later tonight."

"No, I'll go see him before I go home." When Lincoln frowned, she added, "I think I can get him to talk to me if we're alone."

Reluctantly, Lincoln agreed. After arranging to meet for dinner at her home, he reminded her to pray about Walt's defense. He squeezed her hand and departed.

She watched him go, his broad, square shoulders not bending beneath the burden he carried for her and for Walt.

Someone was starting these fires, and if it wasn't Walt, was it Albert?

Even though she wasn't sure how to do it, one way or another, she had to uncover the truth.

❧❧❀❧❧

The dampness of the jail crept beneath the sleeves of Hannah's shirtwaist, making her skin prickle. She longed to pinch her nose and shut out the odor of unwashed bodies and musty brick walls that mingled in the air. The jailer didn't seem to notice. Did one get used to such a stench?

Since she was alone, the jailer insisted she remain outside of Walt's cell to speak to him. Only because the jailer knew she was working with Lincoln did he even allow her that far. She considered making a fuss but decided that perhaps it was better she remain in the hallway.

As she made her way down the aisle between the cells, she kept her eyes focused on the jailer in front of her, despite the whistles and the requests for her to stop and visit. She sent up a silent prayer on behalf of these men. God knew what they needed even if she did not.

Walt met her at the bars. "You shouldn't be here alone. Where's Lincoln?"

"He couldn't come today." Her hands ached to hold his, but after his declaration, she didn't want to encourage him. "But I had to see you because I have something I need to ask you."

A smile flitted across his face, then vanished. "Me first."

Nerves tingled inside her. Why hadn't she prepared an answer to the question she knew he'd ask?

She licked her dry lips. "All right."

"Have you thought about what I said?"

She studied his expression. Cautious expectation flickered in his eyes. She hated to dash his hopes—especially here, especially now. Still, was it fair not to tell him the truth? If Brother Molden was right about love demanding tough choices, this had to be one of the hardest.

"You don't need to say anything." He clenched his jaw, betrayal lacing his words. "I've known you long enough to read the answer on your face."

"I do care about you, but I—"

"Love him." He forced a smile. "I know."

"I'm sorry."

"Don't say that." He gripped the bars so hard his knuckles whitened. "You should never be sorry for loving someone, and I want you to be happy."

"And you deserve to be free." She swallowed hard. "Now, answer my question. I know you feel like you have to be loyal to your fellow union members, but this man is starting fires all over the city. Will you please tell me who you think is most likely the guilty party?"

"I won't betray those men. I understand what it means to be loyal."

The barb stung, but their dear friendship forced her to focus on the situation at hand. "There's no one who is more loyal than you, but whoever this is, he has no trouble betraying you." She stepped closer. "Good grief, Walt, he started a fire on your old line. He wants this pinned on you."

Stepping back from the bars, Walt paced the room, rubbing the back of his neck. Pressing him had never done any good, so she gave him space to sort through the decision.

Finally, he dropped his hand to his side and approached her. "His name is Donnelly. Joe Donnelly," he whispered. "He's one of the blacklisted men. He works at the quarry now."

Hannah's knees jellied, and she reached for the cold, iron bars to steady herself. What if this was George's father?

Taking a deep breath, she ran a finger along the neck of her shirtwaist and smiled at Walt. "Thank you. I'll check into it."

"Let Lincoln take care of this. That man's a hothead." He narrowed his eyes. "I mean it, Hannah."

"Do you honestly believe I'd interrogate a suspected arsonist all by myself?" She laughed lightly. He did know her well.

"I wouldn't put it past you." He reached through the bars and grabbed her wrist. "Promise me you'll let Lincoln know his name."

His fingers dug into her arm. "I will. I promise."

She'd tell Lincoln as soon as she saw him, but first she needed to know if Joe Donnelly was George's father, and there was only one way to find that out.

41

Uneven paved bricks bounced Hannah's bicycle. One call to the information operator at central had given her Joe Donnelly's address, and she hadn't hesitated to search out the home despite its questionable location near the tracks. Donnelly was a fairly common name, so the man may have nothing to do with George. But for Charlotte's sake, she had to find out. If George's father was somehow mixed up in all of these fires, did George know? What if he, too, was involved?

A barking dog ran out in front of her, and she swerved to miss him. A couple of towheaded children with dirty faces stared at her two-wheeler. Maybe they'd never before seen a bicycle in their neighborhood.

If Lincoln knew where she was, he'd not be happy, and she didn't really blame him. For his own good, she had to do this. If she could attach this Joe to the fires, then she could also dismiss her fears about Albert. How would Lincoln feel if he knew Pete had kept the truth from him about Albert?

Hannah wasn't blindly headed to the Donnelly address. From the time she'd left work until she'd gotten home to check on her sisters, she'd considered the possibility of Joe being the arsonist, and the fact that she was an unmarried woman visiting a man. She could easily pass off the visit if George were indeed the son. All she had to do was say she was checking on the young man since he'd not written Charlotte. But what would she use for an excuse if George wasn't there?

Hannah turned the corner and located the Donnelly house. The wood-sided house, in need of a fresh coat of paint, was flanked by two small but tidy homes. Unlike the other two houses beside it, the Donnelly home lacked any flowers to decorate the stoop.

After leaning the bicycle against the iron mailbox, she hurried up the walk before she lost her nerve. She raised her hand to knock on the door but heard giggling around the side of the house. If the man's daughters were there, then she'd have her answer that this wasn't George's father. She stepped off the stoop and peeked around the corner.

Her cheeks warmed at the sight of a young man and young woman in an embrace. The girl spotted her and jumped away, her face filled with color. The young man whirled in Hannah's direction.

She gasped. "George!"

"What are you doing here?" He stepped between Hannah and the girl as if he could shield her presence with his body. "Libby, go on home. We'll talk later."

The girl dashed away like a frightened deer.

George glared at her. "Like I said, why are you here?"

Eyeing the departing young woman, she said, "I might ask you the same thing."

"It's your fault. Yours and Mr. Cole's. If you'd let me see Charlotte, none of this would have happened."

"You couldn't remain faithful to her for two weeks, and that is our fault?" Hannah's voice grew louder. "She's pining away for you, and you're out kissing other girls in the bushes?"

"What's all the commotion?" a man bellowed behind her.

Hannah turned to face Joe Donnelly. Her pulse raced. The man's size dwarfed hers. He had to be well over six feet tall, and his arms were the size of railroad ties. As if his bulk wasn't intimidating enough, he crossed his arms over his chest and scowled disdainfully at her.

Hannah refused to be bullied, and she knew better than to air George's indiscretion first thing. She straightened her shoulders and smiled. "You must be George's father."

He grabbed George's arm and yanked him to his side. "Whatever the boy's done, I'll take care of it with my belt."

"No, sir. You misunderstand my presence. I'm Charlotte's sister, Hannah Gregory."

"I don't know no Charlotte."

"Well, your son does. He's been courting her for a couple of months."

"Has he now?" His frown deepened. "And when were you going to tell me you been out sparkin'?"

"I don't think he'll be seeing her anymore." She paused and looked at George. Her heart squeezed for the young man and his situation, but she couldn't let Charlotte continue associating with someone so untrustworthy. "I came to tell him that."

"You said it. Now you can be gone." Mr. Donnelly stepped aside and motioned toward the street.

Should she ask him about the fires or about the union problem? As it was, she'd received the answer she came for, but the opportunity to find out more dug at her.

She waited until she was several feet away to turn and ask her final question. "Mr. Donnelly, did you by chance work at the Western Union?"

"Yeah, why?"

"I'm friends with Walt Calloway. Your name sounded familiar. I believe he's mentioned you. Do you know he's in jail for some fires related to Western Union?"

George's eyes became as wide as pie plates, and Mr. Donnelly launched into a tirade about the company who'd treated him so unfairly.

More than once, Hannah almost ducked as he swung his massive arms about. "Given the events of late, I imagine a disgruntled employee might draw the attention of the investigators. Have you been questioned?"

In one stride, he stepped so close she was within arm's reach. He glared down at her. "Are you accusing me?"

"No, sir, why would I do that? Walt's the one who's been charged."

"Good, 'cause he's the one who did it." He motioned with his hand. "Go on. Git out of here and leave us be."

Hannah hurried to her bicycle and turned it toward the path.

George stepped in her way. "You best keep your mouth shut, Hannah, and not stir up any trouble, if you know what's good for you."

"Are you speaking for yourself or your father?"

He looked back toward his father and then at her. "Both."

She mounted the velocipede. "In case you haven't noticed, George, keeping my mouth shut isn't one of my strong suits."

"Charlotte won't believe you even if you tell her about me."

She gave a wry laugh. "We'll see about that."

❧❦❧

Where was Hannah?

Lincoln walked to the end of the block and looked both directions. An uneasy feeling tugged at him. When he'd arrived around six, Charlotte had told him Hannah had taken the bicycle about an hour earlier, saying she had an errand to run. She'd never been late to any of their planned activities before, so what was keeping her now? Did she have an accident on the bicycle somewhere? He could go look for her, but where would he start?

A dot in the distance appeared and took shape. She rode in his direction, and the closer she came, the more he relaxed. She'd probably lost track of time while shopping, or her errand took longer than she'd planned.

She pulled up beside him and stopped. "Is it supper time already? What are you doing all the way down the block from the house?"

"Looking for you." He cocked his head to the side. "I was getting worried. Is everything all right?"

"Yes and no." She dismounted and glanced toward the house. "Can we talk about it after supper? I'm sure the girls are starving."

Everything in Lincoln wanted to make her stay and explain what she meant, but he kept reminding himself that love is patient. He took the two-wheeler from her to push it home while they walked.

"Did you see Walt?" he asked.

"I did."

"And?"

"That's what we need to talk about."

Even though Charlotte had made a delicious supper of chicken and dumplings, spinach, and strawberries for dessert, Lincoln scarcely thought of what he was eating. The possibilities Hannah had implied kept tumbling in his mind.

He prayed Walt had given her a name. Although Lincoln hadn't said anything, he had other fears about whom it might be. He'd considered sharing his concerns with Hannah but decided he didn't want to frighten her with doubtful possibilities.

Ever since their night at the Williamses' home, he'd been second-guessing the fire. Both Cedric and Albert had departed before the fire started, and given Albert's history, anything was possible. He pushed the thought aside. If Pete was concerned about Albert's involvement, he'd say something, and Pete knew his son better than anyone.

After washing up the supper dishes, Lincoln suggested he and Hannah go for a drive. Once they reached Ingersoll Park, he took her hand and directed her down the path leading to the lake. They walked in silence for several minutes.

When they reached the lake, he drew her toward the white bridge that spanned the still, blue waters. Their shoes clattered against the bridge's wooden slats, the only noise save the honking of some geese nearby.

"You've kept me in suspense long enough, I think," Lincoln said. They stopped beneath a latticed cover at the center of the bridge, and he turned to her. "What did Walt tell you? Did he give you a name?"

"He did." Tears filled her eyes.

Lincoln's heart stuttered. "Hannah, who is it?"

"One of the men who'd been blacklisted by Western Union—Joe Donnelly."

"And?" He kept his voice calm, as he'd learned to do when a reluctant witness was on the stand. But why did this upset her to the point of tears?

"He's George's father."

"There are other Donnellys in the city. Are you sure?"

She nodded and turned toward the lake. Placing her hands on the railing, she stared out an arched window in the bridge's covering. "I know because I went to his house and checked."

"You went there? Alone?" A vice gripped his chest. How could Hannah do something so dangerous? His voice rose. "He could be the arsonist. What were you thinking?"

"For Charlotte's sake, I had to know if he was related to George." She let go of the railing and crossed her arms over her chest.

"And you didn't think I would go to his house to find out if it was George's father, or even that we could go there together?" His chest heaved, and he struck the railing with his fist. The lattice overhead vibrated. "No, of course you didn't think that, because you're so all-fired determined to do it all on your own. Like always. When are you going to realize you're not on your own anymore? How are we ever going to have a relationship if you keep living as if I'm not there for you?"

"You're blowing this out of proportion."

"Am I?" He held her shoulders. "Don't you realize the kind of danger you put yourself in? If he's the arsonist, he likes to blow things up for fun, and now he knows you suspect him."

She turned, lips drawn tight like the strings of a purse. "I'm not ignorant. I let Mr. Donnelly believe I was there because of Charlotte and George's relationship."

"Then you said nothing about the fires?"

"I only asked if he once worked for Western Union, as Walt had said he did, and pointed out that a disgruntled former employee might draw some attention in a case like this."

"You didn't." He rubbed his aching temple. "Hannah, you might as well have accused the man."

She stiffened. "But I didn't accuse him."

"Then what did he say?"

"He said Walt was guilty." With steely determination, she met his gaze. "And he suggested I leave."

"That's all?" He narrowed his eyes. Hannah was hiding something. "Did George add anything?"

Her eyes flicked downward, then back at him. "He might have told me to keep my mouth shut—but I believe he was mostly referring to what I'd seen involving him and not the fires."

"What are you talking about?"

"When I arrived." Her cheeks reddened. "I found him kissing a girl outside the house."

"The cad." He rubbed his collarbone, his breath coming quick. "The sooner he's out of Charlotte's life, the better." Never before had Lincoln wanted to tear something apart with his bare hands as much as he did at this moment. He needed the facts, and he needed to get them now. He knew only one way to do that.

"So." He assumed his courtroom persona. "Let me get this straight. After weeks of Walt refusing to give us the name of the man he believes might be setting the fires, you got him to finally disclose it. Then, without telling anyone—especially me, his attorney and the man who loves you—where you were going, you found the man's address and went there, only to discover that his son, who's been seeing your sister, was kissing another girl."

She started to speak, but he held up his hand. "Then, instead of simply leaving, not only did you let the suspected arsonist know that you are friends with the man who's accused of setting the fires, but you also made sure he was aware he'd make an excellent suspect."

His mouth rigid, his jaw flexing, he went on. "And I'm taking a wild guess here, but when George told you to keep your mouth shut, he did mean both about his dad and about his little kissing scene, and you let him know you had no intention of being quiet about either. Would you say that was an accurate summary?"

She flinched, then squared her shoulders. "Don't make it sound like I'm on trial."

His voice, hard as steel, grew louder. Anger tinted his words. "I'll do what I want. You certainly do."

If her glare could start a fire, he'd be ablaze.

Let her be mad. Let her stew about it. It served her right.

Love is patient. Love is kind.

The words hit him again. Obviously, Paul hadn't dealt with a Hannah Gregory before he wrote that.

He drew in a long breath and released it slowly. When he spoke, he forced his voice to come out softer. "Why didn't you let me take you? Then we could have gone to talk to him together."

"You wouldn't have let me go with you to talk to him if I'd spoken to you first, and we both know it."

He rubbed the back of his neck. She wasn't making this easy. "But Hannah, don't you see what you've done? You've given him a warning. If there's any evidence at his home linking him to the crime, he'll know to destroy it now, and if he is questioned or arrested, he'll be pointing his dynamite-holding fingers right at you."

She blinked, and her voice grew quiet. "I didn't think about that." Her chin quivered, and she covered it with her hand. "George knows where we live. If something happens to Charlotte or Tess—"

He drew her into his arms and tucked her head against his shoulder. "Shhh. We'll figure this out. You're right, I wouldn't have let you go, and then we'd not have learned about George and the other girl. That's important too, but we've got to learn to trust each other."

"I know," she mumbled into his shirt. "What if he comes to the house?"

"It'll be okay. I don't think he'd do anything to hurt you or the girls, but I wanted you to see how much danger you put yourself in."

She tipped her head up toward his, her hazel eyes awash in tears. "I'm sorry. I should have come to you."

"Do you like my hair?"

"What?" She tilted her head to the side, revealing her creamy neck. "Why are you asking that now?"

"Do you?"

"Yes, very much."

"Good. Next time you think of going off all by yourself on some tangent, think how my nice head of brown hair will be turning gray if you don't stop scaring me."

Her lips curled in a genuine smile. She lifted her hand and touched the hair at his temple. "I think I'd like you gray too."

He captured her hand in his and kissed the fingertips. "And if I have my way, someday you'll get to find out if you do."

A look that gave Lincoln goose bumps crossed Hannah's face. She moistened her lips with the tip of her tongue, and he could no more keep from kissing her than keep her from taking chances. His lips claimed hers in a hot, velvety moment. Could she feel his love? Did she realize he'd do anything to protect her? Would she ever trust him with that corner of her heart just beyond his grasp?

He wrapped his hands around her waist, drawing her closer, letting his lips say what his words could not. He dotted kisses on her jawline, and she tipped her head, giving him access to her neck. His lips moved restlessly across her neck, and he felt her body shudder against him.

Drawing on every ounce of self-control, he cupped her face in his hands and pulled away. Her flushed face and swollen lips made him want to take her in his arms all over again, every day, for the rest of his life.

She looked bewildered at the loss of his kisses. Lincoln smiled. Hannah had no idea what she stirred in him.

He touched his lips to her forehead and drew her against his chest. The almond scent of her maple-syrup-colored hair reached him. Gently moving his thumb, he drew circles on the back of her neck.

When had she won his heart? That first day they met, when she so bravely spoke to him? When she came to ask for help for her friend? When she pulled him into the lake?

It wasn't one moment. It was a hundred little ones. And he hoped there'd be a lifetime more to come.

42

Another kiss at the door left Hannah breathless. She entered the house, closed the door, and leaned against the solid wood. She pressed two fingers to her lips while she held her other hand against her stomach, and warmth shot to her still-tingling limbs.

Lord, please help me be worthy of Lincoln's love.

She wanted his love more than anything, but she could feel a reluctant tug even in the afterglow of his touch. How did she explain what was holding her back? Would he understand she was afraid of losing herself? What if she had to give up all control to a man? Even if it were Lincoln?

"There you are." Tessa rounded the corner. "When did you get home, and why are you standing there looking all weird?"

Hannah pushed away from the door. "Did you need something, Tess?"

"I wanted to show you the new headline and story I found." She held out a clipping.

The headline drew Hannah in—"Boy tells of awful plotting." Hannah scanned the article. At the top, Tessa had penciled in a February date. Hannah was shocked to learn about a son reporting that his mother planned to murder many with her infernal machine of terrible power.

She glanced at Tessa. "Have you seen other articles on this court case?"

"Oh, sure, they were in the newspaper all the time back then." She pointed a finger toward the clipping. "But this one had the best story and description of the infernal device. Can you imagine a woman plotting to kill a judge?"

Could their arsonist have read articles like these? Enough detail was given that someone with some knowledge of science and a bit of creativity could construct one of these devices. She closed her eyes and tried to picture what she'd seen in Albert's workroom. It all seemed like a blur. Perhaps if she could speak with Albert alone, she could feign an interest in these articles and gauge his reaction.

"Thank you, Tessa. I'll show this to Lincoln to see if it might be related to the arson case." She kissed her sister's cheek. "You head off to bed. I want to talk to Charlotte alone for a few minutes."

Tessa frowned but trotted up the stairs.

Hannah sent up a silent prayer of thanks and headed into the parlor. Charlotte sat in an armchair, reading a copy of *Ladies' Home Journal*. Rosie had brought over several issues the other day.

Charlotte looked up and smiled. "Did you enjoy your drive?"

"Yes, we did." Hannah sat down on the couch. "How are you doing? I know you were angry with me. Are you still?"

Charlotte closed her magazine. "Mostly not. I can see that maybe I wasn't really acting like myself."

"That's good to hear." Hannah sighed. How should she proceed? Charlotte was going to be devastated. Hannah prayed God would give her wisdom and temper her words. "Have you heard from George at all?"

Her sister shook her head. "He doesn't care much for writing, even in school, and this time apart has given me a lot of time to think."

"I'm glad, but you should know I went to George's house today."

"You did?" Charlotte's round eyes lit up. "Did he send a message?"

"Sort of."

Charlotte's brows drew together. "Hannah, what is it? Is something wrong?"

"When I arrived, I saw him kissing another girl."

"Maybe she was a cousin." Charlotte's voice caught. She stood and walked to the mantel. Unshed tears filled her eyes.

"You don't kiss a cousin in that manner."

Tears rolled down Charlotte's cheeks. After a few seconds, she swiped them away with the back of her hand, took a deep breath, and pushed her shoulders back.

"It's not me." Her eyes were wide. "There's nothing wrong with me." A bubble of laughter erupted from her throat.

Was her sister going insane? "Charlotte?" Hannah asked. "Are you okay?"

"I'm perfect." She stood and spun in a circle like a little girl in a meadow. "Don't you see? I'm perfectly fine the way I am."

"Honey, what are you talking about?"

She stopped and clasped her hands to her chest. "All this time, I've been trying to be what he wanted me to be. I was trying to make him happy. But it isn't that I wasn't good enough or pretty enough or fast enough. I let him try to remake me. I tried to become more lovable for him, but it would never have been enough. I wasn't even there this time, and he didn't care enough to wait two weeks for me."

"That's exactly right, but—"

"Never again." Charlotte took Hannah's hands and pulled her to her feet. "From here on out, I'm not changing for anyone, ever again. I'm going to be who God made me to be. Period."

"And what does this new woman want?"

Charlotte lifted her chin. "I'm Charlotte Gregory, and I want to go to Fannie Farmer's School of Cookery."

"And I promise to see that you do."

⁂

The bright June sunshine contrasted with the dark interior of the jail. It took Lincoln's eyes a few minutes to adjust before he could ask to see Walt Calloway.

The jailer's keys jangled as he unlocked the cell and motioned Lincoln inside. After snagging a chair from the hall, Lincoln entered and set the chair down. The door clanged shut, and he heard the familiar rattling of keys as the jailer locked the door behind him.

Walt sat up on his cot. "Good news?"

"That's up to you." He straddled the chair. "Do you know what Hannah did after you gave her Donnelly's name?"

"I told her to tell you." Walt rubbed his whiskered chin. "But I can tell by the look on your face she didn't. Please tell me she did not go there alone."

"She did."

"I can't believe she did that. I specifically told her not to."

"And you thought that would work? How long have you known her?" The muscle in his jaw ticked, and his frustration threatened to give way to anger. But his anger would be misplaced. No matter how hard he wanted to make it Walt's fault, Hannah had put herself and the case at risk, not Walt. She'd made the choice all on her own, and she'd do it again if the opportunity arose. That was why he had to convince Walt to cooperate with him.

Lincoln drew in a deep breath. "Listen, we both care about Hannah, and we both know she's not going to stop looking for an answer until you're out of jail. So if you're willing to work with me, I think we can protect Hannah's safety and your freedom."

"How?"

Pushing off the back of the chair, Lincoln stood. "You'll have to tell the police what you know."

"Couldn't you give them Donnelly's name?"

"No, it would be hearsay." He held Walt's gaze. "If you won't do it for yourself, do it for her."

"You really love her, don't you?"

"With all my heart."

Walt pressed his hands to his knees and stood. He offered his hand to Lincoln. "I'll do it—for her."

Lincoln clasped his hand and shook it firmly. "Thank you."

"No, thank you. I can see you love her, and I know she loves you. You're a lucky man." Regret flickered in Walt's eyes.

Lincoln didn't blame the man. He'd counted on Walt's love for

Hannah to make this work, and dragging it out would be uncomfortable for both of them. He called for the jailer. "I'll go speak to the detective, and then we can get this over with." Outside the cell, he turned back to Walt one final time. "Walt, thanks again."

⁓⁓⊙⊙⁓⁓

After lining up the shot, Lincoln took a deep breath and drew his golf club back. The lofty drive ended with the ball rolling several yards on the fairway.

Pete leaned back and patted his round belly. "Well, well, well. Love has improved your game, son."

"I've never told you I was in love."

"You didn't have to." Pete's eyes twinkled. "You aren't the only one who can read a person's body. It's in the way you walk. It's in the way you talk. And it's obviously in the way you play." Pete took his turn positioning himself before the ball. He swung hard. "You found a good woman."

"So did you." Lincoln slipped his club back in his bag. "Speaking of Hannah, I got her friend Walt out of jail. Yesterday he gave us the name of the man he suspects. The detective and fire marshal looked into it, and they arrested Joe Donnelly. They found sticks of dynamite and gasoline in his house. His son is staying with neighbors until I can find him a new home."

"You're finding him a home?"

Lincoln shrugged. "I figured it's the least I can do."

Pete hiked his bag onto his shoulder and followed Lincoln. "That takes care of the arson cases then. We can all rest a little easier."

"Except—"

"Oh yes, your theory of a second arsonist." Having reached their golf balls, Pete set down his bag, then leaned against it while Lincoln prepared to chip his ball onto the green. "Did you mention it to the fire marshal?"

Lincoln took his shot and watched as the ball bounced on the putting green and rolled toward the hole. "He wasn't interested in my amateur theories."

"Guess that settles it then." Again Pete hefted his bag onto his shoulder.

"I don't know about that." They walked onto the putting green, and Lincoln easily sank the putt. He scooped out his ball and leaned on his club. "You said something the other day that got me thinking. You mentioned the Western Union link was weak on the Grennen fire. Sure, she's the daughter of a manager, but the other fire was at the home of an actual employee or at a Western Union building. So I decided to look for any other connections."

Pete's nostrils flared. "And you found something?"

"Of the arson cases, the Grennens and the Western Union manager are both clients of Cedric's, and he's trying to get us retained by the fire insurance companies."

"Now you're accusing Cedric?" Pete chuckled. "I know you dislike the man, but I don't think that's going to stick." Pete finished the hole, and they walked on to the next.

"I don't think Cedric is the other arsonist, but I think there's something we're missing."

"Let it go, son. Enjoy the fact you won." He raised his eyebrows. "And get ready to entertain that aunt of yours. She'll be here tomorrow, you know."

"How could I forget?"

They finished their game without any more arson discussion, but Lincoln couldn't shake the niggling feeling that there was still another firebug out there. When he'd tried to mention the complexity of the infernal device and asked Pete if Albert could explain how one would be created, Pete had changed the subject to his aunt's visit and the upcoming ball at Terrace Hill.

Maybe Pete was right. He should focus on Hannah and his Aunt Sam. After all, tomorrow the two women he loved most would meet for the first time. Would there be instant fireworks or friendship? With Aunt Sam, anything was possible.

43

Steam hissed and brakes squealed as the train pulled into Union Station. Since the train station was directly across from Court House Square, Hannah had no trouble meeting the arrival of the 5:20 train. At Lincoln's insistence, her sisters had taken the streetcar to join them.

Now, as she stood beside Lincoln, butterflies the size of bats fluttered in her stomach. What if Aunt Sam didn't approve of her? After all, she'd not invested all that money in her nephew only to have him marry a working girl like her.

Jo had told her not to worry about that. Ruth and Boaz were from two different worlds too. She'd said, "God can put together whoever he wants, whenever he wants."

Hannah guessed that was true, but she still didn't feel settled.

As if he sensed her discomfort, Lincoln took her hand in his and squeezed it. "Remember what I said? Aunt Sam is her own person. Just be yourself, and she's going to love you."

"Yeah," Tessa said. "We love you despite your flaws."

Charlotte swatted her arm with the back of her hand but giggled too.

The porter stepped down and assisted the first passengers from the train. Would Hannah recognize Aunt Sam when she saw her? She'd probably be wearing a fine traveling outfit. Perhaps she'd even come in the Pullman Palace car at the end of the train.

"There she is!" Lincoln pulled Hannah toward those exiting the passenger car. The woman on the steps wore a plain, chestnut-brown, tailor-made suit. Wavy gray hair curled around her face and was topped by a modest hat. Despite the wrinkles around her eyes and lips, a youthfulness exuded from her head to her toes.

Hannah gasped. Oh my. Was she wearing cycling bloomers? Though some people found the attire scandalous even for those who enjoyed cycling, Hannah thought the pantaloons a necessary and intelligent article of clothing for women. How many times had she gotten her own skirt caught in the chain in the last few days? But to travel in?

With a quick glance, Hannah gauged Tessa's and Charlotte's reactions to the traveling apparel. Charlotte's eyes grew as large as oversized buttons. Hannah stifled a giggle.

Tessa grinned. "I love her already."

Hannah did too.

Angling both himself and Hannah through the crowd, Lincoln let go of her hand when he reached his aunt. He enveloped the matronly woman in a long hug, then glanced at Hannah.

"Mrs. Samantha Phillips, this is Miss Hannah Gregory."

"Our future attorney." Aunt Sam pulled Hannah into a hug before she could protest. "Good for you."

"I . . . I'm not pursuing that anymore, Mrs. Phillips."

"We'll see about that." She linked her arm in Hannah's. "And you're all to call me Aunt Sam. These darlings must be your sisters. Let me guess. You're Charlotte and you're Tessa."

Hannah's heart warmed. Not only had Lincoln told his aunt about her, but he'd also told her enough about her sisters for the woman to recognize them on sight.

"A pleasure to meet you." Charlotte bobbed in a little curtsy. "Aunt Sam."

"Now, what do you ladies say about the four of us going shopping? I hear there's a ball going to be thrown in my honor and I need something to wear. Besides, I've never had any girls to spoil."

She glanced back at Lincoln. "Sorry, Linc, you can't come along. Mustn't see a lady in all her finery before the event."

"But you've just arrived." Irritation laced his voice. "What about getting your things and getting you settled? I know you like your privacy, so I booked you a room at the Kirkwood Hotel."

"Don't whine. It's not polite." She rolled her eyes in Hannah's direction. "I did my best with him. Are you sure you want to be saddled with a whiner?"

"He doesn't whine very often." Hannah had to hurry to keep up with the woman.

"I don't whine at all." Lincoln, sounding exasperated, followed behind.

Aunt Sam winked at her, and Hannah chuckled. The older woman suddenly came to a halt and looked at the watch pinned to her waist. "A new record, I believe. I've flummoxed my nephew in less than five minutes." She turned to him. "And Linc, I'm not staying in some stuffy hotel. I'm staying with you. Maureen will see to my things. She has the address and fare for a hansom cab. So, where is that automobile of yours? I need to freshen up before we take these lovely girls to dinner."

"But I thought you said—"

She glanced at Hannah. "Are you sure you want to put up with this? His mind seems to be slipping already."

"Aunt Sam, please, behave yourself."

She quirked a smile in his direction. "And where's the fun in that?"

❧◈❧

After picking Hannah up promptly at nine thirty on Saturday, Lincoln drove her to meet his aunt at Younker Brothers Department Store. Last night, Aunt Sam had decided she'd like separate shopping excursions with each of the girls, and she'd start with Hannah.

"She said she'd meet you in the dress department. She wants your opinion on a new gown." Lincoln kissed Hannah's cheek as he helped her from the Reo. "Thank you for being such a good sport about all this. I know she can be a lot to take when you first meet her. I've always said that loving my aunt was like hugging a tornado."

"She's delightful, Lincoln."

"Well, I hope you can say that by the time we meet for lunch today." He held the door to the department store for her. "And Hannah, one more thing. She handles 'no' as poorly as you, and she likes to win as much as I do."

She flashed him a cheeky grin. "What's that supposed to mean?"

"That it's easier to say yes than argue with her."

Inside, Hannah found her way to the dress department. Hearing Aunt Sam's voice, she headed toward it, only to find herself in the midst of gowns.

Hannah stopped to stare at the ones on display. An ivory satin gown draped in lace. An ice-blue one with a V-neck—dropped much too low—with stunning dark blue embroidery work. And a charcoal-gray chiffon edged with turquoise silk and bearing a peacock feather motif.

"There you are!" Aunt Sam, now dressed in a sunny yellow tailor-made suit complete with a narrow skirt, took her hands. "I've taken the liberty of selecting the first five for you to try on, but if you don't like them, there's plenty more to choose from. If you don't like any here, we'll go to the next store."

"Ma'am, I thought we were here to pick out your gown."

"Nonsense. I have plenty the good folks of Des Moines have never laid eyes on." She squeezed her hands. "Please, Hannah, don't take offense. I've never had a daughter, and I can't wait to see Lincoln's eyes when he sees you in one of these creations."

A middle-aged lady in a similar traveling jacket and skirt moved next to Aunt Sam. "Are you ready, miss?"

"This is my personal maid and dear friend, Maureen. She can do wonders with a needle if any alterations need to be done." Aunt Sam motioned Hannah toward the dressing room. "Try the peach first. I think it will look lovely with your hair."

Hannah slipped into the luxurious fabrics one at a time, with each dress prettier than the last. How would she ever choose? Thankfully, Aunt Sam and Maureen vetoed most of them before she had a chance to seriously consider them. The ivory satin was too traditional. The ice-blue too radical. The charcoal-gray too dramatic.

"How about this one, miss?" Maureen held up a stunning dress the color of eggplant, with a hand-crocheted lace yoke.

Hannah sucked in a breath. "It's gorgeous."

Maureen eased it over her head and fastened the waistband. "The button is hidden behind a cluster of lavender rosettes back here. See?" She pointed to the angled mirror the store had set up in the dressing room so patrons could see the front and back of their gowns.

"I love how the reverse side of the dark purple is lined with the light purple silk that cascades down the back," Hannah said.

"And that matching drape in the front is tied at the bottom with rosettes too." Maureen tugged at the extra fabric at the waist. "It would need to be taken up a wee bit, but that would only take a few minutes."

"Let's go show Aunt Sam."

Hannah loved the swish of the skirt and the softness of the velvet and silk. And with no train, the gown was easy to move about in.

She stood before Aunt Sam, who was seated on the love seat. Aunt Sam motioned for her to spin around. When she faced her again, the woman had tears in her eyes. "My dear girl, do you realize how much joy it will bring me to see you in that dress at the ball? You are a vision to behold, and Linc won't be able to take his eyes off you." She motioned for the clerk. "We'll need all the trappings to match this—shoes, hats, etcetera. And she'll need a brooch to wear with that collar. Please arrange a selection of all of these items to be brought up here."

Hannah blinked. Was she in a dream? How could she accept such extravagance? "Aunt Sam, that's too much."

"Nonsense." She stood and called to the clerk, "And we'll need a proper cycling outfit. Have some of those brought over as well."

Hannah's jaw dropped.

"Well, I can't very well go riding alone," Aunt Sam said. "And you can't keep up in a skirt. It's all rather selfish of me, you see."

By the time they met Lincoln for lunch in the store's tearoom, not only had Aunt Sam purchased a gown and a cycling outfit for Hannah, but she'd also added two corsets—one of which was modified for cycling—a pair of shoes, a silk hat, earrings, and a brooch to match the dress, and a jewel-studded hair comb that Aunt Sam said Hannah had to have.

Lincoln kissed his aunt's cheek, then Hannah's. "Was the shopping trip successful?"

"Very." Aunt Sam spread her napkin over her lap. "And your Hannah has blessed my stockings off."

Lincoln glanced at Hannah.

She averted her eyes. Would he think she'd taken advantage of his aunt's generosity?

"Did she now?" He captured Hannah's hand under the table. "Thank you for making my aunt a happy woman, Hannah. She likes nothing more than to give gifts, and you bless her by being a gracious receiver."

"Our heavenly Father lavishes blessings on us. Why should I not do the same for those I love?" She looked directly at Hannah. "And yes, dear, that includes you." She lifted her menu. "Now, let's order. I think I'll have the cucumber sandwiches."

Hannah glanced from Aunt Sam to Lincoln. She'd read Lewis Carroll's *Alice's Adventures in Wonderland* again a few months ago. If she didn't know better, she would think she'd stepped into Wonderland, and now she was sitting at a tea party with the Mad Hatter and the Queen of Hearts. At any minute, she expected the queen to shout, "Off with her head!"

But the blow never came. Only pleasant conversation, excellent food, and frequent laughter filled the table. More than anything, Hannah found herself feeling a part of Lincoln's family. Could she really become Mrs. Lincoln Cole?

She bit the inside of her lip. Not unless she told him everything.

"Hello, Courthouse Main. Number, please." Hannah connected the call and leaned back in her chair. She removed her earpiece and rubbed where the apparatus had chafed.

The light on her panel lit up, and she inserted the plug. "Hello, Courthouse Main. Number, please."

"The only number I want is yours, Miss Gregory."

"Lincoln," she whispered, "you aren't supposed to call me here."

Jo cast her a sidelong glance and mouthed it was fine.

"Hey, when love calls, you have to answer." He was quiet for a second. "I hate to admit this, but I'm a little jealous of my aunt. You've spent so much time with her, we've barely had a moment together."

"We've been together."

"Not alone."

How true that was. She'd wanted to tell him about the call she'd overheard, but there'd not been a good time to do so. She missed him, but Aunt Sam would leave soon, and then they'd have all the time in the world.

She tried to make her voice sound light. "I miss you too."

"Then how about I pick you up after work."

"I'm going cycling with your aunt. She has a call she wants to make too."

"Hannah . . ." he moaned.

"You'll live." She leaned close to her mouthpiece. "And I'll see you in my dreams."

"If you think that silky voice of yours is helping, you are so wrong. If you're not careful, I may have to kidnap you."

"You'll have to find me first." She laughed. "See you tonight. I've got to go. Love you."

"Love you too. Bye."

After connecting the next call, she glanced at the clock. Another half an hour and she'd ride her bicycle to Lincoln's to meet Aunt Sam. Where should they ride today? Ingersoll Park?

Hannah's cheeks warmed at the memory of Lincoln's kiss on the bridge.

On second thought, perhaps they should stick to the streets.

❧❧❧

When Hannah arrived at Lincoln's house, she took the time to switch into the cycling bloomers she'd brought with her. According to Lincoln, the dark trousers looked quite fetching.

"I'll go pick up your sisters while you're out riding." He pulled her close and pressed his lips to her ear. "And you and I *will* sneak away for some quality time tonight."

Even in the breeze, her cheeks flamed.

"Is he whining again?" Aunt Sam cast her a knowing glance. "What are we going to do with him? You'll have her all to yourself tomorrow." She waved her fingers at Lincoln and started down the path. "Time to fly, Hannah."

"Like you need any encouragement to fly." He kissed Hannah's cheek. "See you later, and be careful."

"Aren't I always?" She shoved off and started pedaling behind Aunt Sam. "On second thought, don't answer that."

44

Since Aunt Sam hadn't asked Hannah directions as she often did, Hannah was left to assume the woman had a plan and knew exactly where to go on their bicycle excursion.

They turned on Grand Avenue and rode without stopping for several blocks. Hannah marveled at the older woman's fitness. When they finally paused at a corner, Hannah was puffing, but Aunt Sam had no trouble speaking.

"I apologize for the hilly ride, but I wanted to drop by Elise Williams's and check on her spirits. Lincoln said Pete mentioned she'd slipped into another one of her melancholies."

Hannah's heart thudded against her ribs. Was it because of her worries about the fire?

A short time later, the maid showed them into the parlor, where Elise sat beside her electric machine. She barely glanced up when they entered.

Aunt Sam snagged the footstool and placed it directly in front of the unresponsive woman. "Hello, Elise. I've brought Lincoln's Hannah with me. Remember, you met her at your dinner party."

She glanced up at Hannah, and recognition flickered in her pale green eyes. "The night of the fire."

"Yes, there was a fire."

Tears filled Elise's eyes. "So many flames. So much smoke."

"You go right ahead and cry, Elise. Wash the sad right out of you." Aunt Sam dabbed at the tears with the corner of her handkerchief. "Hannah, why don't you ask the maid to bring her some water or tea?"

Hannah nodded and slipped from the room. In the hall, she listened for the sound of clanging pots to indicate the direction of the kitchen. Hearing none, she started down the hallway. She paused at the first open doorway—a study.

"What are you looking for now?"

She whirled to see Albert. How had he snuck up on her?

"I was looking for a maid. Your mother needs a glass of water or some tea."

"My mother needs a lot more than a glass of water." He pointed down the hall. "The kitchen's down there."

Hannah's pulse raced. Here Albert stood before her. Was God giving her the chance to ask him about the fire?

Squaring her shoulders, Hannah placed a hand on the wall to anchor herself. "Albert, may I ask you a science question?"

Distrust filled his blue eyes. "I suppose."

"I've read about fires started by an infernal device." She licked her dry lips. "How could one trigger such an explosion?"

His face reddened, and he glared at her. "Did Lincoln put you up to this? Tell him I'm fine now. That's all behind me."

"What?" Hannah took a step back. "I didn't—I mean I don't mean to offend you. Lincoln has nothing to do with my question. I only thought you'd know because you're so intelligent."

"Give your beau a message, Miss Gregory. My father doesn't need him to be the son I never was anymore. You got that?"

"Yes, but—"

"And you'd both be wise to stay out of my business."

Chills crept up her spine at the look in Albert's eyes. How could she define the look? Hatred? Yes, that was it. He appeared to hate Lincoln, and that hatred was rooted in Lincoln's relationship with Pete. Was Lincoln aware of Albert's feelings?

She went over the bizarre exchange again as she found the kitchen and asked for water. What had Albert meant about telling Lincoln he was fine now? What was all behind him? Surely if Lincoln knew Albert had any kind of firebug past, he'd have said something.

Halting so fast she almost spilled the water in the glass, Hannah sucked in a breath. What if Lincoln was also covering for Albert? He loved Pete like a father. Wouldn't he do anything for the man to protect him? And if that was the case, did she really want to share what she'd heard?

We've got to learn to trust each other. Lincoln's words filled her mind. She wanted to trust him, but if she really loved him, shouldn't she keep this secret too?

❧ ⁓ ⁓ ◌ ⁓ ⁓ ❧

Heat singed Hannah's scalp, and she pulled away from Maureen's ministrations. Aunt Sam had suggested Hannah get ready at Lincoln's home so Maureen could do her hair. Her sisters had come along as well, and Mrs. Reynolds promised to make them a delicious supper.

Aunt Sam had kicked her nephew out of the house, telling him not to come back until it was time to pick them up. How odd it felt to be dressing in Lincoln's home.

"Sorry about that, lamb. I got a little too close with the curling iron." Maureen unrolled the device, clipped it back inside the chimney flue on the lamp, and blew on the hot curl. "Can you believe you're going to a ball at Terrace Hill?"

Hannah pressed a hand to her side. Beneath the fancy stays in her new corset, her stomach whirled like a pinwheel in the wind. Mr. and Mrs. Frederick Allen Hubbell hosted many events at their mansion, Terrace Hill, but Hannah certainly had never imagined attending one. The only part of Terrace Hill she'd ever seen was the ninety-foot tower on the front of the house, which was impossible to miss from the sidewalk.

"What if I make a fool of myself?"

"And how could you possibly do that?" Maureen pinned another curl in place. "There. What do you think?"

Hannah angled her hand mirror so she could see all of her hair.

Maureen had formed a long coil and fastened it at the back of Hannah's head. More coils added height. She'd also left a generous amount of hair hanging in loose ringlets down Hannah's neck. She tucked the new jeweled hair comb in like a coronet.

"It's perfect. How can I ever thank you?" She stood and gathered her dress.

"You can thank me by remembering every detail of tonight. I want to hear it all, from the color of the carpet to how many sconces are hanging on the wall to how many men Lincoln has to fight off to dance with you." She took the purple dress from Hannah and carefully eased it over her head.

"I'll certainly do my best to recall every detail." Hannah shifted the dress into place and turned so Maureen could button the waistband.

Once a bit of cheek color, shoes, jewelry, and gloves were added, Maureen pronounced her ready.

"Oh, wait, do you have any fragrance?" Maureen scanned the top of the dressing table.

"No. I didn't bring any."

Charlotte stepped into the room. "I did." She held out an atomizer. "It was Mother's." After giving Hannah a spritz, Charlotte stepped back and smiled. A spicy floral scent filled the room. "Whenever you smell it tonight, think of her as being with you."

Aunt Sam glided into the room in a gauzy, rose-colored gown. She motioned for Hannah to stand. "Let me take a look at you, dear."

Hannah stood and slowly turned around.

Aunt Sam applauded. "Maureen, you've outdone yourself, and Hannah, you are such a natural beauty." She drew on her own long gloves, and Maureen hurried to button them.

"Where's Tessa?" Hannah looked about the room.

Charlotte leaned into the hall and called for her. Seconds later, Tessa bounced in. "He's coming, but Hannah, you wait up here until he arrives. There's nothing like a lady's grand entrance to get a man's blood flowing."

The ladies laughed, and everyone departed, leaving Hannah alone for the first time.

Please, God, teach me how to love Lincoln with all of my heart. Show me why I'm not letting him in completely.

Even though the clamor of activity downstairs announced Lincoln's arrival, she waited until Maureen summoned her. A glance out the window told her Lincoln had rented a fancy carriage. Why hadn't she considered that she and Aunt Sam wouldn't both fit in the Reo?

Maureen tapped on the door. "Are you ready, lamb?"

"I certainly hope so."

Keeping her gaze fixed on Lincoln, Hannah descended the stairs. Dressed in a black swallowtail coat, white waistcoat, and black bow tie, he'd never looked more handsome.

He held out his hand, and at the sight of his smile, a delicious heat spread through her. Her knees weakened under the intensity of his gaze.

"You take my breath away." His voice was husky.

"Yes, yes. She's beautiful. You're handsome." Tessa placed a hand on each of their backs. "Now go to the ball and come back with some good stories, and I don't mean who danced with whom. I want real juicy stories."

Lincoln laughed and offered Hannah his arm. "You heard the lady."

Hannah glanced at Aunt Sam. The older woman beamed, and Lincoln held out his arm to her too. "I think I'll be escorting the two loveliest ladies of the evening. Come, your carriage awaits."

❧⁓⁓⦿⁓⁓❧

If Hannah didn't already feel like a princess, she certainly did once she stepped through the front doors of the Victorian mansion.

In the vestibule, the butler greeted them and said he'd show them to the reception room. Hannah and Lincoln trailed Aunt Sam, the guest of honor.

"Look at these!" Hannah whispered as they passed through the massive doors leading down the hall.

Lincoln patted her hand. "According to Aunt Sam, together they weigh around three hundred pounds."

Because Aunt Sam had to be there before the other guests arrived, Hannah and Lincoln had time to look around after meeting the Hubbells. From the reception room to the drawing room to the music room, every space on the first floor seemed more beautiful than the last. All the doors that linked the rooms opened to create one great hall.

The string quartet played in the music room, and Hannah hoped someone would also play the magnificent Steinway piano. She so wanted to hear it. In the formal dining room, maids rushed to put the finishing touches on the buffet.

As other guests began to arrive, Lincoln reached for a sugared plum and popped it in his mouth. Hannah gave him a mock glare, and he pulled her close and kissed her temple.

She should talk to him now about Albert while they were alone. She swallowed. How did she start?

Before she could say anything, the butler suggested everyone move to the drawing room so the festivities could begin. Hannah sucked in her breath when they entered the room. Both walls and furniture sported a rosy-pink color. The rug had apparently been rolled up and removed to make dancing easier, and the chairs had been pushed to the edges of the room. Everywhere she looked, from the hand-painted mural on the wall to the white marble fireplace, made her feel like she'd stepped into a dream.

And when she found herself twirling beneath the crystal chandelier in the arms of the man she loved, she prayed she'd never wake up.

"Do you have any idea how lovely you are tonight? I think every man here has his eye on you." Lincoln spun her in a circle. "I hope you'll squeeze in a few more dances with me."

Her skirt swished against her legs. "If it was up to me, you could have them all."

"I wish I could. But even with her modern ways, I'm afraid my aunt would point out that faux pas." He drew her closer. "Just remember who you belong to."

Belong to? Normally such a phrase would raise Hannah's hackles, but she found it stirred something entirely new inside her. She risked a quick glance upward, her heart hammering in her throat when she caught a glimpse of the heat in his eyes.

All too soon, the waltz came to an end, and Lincoln surrendered her to the next gentleman. To her surprise, Cedric claimed the next dance. He apologized for his boorish behavior at the Williamses' dinner party and begged her forgiveness.

Shortly after that dance, Albert asked her to join him on the dance floor. Although reluctant at first, she agreed and found him to be a remarkable dancer.

Near the end of the dance, he tightened his hold on her. "Did you give Lincoln the message I gave you the other day?"

Hannah looked into his eyes, trying to guess if this question was coming from the angry Albert or the friendly one who'd been making polite conversation. She decided it was the latter. "He's not trying to replace you as Pete's son, Albert. Your father is his mentor and friend. He cares about your whole family."

Albert swung her in a wide circle and laughed wryly. "It doesn't make a difference anymore."

"Because you'll be returning to college this fall?"

"No, because I've got things under control now." He laughed again. "Miss Gregory, I've learned to accept the way things are and deal with them accordingly." He whirled her around, his eyes alight. "You're truly a vision. I can see why Lincoln is so enamored with you. He's a lucky man."

"I'm the lucky one."

"I suppose that's true as well."

Did he mean that? She studied his features, but he gave nothing away. She found herself relaxing as they danced. None of the strangeness that sometimes accompanied Pete's son seemed to be present tonight. Was this the young man who'd been accepted to Yale? Perhaps Lincoln was right about him being cured.

Still, she didn't want to be naive. If he was the arsonist, she had to know. A few questions and she'd have her answers. Lincoln would chastise her for taking chances, but if Albert were guilty, he'd never do anything to her here.

"Albert." She swallowed. "May I ask you something?"

"Anything."

"What kind of person do you believe is setting the fires?"

His eyes never left hers, nor did his body stiffen in response to her question. He smiled and let out a chuckle. "I suppose the man must be mad. Am I on your list?"

"No, of course not."

"Come now, Miss Gregory. I'd understand if I was." The song neared its end, and their steps slowed. "But I can assure you, my dear, you have nothing to fear from me."

Relief flooded over her. Surely she didn't need to speak to Lincoln about this man if he could speak so sincerely in answer to her question. Lincoln himself had taught her to watch a person's body for clues to see if they were lying, and she hadn't seen one flicker that indicated subterfuge.

She released a slow breath and sent up a silent prayer of thanks. She'd handled the situation without Lincoln ever having to know her fears.

When the dance concluded, Albert bowed over her hand. "Thank you. And if you find yourself in need of a partner in the future, I'd be happy to accept the position."

Needing a reprieve, Hannah sat the next dance out and found an empty chair in the reception room.

Lincoln spotted her and brought her a cup of fruit punch. "Are you enjoying yourself?"

"Very much, but my feet needed a break." She glanced down at her new slippers peeking from beneath the hem of her gown.

"Yours?" Lincoln laughed. "You didn't dance with graceless Grace."

"That bad?"

"Worse." He took her empty cup and set it on a servant's silver tray. He held out his hand to her. "Shall we?"

She slipped her hand in his and smiled. "If I step on your toe, are you going to start calling me Hannah the horse?"

"Nay." He mimicked the sound of a horse.

With a giggle, she let the magic carry them away once again.

Tired but happy, Lincoln helped his aunt out of the carriage, then Hannah. The plan was to drop Aunt Sam off at his home and collect Tessa and Charlotte, who'd spent the evening there with Maureen.

"We'll probably have to waken my sisters." Hannah stifled a yawn behind her gloved hand.

Beneath the full moon, Hannah's face shone like an angel's. What a lucky man he was.

He started up the walkway toward the house and halted. Why was Albert out for a walk in his neighborhood?

Aunt Sam spotted him too. "Is that—"

Hannah gasped.

Boom!

He flew backward and hit the ground hard. The earth shook.

Rolling over, he searched for Hannah and his aunt. He found Aunt Sam first. She'd ended up a yard from him. "You okay?"

"I think so." She looked around. "Where's Hannah?"

He spotted her in the yard—lying dark and still.

45

Fuzziness faded. Hannah sat up and rubbed her aching head with the palm of her hand. What had happened?

"Are you all right?" Lincoln sounded far away.

She shook her head and it cleared. An explosion. Albert. The house.

Her sisters!

She jumped to her feet and stumbled. Lincoln caught her.

Flames engulfed the porch.

"Let me go! They're in there!"

"You can't go in that way. I'll get them." He thrust her into Aunt Sam's arms. "Stay here."

She fought Aunt Sam's hold.

"He'll get them. Trust him, Hannah."

Trust him. The words hit her like a second blast, and her body trembled. If she'd have trusted him, none of this would have happened. Why hadn't she told him what she knew?

Aunt Sam pulled her close. "He'll get them all out."

The clang of the fire bell sounded in the distance, but she barely heard it over the din of her own heartbeat in her ears.

Please, God, don't take them too!

Throwing the back door wide open, Lincoln plunged into his home. Smoke billowed toward the opening he created.

"Charlotte! Tess! Maureen!"

No answer. What if they'd been knocked out by the explosion? Where would they have been?

Keeping low, he felt his way through the kitchen and into the dining room. Despite his lungs aching for fresh air, he pressed harder. He'd promised Hannah. "Charlotte!"

"Here."

The voice was faint. In the parlor? Of course. None of the three were familiar enough with the house to know how to get out any way other than the front door.

He found Charlotte and Maureen first. Thankfully, the women had had the sense to cover their mouths and keep to the ground. "Stay down. We'll crawl out. I'll lead you." Passing through the hall, he felt the heat from the fire destroying the front of his house. "Hurry."

At last they reached the back door. He helped Charlotte and Maureen out. Where was Tessa?

His lungs burned, but he had no choice. After taking a deep breath, he plunged back inside and found Tessa lying yards from the door. Lifting her into his arms, he bolted for the door.

Lord, save her. Hannah can't lose anyone else.

Tessa began to cough as soon as they rounded the corner of the house. Hannah ran to meet them. As soon as he deposited Tessa on the ground, Hannah helped her hacking sister sit up. Still sounding nearly hysterical, she said, "This is all my fault. This is all my fault."

Dropping his hands to his knees, Lincoln drank in great gulps of air. Smoke clogged his throat, and he fought to clear it. He couldn't let Hannah go on like this. He placed a hand on her shoulder, and a coughing spasm seized him. It seemed like eternity before it passed. "This is not your fault."

She looked up at him. Even in the moonlight, he saw the anguish in her eyes. "It is. I knew Albert was the arsonist."

"You knew? How could you know?"

"I overheard someone on the phone. They were worried it was him."

Anger and confusion surged through him like the fire consuming his home. She knew? And she'd kept quiet about it? Why would she do that?

Because that's what Hannah did. She liked to be in control, and because of that, her sisters had almost died.

"Who?" he demanded, broiling inside. "Who did you overhear?"

"Please don't make me tell you." Her voice cracked.

"Who did you overhear?" His voice grew louder, and he shook off Aunt Sam's restraining hand. "Tell me, Hannah!"

"Pete and Elise," she sobbed. "I'm sorry. I should have told you. I should have trusted you. It's just—"

"You thought you could handle it all on your own—again." He jabbed his finger toward the firemen fighting the flames. Betrayal, raw and cutting, sliced through his heart. "And now look what you've done."

46

Heart splintering, Hannah removed her smoky purple gown and sank onto her bed. Tears spilled down her cheeks, and she made no effort to wipe them away. She squeezed her eyes closed, hoping to block out the image of the fire. Instead, the expression of betrayal on Lincoln's face was branded on her memory.

In the far bed, Tessa still coughed, but the doctor said she'd be fine. Even in his anger, Lincoln had seen that the three of them were taken home and had sent a doctor to check on them. She'd waved off the physician's ministrations but was quite relieved to hear her sisters wouldn't suffer any long-term effects from her mistakes.

But she would.

Even if Lincoln could somehow forgive her, she'd never be able to forgive herself. She recalled the flames devouring Lincoln's home. The firemen had put the fire out before she'd left, but the porch was gone and the front of the house was badly damaged. Could it be repaired?

Probably much more easily than her relationship with Lincoln.

Fresh sobs wracked her body. Finally, her energy spent, she let exhaustion claim her. Tomorrow she'd face the day like she always had—alone.

The room at the Kirkwood Hotel had a most inviting bed, but Lincoln couldn't imagine going to sleep right now. He sat down on the bed and removed his shoes. He tossed them across the room, harder than necessary. First one and then the other clunked against the wall. His home was near ruins. He'd been targeted by his mentor's son, whom the detectives would soon arrest, and the woman he loved had withheld the knowledge that could have prevented the whole fiasco.

Why?

He yanked at his bow tie and let it fall to the floor. His lungs hurt, but not half as much as his heart. That same independent spirit he loved in Hannah now made him cringe. It made her believe she had to take on the world and prove herself. She thought she had to conquer any obstacle and take any risk that came her way. Well, he'd tried to convince her otherwise, and he was tired of his words not going any deeper than the blister on his hand. Loving her cost him too much, and he wasn't referring to his home.

Falling back onto the pillows, he sighed. Always, Hannah clung to a little piece of herself—a stubborn, "I can handle it" attitude marked by an inability to trust him.

He punched the pillow beneath his head into submission. If he couldn't have her whole heart, he didn't want any of it.

❧⟨⟨◯⟩⟩❧

Every muscle on Hannah's five-foot-six-inch frame still ached from being thrown by the explosion, but her greatest ache ran much deeper. She took her place at the courthouse switchboard and adjusted her headset without a word.

Jo eyed her critically. "All right. Out with it. What happened?"

"Even if it involves something I overheard on the telephone lines?"

"Yes, even then." Jo settled back, apparently ready to listen.

Hannah briefly gave her fellow operator and friend a description of the weekend, including her own role in not telling anyone what she'd overheard on the telephone lines.

"It was the rule, and I couldn't break it." Hannah knew Jo, of all people, would understand.

"Interesting."

"Why do you say that?"

"I find it surprising that a woman who breaks the rules whenever she sees fit chose to obey this one."

"But—"

Jo broke her off to connect a call. When she'd completed it, she turned back to Hannah. "Answer this. Did you pray even once about whether you should tell me or Lincoln or anyone else about this call?"

"No, there was nothing for sure. I thought I could find out if it was true or not."

"*You* thought *you* could find out the truth?" Jo gave her a weak smile. "Hannah, I think you've got a bad case of self-reliance and not God-reliance."

"But what's wrong with that? Ruth was self-reliant. She insisted on going with Naomi. She gleaned in the fields. She went to the threshing floor."

"And she listened to the council of Naomi and to Boaz, and she made Naomi's God her God." Jo patted Hannah's arm. "Your world got turned upside down when you lost your parents, and you were doing everything you could to get it back in control. But I think if you look inside yourself, you might see that Lincoln wasn't the only one you stopped trusting."

Hannah moved too quickly and winced. She bit her lip. "You think I stopped trusting God?"

Jo pointed to Hannah's switchboard. "I think you've been holding the plug in your hands but not completing the call. You're scared."

Was Jo right? Why hadn't she prayed about whether to tell Lincoln, and why hadn't she broken the rules? It didn't make sense.

Could she be scared? Had she been afraid to take the biggest risk of all—giving her heart away?

She rubbed her aching temples. She'd asked God to help her learn to love Lincoln completely, but if this was the answer to her prayers, why had it come too late?

47

Poking at the rubble of what had been his front porch, Lincoln heaved a sigh. It had been a week since the fire marshal had done a thorough search, but Lincoln needed to examine the area for himself. He needed closure, and the ashes seemed an appropriate place to do so since his life had gone up in smoke.

To his surprise, most of the house was salvageable. There'd be new siding to put on, a new porch to build, and some other damages to fix, but he'd already contacted workmen. They were set to begin next week.

His aunt stood in the yard. "For a busy attorney, this is a strange place to find you."

"I'm not in the mood, Aunt Sam."

She marched over, her hands propped on her hips. "Well, it's time someone told you to stop moping about."

"I've been betrayed by my best friend and the woman I love. I think I have a right to mope."

"Pete didn't betray you. I've spoken to him, and he had no idea his son would do something like this. He was protecting Elise, and he didn't want to believe his son could be the arsonist." She cleared her throat. "Do you blame him?"

In truth, Lincoln did, but her words pricked his hard heart. "I guess I wouldn't want to think my son was capable of this either."

"He's hurting, Lincoln. He feels like he's lost both of you now."

Lincoln shrugged. "I don't know if I can go back to what it was."

"Then go forward." She took his arm and pulled him toward the bench in the yard. When she sat down, he joined her. "Lincoln, I can see the guilt in your eyes. Why are blaming yourself for this?"

"Because I knew what Albert had done at Yale. He was asked to leave because he set fire to a lab."

She touched her chin. "Did you tell Hannah about it?"

"No, I didn't want her to be scared of Albert. I thought—I hoped—he'd been cured."

"So you were protecting her?" Aunt Sam's brows lifted. "And she was protecting you. I'll never forget the anguish in her voice when she had to tell you she'd overheard Elise and Pete talking about Albert. Didn't you hear it? Maybe a part of the reason she didn't tell you was because she tried to handle it alone, but the other part was because she loves you and didn't want to hurt you."

Lincoln released a long sigh.

"One more thing." She stood and faced him. "Knowing you, you've been pushing her. I bet you think that she should trust you and that she should turn to you, right?"

"I want her to let me help her!" He raised his hands in exasperation.

"I understand. But Hannah can't change overnight. She's independent and strong, and she's been the responsible one in her family all her life. It's going to take time to learn how to turn to you, and that kind of trust can't be demanded, it has to be earned."

Lincoln stood and rubbed the back of his neck. "Aren't you supposed to be on my side?"

"I am on your side, and I'm on mine too. You're miserable, Pete's miserable, and Hannah's miserable. And you're all making me miserable."

"I don't know where to start."

"Start here." She covered his heart with her hand. "Delight yourself in the Lord, and he will give you the desires of your heart."

With a prayer on her lips, Hannah turned to the book of Ruth. She'd cried an ocean of tears in the last week, but the ache in her heart hadn't lessened one bit. Now it was time to find some direction. If Ruth's journey mirrored her own, then it had to have the answer of what to do now.

Her gaze landed on chapter 3, verse 3. "Wash thyself therefore, and anoint thee, and put thy raiment upon thee, and get thee down to the floor: but make not thyself known unto the man, until he shall have done eating and drinking."

Hannah stared at the passage. Was this a prescription for her as well? Like her, Ruth was trying to survive in a difficult time. She needed to start over, and she needed Boaz to cover her. How Hannah had chafed at that thought before, and how she ached for it now.

Taking the verse apart, she started at the beginning. "Wash thyself"? Could she take that as spiritually purifying her heart? As asking for forgiveness?

"Lord," she prayed aloud, "I've been stubborn and prideful. I didn't turn to Lincoln, but worse, I didn't turn to you. Please forgive me. Purify my heart. Set me on the path you want for my life."

She then placed her finger beneath the words "anoint thee." She recalled the woman who'd anointed Jesus's feet with costly perfume. Hers was a risky love. Hannah had no intention of drizzling oil over her head or taking a bath in perfume, but could she offer thanksgiving—incense to the Lord?

For the next few hours, she thanked the Lord for his provisions and asked him for mercy. Even when things seemed darkest, he'd held them in the palm of his hand.

"Put thy raiment upon thee"? While she could put on her Sunday dress, she didn't think that would apply here. She decided to consider it putting on Christ. She'd obeyed the gospel nearly five years ago and put on Christ in baptism. A thrill spread through her as she recalled the day she'd said yes to him. He was her raiment now. He was her life.

Finally, she read that Ruth wasn't to make herself known. She was to wait.

Hannah took a deep breath and stared at the phone. She'd have to wait for love to call.

~⌇∽⌇∽⌇~

The telephone rang, jolting Hannah out of a delightful dream. She scrubbed her face with her hands. Sunlight streamed through the window. She must have dozed off.

She gripped the candlestick phone in her hand, then lifted the earpiece and held it close. "Hello?"

"Hannah?"

Her heart skipped a beat, and tears clogged her throat. "Lincoln, I'm so sorry. I should have—"

"Shhh," he said softly. "Just listen for a minute. I love you. I don't want to change you, and I don't want to run your life, but I do want to share a life with you. I want to be your partner in every way, and that can only happen if you trust me and I trust you."

"I do trust you."

"You do?" The connection crackled.

She twirled the cord in her fingers. "A hundred percent. I knew it would hurt you to learn Pete was keeping this secret, but I should have told you anyway. I wanted to handle it on my own. I wanted to handle everything on my own."

"And now?"

"I want God and you to cover me." She swallowed and waited until the popping noises on the line cleared. "But can you trust me after all I've done?"

"You were trying to protect me, and I was trying to protect you."

His voice sounded so gentle, Hannah pictured his dove-blue eyes softening.

"I knew about Albert's history, and I didn't tell you. I'm sorry too." His voice warbled, and he cleared his throat. "Hannah, I asked you this before, but I'm asking again. Will you take a risk on me?"

48

Standing before the mirror, Hannah stared at her reflection. The soft ivory dress layered with lace fit her waist snugly. The impulsive girl who'd left college to take care of her sisters was gone, only to be replaced by a woman who was learning to rely on the Lord.

"Aren't you ready yet?" Tessa stuck her head in the door.

"Almost. Will you ask Charlotte to come here a minute?"

Tessa disappeared and returned with Charlotte in tow. "You look beautiful."

"Thank you. Can you help me do up the buttons on these gloves?" Hannah held out her hand to Charlotte.

Charlotte slipped the pearl buttons through the holes. "I can't believe you trust Lincoln with something as important as the location of your wedding."

"I think it's very romantic." Tessa pulled back the curtain. "And the carriage is here to take us there. Are you ready now?"

"As soon as I tell you both how much I love you." Hannah reached for their hands. "And to thank you. You both have been gracious about our move to Saint Paul, and Lincoln is excited about opening his own practice there." Hannah's heart tugged as she recalled Lincoln explaining that Pete was giving up his law practice to spend more time with Elise, now that Albert was being sent to the asylum. The decision meant they'd all be starting over.

"And you'll be by Lincoln's side once we get there." Charlotte beamed at her.

"Yes, after I finish law school."

Tessa's eyes twinkled. "You mean *if* you finish."

Charlotte repinned one of Hannah's curls. "She'll finish. We'll make sure of it."

⁂

The carriage stopped, and Lincoln opened the door. Tessa popped out first, followed by Rosie and then Charlotte. Finally, Hannah appeared, and he took her hand. The blindfold he'd asked her to wear still covered her eyes.

"Easy." He helped her alight and tucked her hand in the crook of his arm. "Trust me. I've got you covered."

"I know you do."

They came to a stop, and he motioned for everyone to be quiet. "We're here."

⁂

Had they gone inside and she didn't realize it? No, Hannah could still hear the trills of birds and the rippling of leaves.

Lincoln tugged off the blindfold.

She blinked, then gasped. Before her stood the heavy wicker basket of a hot air balloon. Her eyes climbed higher, and she felt dwarfed by the huge, multicolored balloon overhead. Brother Molden waited for them inside the basket.

She turned to Lincoln. "We're getting married in there?"

"It seemed like the appropriate place for my Hello Girl with dreams of flying. Do you like it?"

"Lincoln, it's perfect."

He scooped her into his arms and carried her to the basket. After setting her inside, he climbed in, and the balloonist released the tethers.

The balloon began its ascent, and Hannah could scarcely breathe. She waved to her sisters, Rosie, Pete and Elise, Jo, and Aunt Sam. Walt was there with his parents. They'd brought George too. How kind it was for them to take in the boy while his fa-

337

ther was incarcerated for the fires he'd set in the Western Union buildings.

They rose above the trees and the fields, and their family and friends below grew smaller, as did the city's buildings. She glanced at Lincoln. His gaze seemed fixed on her and not the sights. Heat spread over her face and neck.

"Are we ready to begin?" Brother Molden asked.

Hannah nodded, and Lincoln took her hands. "Yes, sir, I'd certainly like to make this lady my bride."

Brother Molden grinned. "Dearly beloved, we are gathered up here . . ."

She didn't hear most of what the minister said. She said her "I do" in the right place, repeated the vows, and exchanged the rings, but her mind was focused on the feelings exploding inside her. Like the rising balloon, her heart swelled with love until she feared it might burst.

"Lincoln, you may kiss your bride."

And there, amid the swooping hawks and the billowing clouds, she felt the fan of his breath on her lips. Then, as if he had all the time in the world, he kissed her with a tenderness that filled her heart.

Love had called, and she'd gladly answer it every day for the rest of her life.

Author's Note

Many readers might be surprised to know that this book was born after I viewed a YouTube video. When I first discovered the Hello Girls video, I was fascinated. After that, I found several wonderful videos from the AT&T and Bell Telephone archives, chronicling the life of the early switchboard operator and explaining how the switchboard worked. Archived newspaper accounts from across the nation, which featured the day-to-day life of the switchboard operator, her training, and some of her humorous experiences, were priceless.

By 1910, New York Telephone alone had over 600,000 switchboard operators. Across the country, these young women, with their low, melodious voices, provided exemplary services to both pleasant and obnoxious patrons with unparalleled grace, despite crackling lines.

These women, and all those who worked as operators in the following years, are the real heroes of this book, and I want to thank them for their service. And thank you, dear reader, for blessing me with the opportunity to share their story with you.

Acknowledgments

Setting this book in Des Moines gave me the opportunity to learn more about Iowa's state capital. A special thank-you goes out Rosie Springer and Shari Stelling of the State Historical Library of Iowa for your help in my research efforts, and to the Council Bluffs Public Library.

I'm also extremely grateful for the Lost Des Moines Facebook group. Thanks to Arnold Brown, Cataldo Punelli, Michael O'Brien, and all the other Lost Des Moiners for keeping the city's past alive, for sharing your wonderful photos, and for providing invaluable information.

Thank you, Revell team, and especially my editors, Andrea Doering and Jessica English, for believing in my work and supporting me. Thank you, Judy, Shannon, and Brenda, for your insightful critiques. Thank you, Dawn, Laura, and Sandra, for your treasured friendship.

Thank you, Caroline, my middle daughter, for being the last one to read my manuscripts before I send them off to the editor and for your great catches, and thank you, Parker and Emma, for being my cheerleaders. Thank you, my beloved David, for making every day a real-life romance.

Most of all, thank you, Lord, for the honor of writing the stories you place on my heart.

A history buff, antique collector, and freelance graphic designer, **Lorna Seilstad** is the author of *Making Waves*, *A Great Catch*, and *The Ride of Her Life*. She draws her setting from her home state of Iowa. A former high school English and journalism teacher, she has won several online writing awards and is a member of American Christian Fiction Writers. Contact her and find out more at www.lornaseilstad.com.

Lake Manawa Summers Series

"Buckle up! With a sparkle of humor, heart-pumping romance, and a writing style that is fresh, fun, and addictive, Lorna Seilstad takes you along the fun-filled shores of Lake Manawa."

—JULIE LESSMAN, award-winning author of the Daughters of Boston and the Winds of Change series

Look for the second book of

THE GREGORY SISTERS
SERIES

to be released in 2014

LORNASEILSTAD.COM

Revell

a division of Baker Publishing Group
www.RevellBooks.com